MW00353741

Braxton's Turn

Watch Out Washington

Stephen R. Marks

@2022 Stephen R. Marks. All rights reserved. No part of this publication may be reproduced, stored in electronic format or transmitted in any form, by any means electronic, mechanical, or photocopied, recorded or otherwise without express written consent of the author.

This work is a work of fiction. Names, characters, businesses, places, events, and incidents are either the products of the author's imagination or used in a fictitious manner. Any resemblance to actual persons, living or dead, or actual events is purely coincidental.

ISBN (hardcover): 978-1-7373038-6-2
ISBN (paperback): 978-1-7373038-7-9
ISBN (ebook): 978-1-7373038-8-6

Madison

May you know you and your fight
are never far from my thoughts

Nancy
Melissa
Shayna
Remington

May you know my love for you

To The Type 1 Community

May my words make a difference
somehow, some way
May the cure be upon us
tomorrow, if not today

Turn

Verb
To cause to move upon a center
To present a different side
To change from a given use
To convert
To transform

Noun
Successive course
Change of direction, motion or position
A place where a change of direction occurs
A period of participation
A chance or opportunity

One

His sleep-filled eyes popped open.

His torso blasted off the bed, leaving him sitting upright and staring at the wall across the room. Now fully awake, in a cold sweat, the distant memories of his foster brother thrust back into his consciousness, again.

He looked to his left to see if he had awoken his wife. He hadn't. Good.

He slowly reclined his body back to the bed, placing his now clasped hands behind his head. He stared at the ceiling recalling the two memories revisiting him often recently. Two memories from the age of four and only five months apart. The first one of the first time he saw Monty. The second one of the last.

─────≋─────

"Jon, honey, why don't you sit at the kitchen table and work on your coloring until they get here? They should be here soon." He took a seat facing the small front entry area.

Suddenly, the doorbell. Mary Shannon, the foster mother of Irish descent who had been caring for Jon the last six months, went to answer.

"Mrs. Shannon, I'm Adam Boyd from the Department of Child Services. I believe you're expecting me."

"Yes, Mr. Boyd, I am. Please come in. And you have Montgomery with you. Montgomery Wells, hi sweetheart. It is so nice to see you again. Welcome to your new home. Come in and say hello to Jon, your new brother."

Jon knew they had a new boy coming to live with them but was not expecting someone younger than himself—nor expecting his new brother to be black. In his four short years of life, Jon had never been in the presence of a black child before. The smallish three-year-old was petrified when he entered the house and looked around in fear, still holding Adam's hand. His eyes then settled on Jon, who was looking at him inquisitively from the table. Monty saw it as a smile and relaxed a tad.

Jon had been living in Mary Shannon's modest five-bedroom Sylmar, California foster home with four other girls since he arrived. Two were Mary's young daughters, both slightly older than Jon. And the other two were foster children, like Jon. Both slightly older. Jon was uncertain why he had been placed in the home. He was with a babysitter when a man like Mr. Boyd came for him. He was told his mother and father had to leave for a while and would return at some point to take him home—a lie he was not made aware of for another four years.

"Now, Mrs. Shannon, I understand you went through training for administering Monty's insulin, but it is part of my responsibility to verify that you are capable and comfortable making sure his blood sugar levels are always monitored and controlled. I'd like to see you take blood from him now and test it. Are you OK with this?"

"Yes, Mr. Boyd. I've dealt with many diabetic children, so I know the drill. Did you bring any supplies with you? I have my own if you didn't."

"I did," said Boyd, though relieved to hear Mary Shannon was prepared. He opened a small luggage bag and retrieved a small, handheld glucose monitor, four dozen strips for blood droplets to insert into the monitor, twenty-four small needles to prick Monty's tiny fingers, twelve syringes, and twelve vials of insulin. He set them on the table in front of Jon. Jon stared intensely as Mrs. Shannon brought Monty to the table to execute a routine which she would follow at least three times every day for the rest of Monty's short life. She pricked his finger, extracted a small droplet of blood onto the strip, and placed it into the monitor. It read 180 milligrams. She turned to Boyd. "His glucose level is high. I'll give him a shot."

Boyd nodded and Mary unwrapped one of the syringes and one of the vials of insulin. She drew the appropriate amount into the syringe and asked Monty to stand next to her and lift his shirt. He started to whimper but was in no state of mind to resist. She plunged the small needle into his abdomen and released the life-assuring liquid.

———— ≈ ————

Jon was grateful to have Monty to share experiences with. He was having difficulty relating to the four older girls. With Monty he had a younger companion with somewhat similar small boy interests and with whom he could be in charge.

One of their routines was playing kickball in the front yard. The Shannon home was completely enclosed by a chain-link fence. There were two gates in the fence. One was for entry from the sidewalk to a path that split the front yard lawn and led to the home's raised front door. The other gate was for access to the driveway on the west end of the small lot. It led to a detached garage at the back of the property. Mary Shannon was always checking to make sure both gates were closed, especially when any of the children were playing in the front yard.

Jon did not mean to kick the ball towards the driveway gate. Inexplicably, that gate was not fully closed that day. The ball caromed off the outside of Jon's right foot and rolled through the open gate, towards the street. Monty started in pursuit.

"No, Monty!" Jon screamed and ran frantically towards the open gate after him. "Stop, don't go into the street!". The car that struck

Monty was not going fast, and it was not the impact that killed him. His body was still squirming when the front right tire rolled over him, with Jon witnessing from ten feet away.

Two

The 1992 to 2000 U.S. Presidency of Democrat Wilton Carrington, and the twelve years following his two terms in the White House, did nothing to quell the political ambitions of the former first lady, Heather Wilson-Carrington.

The South Carolina debutante and daughter of the highly successful and politically well-connected corporate attorney Horace Wilson, young Heather knew the life of politics from a very early age. And she loved every aspect.

She revered her father, captivated by his intelligence and the respect he commanded among his staff, his colleagues, and the numerous political figures who crossed his path. Young Heather was a constant by Horace's side. She was involved early and often with his cases. When old enough, she occasionally travelled with him. She had the opportunity to meet many politicians in the South Carolina state legislature, as well as three South Carolina governors. From age seven through her high school years, Heather Wilson was known and respected within South Carolina's social and political circles. At age seven, she formulated her lifetime goal.

"Daddy," she proclaimed numerous times before the age of ten, "I'm going to be the first lady President of the United States."

In high school, Heather involved herself in groups, clubs, and elections. Her moral compass pointed dead center at public service and political activism. She was articulate, knowledgeable, and well-spoken on many political issues of the day. And, exceedingly ambitious. Her grades were all A's.

Heather and Horace decided an Ivy League college education would be appropriate, and she enrolled at Princeton University in 1965 at the age of 18. After four years at Princeton, she moved to Harvard Law School. During her second year at Harvard her path crossed with a tall and charismatic Wilton Carrington, a third-year law student from Arkansas.

Wilton was dynamic, inspirational, and a charming presence at Harvard Law. His ability to articulate issues and win over the minds and opinions of his classmates would build a legacy eventually culminating in the United States Presidency.

———— ≈ ————

In October 1971, the Harvard Federalist Society hosted a debate event to promote and hear arguments for and against the preservation of the First Amendment in the face of rising government dissent. A constitutional law professor teaching the second-year law students and one teaching the same to third-year students, saw the Society's call for debate teams as a great opportunity for their respective students. Each made it a class assignment.

The topic for debate was the Supreme Court decision in June 1971 which centered on the viability of the First Amendment to the Constitution in the face of national security concerns. The case of the United States Government v The New York Times and The Washington Post. Also known as the 'Pentagon Papers Case'. At issue was the leaking of sensitive Defense Department documents shedding unfavorable light on U.S. strategies and relations in Southeast Asia.

Both professors used a ballot system to elect their six-member debate teams. One of the six would then be chosen by secret ballot from the team to serve as 'captain' and orator of the team's final argument. The third-year class team captain votes were in. Wilton Carrington was the unanimous choice.

The second-year class travelled a different path to select their captain. Heather was chosen for the debate team and immediately began campaigning for the captaincy. But she had a viable competitor. A young Californian named Aaron Wheatley expressed interest and was lightly lobbying his teammates.

Aaron was likeable, but overly studious. Most of the second-year class felt he was their most intellectual member. But he was also seen as an outcast. He did not share his classmate's propensity to party during the few opportunities the second-year students were presented. Most needed an outlet from the rigorous curriculum to get high or drunk after a set of tests or reports were completed—and before the next round of torture began.

The four young ladies were turning the heads of their male classmates as they walked briskly thorough the open courtyard area back inside to their dorm hall. "That tall guy" one of them mused, "in my tort law class is so gorgeous. I so want to run my lips all over him."

"Julie, stop, you're going to make me blush."

"Yeah right Ashley you couldn't blush even if you wanted. Besides I see you in the room with me and gorgeous looking for the leftovers."

Three of the ladies giggle. Heather only smiles as they reach her room.

Julie sought to confirm their evening plans. "We're meeting at nine tonight at Shay's to shoot pool and hunt love. You'll be there?"

Heather declines. "Sorry bitches. Can't make it. Too much reading to do. See you tomorrow."

She entered her dorm room and moved straight for the phone. She dialed her father.

"Horace Wilson."

"Hi daddy."

"Is this my darling daughter, the first female president of the United States."

"Yes daddy." She was not in the mood. "That's exactly who this is."

"Uh oh. What's up, sweetheart?"

"I need advice. My Constitutional Law class formed a debate team to argue a Supreme Court case against the third-year class. I'm on the team, and next week the six of us vote by secret ballot to select the captain. I really want the job, daddy. But there's a guy from California who might win. He's a nice guy, but kind of nerdy. He's very smart, and I know there are some on the team who want him. I'd be a much better captain, but I'm not sure what to do to win over my teammates."

After a few seconds of silence Horace advised his daughter: "OK sweetheart, here's what we need you to do."

Horace Wilson proceeded to give his daughter some early lessons in leverage and influence. Heather reported back to Horace the next day that Aaron was interning at the Boston Law Firm of Shiller, Crosby, and Nash. Horace placed a call to his friend and colleague Gerald Nash. Horace and Gerald worked together occasionally over the years jointly defending corporate clients against class action lawsuits.

The following day was Wednesday. One of Aaron Wheatley's three days a week he holed up in a small research room at Nash's firm. It was four in the afternoon, and he was wrapping up his day's research. Shirley Davis, Gerald Nash's administrative assistant, knocked on the door of the room and, after the third knock, walked in uninvited. She looked at Aaron apologetically and handed him a folded handwritten note on Gerald Nash's stationary. Without any emotion, she turned and left the room, gently closing the door behind her.

Aaron took the note and opened it. '*Aaron, we're reassigning your current task to another intern as of now. We don't have any additional assignments currently. As such, we're putting your internship on hold until some additional work frees up. We hope to call you back in a week or two.*

The notes in your file will reflect this hiatus in positive terms, so please don't worry about any impact on your career. You're a great law student, and we hope to work with you again soon.—Gerald.'

Disappointed but not upset, Aaron chalked it up to it being the way it was in corporate law. His first thoughts were this would free up additional time to devote to his classes and the upcoming debate. He did not mention the occurrence to anyone. It was not important enough for anyone else to know.

The next day, four days before the second-year Constitutional Law class debate team would vote for captain, Heather sought out Aaron. She found him in the law library. He was sitting alone at a rectangular table with six chairs. He was in the chair to the far left, facing the library entrance. She sat down directly across the table from him, staring and waiting for eye contact. He sensed her presence and cranked his head up from his notes. He smiled weakly and she returned it. He returned his attention to his notepad.

Heather tore a piece of paper from her notebook, wrote a few words, folded it, and slid it where he could not help but see her hand. *'Twice in two days, mysterious folded notes?'* He looked at her again and then the note. She returned his glance but without her smile.

Aaron returned his eyes to the note, paused a few seconds, then picked it up and opened it. *'Sorry about your suspension from SC&N yesterday.'*

Aaron had to read the note three times to fully grasp Heather knew about his furlough. How could she? He hadn't mentioned it to anyone, and he had no reason to believe Heather Wilson was connected to the firm. His quick internal processing of these thoughts caused a gurgitation in his stomach and weakness in his joints.

Heather's smile returned. She leaned forward and spoke her words softly. "Mr. Nash wants me to captain our debate team and is asking you to drop from consideration. That is, if you want your internship reinstated."

Heather got up, turned, and walked out of the library, leaving Aaron stunned.

As she exited, she felt as if walking on air, exhilarated by the experience of climbing to her goals on the back of an unsuspecting soul. It was a fitting emotion to her first experience of exercising power. She savored it wholeheartedly.

———≈———

The debate was a spirited affair. Both sides argued and counterargued their respective points with passion and purpose. Heather's second-year team represented the defendants, opposing the position of the executive branch. The Year-Twos, under Heather's captaincy, made all the right arguments for rejecting the government's claims that an injunction should be granted to prevent the leaked documents from being published. They deconstructed the government's claims about checks and balances and separations of power. Claims to influence the Supreme Court to render the judicial branch of the U.S. government did not have rights to handcuff the executive branch's ability to defend the country.

Heather's team also effectively argued in favor of the Founding Fathers' intent to use the First Amendment as a tool to protect the republic from dangerous power-grabs by either the executive or legislative branches. They used their quotes and previous Supreme Court rulings to make their case. Their points landed strongly with the three law school professors scoring the debate. And with the 300 law students in attendance.

Archie Davis, from Heather's team, passionately made the case for freedom of speech and freedom of the press by reciting quotes from the founding fathers on the matter.

"If the freedom of speech is taken away, then dumb and silent, we may be led like sheep to the slaughter—George Washington."

"Without freedom of thought, there can be no such thing as wisdom, and no such thing as public liberty, without freedom of speech— Benjamin Franklin."

Debbie Hansen was precise claiming the Supreme Court had twice previously rejected the power of the court to impose restraint. To grant the Justice Department's request in this instance would be equivalent to enacting law, clearly forbidden for the judicial branch by the Constitution. She reinforced the point reciting the First Amendment text detailing the restriction on the legislative branch to enact any law relating to restraining the freedom of the press.

As the debate proceeded, it was clear Heather's team was well prepared, well coached, and performing admirably. This was not unnoticed nor unappreciated by her tall, charming opponent. Wilton Carrington's third-year team was also well prepared and articulated its points and counterpoints with clarity and purpose. While they had the less popular argument, their emphasis on country and the responsibilities of the executive branch to protect the security of the republic in its handling of foreign affairs was also resonating.

Wilton shared his tempered view that this case should not be considered an egregious overreach by the executive branch. While he shared the viewpoints of his classmates the Vietnam War was nasty and evil, he was also a realist. His team made strong arguments the threats posed by the spread of communism were dangerous to the country. His team expanded the argument this judicial action was not a cut-and-dried case of protecting the integrity of the First Amendment.

Wilton had the unpopular task of defending the Justice Department's arguments, which he personally felt were weak. Though his line of reasoning did not in itself justify the war in Southeast Asia to him or his teammates, it provided a foundation upon which they could build their talking points, their case, and their final arguments.

Wilton felt his only chance to win the debate was to change the argument. His strategy was making the case the Supreme Court had a responsibility above and beyond protecting the Constitution. They were also responsible to protect the union. The strategy he laid out for his team followed this thinking.

It was time for final arguments and the Year-Two's were first. Heather Wilson strode to the podium. She was dressed conservatively and radiating confidence. Her long, blondish, lightly curled hair was pulled back on both sides of her face to form a small ponytail layered on top of the rest of her mid-back length locks. She was wearing a fashionable lady's light-green business suit with a skirt that just topped her knees. Her blouse had a V-neckline, coming to a point just above her modest breasts. Wilton Carrington took his first real look at Heather Wilson.

She was methodical, composed, and confident in restating her team's defense of the Supreme Court's ruling in this matter. She had total command of her arguments and the facts to support them. She recapped many statements of the Founding Fathers that served to illustrate the importance of a free press. She recapped many previous Supreme Court rulings that had protected First Amendment rights in a variety of cases where circumstances created challenges. She recapped a series of examples in other countries where limits and prohibitions of a free press served to undermine the freedom of the populace and lead to abusive government control.

She brilliantly closed by arguing the Supreme Court's conclusion, while there were potential national security interests at stake in the publishing of the documents, the Justice Department had not made a valid case the restraint was justified. She closed with, "the court ultimately had no choice but to uphold the rulings of the two U.S. Courts of Appeal in rejecting the request for injunction against the Times and the Post."

Heather strode confidently back to her seat on the left side of the stage to a rousing round of applause. Wilton never took his eyes off her as he thought about making passionate love to this incredibly bright, attractive, and articulate second-year law student. With that thought in mind, he rose and sauntered confidently to the podium as his name was announced.

"Ladies and gentlemen, my opponent has argued a spirited defense of the United States Supreme Court's ruling in the case identified as 403 U.S. 713, The New York Times Co. vs. the United States. But my opponent's argument is flawed and shallow. Allow me to explain."

Heather had returned to her seat and was still accepting kudos from her teammates when Wilton's opening remarks silenced the debate hall. Many were surprised by his audacity.

With the hall now silent he continued. "Our opponents in the year-two class have argued the Supreme Court had no choice in this case but to rule in favor of the lower court's decision to refuse granting an injunction against the defendants. They have based this position on the words of the Constitution, the arguments written by the judges supporting the majority opinion, and on previous Supreme Court rulings."

"In considering the court's ruling, I believe it important to understand some supporting material facts. First consider, while the ruling was a six-three majority, there was no clear majority opinion authored. In fact, Chief Justice Berger was one of the three dissenters. The brief opinion offered for the record displayed a wide variety of opinions of the nine judges. Even amongst the concurring opinions there existed a large disparity. Justices Black and Douglas offered strong arguments in defense of the absolute superiority of the language in the Constitution protecting the freedom of the press. Yet the written opinions of Justices White and Stewart proclaimed latitude for offering restraint and discussed a burden of proof requirement."

"Justice Black, in offering his opinion to protect the right of The New York Times to publish illegally obtained documents, under the protection of the First Amendment, cites the absolute superiority of the First Amendment."

"He writes: 'In response to an overwhelming public clamor, James Madison offered a series of amendments to satisfy citizens that these great liberties would remain safe. In the First Amendment, the Founding Fathers gave the free press the protection it must have to fulfill its essential role in our democracy. The press was to serve the governed, not the governors. The government's power to censor the press was abolished so that the press would remain forever free to censure the government. The press was protected so that it could reveal the secrets of the government and inform the people. Only a free and unrestrained press can effectively expose deception in government.'"

"He also writes: 'I do not believe that any federal agencies, including Congress and the court, have power or authority to subordinate speech and press to what they think are 'more important interests.'"

"Justice Douglas concurs, adding: 'While I join the opinion of the court, I believe it necessary to express my views more fully. It should be noted at the outset that the First Amendment provides that "Congress shall make no law . . . abridging the freedom of speech or of the press." That leaves, in my view, no room for governmental restraint on the press.'"

"Yet Justice White cites there is a less absolute standard. He offers that there are circumstances where the First Amendment is not absolute and that there is a latitude for judicial restraint if the government can meet a substantial burden of proof."

"He writes: 'I concur in today's judgments, but only because of the concededly extraordinary protection against prior restraints enjoyed by the press under our constitutional system. I do not say that, in no circumstances, would the First Amendment permit an injunction against publishing information about government plans or operations. Nor, after examining the materials the government characterizes as the most sensitive and destructive, can I deny that revelation of these documents will do substantial damage to public interests. Indeed, I am confident that their disclosure will have that result.

But I nevertheless agree that the United States has not satisfied the very heavy burden that it must meet to warrant an injunction against publication in these cases.'"

"Justice Stewart writes: 'It is elementary that the successful conduct of international diplomacy and the maintenance of an effective national defense require both confidentiality and secrecy. Other nations can hardly deal with this nation in an atmosphere of mutual trust unless they can be assured that their confidences will be kept. And, within our own executive departments, the development of considered and intelligent international policies would be impossible if those charged with their formulation could not communicate with each other freely, frankly, and in confidence. In the area of basic national defense, the frequent need for absolute secrecy is, of course, self-evident.'"

Wilton continued: "It is clear from these contrasting majority written opinions that the court itself is unclear to what degree the First Amendment should be applied. And from this conflict, we argue that the court itself, in its duty to uphold the sanctity of the Constitution, should have ruled differently. We are not arguing that the court's ruling in this case to reject the government's request for injunction was incorrect. We are arguing that the rushed manner in which this case was decided was improper and the ultimate failure of the court to author a clear and concise rationale for their ruling represented a failure of the court to uphold its most important judicial responsibility. The dissenting arguments in this case serve to illustrate our point."

"Chief Justice Berger writes: 'In these cases, the imperative of a free and unfettered press comes into collision with another imperative: the effective functioning of a complex modern government and, specifically, the effective exercise of certain constitutional powers of the executive. Only those who view the First Amendment as an absolute in all circumstances—a view I respect but reject—can find such cases as these to be simple or easy. These cases are not simple for another and more immediate reason. We do not know the facts of the cases. No district judge knew all the facts. No court of appeals judge knew all the facts. No member of this court knows all the facts. Why are we in this posture, in which only those judges to whom the First Amendment is absolute and permits no restraint in any circumstances or for any reason, are really in a position to act? I suggest we are in this posture because these cases have been conducted in unseemly haste.'"

"Justice Harlan writes: 'With all respect, I consider that the court has been almost irresponsibly feverish in dealing with these cases. Both the Court of Appeals for the Second Circuit and the Court of Appeals for the District of Columbia Circuit rendered judgment on June 23. The New York Times' petition for certiorari, its motion for accelerated consideration thereof, and its application for interim relief were filed in this court on June 24 at about 11 a.m. The application of the United States for interim relief in the Post case was also filed here on June 24, at about 7:15 p.m. This court's order setting a hearing before us on June 26 at 11 a.m., a course which I joined only to avoid the possibility of even more peremptory action by the court, was issued less than twenty-four hours before. The record in the Post case was filed with the clerk shortly before 1 p.m. on June 25. The record in the Times case did not arrive until 7 or 8 o'clock that same night. The briefs of the parties were received less than two hours before argument on June 26. This frenzied train of events took place in the name of the presumption against prior restraints created by the First Amendment. Due regard for the extraordinarily important and difficult questions involved in these litigations should have led the court to shun such a precipitate timetable.'"

Wilton paused for effect. He turned his gaze to Heather. He noticed she was laser focused on him. He offered a smile in her direction, and she returned it. She had been listening closely to Wilton's presentation and recognized his strategy to win the debate. She was highly impressed, feeling as though she were listening to her father.

Wilton continued: "It is our opinion that the court acted erroneously in its rush to a decision and in its lack of judicial providence in fully understanding the ramifications of the release of this information."

"Ladies and gentlemen, the Supreme Court of the United States, within their sworn duty, has the monumental task of protecting the Constitution and the intent of the Founding Fathers against the litany of challenges our judicial system offers for clarification and dissenting viewpoints. It is a job fit for only the greatest legal minds the country can produce. But I argue that while the protection of the Constitution is a primary responsibility of those great legal minds sitting on the bench, it is not their only responsibility."

"The Constitution exists for one reason, and that is to protect our union. Without our union there is no need nor place for our Constitution. I argue that protecting our union in light of the potential national security implications and potential harm to the well-being of U.S. citizens in the release of this illegally obtained information required the court to review this case more deliberately and offer more than the simple decision it rendered to support the ruling of the two lower courts—a decision it made without offering a clear statement on the First Amendment law as it relates to prior restraint."

"In consideration of these facts and of our position, we reject the position of our opponents. We believe the majority opinion rendered by the Supreme Court in the case of the United States vs The New York Times and The Washington Post was improper. Because this case represented the most significant challenge to the absolute superiority of the First Amendment of the Constitution in our country's history, we believe the court failed in this case in: one, rushing its opinion without proper diligence in understanding the true ramifications of its ruling; two, failing to author a clear defense of its position of the superiority of the First amendment; and three, failing in its highest priority to protect our union, known as the United States of America. Thank you."

The hall erupted into thunderous applause, with Wilton's third-year Law mates adding the requisite hooting and hollering. Wilton sauntered back to his seat among his team to the right of the podium with a look of confident smugness as he accepted their pats to his back. He then turned his head to find Heather. She was on the other end of the debate stage accepting congratulations. Their eyes met. He started walking in her direction. As he approached her, he was overcome by a strong physical yearning, a yearning he was finding difficult to suppress. He moved directly toward her with a sense of purpose. As he grew closer, his physical desire was now all consuming. His breathing intensified. His heart pounded.

"Hi, Heather. I'm hungry. Let's get some food."

Three

He first noticed her in the quad area talking to a friend and was struck by her beauty and grace. He arrived on campus early to find the route to his first class but was now distracted. She and her friend parted company, and she began her walk to class. He decided to follow.

"Cool. She's heading for the building my class is in," he said aloud to the only one listening to his thoughts.

He was pleasantly surprised when he saw her enter the same lecture hall he was headed for. She strode purposefully, twenty-five minutes early, into the lecture hall for her first class in her first quarter of her freshman year at UCLA.

"All right then, we're in the same class."

She entered at the top row and surveyed the room. It was empty except for twenty descending rows of fifteen individual seats with attached desktops. She decided, then descended the six-inch stairs to row ten. She turned left and headed to the far left-hand seat against a window overlooking a grassy area.

She was dressed down for her first day of college to avoid the inevitable leers and advances, to which she had become accustomed, from uninteresting and overzealous young men. She was dressed in a long, pleated skirt. A conservative, high-neckline blouse. And nondescript sandals. Against the window, her only concern was the seat to her right being populated. She pulled out the novel she was into and began reading.

He was a minute behind when he entered at the top row. He saw her sitting alone.

She had not noticed the second student to enter the lecture hall until he was standing behind the seat next to hers.

"Excuse me, is this seat taken?"

She looked up to her right to see an unkempt and shabbily dressed young man. She then glanced around the room, seeing no other seats filled.

"Yes, it is. I'm holding it for my friend."

Undeterred, he sat down. "OK, I'll move when he gets here."

"What makes you think it's a he?"

"I'm not sure but if he is a she I'm going to consider this the luckiest day of my life."

The young woman, all of nineteen, of Japanese descent, tall, statuesque, with looks of supermodel quality, was now annoyed. Her usual reaction when guys tried using their lines on her.

"I must say, you have the most beautiful hair I've ever seen."

Ahhh that does it, she thought to herself, deciding the conversation with this jerk was over as she returned her focus to her book.

Unfazed by the silent treatment, in a serious voice and flashing a straight face. "And what do you think of mine?"

She turned to look at his hair more closely, and could not help but laugh at his long, curly, sandy-brown, unwashed shoulder-length mange.

"Your hair's disgusting."

"I'm glad you like it," the young man dressed in blue jeans with holes at the knees and a worn, undersized white T-shirt said, extending his right hand. "I'm Jon."

"Angela," she said as she took it and shook it, glancing only briefly at his scruffy beard and engaging smile.

"Nice meeting you, Angela." He let go of her hand, nodded, smiled, and reached into his backpack for a book. He started reading, leaving her to stare at him.

Angela Aoki was born in Redondo Beach, California, to first-generation Japanese immigrants in 1972. She was an only child and raised in a traditional Japanese home in the middle of the Southern California sprawl. Her father, Tanoro Aoki, and mother, Taka, had migrated to California in 1963 for Tanoro to pursue an engineering degree at UCLA and Taka a teaching career. They were both industrious, intelligent, hard-working, and passed those traits along to their only child—a child they purposefully gave an "American" name to enable her to better assimilate into the society they planned to be a part of their entire lives.

Angela grew to be tall and beautiful. Her striking facial features, curvaceous figure, and long silky hair were of cover girl quality. But she was a serious student and led a relatively modest life, focusing primarily on her studies and her close cadre of girlfriends from Redondo Beach High. She never dated much. She had very high standards and most of the boys she met at Redondo Beach High were of no interest.

In the fall of 1991, Angela enrolled in UCLA interested in studying human behavior and exploring a potential career path to become a social psychologist. She had no idea when she arrived for the first lecture of her freshman Psychology 101 class that she would be meeting a human subject who would come to fascinate her.

Ten minutes of silence passed between the two before the hall filled up and the professor arrived. Angela couldn't decide if she was upset Jon stopped talking to her or relieved he was content in leaving her alone. She stared closely at his profile momentarily while he was into his read, took note of his handsome features and had a fleeting thought about what it would be like to have an extended conversation with this odd young man. She then joined him in focusing on the lecture.

Ninety minutes later, both Jon and Angela had experienced their first taste of freshman year psychology. Class had been dismissed, and both were packing up to leave. Before Angela could stand, Jon broke the silence: "Angela, now that we're friends, can I give you my number?"

"No." She stood and rushed away.

The following Wednesday, Angela again arrived twenty-five minutes early for Psych 101, wondering if she would be interacting again with that 'weird kid', as she had described Jon to one of her friends. Upon entering the lecture hall, she saw only one seat taken. As on Monday, she descended to row ten and strode to the seat to the far left, next to the window, and sat down. She turned to her right to the seat next to hers.

"Hello, Jon."

"Hey, Angela. Uh, excuse me, but that seat you're in is reserved."

"Oh really? Then I'll consider this the luckiest day of my life that I don't have to sit next to you." She had no intent in moving.

"So, you're not really that lucky because I was saving it for you."

"And why would you do that?"

"I'll never tell unless you buy me a cup of coffee."

Angela and Jon met for coffee the next day—and for every day of their freshman year together. First it was morning coffee together, and soon after, everything together. It was not long before they had fallen for one another; the conservative, studious, serious, and statuesque young Japanese beauty—and the Valley-bred, scruffy, care-free, surfer-type dude. They made an odd couple, but an incredible team—their friends referring to them as "Beauty and the Beast."

As Jon grew to love Angela, he began transforming from the quirky, sloppily dressed, poorly groomed, unrefined boy genius into a still quirky, slightly better-dressed, much better-groomed force of nature. He was willing to sacrifice being what he was to be what she wanted him to be. And she didn't want much to change, other than for him to clean it up a little bit. Instinctively, he knew this and ran with it.

Jon's carefree, yet insightful personality combined with his total lack of inhibition, ultimate confidence, supreme intelligence, and uncanny people skills were taking him to success in all his endeavors, including his relationship with Angela.

During their careers at UCLA, they both pursued their fields of study with vigor and passion. Angela continued her pathway toward an undergrad degree in psychology, while Jon realized he was most interested in engineering and moved to a major with lots of math and technology courses.

During sophomore year, Jon found a job in the burgeoning e-commerce industry a few miles south of UCLA in Torrance, California. The company was called Spectre Systems. Spectre had been in business three years at the time, designing and building customized network servers to process e-commerce transactions in a fast, efficient manner. The business was small, twenty people, and struggling, with only eight systems sold in 1992. The owners of Spectre were two brothers, Boris and Bogdan Mitrovich. Boris was the business guy, Bogdan the software wizard.

The firm's struggles centered on hardware. Bogdan's programs were well written and stable.

But engineering the right hardware to take full advantage of the software's capability was proving to be a challenge. Jon was hired part time to help the hardware team do low-level prototyping, testing, and documentation. The position suited him perfectly, allowing him time to pursue his studies and his girlfriend. It wasn't long before he discovered the root causes of the hardware problems and began proposing changes to the firm's designs.

The value of the changes Jon proposed were recognized by the Mitrovich brothers, and many were put into production. The positive results of Jon's changes translated into improved performance, stability, and customer satisfaction. As a result, sales started growing in the summer of 1993. Jon was given special recognition by Bogdan, soon became his protégé, and nicknamed 'JB'.

But Jon's success and recognition created friction on the engineering team. A few key hardware engineers, feeling upstaged by

JB, left the company. This created numerous internal inefficiencies and customer service glitches. As the number of customers grew, along with the financial requirements to keep the company operating, Boris' management weaknesses were exposed. There were also issues with company funds disappearing, and a serious rift grew between the Mitrovich brothers. Despite having developed a marketable technology for a burgeoning industry, the company was on its way to collapse.

Jon was aware of the company's struggles and wanted to become more involved in strategic decision-making. He developed keen insights into why the company was floundering and how to rectify its hardware, operational and customer service issues.

His relationship with Angela was having no such issues and was growing deeper and more intense. In early 1994, Jon proposed. She couldn't say yes fast enough when he popped the question during a Valentine's Day couple's massage. They were next to each other on two massage tables, face down, each being rubbed down by a masseuse. He had his head turned to the left, and she had hers to the right. They were looking at one another. He extended his left hand for hers, and she reached for his left with her right.

"Remember when we met that first day in Psych? You said you were holding the seat next to you for your boyfriend."

"I didn't say that."

"OK, so I said that, but you didn't deny it."

She smiled.

"Remember when I said if you weren't holding the seat for a boyfriend, it would be the luckiest day of my life? Let's make that day the luckiest in both our lives. Let's get married."

———— ≋ ————

"Angie, I like Jon. I really do. But you are so young. Too young to marry. Give things more time."

"Dad we love each other and want to start our life together. If you're concerned about Jon being a good provider, there's no need. He's very intelligent. He's really helping Spectre work through their problems. He's great with technology and has a bright future in front of him, and we both want to be a part of it, together. He makes me laugh and he makes me happy."

"But Angie, I'm not saying don't marry him, I'm just saying not now."

Taka wanted what her daughter wanted. She'd had enough. "Tanoro, stop! Go watch TV."

She then took Angela's arm and squeezed. "When's the wedding?"

———≈———

Jon and Angela married early in their senior year, with Tanoro's and Taka's blessings. As they had only Jon's part-time income from Spectre, Jon was welcomed into the Aoki home. Fueled by his love for Angela and his sincere affection for her parents, he adopted Tanoro and Taka as his own parents. They immensely enjoyed the presence of their new son-in-law, who was making their precious daughter so happy.

While Jon enjoyed living under the Aoki's roof, he knew it would soon be time for he and Angela to go out on their own. Jon was now thinking in terms of making a living and raising a family. With those thoughts, he started looking at Spectre in a different light.

"Dad, I think we should buy the company." Jon proposed to Tanoro one night at the dinner table. He had already been discussing this possibility with Angela, and she encouraged him to approach his father-in-law. Tanoro was aware of the happenings at Spectre, as Jon would fill him in on occasion. But the idea of acquiring the company had never been discussed.

"What makes you think the brothers want to sell?"

"What I know is they don't know what to do. Even with their good core of customers and their systems showing promise, the company's heading into bankruptcy. If a decent offer came along to put them out of their misery, they'd take it. That is, if they didn't kill each other first. If a sale can give them a way out and provide them at least a little return on their investment, they'll go for it."

"But the company is not doing well financially. Why do you feel it would be a wise investment?"

"Dad, are you following what's going on in e-commerce today? The market is exploding. Any business wanting to sell online needs a platform to manage that commerce. For all Spectre's issues, Bogdan's software is incredibly powerful. I know why the hardware's failing, and I know how to fix it. I've given them the answers to the performance issues, but their relationship is so dysfunctional they can't implement the changes. With that software and the right hardware design, I could take the company to ten million in three years, easily."

"How would they feel accepting an offer from you, being so young and inexperienced? Would they take it seriously?"

Before Tanoro could finish asking his question, the answer had already become clear. His facial expression unmistakably conveyed to everyone at the table he would have to be, not only the financier but, actively involved in the negotiation. His wife, daughter, and son-in-law all saw him come to that realization and were relieved they didn't have to spell it out for him.

"Angie" Tanoro asked, "what do you think?"

She looked over at her husband, taking her hand from her lap and putting on top of his left hand, which was resting on the table with a fork in it.

"Dad, let's give Mr. JB a shot."

Jon's perception was prophetic. The Mitrovich brothers put up lots of arguments why they felt Tanoro Aoki's bid for the company was too low. Eventually reality came into focus and the deal was consummated in the spring of 1995 for $750,000. Three months prior to Jon and Angela's graduation from UCLA. The deal included all rights and ownership of Spectre's source code and three-year non-compete agreements from both brothers. Jon laughed when Tanoro had insisted on the non-competes, saying he'd welcome them back into the market as a competitor remarking, "We'd never lose a single sale, and they'd only make us look better with their incompetence."

It wasn't long before Jon started turning Spectre around. He crafted a new mission statement the day he took control. "As of right now all our efforts are focused on being 'The Uncontested Leader in the Industry for High-Performance Integrated E-Commerce Server Solutions'."

Next was his objective to build a competent team whom he could work with to implement the numerous ideas he had to accomplish their mission. It required letting most of the current staff go. He retained only five of the eighteen people employed at the acquisition.

Next, he began to rebuild the hardware design for their three current production systems from scratch. He promised all forty of Spectre's current customers that the company would provide them with brand new hardware platforms for no charge to replace their current models once they had been proven stable and reliable.

Tanoro fought this. But Jon convinced him they needed these new systems in the field quickly to do real production testing and to stay ahead of any potential competitors in pursuit of their market.

He also decided to suspend all current sales of existing systems until the new hardware platforms were ready. He and Tanoro debated this strategy as it would create a cash flow burden. Jon convinced Tanoro to take the long view.

Jon knew his father-in-law would be concerned with the cash

flow ramifications of going into sales hibernation. In anticipation of adopting this strategy, Jon had been working on new hardware designs for months before the sale. He convinced Tanoro they would be ready to resume system sales within six months of the transaction. He shared with his father-in-law all the design plans. He showed him the performance modeling with early prototypes. He crafted a contingency plan considering all potential setbacks or failures of the new designs. And the next steps needed should they have to redesign or re-architect, all with cost estimates and timelines.

Jon worked out cash flow models using both six month-to-market and nine month-to-market timelines, with very conservative sales numbers.

He did his homework on market trends. He hired a friend he met during sophomore year in one of his engineering classes to do the research. For the three months prior to the sale of Spectre, Jon's friend had been independently surveying current and prospective customers on what they liked and disliked about their current e-commerce integrated server and software solutions, and what levels of performance, scalability, and reliability they would look for in their next purchase. Jon had all this data the day he assumed operational control. The transformation was underway immediately.

Staff changed significantly during the first months of Jon's ownership, but the JB nickname stuck. Jon and the new Spectre team quickly completed the design of the SS-50K and went into limited production. The SS-50K system was targeted for Spectre's current customer base, e-commerce companies processing a maximum of 50,000 transactions per month.

By July, Spectre had shipped ten newly designed systems to ten of their existing customers. Customers whose environments would provide the best test for the new system's performance and reliability. In August, they shipped another ten, and in September, another twenty—fulfilling Jon's no-cost upgrade promise to Spectre's forty customers.

By October 1995, having the benefit of true market performance data and the time to incorporate the changes dictated by the relatively few issues encountered in SS-50K production, the company was again shipping systems for revenue.

Jon's estimate to Tanoro that Spectre would resume generating revenue within six months of the acquisition was on target. The October SS-50K shipments to new customers, complete with a new catalog of software features and thirty-seven highly satisfied customers as references, was an instant success.

Jon also convinced Tanoro to accept a new sales model he crafted. A model where customers were charged a small base fee for hardware and software use and support, plus a monthly incremental fee based on the number of e-commerce transactions processed. Customers found the model attractive as they could scale their costs to match current transaction levels.

But Tanoro needed convincing. It represented risk if a system did not perform, or the customer did not grow. Jon used the argument with both Tanoro and prospective new customers that, under this model, Spectre would be highly motivated to continue innovation and development of new performance-enhancing features.

"We're partners. If you don't grow by increasing processing transactions, we're both impacted. We'll be highly motivated to continue development to increase both our chances of success."

It was a true partnership-driven model none of Spectre's competitors had considered. It was possible some sales could result in a loss. But the flip side was the tremendous loyalty Spectre would build with customers who were able to grow while scaling costs. Jon saw it as a barrier to entry for future competition.

Once Tanoro was presented the big picture vision he stopped objecting, marveling at the business insight his twenty-three-year-old son-in-law possessed.

The combination of the new SS-50K's performance specifications with Jon's innovative pricing model made the product very successful. Within the first month of new production sales, Spectre received twenty orders, with projected first year revenue including the estimated transactions processing, of $175,000 per system. The mission statement was taking root.

Spectre shipped the twenty systems within sixty days. In customer production environments they exhibited high performance and reliability. With the success of the SS-50K, Jon finished his designs for the higher capacity SS-100K and SS-250K.

In February 2006, Spectre released both higher capacity systems, launching the company closer to Jon's $10 million forecast for 2007. The rise of Spectre continued for the next three years, with the company growing to $30,000,000 annual revenue in 1999 as the dot-com era matured. But Jon was growing concerned with Spectre's lack of diversification. He was keenly aware many dot-com companies were built on flawed business models. He was also aware the enormous growth in the U.S. economy was tied to them. He anticipated the looming 2001 recession ahead of most.

Spectre enjoyed solid growth in 1999, and Jon embarked on a strategy to diversify the company into computer components and systems distribution. As part of that diversification and the need to expand facilities, Jon and Angela moved the company north to Ventura County into a 150,000 square-foot facility. They hired 150 new people. Angela and Jon bought a modest four-bedroom ranch-style home five miles from headquarters in the nearby Lynn Ranch community. Shortly after the company's move, Angela and Jon welcomed their newborn son, Lucas, into their lives.

In November 1999, as the company was heavily recruiting, a warehouse candidate entered the Spectre main lobby and approached the receptionist.

"Welcome to Spectre. How can I help you?"

"I've got an eleven appointment with Miranda Sanchez."

"An interview for employment?"

"Depends."

"On what?"

"On if we get along."

"OK, please have a seat. I'll let her know you're here."

The receptionist dialed Miranda's extension.

"What's up Betty."

"You're 11 o'clock interview is here. Abby Martin. I think you're going to like her."

Four

Wallis Kriss, the ratings leader of the Sunday morning cable news programs broadcast from within the DC beltway, fresh from a ninety-minute makeup session with the set's cosmetics expert, walked briskly towards the set. As was his custom, barking instructions.

"C'mon people. Showtime in 2 minutes. Let's get our asses in gear and start 2012 off on the right foot."

Wallis reached the stage and effortlessly glided into his seat. Staff was still fussing with his hair and makeup as he adjusted his earpiece and lapel microphone. The pompous lead-in music concluded. The staff scurried off. The red light went on and the broadcast was underway.

"Good morning from Washington, D.C. It's Sunday, January 7. I'm Wallis Kriss, and welcome to Big News Sunday."

"Our first guest today is Wall Street Journal opinion columnist Bridgett Masterson. No stranger to this show, Bridgett had her latest article, entitled 'The Country is So Ready,' published today. She's here to tell us why she felt the need to write this piece and what she thinks the country is so ready for. Bridgett, welcome back to Big News Sunday."

"Thank you, Wallis. Happy New Year to you and your audience."

"And Happy New Year to you. The country is so ready? Ready for what, exactly?"

"Effective federal government leadership, Wallis, plain and simple."

"We have leaders, and they are leading. Don't we already have leadership?"

"I guess you can call it leadership. But I'm more interested in the adjectives you would use to describe it. In considering the leadership our executive and legislative branches of government exhibit, what adjectives would you use?"

Kriss smiled and lightheartedly replied. "Bridgett, you've likely been spending a lot of time thinking about this. Please, tell us yours."

"Well, we can use adjectives to describe what the leadership attributes of our current leaders are or adjectives to describe what they are not. I already gave you one example of what I believe they are not. 'Effective' is not a word I would use to describe the policies we've seen come out of Washington the last twelve years. Nor would I use 'bold,' 'imaginative,' 'creative,' 'fiscally responsible,' 'comprehensive,' 'decisive,' or 'focused.'"

Kriss knew Masterson was not an advocate of the current administration. He tried to pin her down. "Where do you feel the root cause lies Bridgett, with the White House or Congress?"

"Both, Wallis. They're equally to blame for the lack of effective federal government leadership."

"OK. In your view, we have a leadership void in our federal government. Let me go back to my first question: The country is so ready for what?"

"Wallis, in my article I write about four years from now, 2016, being a transformational year in U.S. politics. There's no question in my mind Barack Obama will be reelected to a second term later this year. I don't see the Republicans being able to mount a serious challenge. They won control of the House in the 2010 midterms by a resounding margin but have done nothing positive with that victory. The leadership they have displayed in working with Democrats for the good of the country has been appalling. I see absolutely no chance for Republicans to win the White House this year. I see Obama being reelected decisively. I also see the Republicans losing their majority in the House this year."

"OK, Bridgett, we see your 2012 vision. What do you foresee for 2016?"

"Wallis, this is what I cover in my article. I see Heather Carrington being the Democrat nominee in 2016, no surprise there. But on the Republican side, I'm expecting something unusual. There will be a fallout from the lack of current Republican Party leadership. If you consider the Tea Party movement from a couple of years ago, I believe that sentiment is still inherent for many in this country. And I believe it will become more pronounced over the next four years. In 2016, because of lack of trust by Republican voters in the party's leadership, I'm predicting the Republican presidential nominee in 2016 will not come from political ranks. I believe half the country will be ready for something different, something not normal in the traditions of presidential candidates or politics."

"If the Republican nominee will not be a politician, from where will he come from?"

"It's a good question. First, let me say there is a distinct possibility the Republican nominee will be a woman. As to what walk of life she comes from, it could be from anywhere. She could be a sports superstar, someone from entertainment, from business, or from the financial community. This is not terribly far-fetched. Remember, we've seen this phenomenon in the recent past with Ross Perot and Steve Forbes. But the country wasn't quite ready for this kind of tectonic shift when they ran. In 2016, I believe the country will be ready. And it could very well be a woman who wins the Republican nomination to run against Heather Carrington. But one thing about this candidate I feel comfortable in predicting is that she, or he, will have one core fundamental issue that will drive their motivation and their campaign."

"Bridgett don't leave us hanging. Who will be the Republican nominee in 2016? We won't hold you to it. Just give us an idea who you would put your money on right now."

"Carly Fiorina, the former CEO of Hewlett Packard. I would give her a fifty-fifty shot for defeating Carrington."

Five

S parks Steak House on East Forty-second Street between Second and Third Avenue in Manhattan was one of the favorite New York restaurants of the brothers Carlton and Cornelius Hale.

It was a brisk mid-February evening in 2012 as Carl and "Corny" decided to rendezvous in the city to talk about the recently started 2012 Presidential primary season. Both Hale brothers were concerned about the Republican party field of candidates.

Carlton chauffeured down from his home in Boston specifically for this hook-up with his younger brother. Earlier in the day, Cornelius flew into Philadelphia from his home in Greenville, South Carolina, for a meeting with the directors of the Liberty Bell Foundation, an inner-city youth-focused organization founded by a local pastor. The foundation served to improve the lives of underserved young people in the community, teaching values that aligned with the Hales.

They had been supporting the foundation's efforts the last six years and the directors wanted to pitch Cornelius on some new ideas they had. After his meeting concluded at one, he commissioned a limo to take him directly to Sparks.

The Hale brothers enjoyed a successful business legacy and owned at one point the second largest privately held company in the U.S., The Hale Group. Carlton Hale was born in 1943 and Cornelius in 1947. Their father, Dickson Hale, amassed a large fortune in his lifetime as the founder of The Hale Group, which emerged from Dickson's invention of a new water management system to help oil refineries reduce the amount of water used for cooling in the process of refining oil into gasoline.

As a chemical engineer in the oil fields of Oklahoma in the early 1950s, Dickson recognized an opportunity. His invention was an instant success and widely adopted both domestically and internationally by the petroleum refinery industry. The company he formed to bring the technology to market, Halenomics International, became a Fortune 50 company in 1974 when its valuation reached $200 billion. His success led to amassing a considerable fortune, a fortune he willed in equal parts to his two sons upon his death in 1978. Carlton and Cornelius took over the reins of Halenomics after Dickson's passing and managed the company's continued growth until it reached $350 billion in valuation in 1996. At that point they decided it was time to exit and turn their attention to using their considerable wealth for philanthropic and political purposes.

The two power brokers settled into their booth at Sparks and exchanged the usual pleasantries one might expect between two elderly brothers. With the pleasantries dispatched, Carlton started his lament.

"You know Corny, I don't like our chances for winning the White House this year. I don't like any of our guys. Huckabee, Santorum, Romney, Perry, Ron Paul. I don't see any of them beating Obama."

Cornelius listened to his older brother with a respectful, focused silence, letting him get his thoughts out without interruption. Instead of responding directly, he readied the questions he had for his older brother to make the case he had been contemplating for many weeks. His recent thoughts were focused on how to get the country back on what he felt was the right track. He knew convincing his elder brother on the merit of his ideas would be a challenge.

"Yeah, I agree, all the horses in our stable are ugly. So, my dear big brother, what kind of background would a prospective conservative candidate need to pose a real threat to Obama this year? Or to Carrington in 2016? Would it have to be someone in politics or someone from a different industry, say a corporate CEO like John Chambers? Someone from inside the beltway but Hispanic—Rubio? Would the best candidate for us be a woman—Susan Martinez? Does it need to be a governor, as opposed to a senator or congressman? What does a winning 2012 Republican candidate look like in your eyes?"

Carlton took a long sip from his Hendricks Gin Gibson and considered Corny's question. It was a question that had been troubling him since the 2008 election with the failure of John McCain not only to win, but also his failure to articulate the messaging and motivate the passion for the shared values of the Hale brothers.

"Well, my young brother, instead of me answering your questions—because knowing you the way I do, you usually ask questions for which you've carefully, in advance, formulated your answers—you go first. What does our next successful Republican Presidential candidate need to look like?"

"Carl, that's a cop-out. Come on, give me your thoughts. I'm relishing the thought of debating you on this because I'm pretty sure we're not aligned on this one. But seriously, I want to know what you think our 2012 or 2016 candidate should be all about."

Carl accepted the invitation. "For this year, best I can tell, the election's going to come down to a few battleground states. Florida. Ohio. Colorado. Iowa. North Carolina. We need people on the ticket who can help carry those states, whether it's the top spot or the VP. McCain-Palin had zero shot in any of those states. We win a majority of the battleground states, and we have a chance. We can't afford the same oversight this time. What we need Corny is a ticket where both candidates have strong connections or relationships with the real movers and shakers in the battleground states. Easier said than done, but that's the opinion I gave to the RNC last month."

Carl continued: "You know, Corny, besides the tactical strategies, we really need someone who can better articulate what will move conservatives to vote. Most of the politicians today, I'm sick of them.

They're too busy lining their pockets by peddling influence to stand up for what's best for the country. What we need is another Reagan. But I don't see him out there. We should focus on congressional elections again. It served us well last election. Taking back Congress saved our ass. And we need more, good conservative governors. Mike Pence is a good man, and he'll be in a dogfight to succeed Daniels in Indiana. Rick Hill has a shot in Montana. That would be a net gain. Scott Walker will need all the help he can get in Wisconsin. Listen to me. I'm talking about Montana and Indiana and Wisconsin, and not Washington DC. We're so screwed."

Corny laughed. It always amused him when his older brother was trying to think out loud on a subject that was obviously confusing him. He was especially amused when his esteemed older brother resorted to slightly salty language.

"Carl, remember when you were thirteen and I was ten, and we were shooting hoops in the backyard, and I was smoking hot from the outside? I was shooting from the top of the key and the corner and couldn't miss. I was a basket away from beating you for the first time. Then you stop the game and said we need to make a rule change because the wind was starting to blow. Your rule was neither of us could shoot more than two shots outside the key in a row. You didn't want the wind affecting the game, and if we shot from inside the key, the wind wouldn't affect our shots. You said the game was over unless we used this rule. The fact that you were four inches taller I'm sure had no bearing on your change." Corny paused to let that comment hang in the air. Both brothers smiled from the memory.

Corny continued: "I so badly wanted to beat you, and I didn't want you to quit, so I said OK. You started blocking my shots and that completely turned the game around. You ended up winning, and I never had another chance to beat you in B-ball."

Carl laughed aloud loud at the pleasant memory. "I always felt grateful you fell for that one, little brother, so I could retire undefeated in hoops against you. What's the point?"

Corny obliged: "Well, I agree with you about this year. None of the Republicans in the field have a chance in hell. We're outflanked. The Democrats know exactly what they need to do to get their voters out in a Presidential election. They win the larger states, they wrap it up. They have a playbook we're hopeless against. They set us up every time. When our side comes out on an issue, they know exactly how to spin things to make us look heartless and, greedy. They play on the emotions of our guys and push their buttons, getting them to say something stupid. It gets on the nightly news. It inflames the Democrat base, and they cough up more money for the campaigns. It rallies their troops, and they can play that card whenever they need. As I see it, we have no chance for the White House this year. We don't have the right horse, we don't have the right message, and we don't have enough time to change things. We should set our sights on 2016, and realize our only chance, with Heather Carrington the likely candidate, is to change the game."

Corny was now almost shouting and ended his diatribe with a slap to the table from his open left hand, rattling the glassware, attracting the glances of some of the others in the Sparks main dining hall. "We've got to get them to play our game. But the game has to be a new one, a different one so we can mobilize the people in this country who think like we do to vote."

"Easy there, little brother. Talking about having their buttons pushed, what's gotten into you?"

"Too many things just eating at me. Like a call I took in February. A woman in Houston. She's working at a polling booth in 2010 for a local election. She sees numerous voting irregularities and brings them up to local voting officials. She waits for months, hears nothing and they ignore her follow ups. She starts a political activist group to alert the community about voter fraud. The response is strong, and she takes her fight to the next level. She wants to build a website and produce materials to educate the public. Classic First Amendment stuff."

"She wants to raise funding to educate the public and wants to do it all legit, so she applies for tax exempt status and then KABOOM!!! The huge fucking hammer of the federal bureaucracy comes down on this unsuspecting, unfortunate patriotic woman. She has no idea she's going to be dragged into hell for no other reason than she loves her country. The FBI comes calling. The domestic terrorist arm of the FBI starts investigating one of their members. The IRS audits their small manufacturing business and their personal taxes. To top it off, BATF and OSHA hit them with fines and bureaucratic audits."

"This woman was not political until 2008. She decides to get involved. She promotes a cause and finds others to join her. But she's on the wrong side of the fence. I tell you Carl, if something's not done, we'll end up like China."

"Corny, I've never seen you so animated. Maybe you shouldn't answer your phone and take those calls. You say change the game. How?"

"We have to turn things on their head. Change the way we find and elect our leaders. The current system breeds career politicians and they put their careers in front of what's best for the country. If it doesn't change, I think we're doomed. Democrats, Republicans, there's a difference in ideology, but doesn't seem to be a big difference in the character of the people running and being elected."

Carl leaned in with a little smirk on his face, staring his brother straight in the eye and half seriously says, "Alright, little brother, how do you propose we do this?"

Corny sat back in his chair, exasperated. "I don't have the faintest idea, yet."

Carl nodded, letting Corny's rant hang over the table. After a brief moment of reflection, with both powerful men in thought, he broke the silence.

"By the way, how was the LBF meeting in Philly today?"

"Unproductive. Their board doesn't seem to connect with Jeffrey. They had no new good ideas. They're having budget issues and the facilities don't seem to be in good order. I wrote them a check for $300K."

"No wonder your muffins are toasted. Here, I'll make you feel better. We're going to California in six weeks. Ventura County Economic Development Conference. Favor for Earl Gregory. Felt we owe it to him since I think this might be his last run. That district of his is going to miss his presence in Congress."

Six

"Abby, hold my calls for thirty minutes."

"Of course, your lordship. May I ask why?"

"Of course, you can, and I'll discuss it with you as I'm handing you your pink slip. Come on in whenever you can pull yourself away from figuring out how to annoy me."

"You're sounding a little tense today, Mr. Braxton. No need to fill out the pink slip. Allow me to guess what's got your boxers in a wad. It's the beginning of April and I haven't heard you boasting with your fantasy baseball cronies. I'll say you're late drafting your team. Just make sure you take Matt Kemp this year. He's going to have a monster season."

"Abby".

"Yes, mi' Lord?"

"You scare me. Just hold my calls for thirty minutes, OK?"

"Yes, sir. Remember, you've got Randy Boswell from the City at eleven today."

As busy as Jon Braxton's days typically were, his daily routines included many quirks. No matter how difficult, stressful, or tenuous the business dealings of the day were, Jon was often simultaneously engaged in something trivial or totally detached from the day's business affairs—his commitment to the younger guys he had been involved with the last ten years playing fantasy baseball being one such distraction.

At first these quirks drove Abby crazy, but over time she realized these diversions were one of the many reasons Jon was so successful in running Spectre. He always had a lens at his disposal to view a business situation no one else had. This lens provided him an image of great clarity. He always had an unfair advantage in a difficult or competitive situation. He always had the right words or actions to move the ball down the field. Whether it was a sales negotiation or a disagreement with a vendor or having to moderate a disagreement between employees, Jon had a knack for generating positive outcomes.

"Abby?" Jon's voice resounded over the intercom.

She looked at her computer screen and saw he put two business calls on hold to buzz her. "Yes, your highness?"

"Are you sure Kemp's fully recovered from the shoulder issues at the end of last season?"

Abby Martin had been working for Jonathon Braxton and Spectre Systems for thirteen years. The last eight as his executive administrative assistant.

As with all Spectre's early employees, Abby got to know Jon well in the formative days of the company. In those early years, he was highly focused on firsthand interaction with all his staff. As the company grew, it became a challenge to maintain that touch. But he always managed to keep his eyes and ears open to stay close to what was going on with his people.

Jon was involved to some degree with everyone, from the warehouse staff to his vice presidents. If there was any one constant that shaped his management style, it was his belief the best opportunity for his employees to reach their maximum potential at work was to have their personal lives in harmony. In the early years, he made it a point to know each of his employees personally and to help in any way he could when there was turbulence.

As Spectre grew from a local company in Thousand Oaks, to an 800-person nationwide enterprise, hands-on interaction with everyone in the company became impossible. But the company managed to find unique and innovative ways to maintain a highly productive and engaged workforce. Abby was instrumental in scaling Jon's people-first philosophy. Jon recognized Abby's talents shortly after she started with Spectre. She saw his unique management style and personality and adopted him as her mentor. She witnessed how his management style bred loyalty, satisfaction, and productivity. Without any specific direction, she started executing his policies, often coming up with her own creative approaches. Not unnoticed by Jon.

Abby quickly rose through the ranks of the company, eventually becoming Jon's executive administrator and most trusted confidant. They and their spouses became great friends. Abby was never attracted to Jon in any way other than how a little sister might feel about a big brother.

Jon and Abby complimented one another perfectly. He was a business strategy genius with an uncanny knack of being able to understand the dynamics of any business or personal situation. He consistently and successfully solved complex problems, many times with unorthodox solutions.

She was his grounding wire and sounding board. Abby Martin, now thirty-five, had grown into a highly competent business executive in her own right. She often acted as Jon's proxy in meetings and at trade shows. She gained the respect of numerous executives throughout the electronics and computer systems industries. When travelling for company business, she was often approached with new career opportunities. Many executives commented to her she deserved more credit for Spectre's success. She deserved a title befitting her talents and capabilities, a corner office, more recognition, more money.

When approached with employment offers from vendors, customers, or competitors, she'd always nod and politely decline, diplomatically responding Jon was very good to her and she was perfectly content as his executive assistant. She explained she didn't want more responsibility. Maintaining a good work-life balance for her husband Mark and her two young children was more important.

She'd always relate the informal job offers back to Jon. She adopted his philosophy early on. How could she maintain his trust and respect if she were not totally honest and truthful with him? In his eyes, the basis of any successful relationship was total transparency.

"You know, Bob is right. You should get a promotion and a title and a raise. Let's make you Eastern Region VP and have you work out of Boston, and then I can finally enjoy a tuna sandwich in peace."

"No freaking way. You think I'm going to leave you here by yourself so you can screw up the good thing we've got going? Uh-uh. Sorry, but I'm keeping my seat right outside your office so I can keep an eye on you—wait, make that both eyes and both ears."

Jon knew Abby was coveted by many other companies and was willing to endorse her and support her taking another position in the industry if she wanted. He did not want that to happen, but he didn't consider himself in the equation. If she felt a career change was in her best interest, he knew her well enough to know that she had weighed everything and was making the best decision for herself and her family.

Abby knew Jon would not stand in her way, would support her, and remain her close friend if she decided to leave his side. She never seriously considered any offers to do so.

———— ≈ ————

"Mrs. Martin, Randy Boswell is here" read an instant message window on Abby's computer screen.

"Thanks Joni, send him up," she replied instantly, with keystrokes typed so fast it might have been a one-key shortcut.

"Abby, you look marvelous today" chirped the Thousand Oaks city business manager as he walked purposefully into Spectre's executive offices reception area, furnished by Abby's desk adjacent to a comfortable sofa and two chairs.

"Ah, Mr. Boswell, wish I could say the same about you," she said playfully. "But you look like crap. Why didn't you shave last night? And Jesus, Randy, that suit? You know when you're coming to meet with the king to ask him for some treasure—I assume you're here to ask for something—the least you could do is clean it up a little."

"Abby, have I ever told you how much I love you?"

"Uh, no, Randy you never have, but I wish you would".

"Wonder why that is?" Randy feigned as they shared a smile.

"OK, I'll let his majesty know you're here."

Abby picked up her phone handset, keeping her eyes on Boswell, somewhat curious the reason for this meeting. She pressed the blue button on her phone, giving her access to a speaker on Jon's desk. "Your highness, Mr. Boswell is here."

"Thanks Abby, send him in. And while you're at it see if you can get some work done today for a change," loud enough for Boswell to hear.

She made eye contact with Randy and smiled as she replied to her boss. "Yes, your lordship, your wish is my command. Go on in, Mr. Boswell."

"Thank you, Mrs. Martin."

Randy opened the door and walked into Jon's office. He stood slimmer and taller than Randy, dressed in gray, pleated woolen dress pants and a long-sleeved blue button-down collared dress shirt. He was in front of his desk awaiting his friend. Randy closed the door behind him. The two greeted each other warmly. They exchanged a brief power hug followed by a firm handshake.

Randy Boswell was one of many local civic leaders in the Jonathon Braxton fan club. He had been the City Manager of Thousand Oaks since 1999, the year Spectre moved into town. He had seen many economic cycles over the years and was grateful his city was the home of Jon's enterprise.

Jon's business provided Thousand Oaks with numerous outreach and philanthropic benefits and had become the become the city's second largest employer behind Amgen Pharmaceuticals. Spectre was highly profitable and paid their people above industry average wages and lucrative bonuses, contributing to the community's quality of life. In addition, Jon was always assisting various charities and causes with ideas, money, and people.

One program Jon created in 2006 monumentally successful in supporting the city was the company's Charity Sabbatical Program and corresponding Mission Fund.

Every Spectre employee had the option to volunteer two weeks of time every year, fully paid, to work with local charities. The perk engineered feelings of pride and purpose. It was one of many reasons employee morale and productivity at Spectre was high. Why turnover was low. And why the company was so highly regarded by its customers and business partners.

After donating time to the authorized cause of their choice, employees were encouraged to identify noteworthy fund-raising projects for funding by the Mission Fund. For a candidate project to be approved, the Spectre employee had to write a business plan detailing the use of the funds and clearly outlining the benefits to the charity.

Spectre employees deciding to write business plans to qualify for funding were encouraged to be creative. The business plans had a better chance for approval if they were novel and innovative.

Employees were encouraged to grow into important roles within the causes they chose for their sabbaticals. Spectre further encouraged these personal growth opportunities by sponsoring classes at Spectre headquarters to educate employees how nonprofits operated and their best practices.

The goodwill and tangible benefits generated for Spectre employees, for the company, and for the city were immeasurable. Randy Boswell was ever grateful.

Jon motioned Randy to take a seat in one of the four chairs surrounding a circular coffee table in the corner of the twenty-by-twenty-foot office.

"Randy, it's great to see you. What's up?"

"You know JB, if you ever let Abby leave this place, I'll never forgive you."

"Sounds like she worked you over this morning —and you might have enjoyed it?"

"Just a little," Randy offered with a smile.

He continued: "Thanks for taking the time to see me. First, I wanted to personally thank you for everything you did to support Miranda Sanchez and the work she did for Food for the Hungry during the Christmas season last year. Thanks in large part to her efforts, food donations were up sixty percent in the fourth quarter over the previous year."

"Doesn't surprise me. Miranda is very talented. She started in the warehouse, just like Abby. Could barely speak English the first year she worked for us. Now she's the managing director for the Spectre component warehouse. Her division's stock price is up over forty percent from last quarter. The whole company is investing in her."

"JB, what the hell are you talking about? Spectre component warehouse? Managing director? Stock price up forty percent?"

"Long story, Randy. I'll tell you about our new internal company equity market someday over a beer. What brings you here today?"

Boswell, who was sitting back in his chair, leaned forward.

"JB, look, I know I ask a lot of you, more than I ever should, given everything you do for the city. But this request isn't coming from me—although I do hope you accept. I was asked by Mitch Greenway from the Ventura County Board of Supervisors to ask you to be a keynote speaker at the County's Economic Development Conference coming up next month. I know you don't like speaking about the things you do. I know you like the results to speak for themselves. I know you like your people to get the credit for the ideas you come up with and the programs you put together. I know, I know. But consider this one. There'll be a lot of influential people from out-of-county and out-of-state potential employers attending. The county is undertaking a concerted effort to grow its employment base. The plan for this conference is to introduce the county, all its attributes, and some economic incentives to attract new employers. I know you're always looking for ways to help the community. For the good of the region, we need the conference to be a success. The county needs to make a good showing, and we know you can help us. Greenway asked me to ask you." With that last word, Boswell leaned back in his chair, crossed his legs, and outstretched his arms, palms up in Jon's direction, gesturing *'Thoughts'?*

Jon silently considered Randy's ask. Boswell was hopeful Jon was strongly considering it.

"Randy?"

"Yup."

"What kind of season is Matt Kemp going to have for the Dodgers this year?"

Randy tried to maintain his serious demeanor, unsuccessfully. "Ahhh. It's fantasy baseball time. I think he'll have a good year. What does your team GM Abby think?"

"She's in love with his butt and thinks he's going to have a monster season. Send me the dates and agenda of the conference and I'll get back to you."

Seven

The intercom came alive on Abby's desk. "Abby, it's Miranda". We've got trouble in the warehouse. Please get Mr. Braxton down here fast. I'm worried something bad is about to happen."

Composed but firm Abby responded: "OK, hold on Miranda, I'll interrupt his call."

Abby typed out an instant message that popped on Jon's computer screen. '*Need you to take a call from Miranda in the warehouse, NOW. She's got an urgent problem.*'

Jon learned over the years to trust Abby's judgment and told Joe Spangler, his East Coast region operations manager, he'd have to call him back.

'*OK, I'm off the phone. Transfer her on and come in,*' popped on Abby's monitor.

In a few seconds, Jon had Miranda on the speaker phone, with Abby sitting across the desk listening in. "Mr. Braxton, there was a bad argument between two of my guys a few minutes ago, Lloyd Culver and Jamie McKewen. Lloyd was screaming at Jamie, something about how could he do this to him? I think it's about Lloyd's girlfriend. One of the other guys told me Lloyd and Jamie are friends, and they hang out together with their girlfriends. But he thinks Jamie's got a thing for Lloyd's girlfriend and has been hitting on her. Lloyd overheard Jamie talking to one of the other guys about them sleeping together and he went ballistic. Two of my guys broke up the shouting, and Lloyd ran out to the parking lot to his car. He was screaming that he was going to kill Jamie. I can see him now through my window. He's heading back towards the warehouse. It looks like he's holding something under his coat. It might be a gun."

"Call 911. I'm heading down. Lock the warehouse door to keep Lloyd out. Tell Jamie to leave the building through the front door and get away from the area."

Jon bolted from his desk, running at full speed down the hallway past Spectre's executive offices. Abby was in quick pursuit. He approached the flight of stairs to his right, grabbed the stair rail to swing a ninety-degree turn. He covered the single flight down in two seconds. The stairway from the second floor let out on the first floor in the product manager's office area. The entrance to the component warehouse was a straight shot of thirty yards through the product management and customer service departments. Jon covered the ground in six seconds. Abby was no more than two seconds behind.

Miranda couldn't get to the warehouse door in time to lock Lloyd out. When Jon and Abby entered the warehouse, Lloyd Culver was semi-crouching in an attack position. He was facing Jamie McKewen who was twenty feet away, backed into a corner. Jamie had his hands up, pleading with Lloyd. There were fifteen other Spectre employees watching from a short distance, a few of them urging Lloyd to drop the knife. Jamie pleaded: "Come on, man. What are you doing? Shit, Lloyd, put the knife down, man."

Tears were flowing down Lloyd's face. "You asshole, Jamie. I fucking trusted you and you hit on Carla. You slept with her? I'm going to kill you."

Lloyd was processing the situation trying to decide what to do. He was not one to partake in violence. This situation was confusing him. His emotions had taken over, but his logical mind was still in the picture, trying to wrest control.

Jon had interacted with Lloyd over the two years he'd worked at Spectre. He'd been a model employee, and Jon liked him. On more than one occasion, they had conversations about the future and what Lloyd wanted to do, career-wise. They had talked about Lloyd's girlfriend Carla, and Lloyd confided to Jon how much he loved her. But he was insecure about the relationship, fearing he might not be the career man she wanted. Lloyd was a hard worker and came from a blue-collar family. He had a high school education and was relatively well spoken, but not overly intelligent nor ambitious.

"Lloyd, what's up?" Jon said calmly, breaking Lloyd's intense focus on Jamie. He walked slowly towards the distraught young man. Jon had his arms down by his waist, palms up. Lloyd was shaking and still dangerous, now spreading his focus between Jamie and Jon.

Jon walked to a point between Lloyd and Jamie and made eye contact with Lloyd. "It's not worth it, Lloyd. You hurt Jamie with that knife and your life goes down the drain."

"I don't care, Mr. Braxton. Stay out of this. That asshole slept with my girlfriend. I'm gonna kill him."

"Whoa, Lloyd, what are you thinking?" Jon was taking a chance there was nothing between Jamie and Carla. He wasn't sure but hoped to cast some doubt. "How do you know that's true?"

"You think something's going on between Carla and Jamie? I don't think so. From what you've told me about her, I think she loves you and there's nothing to be fried about."

"I overheard him talking to Jose about sleeping with her." Lloyd's anger was growing again as he heard himself say the words. His grip on the knife tightened. "Get out of the way, Mr. Braxton."

"Not going to do that, Lloyd. Not going to let you ruin your life. If you love Carla, you give her the benefit of the doubt. You love her, right? You've got to find out for sure. If it's true, then you deal with it. Like a man and not with a knife. But don't do anything before you know what's really going on. Get all the facts. C'mon Lloyd, think clearly. Let's you and I find out what's really going on. Whaddya say? Let me help you."

He made eye contact with Lloyd and gave him a reassuring nod. He slowly turned to face Jamie for a second and then turned his gaze back to Lloyd. While watching Lloyd's eyes, Jon spoke forcefully: "Jamie. Walk behind me and keep on going out of the warehouse and leave the building. Don't come back to work until I call you and we talk, got it?"

"Yeah," said Jamie, also watching Lloyd intently ae he walked towards Jon's back on the way to the door Jon and Abby burst through a moment ago.

Jamie made his way out. Lloyd dropped his right arm and was barely maintaining his grasp on the knife. His head was down. He then raised it to face Jon. "I'm sorry, Mr. Braxton."

"Lloyd is that your fishing knife? The one you mentioned when you told me about the time you and Carla went fishing off Channel Islands a few months ago and had a shark on your line?"

Jon's memory soothed Lloyd, but he remained distraught at the thought of losing Carla and the trouble he had just caused with his jealousy. He could not respond.

Jon walked towards him cautiously. "Lloyd, please hand me the knife and let's go upstairs and talk." Lloyd did what was asked, and Jon put his arm around his shoulders to console him. Jon handed the knife to Abby as the two of them started towards the interior warehouse door leading back into the office area.

At that moment two Ventura County Sheriff's deputies burst into the warehouse through an exterior door and entered the warehouse at a point forty feet from where Jon and Lloyd were. They had their service revolvers drawn. "Who's Miranda?"

Jon turned to face the officers. Lloyd stiffened in fear as he realized what was happening. One of the officers recognized Jon. "Mr. Braxton? Everything OK?"

Jon did not recognize the officer, but many in the Ventura County Sheriff's Department knew Jon from his involvement with the Win-the-Day Foundation, a foundation Spectre had started five years ago to work with underprivileged youth in Ventura County. It was a foundation that worked closely with the Sheriff's department and Officer Sanders had participated in some activities with the foundation over the years.

"Officer, everything's fine. Just a small misunderstanding. It's under control. We don't need your services but thank you for getting here so quickly."

"I'm sorry, Mr. Braxton, but we'll need to talk to you or Miranda regarding the 911 call. She mentioned there was a life-threatening situation, and it's policy we write a report."

"I understand but this young man is not feeling well, and we need to help him a little bit. What's your name, officer?"

"Jerry Sanders."

"Jerry, thank you for understanding. Please call me tomorrow, and I'll fill you in on what happened." Jon stared at Sanders with firm resolve to protect Lloyd from any repercussions. At least until he fully understood all the circumstances.

Officer Sanders looked back at Jon. He knew he should take control of the situation and demand cooperation in gathering the information for their report. The two men stared at each other for a moment.

"OK Mr. Braxton, I'll call you tomorrow." The officers put their service revolvers away, turned, and left the building. Lloyd breathed a sigh of relief.

"Lloyd, give me a minute." Jon took his arm off Lloyd's shoulders and walked over to Abby standing twenty feet from Lloyd. Speaking quietly out of Lloyd's earshot, "get Carla's cell number and send her a text to call you, and then let me speak with her. Keep it quiet."

Jon trusted Abby's resourcefulness. He knew she would know what to do to come up with Carla's number. She'd take to online social media. Look for a Facebook page. Talk to others in the company. She'd find someone who knew her. He knew she'd come up with the number, and it would be quick.

"Uh, Mr. JB, Braxton, sir. Can you ask Lloyd to give me his cell phone?"

Jon walked back over to Lloyd. "Lloyd don't ask me why, just trust me. Let me have your cell phone for a few minutes." Lloyd, still in a state of remorse and embarrassment, was in no state to resist. He reached into his pocket, pulled out his cell and handed it to him.

Jon walked back to Abby handing her the phone, smirking. "Smartass." He walked back to Lloyd, put his arm around his shoulders and the two of them started walking towards Jon's office.

They reached his office and entered. Jon closed the door behind them. He motioned Lloyd to have a seat in one of the four guest chairs surrounding the conference table and walked over to a small refrigerator, pulling out two bottles of Aquafina. He sat in the chair directly across from Lloyd.

"I'm going to do whatever I can to help you avoid any consequences with the law on this. But you've got to be straight with me. If I'm going to help you out on this, you've got to help me not step in it myself. If you give me any BS, I'm out. Deal?"

"Yes, sir."

"OK first, how are you feeling right now? Do you have a grip?"

"Yes, sir. Just really sad. The thought of Carla and…" Lloyd lowered his head, unable to finish the thought.

"Do you have any reason to believe there's anything going on— other than what you overheard? You know some guys like to embellish a little bit when it comes to their machismo. I don't know Jamie at all. Have never spoken to him, so I don't have a feel for his deal. But I know you and what you've told me about Carla. You've got to give her the benefit of the doubt at this point, right? So let me ask you again, do you have any reason whatsoever to believe what you overheard is true?"

"No, sir."

There was a knock on the door, followed by Abby's head sliding in through a slight opening. "Mr. Braxton, that important call you were waiting for—I've got them on the line."

"Thank you, Abby. Excuse me Lloyd." Jon got walked out to Abby's desk. She handed him Lloyd's cell phone.

"Hi Carla, this is Jon Braxton at Spectre Systems. Lloyd works for us."

"Hi, Mr. Braxton. I know, Lloyd talks about you a lot. Is there anything wrong?"

"Carla, only you know the answer to that. First, Lloyd is OK. It's clear he's crazy about you. He overheard a conversation here about something going on in your relationship and he had a bad reaction to it. It's none of my business to know what you do, but as a friend to Lloyd, I felt I should let you know that you might have a little work to do on your relationship. And if you want to start that work, I'd like you to come to the office and pick him up and take him home. We want him to take a little time off."

Jon felt he could best help Lloyd by flushing out the truth. If the relationship was on solid footing, Carla would come. If not, she'd make an excuse not to.

"I work just a few minutes away. I'll be right there." Jon winked at Abby and flipped her Lloyd's phone, which Abby caught without effort.

"Carla's on her way. Put her in the conference room and let me know when she arrives—but don't say her name. Don't want Lloyd to know she's here."

Back in his office, he started to work on building Lloyd's confidence. He didn't know what Carla's story was yet, but felt Lloyd needed to be in a good place mentally to hear it. Good or bad.

"Lloyd, when's your next performance review with Miranda?"

"Next month. It will be two years since I started here."

"I was thinking it was about two. What's your objective for the review?"

"My objective?"

"Yes, your objective. Every time you meet with your supervisor, it's an opportunity to advance your career. I'm guessing you want to advance your career. I'd like you to advance your career with us."

"I haven't really thought about it that way."

"Well, this is the kind of thing you've got to start thinking about. You're what, twenty-eight, twenty-nine years old now?"

"Twenty-eight."

"OK, here's what we're going to do. We're going to work together on developing an objective for your review. First you need to write down your personal and professional goals. If I give you a worksheet, will you do that for me?"

"OK."

Jon got up and walked over to a filing cabinet. He pulled out an information form printed with the title, 'My Career Plan'. He walked back to the table, handed it to Lloyd, and sat down across from him again. "Read it all the way through."

As he started reading the worksheet, for the first time in the last thirty minutes, Lloyd took his mind off Carla. "Mr. Braxton, I've never really thought too much about the future and what I want to accomplish. I sort of live day by day. I might need some time to come up with the answers to these questions."

"I understand and that's fine, but let's get the process started. Let's have you take a crack at answering them and then we'll review together, and between us we'll come up with your plan. Once we have your plan dialed in, we'll work on the upcoming review and develop your objectives. Life can be very rewarding if you figure out what you love to do and then set a course to put you in a position to do what you love."

A light bulb suddenly went off in Lloyd's head. He realized why he had been so insecure in his relationship with Carla. She wanted from him exactly what Jon was now asking, she just didn't know how to get it across. The discussions they had about their future always ended in frustration for both. Lloyd now understood what Carla wanted. She wanted Lloyd to come up with the answers to the questions that were right in front of him on the "My Career Plan" sheet. He sighed at the realization.

A knock on the door interrupted the moment of silence. Abby cracked the office door and peeked her head in. "Sorry Mr. Braxton, I have another call you were expecting."

"Sorry Lloyd, excuse me again." Jon took a pen out of his pocket and set it on the round meeting table in front of Lloyd. He got up and walked out the office door, closing it behind him.

"Carla's in the conference room".

Jon entered Spectre's executive conference room. It was a nicely, but not overly opulently appointed fourteen-by-twenty-two-foot meeting room with an oval conference table that could accommodate sixteen. The conference table was made of solid mahogany, and the sixteen chairs were of black mesh ergonomic material. There were two thirty-two-inch monitors mounted on the north wall and a sleek modern brushed-steel video conferencing equipment cabinet along the wall opposite the glass wall that bordered the open hallway traversing Spectre's executive offices. The blinds on the glass wall were drawn shut.

Jon closed the door behind him. He had never met Carla and spent a few seconds watching her as he made his way to a seat. He was hoping she would tell him the truth, and he was trying to use this first impression to help him conclude if she would. She was sitting nervously as he introduced himself. He noticed her small stature and sensed her unease. "Hi Carla, I'm Jon Braxton. Nice to meet you and thank you for coming by on such short notice," he said in a friendly but firm and even tone. She stood up to greet him. Jon extended his hand, and they shook. "Please, have a seat".

"Carla, I'll get right to the point, OK?" He gave her the opening to respond to help break her tension.

"OK," she replied cautiously.

"Look, like I said on the phone, your relationship with Lloyd is none of my business, so this is a little awkward. But Lloyd's mental state while he's working here is my business, and that's why you're here. Let me first say that everything is OK physically with Lloyd. But whether Lloyd's OK otherwise depends on what the truth is about anything going on romantically between you and Jamie McKewen. If you don't want to talk to me about this, that's fine and I'd understand. It's entirely up to you. You're welcome to get up and leave right now, and Lloyd will never know you were here and the two of you can figure it out."

Jon looked at Carla without emotion. She was sitting upright with her two hands interlocked and resting on the conference room table. The mention of Lloyd and Jamie in the same context caused her to shake. She looked back at Jon briefly and then turned her gaze into the table, her hands still in the same position, making no movements that indicated she was ready to walk out.

After a few seconds of silence, Jon continued: "I know, and I mean I know, that Lloyd loves you. He and I have talked about you, and he's shared his feelings. Earlier today he overheard a conversation where Jamie was talking to another guy in the warehouse, saying something about him and you."

He paused to give Carla the chance to respond. She remained silent. "If it's true, it's between the two of you and you can choose to leave, and Lloyd will never know you were here. If it's not true and you want my help talking to Lloyd about it, I'll help, but only on the condition that you tell me the full truth. I told Lloyd he needs to give you the benefit of the doubt. I asked you to come here without him knowing because I care about him, and he cares about you. If it's not true about Jamie and you want my help to fix this, I will. It's up to you."

It was time for Carla to speak and he gave her the opportunity, sitting back in his chair, looking at her in a way that he hoped would build some trust.

With her hands still locked and her head still down, staring at the portion of the conference table directly in front of her, she was ready to respond. "Mr. Braxton, I've never mixed it up with Jamie, but he has been flirting hard with me lately when we've been out with him and his girlfriend."

Carla's voice was cracking with a combination of anxiety and shame. "I told him no." Carla looked up at Jon and a few tears were streaming down her cheeks. "What did Lloyd do?"

"Carla, what are your feelings towards Lloyd?"

"I love him, and I feel sick that he heard Jamie lie about us."

"Do you want my help fixing this?"

She looked at Jon and nodded. They spoke for another minute and then Jon led her to his office. "Lloyd's in here. Good luck." He opened the door for her, motioned her to go in and then closed the door to leave the two of them alone.

Jon walked over to the desk chair across from Abby and sat. She was heads down working on email. She was staring intently into her computer monitor, not giving any indication she knew he was there. Without any break in her focus, "don't forget you left Joe Spangler hanging. Want me to get him on the phone?"

"No, I'll get back to him tomorrow. Go ahead and finish your shopping." She smiled, nodded at the monitor, and let the banter, for the moment, end there. They sat in silence, Abby writing effective and important emails. Jon waiting to give Lloyd and Carla a few minutes alone.

As Carla entered Jon's office, Lloyd turned. He was surprised to see her and stood to face her. She ran to him and hugged him fiercely, sobbing. "I'm sorry, baby. I'm sorry. It's not true. Nothing's going on between that bastard and me. Please believe me." She was in an all-out cry.

Lloyd took hold of her shoulders and pulled her back to see her face. Tears were streaming down. He had Jon's words of giving her the benefit of the doubt in his mind and decided he believed her 100 percent. He moved his hands from her shoulders to her cheeks, moving in for a kiss which she accepted gratefully. "I love you," Lloyd whispered.

They were in an embrace when there was a knock at the office door. "Guys, OK for me to come in?" Lloyd left his embrace with Carla and walked to the door to let Jon in. He walked over to his desk chair and motioned Carla and Lloyd to sit in the two chairs across the desk facing his.

"You guys have any plans tonight?"

Carla and Lloyd looked at each other a little puzzled. "No, sir," Lloyd responded.

"OK, what restaurant in town have you talked about going to but haven't yet?"

"Uh, I don't know Mr. Braxton."

"Carla?"

"Well Lloyd talks about Mastro's every once in a while, but we really can't afford it."

Jon took a key from his pocket, unlocked his lower left desk drawer, pulled out a $200 Visa gift card, and handed it to Lloyd. "Seven o'clock at Mastro's tonight, OK? I'll have Abby make your reservation."

Lloyd and Carla looked at each other puzzled, still holding hands across the two chairs. Lloyd turned back to Jon. "OK, thank you."

"Great. And Lloyd, I want you in my office at eight sharp tomorrow morning. I want you to tell me what you both had for dinner and how you liked it. Then we'll to start work on your plan. Deal?"

"Yes sir."

"Good. Now go on home and have a great time tonight. Carla, nice meeting you. Lloyd, see you tomorrow."

Jon stood and walked over to his office door, opened it, and showed

Lloyd and Carla out. They were still holding hands as they walked by Abby's desk. Abby had Lloyd's cell phone ready and handed it to him as he walked by. "Bye, Lloyd. Bye, Carla."

"Bye, Mrs. Martin."

Jon had already returned to his desk to catch up on email. Abby walked to his office door, knocked twice, cracked the door, and peeked her head in. "Well done, your highness.".

Eight

arl Gregory had served the twenty-sixth California Congressional District as its House Representative since 1984. In early 2012, he was contemplating his future. If he were going to run for reelection he had to decide quickly. If chose to run, he knew it would be his last.

As was his custom, Gregory was home for the weekend. His normal schedule when Congress was in session was, on Thursday afternoon, flying to Los Angeles from Washington and then limo from LAX to Thousand Oaks. A seven-hour door-to door trip. On Monday afternoon he would reverse course and return to Washington.

It was a grueling schedule for the seventy-six-year-old Gregory, but he loved being home and was willing to endure the travel to spend time in his district and near his family.

One Friday in mid-April, Gregory was grateful to be in his home district Thousand Oaks office and away from the bitter cold that had been gripping Washington DC the last ten days. He was readying for a 9 a.m. meeting scheduled with his California chief of staff for the last eighteen years, Rob Wiley. Wiley, along with Gregory's activist wife of forty-six years, Jeanine, were the center of his trusted advisor team.

Gregory was already seated in the conference room, reading the Washington Post, when Wiley walked in at 8:55 a.m. Gregory popped to his feet and extended his hand. The two men shook as they reached for each other's biceps with their left hands.

"Rob, good to see you. How's Barbara and the rest of the clan?"

"Everyone's fine, Earl. How was the flight in from DC yesterday?"

"Grueling, as usual. Worked on the plane all the way catching up on all the new legislation in play, as well as proposed legislation from last year we're still trying to get to the floor. Getting things done these days is harder now than I ever remember it being. I tell you, Rob, this last session has been the most frustrating of my career. The climate in the House is so hostile. Nobody trusts anyone. Nobody is willing to talk or compromise. Everyone is too concerned about their image and their nightly news persona."

Rob saw and felt Earl's frustration. The two of them had numerous conversations about the dysfunction of the 112th Congress over the last few months. He knew Earl was losing his will to continue the fight and realized the end of the road for Earl Gregory's Congressional career was near.

"What's the latest with 3630, Earl? That has good stuff, right? Will it make it to the floor and pass? Middle class tax relief, isn't that something everyone can get behind?"

Earl Gregory shrugged with a slight laugh. "Pfff, 3630? Were now calling the bill 'The Middle-Class Tax Relief and Jobs Creation Act of 2012.' If you read the current draft, the very first statement describes the Bill as 'an act to provide incentives for the creation of jobs and for other purposes.'"

Earl looked at Rob and shook his head.

"It's more of the same BS, Rob. We start with something good and then end up with shit, with no path to work it out because both sides are so lathered up with each other that there's no useful dialogue. It's so unfortunate."

"You were bullish on 3630 two months ago. Are you saying you're not going to vote for it now?"

"The bill has a lot of good things I'm for, but now I'm on the fence. There's too much useless pork and waste. I feel we can do better, and it bothers me to put my stamp on a bill that I know will cost the taxpayers a lot."

"So nothing good gets done because no one wants to compromise? Can't you weigh it out and put the partisanship aside at some point? If the good outweighs the bad, you vote for it?"

"There's the rub, Rob. We start with X. The other side adds Y. We now are forced to vote for X plus Y. But Y sucks. Yes, X is greater than Y, but Y increases the size and reach of government. It's part of a strategy. The bigger government grows, the better the situation for the federal bureaucracy. We know voting for X plus Y has short-term value, but in the long term it's harmful. X plus Y is short term pain relief. It doesn't cure anything. The most frustrating part? The Democrats outflanking us in public opinion. When we don't vote for X plus Y, they rally their base around the fact we didn't vote for X. X is good. X is great, and we said no. They completely take Y out of the conversation. They win the PR game against us every time."

Earl continued. "Rob, you like 3630? Let me tell you why I'm struggling with it. Like I said, the bill is now called the Middle-Class Tax Relief and Job Creation Act of 2012. Sounds good right? The fundamental legislation is great. Title I is about job creation incentives. We've got some Keystone Pipeline language in there. We have some EPA regulatory relief in there. We've got some bonus depreciation in there. All things that make sense. All things that create private sector jobs."

"Title II has the two percent payroll tax cut extension for the rest of 2012 and some extensions on unemployment benefits. The tax holiday extension I like, the unemployment benefit extension not so much, but I can live with it because the bill tightens up language on eligibility. But when you read the fine print, you find 'Demonstration Projects.' A total boondoggle, pure pork. The appropriations committee thinks it's a good idea to have the Labor Department get into the business of re-employment, so the bill includes a provision where the Secretary of Labor works with ten states to test the effectiveness of their own re-employment laws. How? They give them money, what else? The federal government will give money to ten states, chosen at their discretion, for more bureaucracy and more federal influence on the local level. What ten states are going to get the money? Don't foresee any red ones getting any. Wonder how many political favors this abortion is set to repay? And how will the money be spent? When you read the bill that dictates the how, you'll see the ten states will have to grow their infrastructures to comply with all the reporting standards. The whole idea of the 'Demonstration Projects' provision is asinine."

"Title III? Flood Insurance. The bill has a provision to extend the 1968 National Flood Insurance Act for five more years. I went back and read the original act, and it's a good plan. But it hasn't been reviewed in fifteen years. Flood insurance has nothing to do with jobs creation, yet it's included. I'm not saying it's not worthy, but when it's jammed in with something so top of mind like jobs creation, it's not going to get the kind of review it should. The end result? More unvetted spending and more bureaucracy."

Wiley had heard his boss lament the dysfunction of Congress many times over the last four years. This rant was not new. But Gregory's dissatisfaction with the workings of Congress had reached a new level. Wiley realized as Earl was carrying on, he needed to get his boss focused on the day ahead. They had a busy one planned, and Rob turned his thoughts and the conversation to their schedule.

"Earl, speaking of jobs creation, have you given much thought to the upcoming Ventura County Economic Summit? It's four weeks out and Larry Morris at the county is starting to finalize the speaker lineup. He's expecting you to give one of the keynotes. I told him you would. He's got some good-sized prospective new private sector employers committed to attending. He thinks he's got a good shot at adding 1,500 new county jobs."

"Of course, I'll do a keynote. Who else is he working with for the docket?"

"Well, I took the initiative and reached out to the Hale brothers on your behalf. Carl and Corny both committed to be here, and Corny has offered to speak, if needed."

Gregory leaned back in his chair and put his hands behind his head with his elbows pointed out. He looked directly at his trusted chief of staff. "Thanks, Rob. Great job, as usual. Carl and Corny. I love those guys."

"As for other potential keynote speakers, there's one guy Larry wants. You've met him a couple of times. I thought I'd make you aware because I don't think you like him. It's Jon Braxton. He owns Spectre Systems here in town. Larry wants him to speak because he does some unusual things in his business and because of his philanthropy. He's a talented public speaker and Larry feels he's an attribute to the area. He wants to showcase him in front of prospective new employers."

"We're not sure if he'll speak because he doesn't like getting involved with anything flavored with government. But he does make himself available at times for community-related events so there is a possibility he'll agree. Randy Boswell loves him and is working on him. Spectre is funding a few initiatives here in the county that are really making a huge difference. When you look at everything he's doing, it's quite remarkable. Larry wants him involved, but he hasn't yet committed. Just wanted you to know."

The Congressman was trying to remember any encounters with a Jon Braxton. He couldn't recall any. "Why do you think I don't like this Braxton guy?"

Rob Wiley's recollection of the first two interactions between Jon and the Congressman brought a chuckle. Gregory noticed and raised an eyebrow.

"During 2008 the campaign season you met him twice and they weren't altogether positive. You two just didn't seem to hit it off."

"Is he a Dem?"

Wiley laughed at the thought. "No, not at all. He's totally apolitical.

I've spent quite a bit of time with him at various functions around town, and his views on government and politics are not very favorable. Likens government to the mafia. He's not disengaged, just disinterested. He spends a lot of money in the community but picks his projects carefully. When he does invest, it's usually in projects he's involved in shaping and/or managing. He knows I work for you, and he's respectful when I try to discuss the possibility of him meeting you. He likes to say 'Rob, you know I don't do politics.'"

"What happened when I met him in 2008? I don't remember."

"You met him twice that summer. The first time, you and I were out for a quick dinner at Brent's and as we are walking in, I noticed Jon with his wife Angela at a table. I had you walk over with me and introduced you to the two of them. I had never mentioned him to you, so you had no idea who he was until I mentioned his name in the introduction. You said in your finest booming Congressional voice," Rob smiling as he remembers, "'Hello Jon, I'm Earl Gregory. Pleasure to meet you.' And Jon replied with a lot of, well, manufactured emphatic enthusiasm." "Congressman Gregory, how are you? Boy, it's been a long time. How are Jeanine and the boys and the grandkids? How are things holding up in Washington?"

"He was messing with you. You were flustered about him apparently knowing you and you not having a clue who he was. It was funny. You acted as if you knew him. 'Everyone's fine Jon, and I hope everyone is well on your end. I'll let you two enjoy your dinner. Good to see you, Jon, Mrs. Braxton.' And you walked away. As I followed you, I turned around and looked at JB and he was laughing in my direction, knowing he had pushed a few of your buttons."

"And we're calling him JB now?" Gregory asked with a hint of indignation.

"That's how most people who get to know him end up referring to him. It's a form of endearment. The guy is really well loved and respected in the community."

"You said we met twice that summer. What was the second encounter, dare I ask?"

"It was a function at Many Mansions. You were invited to speak about the huge donation that George and Rosemary Stein were making to support one of their new housing projects. Remember?"

"Yes, somewhat. But I don't remember Braxton."

"You left right after your speech and before JB was introduced. Just after you spoke, he came over to shake your hand and to thank you for praising the Stein's contribution. You recognized him, but acted cold, as if you were still pissed at him for pulling your chain at Brent's. I think you two said a few obligatory words to each other and then you took off."

Gregory was curious. "He was speaking at that event?"

"Yep. He was being honored for one of those unique things that he does for the community. JB sponsors what they call their Charity Sabbatical Program. Everyone at Spectre has an option to take two weeks off each year paid and work for a charitable cause. They also can tap a fund that Spectre set up to finance projects that their employees can utilize if they write a business plan that gains approval from an internal Spectre committee. Barbara Jacobs, who was the director in 2008, wanted to honor JB and Spectre for a fundraising project that brought in $110,000 between late 2006 and the end of 2007."

Gregory was impressed. "They brought in $110k?"

"They did. A Spectre employee, Stacy, worked at Many Mansions for two weeks in October 06. She comes up with an idea. Her sister is a real estate agent, and they devise a plan to solicit donations from the two parties in a residential real estate transaction. Each party donates $100 through escrow to Many Mansions. The premise was both parties in a transaction, grateful for closing escrow, would agree to donate to a fair housing cause. She convinces local escrow and title companies to promote the cause and kick in the $100 if either the buyer or seller refuses."

Wiley continued. "Stacy and her sister, with Jon's help, write a business plan to hire a PR firm and start a website—Grateful-for-a-Home.com. The Spectre committee approves the plan and funds the idea with $20k. Before you know it, real estate agents throughout the county are all pitching Grateful-for-a-Home. Pretty soon it becomes hard for buyers and sellers to say no to the $100 donation. The program runs throughout 2007. But not before Many Mansions collected $110,000 through 550 escrows."

Gregory shakes his head. "Braxton's not interested in politics, huh? Too bad. This country could use some brain power like his. I can see why Randy Boswell likes him and why Larry Morris is chasing him. What else is he into?"

"Had a feeling you might want to know more so I've got a meeting for us at eleven in Oxnard. Remember Connie McIlroy? She was with the County Board of Education in the '90s and retired in 2006?"

"Of course I remember Connie. One of the most dedicated educators I've ever met."

"Well, she works with JB now, running his nonprofit Win-the-Day Foundation. In 2007, JB leased one of the middle school campuses the Oxnard school district shut down due to declining enrollment. He helped drive the development of a curriculum to help failing students in Oxnard and Ventura get their act together. Connie runs the operation there. It's very impressive. She's excited to see you again and can't wait to tell you everything."

Nine

At eleven, Rob Wiley and Earl Gregory pulled up to the Win-the-Day Foundation campus in Downtown Oxnard.

As they walked towards the administration building, Rob noticed a three-on-three basketball game underway on an outdoor court, twenty yards to the left of the pathway they were on. He looked at Earl to see if he noticed the action, but he had his vision focused on the walk forward. Rob turned his attention back to the basketball court. It was three-on-three with five tall and very talented young twenty-ish African Americans and a shorter, older Caucasian. He saw the shorter and slower Caucasian put a tricky basketball move on a much younger, taller, and talented defender, ending up in a drive to the basket and a successful layup. Rob smiled to himself, *'Of course JB would be here.'*

"Good morning." Rob said cheerfully to the receptionist manning a desk in the sparsely decorated lobby area. "Rob Wiley and Congressman Gregory to see Mrs. McIlroy,"

"Thank you, gentlemen. I'll let her know you're here."

A moment later, Rob Wiley and the Congressman were seated across the desk from the smiling, upbeat sixty-eight-year-old executive director of the Win-the-Day Foundation, Connie McIlroy.

"Earl, so nice to see you again. It's been too long. How are you and how is Jeanine?"

"Connie, we're both doing well, and it's so good to see you again. After Rob informed me we'd be seeing you today I called Jeanine to let her know. She made me promise to let you know she's thinking about you. I'm pleased you're staying active in education after your long, successful career in the county. We're all indebted to you for your many years of service. I'm anxious to catch up with what you've been up to and to learn more about what's going on here."

"Oh Earl. I'm so fortunate to be involved with this organization. We're doing amazing work and making a substantial difference in so many children's lives. I couldn't be happier. You know I worked for Ventura Unified for twenty-seven years and then the County Ed Office for eight. It was gratifying early in my career, but over time working in public education became such a struggle. As the demographics in the county shifted it became so difficult to deliver a quality education. There were so many obstacles. I was disillusioned when I retired. I lost confidence the COE objectives were aligned between the teachers, parents, and administrators."

"You retired when, 2007?"

"It was 2006, right after Bernie passed. We'd been married for forty-two years."

"So how did you end up here?"

"I ran into Rob one day about five years ago. We caught up with some small talk. After filling him in on my situation and that I had been retired for six months, he asked me if I was looking for something to do. I told him I was getting a little bored and that I might be. He asked if I would meet with a friend of his who was starting a learning academy and was looking for help."

"Don't tell me, let me guess—Braxton?"

"Yes, Rob introduced me to Jon. I admired his vision and joined the organization. Five years later, here I am, absolutely loving what we're doing and feeling more fulfilled than at any point working for public education."

"Alright. What's Win-the-Day all about?"

"We provide an after-school program for struggling students. Our goal is to teach these children how to view life through a different prism. We believe most children failing in school are struggling with many aspects of their lives. Before they can possibly absorb an education, we believe they need a perspective that enables them to desire and embrace learning."

"Group psychology therapy?" Earl said with a hint of sarcasm.

Connie smiled. "Somewhat, but not entirely. Most of our students are just a small adjustment away from getting on the right path. For ninety percent of them, all it takes is showing them different ways to look at the world, to look at themselves, to look at their families and their situations. The turn arounds are miraculous."

"The program's been running for five years now? How did you start?"

"Jon came up with the concept. His son, Luke, was always telling him how poorly kids were doing in his class, yet they seemed smart. That sparked Jon. When he approached me, he shared his vision of creating an academy to help kids want to learn, to help them want to be successful and productive. He had most of it thought out by the time I met him. When he laid it out, from my experiences in public education, I knew he was on to something. And I agreed to get involved."

"Wonder why I've never seen or heard anything about Win-the-Day? Any requests for grant money in this district would have crossed my desk."

That comment brought eye contact between Connie and Rob, and another smile from both—and another notice from the Congressman.

Earl answered his own question: "OK, I get it. Braxton never intended to go for grant money."

"Earl, something you need to know about Jon. He will never ask for nor accept government money. He does not have favorable opinions of government or politics. He avoids anything related. I suggested early on we apply for a grant. He said absolutely not."

Rob Wiley intentionally changed the subject. "Connie, tell us about the curriculum."

"The first six weeks, we have two three-week sessions. We call them 'HOW' and 'WHO'. In 'HOW' we teach our students how the planet operates. Most kids are only concerned with the next moment, the next hour. They have a mini-micro view of everything. Most don't understand the concept of long-view or big-picture perspective. We introduce them to the idea that any successful endeavor in life occurs over time. During our first interview, we ask students their perception of HOW the universe works. We ask them to identify people whom they admire, then discuss HOW those people achieved the things they did. We have them contemplate HOW people from unfortunate circumstances succeed, and HOW people from fortunate circumstances fail. We discuss HOW they became the person they are, and HOW they have the power to change into the person they would like to be. We work with our students to think in terms they never before considered or understood."

"Sounds well-intended Connie, but the students you have here, can they grasp the concepts you're introducing them to? I imagine their parents are not preparing them for the concepts you're introducing, and you're wasting time and effort.

"You sound like a public education administrator with that talk, Earl. These kids are human beings. They have an innate desire to be respected. To be successful. To be loved. You are right when you put the onus on the parents. But let's face it, many children in these situations have parents ill-equipped for parenting. For the most part, those are the kids who fail in public education. But we believed with our hypothesis, and now we know for certain from our results, we can turn most of these kids around. If you look at the before and after testing scores and achievements for our kids, you would be amazed."

"What's the 'WHO' all about?"

"With 'WHO', we probe internally. We discuss WHO our

students believe they are and WHO they want to be. We help them identify their strengths and weaknesses. We discuss their childhood. We talk about WHO raised them and WHO influences them. We discuss WHO they respect and why. We discuss whether they approve of themselves. We discuss the words they use to describe themselves and why. We go deeply into their self-esteem. We build our students a bridge to take them from where they are to where they want to go by teaching them to know and understand themselves better. When they start to cross that bridge, their lives become transformed in ways we could never imagine."

"Impressive," Earl interjected.

"We see great progress in the first semester. We expose our students to things they've never seen or heard, and they eat it up. In our second session, which is three weeks, we go deeper to bring everything we cover in the first session into better focus. We call it 'BELIEVE'. Taking a child who's living a difficult existence and coaching them to transform requires a change in their belief system. In our first semester we help students understand who they are and why. And we help them determine who and what they want to be. In our second semester we teach them a belief system to underpin their transformation. In 'BELIEVE' we teach the importance of self-esteem, and how improve theirs through visualization, affirmations, and meditation. We teach the power of goal setting and the subconscious mind. We teach our students they can become anyone they can believe themselves to be."

Connie paused and checked her watch.

"Earl, it's almost noon and I have a standing meeting every Thursday at this hour with..."

A knock at her office door is followed by Jon opening it and leaning his head in. He is in his basketball clothes, sweating and has a towel around his shoulders. Rob and Earl turn in their seats to face him.

"Hey Rob. Hello Congressman. Connie, I'm going to take a quick shower and then we'll start our meeting in the Conference Room. I had Abby order lunch for four, and it will be here in a few minutes. Rob, Congressman, you'll join us? Lunch is from the new Thai joint a few blocks from here. Abby tried it and said I couldn't handle the medium spicy. We'll see. Meet you in the conference room in ten."

Jon backs out and closes the door. Rob and Earl turn back around to face Connie.

Connie is smiling at Jon's lack of pretention. Rob does the same but lowers his head for Earl not to see.

"I understand you don't like Mr. Braxton," Connie inquired.

"I heard that rumor today as well and it's not the case."

"Good, it's settled. I hope you like Thai."

Ten

C onnie, Rob, and Earl spent a few more minutes in her office before she suggested they head to the conference room to meet up with Jon and their Thai lunch.

As they strode into the sparsely appointed meeting room, Jon, freshly showered and changed into an immaculately pressed blue pin-striped dress shirt and black woolen slacks, was already present and busy organizing. "Hey guys, come on in. The food smells great. Thought we'd do family style. Everyone OK with that?" It was more of a statement than a question, and the Congressman didn't seem to mind. Neither did Connie or Rob.

Jon arranged four place settings of paper plates, plastic forks, and paper napkins at the north end of a fourteen-by-four-foot rectangular conference table. He motioned Congressman Gregory to sit at the head of the table and suggested Connie sit directly to his left. He sat next to her. Rob took the seat to the Congressman's right and noticed both Jon and Connie were left-handed. The seating arrangement was perfectly aligned to prevent any elbow collisions. He made a mental note to ask Jon later if that was his intention. He grinned to himself, thinking—

'It wasn't a coincidence.'

"Rob, whaddya think? Delicious right?" Rob was amused with Jon's focus on the food. Here he was in the presence of a U.S. Congressman, and it had absolutely no impact whatsoever on his behavior.

As the four of them were eating, Jon started the dialogue he had been looking forward to over the past week since Wiley asked him if he wanted the Congressman to visit Win-the-Day. Jon had a job for the Congressman and was anxious to get his cards on the table. He knew he only had an hour until Rob had to usher his boss to his next meeting with Larry Morris at the County Government Center to discuss the upcoming Economic Summit Conference.

"Congressman, Connie and I are pleased and grateful you're here. Thank you for taking the time. I know there are a lot of demands on it. We're very proud of the work we do here and are interested in your perception and your feedback. What do you think of what you've seen and heard so far?"

"Mr. Braxton, I've known Connie a long time." He moved his gaze to her with an affectionate smile. "She's worked so hard over the years to help kids in this county get an education. And I know working in public education during her final years on the job was a demoralizing experience. Yet she never wavered in her commitment. I have the utmost respect for her."

The Congressman returned eye contact to Jon. "Listening to her speak of the work you're doing here, and about you and your passion for this project, well, I must say I'm impressed. I can't give you much feedback because I know very little about what goes on here. Connie gave me an overview, but I have so many questions. Are you open to answering them?"

"Absolutely, where do you want to start?"

"Mr. Braxton, I work in Congress and am sure you know where I want to start. How much is your annual budget and where does your funding come from?"

Without any pause or hint of hesitation, Jon answered the question seemingly before it left the Congressman's lips. "Mr. Congressman, our annual budget is $1.5 million, and we are funded as a private foundation 100 percent by Spectre Systems."

The Congressman was surprised at the speed and directness of

Jon's answer. He was not prepared with a follow-up to such directness, expectant of the kind of answer he typically received from lobbyists or persons seeking to transact influence—doubletalk and/or nonsense. It took a few seconds for Gregory to respond, all the while Jon looked at him directly, making the Congressman a bit uncomfortable.

"Mr. Braxton, if I understand you correctly, you fund this operation completely as a charitable contribution from your company?"

"Yes sir, we do. I say 'we' because it takes more than money to run this place. Many people in my company, and from the community, donate their time as well."

"So currently, Spectre is contributing 100% of the funding. Are there plans to change this?"

"We do have plans to expand funding to grow our program to work with more students. We're in the middle of some efforts with other companies in the area to join our efforts. And we're making progress. It's a relatively easy case to make to these companies that the efforts here are in their interests. Our work is building a local pool of higher-performing future employees. In the meantime, we are receiving lots of help from people volunteering their time."

"But no plans for any government assistance I've been led to believe." The Congressman turned to his left to look at Rob. He caught the Congressman's glance and then looked at Jon with a look communicating—'he's a U.S. Congressman, go easy on him.'

"Mr. Gregory, I'm not a big fan of government, especially the way it's practiced in the U.S. these days. And I'm emphatically opposed to any government funding for Win-the-Day."

Rob was hoping the Congressman would contain his curiosity and move the conversation away from a discussion of government. No such luck.

"Why is that Mr. Braxton? Federal and state governments fund a lot of worthwhile programs that help millions of people in this country. And look, you know I'm a fiscally conservative Republican, one of the more conservative on the hill. I'm not one who likes spending the taxpayer's money foolishly. But the fact of the matter is we have money, and we're obligated to spend it. I'd much rather see it spent on programs that are truly helping people. So perhaps you might reconsider."

"Mr. Gregory, with all due respect, NO. Win-the-Day will not partner with the federal government. We are about our local kids and our local community. In the spirit of a free market, if the program has merit, it will attract local funding from those who are benefitted by the foundation's work. The merit of Win-the-Day should be the determining factor for its funding, not Congressional deal making. The funding will come from those who it benefits the most. Rob may have told you this but allow me to say it in my own words—I'm a 100 percent believer in free markets and free enterprise. I know from your voting record in Congress you and I are closely aligned on that. I know you have the best intentions in offering to help us with government funding, but we will not do it. I don't care for the way government taxes productivity, and I don't care for the fact that it is money and influence, and not common sense, that dictates public policy. With all due respect to you and the well-meaning people you serve with, the workings of the federal government, when it comes to taxing hard-working people and then spending that money based on political expediency, are obscene to me. I won't take money coming from taxes paid by some poor schmuck in West Virginia who has no idea of who we are or what we do, just because you think it's a good idea."

Rob was hoping Jon wouldn't go where he had just gone. He was hoping the Congressman wouldn't take offense and decided the line of conversation needed a change.

"JB, you were mentioning to me the other day how you measure performance. The Congressman would be very interested in your methods. Will you share them?"

The Congressman glanced at his trusted aide with a hint of

annoyance but decided to not stand in the way of Rob's direction change.

While Jon was worked up a bit in his rejection of the Congressman's offer of financial assistance, he harbored no ill will towards Earl Gregory. He knew the Congressman was one of the good ones on the hill and that his suggestion and offer of government money was simply the result of his being mired in the swamp for twenty-six years. It was not something he was going to change in the few minutes they had left.

"Sure thing, Rob," Jon started in a friendly, conciliatory tone. "Mr. Gregory, we rank every student entering our program with a number from one to five. This rank is based on their current personal situation, the quality of their home life, their circumstances, if they have a criminal record, and their performance in school. Those from the most difficult circumstances we rank as a 'one' or '1-in'. Those from slightly better circumstances, a 'two'. And so on. We call this ranking 'inbound'. Currently due to capacity issues, we only accept inbound ones, twos and threes."

"Four weeks after graduation, we interview our students again and rank them with an 'outbound' number from 'one' to 'five'. We base this ranking on how they're doing after going through the program. Are things improving at home? Are they doing better in school? What is their appearance? What is their outlook? Do they remember the teachings from the program? Can they articulate what they learned? Are they working towards their goals?"

"The kids doing the best, are ranked as Outbound Five or '5-out,'. Those a little less accomplished '4-out' and so on. We measure our internal performance on the difference between their inbound and outbound rankings. A minimum of 'plus two' we consider success. If one of our kids is ranked a '2-in' and a '4-out', that's a 'plus+two'. We know we have made a significant impact on that young person's life. Our goal for this coming session is 100 'plus+twos'. In many cases we've taken a kid with one foot in jail or in a gang and turned them around. It's rare, but we have a few 'plus-fours'."

Earl was curious. "Do you know the history of these metrics?"

Jon had them top of mind. "Since 2008, we've enrolled 1,510 kids in our program. Based on the inbound-outbound assessment for every student, we have sixteen 'plus+fours', 122 'plus+threes', 886 'plus+twos', 347 plus+ones, seventy-four zeros, twelve 'minus-ones', and fifty-three dropouts. Sixty-eight percent of the kids we've enrolled in the program are plus+two or better. There results tell us we make a significant difference in the lives of two of every three kids we touch."

The Congressman was incredulous. Connie was beaming.

"Mr. Braxton, besides providing all the instruction for your students, you're conducting all these interviews, preparing the plans, doing the assessments? That's a lot of work and you don't have a big staff. Who is doing all this work? How's all this magic getting done?"

"Connie's the magician. Among her other talents, she's attracted many of her former colleagues here. There are plenty retired or retiring educators looking for new and different avenues to teach. And we have help from Spectre employees and from T.O. City Hall, thanks to Randy Boswell. On any given night, we have ten to twelve volunteers here working on the plans and helping with assessments. So, we're covered, barely, but limited in our ability to scale."

Connie was not interested in taking all the credit. "Earl, this program would never have seen the light of day if not for Jon. Not only has he put up the money, but he's the driving force behind the curriculum and the focus of the program. All the things we're doing and the tremendous results we're achieving are the result of Jon's vision and his direction. Don't let him misdirect you—Win-the-Day is Jon's creation and he's primarily responsible for its success."

There was a momentary silence in the room as Earl Gregory took this all in. He marveled at the accomplishments of this odd couple—

the sixty-eight-year-old retired educator, and the forty-year-old entrepreneurial businessman.

A knock at the windowless, solid wood conference room door broke the brief silence.

"Come in, Jamal", Jon said in a slightly raised voice. The door opened and a six-foot, four-inch, slender, handsome twenty-year-old African American man entered the room. He closed the door behind him and came over to the conference table, standing directly to Rob Wiley's right and directly across the table from Jon. Connie looked at Jamal with pride. He returned her look with a warm smile. Rob recognized him as one of the five Win-the-Day graduates Jon was playing basketball with when he and Gregory arrived on campus.

"Gentlemen, this is Jamal Peterson, a 2010 graduate of Win-the-Day. Jamal, say hello to Rob Wiley." Rob turned to face Jamal and extended his hand. They shook. "And Jamal, this is Congressman Earl Gregory." Jamal maneuvered around Rob to the Congressman and extended his hand.

"Sir, it's an honor to meet you".

"The honor is all mine, Mr. Peterson." The two exchanged a firm handshake.

"Jamal, grab some food and join us for a few minutes." Jon then turned his torso and his eyes back to Earl while Jamal loaded up on Thai.

"Congressman, Jamal is one of our 122 'plus+threes' and has transformed himself into one of the finest young men I've ever met. I'm hoping one day he'll decide to make a career at Spectre, but right now all he wants to do is fly jets for the U.S. Air Force." Jon turned to face Jamal who had taken the chair across from him. "And I believe he ships out to start his basic training next week."

"Yes, sir."

"Jamal, the Congressman only has a few minutes. Would you mind telling him your story?"

As Jamal started to speak, Connie reached into her purse for a handkerchief and dabbed at the tear drop that had formed in her left eye.

"Mr. Gregory, three years ago, my life was a nightmare. My family was fractured. I had no thought or idea of living a productive life. I spent my time with gangbangers and drunks, doing drugs, petty crimes, tagging. I didn't know anything else. When I saw other people happy and successful, I knew that couldn't be me. They were born lucky, and I wasn't, and that was just the way things were. My only expectation was a life in prison, like my dad, or an early death on the streets. There was nothing I could do about it."

"One day three years ago, I happened to be in school. Most days I didn't go, but that day I was in history class when Principal Bailey walked in. He asked me to go with him to his office. I figured the police were there to arrest me or I was being expelled, and I didn't care."

"Principal Bailey walked me into his office, and I saw only Mrs. McIlroy. She said *sit down, Jamal, let's talk*. Principal Bailey walked out leaving us alone. Ms. McIlroy started asking me questions, strange questions. Questions I didn't have answers for because I didn't understand them. The things she was asking, things like, if I could be like any person in the world, who would that be? And she asked if I ever thought about the world and how there was an order to the way things worked. She asked me why the sun came up every morning in the same place and settled down at night. Questions that I'd never been asked and never thought about. And I'm still not sure how or why, Mr. Gregory, but she touched something inside me."

"We talked for about twenty minutes. I didn't say much. Didn't know what to say. She asks if she can come back and talk to me again the next Monday. I said yes and made sure I went to school that day in case she came back. I wasn't expecting her to. Everyone I knew didn't mean what they said. They mostly lied about everything just to get through the day. But she did. Principal Bailey comes into class and has me go back to his office again."

"We get to his office, and Mrs. McIlroy is there again. This time so is Mr. Braxton. I was nervous. I wasn't sure if he was a cop or someone from the DA's office. I questioned who Mrs. McIlroy really was and I went into a shell. I decided not to say anything. Mrs. McIlroy says hello and introduced Mr. Braxton as her friend. He stood up and extended his hand to shake. I ignored him."

"Hi Jamal, I'm Jon Braxton. Please come in and sit down." No response. Jamal sat down and slouched in his chair with both hands gripping the arm rest.

"OK, you probably don't want to talk to me because you don't know who I am and why I'm here. I can't blame you, but I'm going to talk to you about a few things. If you want to jump in and ask me anything, feel free, OK?"

Jamal was silent, arms crossed, staring at the floor.

"First thing, I'm not a cop. I'm not with the school district. I'm not with child services. I own a business in Thousand Oaks that sells computer systems. I'm here because Mrs. McIlroy and I are starting a new learning academy, and we want you to be part of the first class. We are going to teach our students things the public schools don't teach. Things which should be learned at home but rarely are. Things which will help you lead a successful, fulfilling life. There's no money involved. All we're asking for is some of your time and to give us a chance to make a difference in your life."

Jamal had not changed his posture. "It's not going to work. It's bullshit."

"Jamal, look at me please." He raised his gaze from the floor to Jon's face.

"What do you see when you look at me?"

"I don't know."

"I bet I know what you see. You see a rich white guy. Right?"

"I don't know." Jamal returned his gaze to the floor.

"And when I look at you, you probably think I see a poor black guy. Right?"

"Yeah, I guess."

"Well, that's not what I see. When I look at you, I see the same thing I see when I look in a mirror at myself. I see a man with a mind. I see us almost the same. You know what the biggest difference is between you and I?"

"No."

"It's not our skin color or how much money we have. The biggest difference between you and I is knowledge. And the most important thing that I know that you don't know yet is I have with my mind a tool that can make me be anyone I want to be. And with this tool I can achieve anything I want to achieve. This is what we want to teach."

Jamal brought his eyes from the floor and looked at Jon. "That's not going to work. You didn't grow up like me."

"What do you mean?"

"You're not black."

"Are you saying because you are black, you cannot be successful in life?"

"I guess so."

"Sorry man, but I call bullshit on that. Look, I'm not going to blow smoke up your ass and pretend the world is fair. It isn't. Some people are born into a comfortable life, and some are not. That's the way it is in nature with most species. Was I born into a comfortable life? Not really. My parents were killed in an auto accident when I was four and I lived in foster homes until I was seventeen. My only relative was my aunt, and she was a heroin junkie and couldn't care less about me. So how did I make it to this point where I have a good life, a loving family, a successful business, and the opportunity to support worthwhile social causes? Is it my white skin color? If you think that answer is yes, then how do you explain a significant percentage of the white population in this country live below the poverty line? And why is it that many people of color are successful in business and sports and finance?"

"I learned these lessons when I was sixteen and my life was forever changed. I learned the only thing separating a bad life from a good life for me was the way I saw myself. Jamal, no matter how bad you believe your life is right now, I encourage you to not think of yourself as a victim. You are only a victim of your circumstances if you believe yourself to be. The only thing standing in your way to a happy, successful life are your thoughts."

Jamal remained silent. "You play B-ball, right? I heard you have some talent." Jamal raised his eyebrows. The left side of his mouth curled.

"Look at the NBA. Lots of dudes with black skin doing well, right? Why? Because they have talent. How did they acquire that talent? Born with it? Maybe, to a degree. But the guys that make it to the NBA, they developed their talent. There are a million guys with talent that don't make it. Why is that? They don't develop it. And that's why I'm here. I want to help you develop your talent for whatever it is in life you want to accomplish."

Jamal was still staring at the floor. "Why do you want to do this for me?"

Jon had been sitting relaxed in his chair with his legs crossed. He uncrossed them and leaned forward, putting his hands on his knees. His face was now twelve inches from Jamal's

"Jamal, look at me please."

He slowly raised his head and looked at Jon, who was looking intensely into his eyes.

"What's your middle name?"

"What?" said Jamal, grimacing and looking confused.

"It's Montgomery, right?"

"Yeah."

"You were named after your uncle Monty, who you never met because he died when he was very young."

"Yeah, so what?"

"He was three and I was four, and we were friends. It happened right in front of me."

———≈———

Connie, after hearing Jamal relate to Earl his first interaction with Jon, was now dabbing her fully tear-laden eyes with her left hand. She had her right hand on the table next to the Congressman's folded hands. He separated his hands and put his left hand on top of her right and patted it.

Jamal continued. "We talked a little more. Mr. Braxton explained more about the academy he and Mrs. McIlroy were starting. He told me his mission was to help young, disadvantaged kids in the community become better people. He said he knew it would be difficult and he knew that many wouldn't buy in, but he still wanted to try. And he wanted me to help him. He wanted my help! Said he wanted me to be part of the first class. He wanted me to go through the training and then give them feedback on what was working, what wasn't, and how the program could be tweaked to make it better. He asked me, an aimless stupid gangbanger, to help. No one had ever treated me this way and it felt so good to be treated like someone who had something to offer."

"My life has completely turned around since going through the program. From the lessons I learned, I've been able to put my family back together. My mother has been sober for a year. My little brother is off the streets, living at home with us and has gone back to school.

He has a part-time job and has been getting Bs and Cs in his classes, where it used to be all Fs. Even my mother has gone back to school to learn computers. As for me, I came to know myself at Win-the-Day. We focused a lot on working within ourselves to develop our personal dreams and goals. I realized I had a strong desire to fly jet planes. Mr. Braxton worked with me to lay out a plan to get me through high school and into the Air Force. Thanks to Mr. Braxton, it's all happening. I couldn't be more grateful."

Jon felt a little levity was needed to lighten what was becoming a sob fest. "Jamal, if you're so grateful, what was up with that behind-the-back crossover dribble you used on me at the top of the key on the court this morning? You had me twisted up like a pretzel, and my back is still hurting. You use that junk on me again, I'm going to force you to come over to the house again to eat some of Mrs. Braxton's cooking."

"You know, Mr. B, if my punishment for hanging you out to dry on the court is to enjoy some of Mrs. B's cooking again, you're in for some rough games when I get back here on my break from basic training."

"Don't be so sure, Jamal. I'm working on some new moves myself that are going to make you wish you never met me."

"Sir, I don't think the universe has a basketball move like that."

The love in those words resonated with all in the room, and it took a moment for the silence to be broken by the Congressman. "Jamal, you're a very impressive young man and I wish you all the best in whatever endeavor you choose. I've only got a few minutes. Tell me, what was the one thing Win-the-Day taught you that stands out over and above everything else?"

It didn't take Jamal long. "Mr. Gregory, the one thing I have in my head every day and the one thing that I believe has made the biggest difference for me is understanding how great life can be when you live it selflessly. That first day I met Mr. Braxton, he was there giving his time and, as I came to learn, a lot of money to help other people. This was something I had never thought about. The concept of living life as a means to help others. When I first met Mrs. McIlroy and Mr. Braxton, I only understood survival. Life was a struggle every day. My only thoughts, my only concerns were getting money or getting high. Thinking of others? That thought never entered my mind."

"After a few weeks at Win-the-Day and being exposed to different ways to look at life and different ways to look at myself, I started to get it. And inside, I started to understand I wanted to be like Mr. Braxton. He was always so positive and so driven to get what he wanted, even though what he wanted were things for other people. He and I had lots of talks, and he helped me understand the concept of living selflessly. That one concept has made the biggest difference for me."

Jon broke in before the Congressman or Jamal could continue the dialogue. He wanted those last words from Jamal to be the takeaway for Earl. "Thanks Jamal. I know the Congressman needs to get to his next meeting, so let's leave it at that for now. Maybe sometime down the road we can all get together and talk more."

Jon stood up. Jamal followed his lead and turned to his left. He extended his hand to Rob. They shook, and then Jamal approached the Congressman. Gregory was the first to extend his hand. "Jamal, I'd like to stay in touch with you and follow your progress in the Air Force. Would it be OK if I had Connie give me your contact information?"

"Yes sir, of course." The two exchanged a firm, warm handshake. Jamal then proceeded around the Congressman and approached Connie and the two hugged for many seconds. When they released, Connie lip-synced, "I'm so proud of you." Jamal then walked by Connie to face Jon. The two men exchanged a quick embrace and separated.

"Jamal, good luck in basic training. Check in with us and let us know how you're doing, OK?"

"Yes sir, I will, and thank you again for everything you've done for me." Jamal turned to look at the Congressman, gave him a respectful nod, and left the room.

Once Jamal had left, Jon started his close. "I know you're pressed for time. Just a minute or two more if that's OK." He motioned for Earl to sit down. He complied, followed by Rob and Connie.

"Jamal is what we call a 'plus+three'. He came from very difficult circumstances and has become quite an accomplished young man. This is the kind of work Connie is doing here." Jon paused and looked directly into the Congressman's eyes.

"Earl," Jon intentionally using his first name, "I'd like you to join our cause by accepting my invitation to join the board of directors of Win-the-Day. I believe your experiences, your reputation, and your contacts would greatly benefit our organization. And I feel you would gain tremendous personal satisfaction working with us. I realize you have a hectic schedule in Washington and lots of travel, but I'm willing to schedule our board meetings to work with your calendar. My only condition is no government money and no quid pro quo."

The Congressman stood. Rob, Connie, and Jon followed suit.

"Jon, I'll accept your offer on one condition of my own, and that is you agree to speak at the Economic Summit Conference in Thousand Oaks next month."

Jon smiled and extended his hand to his new Win-the-Day board member. "Deal."

Eleven

As Rob Wiley and Congressman Gregory were having dinner that evening following their meeting with Larry Morris to discuss the upcoming Economic Development Conference, the Blackberry of Secretary of State Heather Wilson-Carrington rang with *'CallerID unknown'* in the display.

The Secretary was home and answered cautiously. "Hello?"

"Go Princeton"—the male voice on the other end of the line replied without hesitation.

Heather responded— "beat Rutgers."

With the security handshake completed, Carrington's Chief of Staff, Mark Parker, addressed the Secretary somberly. "Heather, we just got word our embassy in Yemen was destroyed by ground-launched missiles about an hour ago. We're still gathering info from our ground sources, but it appears it was a terror act. The entire compound was leveled. At this point there are no survivors."

"Was Charlie in the embassy?" While a part of Heather's heart was breaking, she fired off the question to her long-time friend and confidant with a resolute tone.

Parker hesitated for a few seconds. "According to our travel logs, yes."

"Goddammit, those fucking savages," Heather screamed at Parker in a tone loud enough to be heard by her husband, the former President, in his personal study twenty feet down the hallway.

"Call a meeting for tonight in the Truman Building, fourth floor, east conference room, at 22:30 for the senior security team. Don't speak to anyone else until we have our meeting. Send a car for me. I'll be ready in twenty."

She abruptly hung up and walked down the hallway to speak with her husband. He was reading the day's The New York Times when she knocked and shakily entered the room at her husband's bequest. Wilton Carrington was sitting in a high-backed reading chair, facing a red-brick hearth fireplace at a forty-five-degree angle. Wilton had only to move his head a few degrees to the right to see his wife's entrance. He raised his line of vision over the top of his reading glasses, perched at the end of his nose, as she stood in the doorway. From her scream a moment ago, he sensed the news was not good.

"Our embassy in Yemen was bombed a few minutes ago. Initial reports are total destruction and no survivors."

"Charlie?" the former President asked, concerned about his good friend Charlie Carpenter, the current U.S. Ambassador to Yemen.

Heather looked directly at Wil, then dropped her eyes to the floor and shook her head no. "All logs had him in the embassy at the time of attack."

"Leila?"

"Not sure yet."

Charlie Carpenter had been a friend of the Carrington's since their days at Harvard Law School. For one semester he roomed with Wilton. When Wilton started dating Heather, he became the third wheel. After graduating from Harvard, Charlie went on to have a distinguished forty-year career as an in-house corporate attorney for Johnson & Johnson.

He and Wilton remained in constant contact over the years, and it continued throughout the course of Wilton's presidency. The President occasionally offered Charlie opportunities to work for him in the White House. But Charlie was happy living in Franklin Lakes, New Jersey, just a forty-five-minute commute to J&J corporate headquarters in

New Brunswick. Charlie was a family man. His kids were well settled in Franklin Lakes, and he never seriously entertained any thought of moving to Washington.

In 2008, shortly after Heather's nomination to Secretary of State by President Obama, she called Charlie. She knew his kids were now on their own and it was just he and his wife, Leila, in their huge house in Franklin Lakes. She wasn't sure if he would be interested in working for her at State but decided to make the offer of the ambassadorship to Yemen anyway. As she stood in the doorway of her husband's study and readied to turn back to their bedroom to get dressed for a stressful and difficult late evening, she replayed Wil's words to her when he learned she offered Charlie the ambassadorship to Yemen: *'Honey, are you sure? It's not safe.'*

Wilton watched his wife struggle relaying what she had just learned and wondered if she remembered his words of caution four years ago. He pondered how she would respond to having contributed to, as it would shortly be confirmed, their close friend's death.

Within fifteen minutes, a driver from State pulled up to the Carrington residence and onto their driveway. Heather was ready and waiting with a cup of coffee at their kitchen table. Wilton had been sitting with her for the past five minutes. Not a word passed between them. When the Town Car arrived, they stood. Wilton put his two hands on Heather's shoulders and looked at her forlornly. "Be strong, Heather. Good luck." He leaned forward and kissed her on the cheek, then headed back to his study.

Within a minute, Heather was in the back seat on her cell phone to Parker. Prior to calling him, she raised the security sound panel separating her from her driver, whom she never acknowledged when she showed her own way into the back seat.

After wrapping her brief call with Parker, and still ten minutes away from State, Heather called her most trusted advisor and confidant, Sidney Rosenberg. Rosenberg had his primary residence in

Manhattan. He was not officially a member of Heather's staff, but had been instrumental during the Carrington Presidency, serving as official Chief of Staff for Wilton's first four years in office. And in an unofficial senior advisory capacity for the last four. When Heather decided to run in 2008 for the Democrat Party presidential nomination, Rosenberg was her most trusted advisor. He served in that unofficial capacity during her failed 2008 run, but recently, the two had reengaged as Heather was contemplating again running for President in 2016.

Sidney answered his phone cautiously. "Hello?"

"Do we always have to do this security handshake bullshit? I just got a call our embassy in Yemen was destroyed in a missile attack an hour ago. I'm on my way to State right now for a briefing. The unconfirmed intel is the embassy was completely destroyed and no survivors."

"Charlie Carpenter?"

Heather took a brief second to compose herself and answered in unemotional monotone. "Travel logs indicate Charlie was on prem at the time of the attack."

"Oh Heather, I'm so sorry. I know how close you and Wilton were to him. Al-Qaeda?"

Heather's resolve was cracking. "Parker's assuming, but it's not confirmed yet. Charlie and Leila are all I can think about, and I can't seem to get my head on right." Now trembling, with her voice quivering, she said, "I still don't know if she was in Sanaa or not. Sidney, I'm about to get butchered and have no clue about how to handle it."

"Heather, as distasteful as this may sound to you, the most important thing for you to do at this moment is protect Obama. For you to have the best chance of winning in '16, he has to win this year. You do not want to run against an incumbent Republican. If we don't spin this story right, it's big enough to screw him, and you, in November."

Heather's focus was elsewhere. "There's another angle to this. We received a lot of reports lately of Al-Qaeda activity in Yemen. We've known our embassy could be targeted. We had a number of meetings at State on this but with so many competing budget initiatives the embassy in Yemen never made it to the front of the line."

"Fuck. What's been getting the attention?"

"We haven't been able to get consensus on security priorities. I've been on Parker's ass on this, but with so much travelling lately my eye's been off the ball. We have meetings scheduled next week for embassy security initiatives. What am I going to tell Leila if she's still alive? Dammit Sidney, help me fix this." The last words screamed, almost frantically, into her Blackberry.

"Compose yourself. The most important thing tonight is deflecting away from Obama. We'll design a narrative to blame Congress. You'll be pressured to make a public statement soon, but we need to buy time. For now, tell the press you're still gathering information. Don't jump to any conclusions. Tonight, find out everything anyone knows, and contain it. Understand? Tell everyone in the room who are targets for the press or Republican probes that no information leaves State until we have confirmation. Call me on your way home. I'll wait up. You might have to take some heat up front, but if we play it right, the story will fade, and we'll plug something else in. Containment of information and leaks is your objective for tonight."

"Damnit, Sidney."

"All right Heather, something else I need to know. I've been getting some bad vibes from you lately and listening to you now, well, I need to ask: Are you really ready for a '16 run?"

"Hell yes," the Secretary lied.

———≈———

Heather's driver pulled into the underground security entrance at State. The Secretary was met by Mark Parker. He opened her door and the two of them made their way alone through the parking garage building entrance to the elevator and up to the fourth floor.

"What's the latest?"

"New intel came in a few minutes ago. One of our ground-level embeds confirmed the Facebook post. The compound was leveled by twenty Al-Qaeda fighters using shoulder-launched surface missiles. First reports are no survivors. We had twenty-eight personnel on prem. Logs show Carpenter in the embassy. Leila was not. She's home in Franklin Lakes. We haven't contacted her. Figured you'd want to. The press is lighting up the phones for confirmation of the Facebook posts. We've stated no comment to all inquiries."

The elevator reached the fourth floor and they exited. The east conference room, now full of State Department embassy security administration staff, was forty feet down a six-foot-wide carpeted hallway. The two began their march down the hallway when Heather pulled Mark Parker into a small huddle room they came upon. She closed the door.

"Mark, who else knows about the intel you have at this point?"

"Just Robbie Biltmore. He's manning the secure communication channel terminal tonight. He called me on cell when the confirmation from our embed came in."

"Do you know if he told anyone else about the confirmation?"

"I wouldn't think so, but I don't know for sure."

She had Sidney's instructions in mind. "Let's go down now and talk to him."

Carrington and Parker exited the huddle room, went back to the elevator, and dropped to the second floor. They exited and went north to 'Comm', the State Department's primary communications hub. They walked briskly through a maze of offices until they reached the office that housed the terminal Biltmore was monitoring. Six-year State Department veteran Robbie Biltmore was scanning various communication arteries when he realized he had two visitors. He recognized Heather Carrington immediately and rose to his feet. "Madam Secretary."

"Hello, Robbie. I understand you're having a busy night."

"Yes, ma'am. Lots of chatter coming in from operatives all over the Middle East. Everyone is sharing whatever they know to help us put the puzzle together."

"Robbie, what were you doing when the confirmation from our embed in Sanaa came in?"

"I was monitoring all our channels. Not long after the Facebook posts about the attack surfaced, there was a lot of inbound communication."

"Was anyone in the room with you when the confirmation came in?"

"No ma'am. I was alone."

"What did you do after the confirmation came in?"

"I called Mr. Parker and reported it to him."

"You used your cell phone to make the call?"

"No ma'am. I used this desk phone."

"And the number you called to reach Mark, was it his cell phone?"

"Yes ma'am."

"How long were you on the phone with him when you relayed the information?"

"Not long. Maybe ninety seconds."

"Did you call or speak to anyone else about the confirmation?"

"No ma'am."

"Are you sure?"

"Yes ma'am."

"Robbie, as a matter of national security, you are not to relay any information whatsoever about the confirmation to anyone until you hear from Mr. Parker or myself directly that it is OK. Do you understand? No information about the confirmation to anyone."

"Yes ma'am"

"Thank you, Robbie. We'll likely get back to you tomorrow. What time is your shift over?"

"O three hundred."

"Please go home directly after your shift is over. Who takes over when you leave?"

"Amanda Baker."

"Do not share our embed's confirmation with Amanda nor with anyone else until you hear from Mr. Parker or myself. Again, you must keep all intel on this situation under wraps until you hear from Parker or myself. And I'll brief Amanda. Understood?"

"Yes ma'am. I understand."

Heather led Parker to an area out of earshot from Biltmore. "Mark, when we get upstairs, you will start our meeting and advise all we have no reliable information as to what happened in Sanaa, and until we confirm the unsubstantiated reports, the official response from State is no comment. Is that clear?"

"But Heather—"

"Mark, is that clear?"

"Crystal."

The two proceeded out of Comm, back to the elevator, and up to the fourth floor. When they entered the east conference room, they were greeted by twelve staffers, nine of whom were members of State's Embassy Security Administration team. They were joined by Ken Patrick, the State Department's Under Secretary of Management, Mary Olsen, the State Department's Under Secretary for Democracy and Global Affairs, and Cheryl Watkins, the Deputy Secretary of State.

Heather took a seat at the middle of the long edge of the conference room table, facing the wall with the entry doors. Mark Parker sat directly to her left. Everyone else found their way to a seat as soon as the Secretary found hers.

She addressed the silent room: "Thank you everyone for assembling here on such short notice. I'm sure all of you have heard UNCONFIRMED reports of an incident at our embassy in Yemen a few hours ago. I emphasize that these reports are unconfirmed. I'm going to ask Mark Parker to fill you in on what we know officially at this moment." She glanced to her left. "Mark?"

"Thank you, Madam Secretary. Everyone, we have no definitive confirmation on any of the news posted online in the last few hours. We've read all the posts and seen all the pictures." Mark hesitated before making his next, knowingly false comment. "Nothing is definitive. It is possible the information online has been fabricated. As you all know, there have been recent advances into the Yemeni government by Al-Qaeda. We are not sure tonight's online reports have any truth to them or if they are part of some other propaganda agenda."

Mark paused. He felt he had finished delivering the message Heather asked him to. Most in the room had friends or acquaintances that were serving in Yemen. The mood was somber.

Heather let the silence settle. "Listen everyone, this event, if confirmed, will be a tremendous setback for us. We are responsible to protect our personnel wherever they serve. If the intel we received is true, we failed our colleagues in Yemen. But as of right now, we have NO confirmation the intel is accurate. You must, I repeat you must all act in a manner reflecting that. You must make your best effort to not comment nor pass any information to anyone outside of this room until Mark or I give you clearance. As of now, and until you hear differently directly from Mark or I, your response to any inquiry from anyone is we have no verifiable confirmation on any reports out of Yemen. No one outside this room hears anything on this from any of us until we know for sure what happened. If you are cornered somehow and asked for comment, respond State is working to confirm, and until such time, it's NO COMMENT. Avoid any interactions with the media to the best of your ability. But if you are cornered and need to say something in response to their questioning, advise the media we have credible information this is propaganda. Understand? We have credible information this is propaganda. I trust this is crystal clear."

"After we wrap here, you are all to go home and get some sleep.

Stay away from any media to the best of your abilities. Tomorrow is Saturday, so we catch a little break. We'll all be hunted down for comment. It's important we're all well rested. Tomorrow, stay away from the office and out of reach until 15:00. Do not answer your cell phones for any calls outside of State. Am I perfectly clear on this? We will meet tomorrow here at 15:00 and assess the situation. If anyone outside this room from State or another agency or the press corners you, you will respond as we just discussed. NO COMMENT as we are working to confirm, and we have credible information this may be propaganda. No 'off-the-record' or 'promise not to tell anyone else' bullshit. Again, am I clear?"

"I know many of you want to ask questions, but it is best if we delay those until we are more rested and we reflect. If anyone does not comply with my instructions, it will be cause for severe reprimand. Keep the chatter among yourselves to the barest minimum. Be as discreet as you possibly can. Do not discuss these events with friends, family, or loved ones until we have everything confirmed. This is a serious national security matter, and you are responsible for being 100 percent discreet. Again, am I perfectly clear?"

She again scanned the room looking for confirmation of understanding. After a moment, she adjourned the meeting. "Mark, stay behind for a few minutes." Everyone filed out silently.

When she and Parker were alone, Heather took a long breath for the first time since the meeting started. Her demeanor changed from that of a strong, decisive leader to an insecure, remorseful reflector. "Do we know yet if embassy security put up any kind of resistance? Did we go down with a fight? Did we get any verbal communication from the embassy while they were under attack? Any verbal from Charlie?" She asked the questions slowly, remorsefully.

"It was 04:00 hours local time when the attack started. We received very little verbal. The verbals we did receive weren't good. We were caught unaware. All the verbals were distress after the attack started and the comm channel wasn't active for long before it was cut. Maybe three minutes."

"Any verbals from Charlie's quarters?"

"Only screams."

"All unofficial, Mark. Delete all the recordings and all log entries that tie to them. They never made it here. Clear?"

"Heather, are you sure?"

"Are we clear Mark?"

He nodded. She gathered her things, got up, and headed for the door of the conference room. Mark remained seated. When she got to the door, she turned to him. "We fucked up. I'll see you tomorrow. Be in my office at 13:00."

In the back of the Town Car on the ride home from State, Heather raised the security panel and called Sidney Rosenberg. It was Saturday half past midnight. He was awaiting her call. She relayed all the intel she was given and described the meeting in detail.

"You delivered the right message. I hope you can trust those people, Heather. If this is mismanaged, it could be problematic, if not catastrophic."

Heather was half listening. Her thoughts reverted to Charlie Carpenter.

"Sidney, I understand we need to spin this, but at some point we need to do what's right for those people who lost their lives yesterday. They and their brave service have to be recognized."

"Heather, you sound really tired. Let's pick up the conversation tomorrow, OK? Give my best to Wilton. Get some rest. Good night."

Twelve

It was the following Monday morning.

"City of Thousand Oaks, how may I direct your call?"

"Randy Boswell, please."

"May I let Mr. Boswell know who's calling?"

"Abby Martin from Spectre."

"Oh Mrs. Martin, sorry I didn't recognize your voice. Let me see if Mr. Boswell's available."

He was and she put the call through.

"Good morning, Mrs. Martin. What a pleasure to be speaking with you so early on a beautiful Monday morning. How will you be abusing and disrespecting your dutiful public servant today?"

"Mr. Boswell, the nightmare is all mine. But I thought I would call to remind you how awesome it is for you to know me."

"Mrs. Martin, there is no need to remind me. It is my habit to thank my lucky charms every morning that you are among the people we have the tremendously good fortune to serve here in our beautiful city."

"Mr. Boswell, thought I would reinforce all those wonderful things you believe about me with some information I feel certain you'd like to have."

"Mrs. Martin, should I bend over, or may I remain in an upright position?"

Abby couldn't help but laugh aloud.

"Oh Mr. Boswell. You amuse me so. Allow me to share some

good news with you then you can choose your position. Mi Lord has decided he will do a keynote at the Economic Summit Conference. Wanted you to be one of the first to know."

"Abby, that's fantastic. I can't wait to tell Larry."

"Larry, I'm sure, already knows. Sir Braxton was asked by Earl Gregory on Friday at Win-the-Day and he agreed. As I understand it, Gregory and Rob Wiley had a pre-scheduled meeting with Larry right after that. Just thought you should know so you can get a jump with Larry to let him know that you know. Thought he'd be impressed you're in the loop."

"JB and the Congressman meeting up? Wow, given their dustups a couple of years ago and JB's disdain for politicians, I didn't think that would happen. Unless, of course, this was your deal."

"Nope, can't take credit for this one. Rob Wiley did the driving and his highness rode along. He had a, how shall we say, job for the Congressman."

"Abby, you're being replaced? Come to think of it, Gregory's going to be retiring from Congress soon and he'll need something to do. He'd make an excellent executive assistant for JB."

"Oh Mr. Boswell, you're so insightful. You make my heart flutter. The other bit of information you can bless me for is that the Congressman has agreed to join Win-the-Day's board of directors. We'll be publishing that shorty."

"Wow, that's tremendous. That'll bring a lot of attention to what's going on out there. Would have loved to be a fly on the wall at that meeting, given the history between those two. Hope Gregory didn't go too deep with politics but sounds like everything ended positively. Great news on both fronts. Seriously, thanks Abby. I'll give Larry a call and congratulate him. You're right, he'll be impressed that I knew before he could tell me. I'll talk to you later."

"Ah, ah, ah, not so fast there, Mr. Boswell."

"Uh oh, what else?"

"We need ten city staffers to volunteer three nights at Win-the Day next week. New semester starting. Quid pro quo. We cool?"

"Yes, Mrs. Martin, I'll handle it."

Thirteen

Early May 2012 in Washington, D.C. was unusually warm. It would end being the warmest May for the nation's capital on record. Things were also heating up on the political front, as the two candidates the country would choose from for President in November were all but settled. Mitt Romney had just sealed the Republican nomination for President. The race would be between the incumbent Barack Obama versus the former Governor of Massachusetts.

Congress was also busy as all members of the House and thirty-three members of the Senate would be up for reelection in six months. Incumbent candidates were busy positioning themselves on the many pieces of legislation being introduced, debated, and brought up for a vote.

Because of all the legislative activity, and since he was also leaning towards running for reelection in November, Congressman Earl Gregory from the twenty-sixth House District in California had not been following his normal regimen of traveling home to Thousand Oaks over the last few weekends. He was staying in Washington to be close to the action. He wanted to insure he was aware of, and reacting to, anything which could influence voters back home. While he had easily won re-election in his conservative district over the last twelve election cycles, he knew 2012 would be a bruiser if he chose to run, and the time of decision was near. The demographics of his District had been changing and his chances were negatively impacted as a result of the recent 2010 redistricting. The twenty-sixth Congressional district of California was now officially purple. Gregory was not a favorite of House Minority Leader Nancy Pelosi, and he knew she would be earmarking lots of funding to defeat him.

While there were no legitimate Democrat competitors from the local pool of potential candidates, an educator from Santa Monica had recently taken an apartment in the district and was planning to mount a challenge. Earl's chances for reelection in 2012 had the Congressman and Rob Wiley concerned more than they had been for any campaign since their first reelection run in 1986.

———≈———

On Saturday morning in early May, Earl was in his Washington, D.C. apartment reading various opinions on upcoming legislation when his cell phone rang.

"Neil, nice to hear from you. How have you been?"

Cornelius Hale was glad to hear the voice of his longtime friend and political ally. "Doing well, Earl. And how are you and Jeanine doing these days?"

"Not bad for a couple of old farts. Neil, I'm glad you called. We have a few things going on that I needed to talk to you about."

"Good but not now, I'm in town. Let's meet for dinner tonight."

Gregory couldn't say no to one of his longest standing and most loyal supporters. "OK."

———≈———

Corduroy on Ninth near Mt. Vernon Square was a favorite DC eatery of Neil Hale's. He was able to secure the most discreet table in the restaurant for that evening's dinner with Earl Gregory. They arrived separately but precisely the same time and were seated together in a small booth in a remote area of the dining room, well off the path to the kitchen and restrooms. The booth offered their best chance of anonymity.

Immediately upon being seated, a tall Bombay and tonic with two lime quarters was placed in front of Neil Hale. The waiter delivering Hale's drink turned to Gregory. "Sir, what is your pleasure?"

"The same as Mr. Hale."

"Very well, sir."

"Earl, thanks for meeting with me on such short notice. I felt it important for us to talk. We haven't really had a good conversation for almost a year."

"You're right, Neil. It's been almost a year and your timing is good. I've been doing a lot of reflecting lately and thinking about the future."

"Good, were in sync here. I haven't had a chance to discuss your 2012 plans with you yet. Are you planning to run?"

"I am," he said, unconvincingly as far as Hale was concerned. "And thinking this will be it. Things are changing and I'm getting a little long in the tooth. The redistricting is going to hurt. New voters in the district have no knowledge of the things I've done and the things I stand for. The demographics of Ventura County are shifting, and it's going to be tough for a conservative to be elected in the twenty-sixth going forward."

Neil listened to his friend with remorse, knowing all too well the Congressman was exactly right.

"It's a shame, Earl. Everything you have done for the people in your district over the course of your career is going to have so little meaning down the road. But both Carl and I believe you have a good shot to be reelected this year, and we're committed to helping you however we can. That's what I wanted to discuss tonight, Earl. What can Carl and I do to get you reelected? You've always been a champion in Congress for causes dear to our hearts, and we feel a responsibility to help you in whatever way you choose to wind down your career."

"Thank you, Neil. I certainly appreciate that, and I can't thank you and Carl enough for the support over the years. Truth be known, I'm depressed and concerned with the way the political winds are blowing these days. I'm sensing our political system is failing us. The way our government makes its decisions is flawed. We don't have the right mechanics to deal with special interests, the bias of the media, and with how the rest of the world is evolving."

"You know, Earl, as you can imagine, I've got some strong thoughts on this myself. Carl and I have been going back and forth on what we can do to best use our resources to restore some sanity in this country. We can't seem to put our finger on what that strategy should be, but I'm confident we'll get there."

"But Earl, what I wanted to talk to you tonight about is you and your district. Carl and I have an idea we want to run past you. Full disclosure, Rob Wiley asked us if we could help better align you for this year's run. He's the one who came up with the idea. He's a bright guy. We should talk about his political potential. Anyway, I wanted to discuss the idea he proposed to us."

The Congressman frowned. "Strange, I don't think I know anything about it. That's not like Rob."

Neil looked at Earl sympathetically. Was his longtime friend starting to lose the handle now that his California chief of staff was starting to make decisions without consulting his boss? He decided to press on, not giving the Congressman's comment any particular notice.

"Earl, what are your thoughts on the upcoming Ventura County Economic Development Conference? I understand you're delivering one of the keynotes."

Neil being aware of the conference and that he was going to be one of the keynote speakers did not surprise the Congressman. He knew Rob Wiley had already invited the Hales to attend.

"I'm excited for it. I'm anticipating it will attract some new employers to the county. We need to grow local employment with new, higher-paying jobs. Our local economy is shifting towards agriculture.

At the same time, the cost of living is going up, and good employers are moving out of state. So are retirees with their disposable income. Our county is a good example of the middle class shrinking, leaving behind a small upper-income class and a larger lower-income class. It's creating pressures on our social fabric."

"I understand all too well, Earl. When the government taxes the middle class to the degree that it's doing today and uses that revenue to create government programs that build dependency, it rips up the foundation underpinning what made this country great. The values of hard work and personal accountability are being replaced by a sense of self-gratification and entitlement."

The waiter returned with Gregory's gin and tonic and with Neil's second. The drinks were placed in front of the two powerful men as they pondered Neil Hale's depressing prediction for the country both men loved. Both took the moment to draw a gulp from their fresh drinks.

"OK, Neil, you've stated the problem. Any solutions in mind?"

"Carl and I are constantly debating this. Unfortunately, we can't agree on an approach. He thinks we have a chance to win the White House this year and having a Republican President with a Republican House will give us the opportunity to turn it around. But the more he hears Romney speak, the less convinced he becomes. As for myself, I'm absolutely certain Obama will be reelected. The Democrats have us outflanked on all sides and all issues. Romney doesn't connect with enough independents or minorities in a way to make them think in terms of values and morality. The demographics and the Electoral College are squarely in the Democrat's favor. As distasteful as their campaign messaging and strategies are, they're extremely effective, and they'll have an easy time demonizing Romney. The Republican Party is where the right ideas are, but as a political machine on the national stage, it's totally ineffective against the Democrats, especially with a candidate like Romney. Personally, I think Mitt would make a great

President, but we won't get a chance to find out."

"My argument to Carl is we play defense until we build the right offense. Our best defense in 2012 is to hold onto the House. As for the offense? I'm not sure what that looks like right now. All the national candidates we have are outmatched against the Democrat machine. If we don't come up with something soon, not only will Obama win this year, but I'm afraid we'll have eight years of Heather Carrington to look forward to starting in '16. And by '24 the political landscape will be so poisoned and torched that the road back to the values that made this country great could be obliterated."

"OK Neil, I understand why you wanted to meet with me now. Where's your head with respect to the twenty-sixth and your defensive strategy? Are you being sincere when you say I have a decent chance to win? Or are you here to ask me not to run?"

"Earl, I would never ask you not to run. I have too much respect for you. When I said Carl and I felt you had a good shot, I meant it. I'm here, as I said before, to understand what you think you have to do to win and to help you."

The two men paused and took the opportunity for another guzzle.

"Neil, you mentioned a conversation with Rob Wiley. Fill me in." Gregory asked, embarrassed having to do so.

"If the upcoming conference yielded a number of companies signing letters of intent before the election to bring jobs to the county, would that translate into votes for you?"

"My first reaction is yes, but I can't say for sure right now. I'd like to consider before I answer. What's behind the question?"

"Rob asked us to fund jobs for companies signing a letters of intent before the end of July, to incentivize new jobs for the county. He wants us to create a foundation and fund it with five million. The foundation would grant out-of-state companies 10k for each qualified job. So 500 jobs. There would be criteria for the jobs, and a limit on funding per company. Maybe 250k, as in twenty-five jobs per company."

Earl smiled to himself, thinking, *'What was Rob taking to grow his balls?'* Asking the Hale Brothers for five million without his knowledge or endorsement.

Earl's mind started racing through the scenarios on how he could leverage the Hale's generosity to his advantage. His train of thought was interrupted by a memory of his time at Win-the-Day a few weeks ago with Connie McIlroy and his new relationship with Jonathon Braxton. As he continued to sort his thoughts, he had one that perhaps JB was behind this.

Earl sat back in his chair. He pressed the fingertips of his two hands together, with the connection of his two index fingers touching his lips. He stared at a painting of a country landscape hanging on a wall directly over Neil Hale's left shoulder. Hale sat back as well, picked up his drink with his right hand, and settled it on top of the right arm rest. He observed his friend Earl Gregory, looking directly into Earl's eyes as they were focused on the painting over Hale's left shoulder.

Both Hale brothers were sincere in wanting to help the Congressman win reelection, but also wanted to be sure they had a strong chance of winning. And that chance was dependent on Gregory and his motivation to fight in what was going to be the toughest political campaign of his career. Neil patiently waited for his friend to compile his thoughts.

The magnitude of the moment was now apparent to Earl, and his thoughts went back and forth from reflecting on his career to the anticipation of the difficult campaign ahead. He was not as confident as the Hales about his chances. He recognized the Democrats, knowing they had the opportunity to displace a long-time ultra-conservative, would be gunning for him. He knew to be successful he would have to campaign long and hard and he would have to raise money, both tasks he never really liked and was now unsure he had the will and energy to pursue to the level they would require.

As Neil continued to observe the Congressman in his thoughts, he could sense Earl's doubt. He was waiting for Earl's response to the idea of his incenting new Ventura County jobs as a window into his mindset and his will. As Neil observed Earl, he too reflected. He reflected on the state of the country and its struggles. He compared the two—a man and a country both born of the ideals of personal liberty and freedom, and both looking into a future where the viability of those values was in doubt. He would not have been surprised if the next words out of his friend's mouth would be an admission that he was not going to run and would soon announce his retirement.

Instead, "Neil, I think it's a great idea! Rob and I will work with you to develop it. And when we have those letters of intent in hand, I'll take them and bash the fucking Democrats with them. I've served the district well for the past twenty-six years and I'm going to continue to do so while I'm still able. And if my reelection is part of your defensive strategy and you want to help me, I'm grateful. Between you and I for now, 2012 will be my last campaign and I intend to start identifying and grooming a potential successor."

Neil digested Earl's response with mixed feelings. He knew the pending campaign would take its toll on the seventy-six-year-old Congressman, but he was committed to helping his friend and his thoughts turned in that direction.

"Great to hear you've still got that fire in your belly, Earl. Why don't we set up a call in a few days to go over the idea and how we can best execute it to your advantage."

At that moment, their waiter arrived with the dinners they had ordered when the last round of drinks was delivered. As they settled into their meal, Neil probed Gregory about who he might know as a potential successor and if he felt Rob Wiley would fit the bill.

"Rob's a bright guy. He's been unbelievably loyal. And he's done an outstanding job managing my staff in California. But you know he's never mentioned an interest in running for office. I sense he wouldn't want it. He's a great administrator but is not comfortable in the limelight. Never been a good campaigner and recognizes it. Over the years, has had opportunities to speak on my behalf at various events, but always finds someone else to stand on the soapbox. He's not the right choice, but I'd highly recommend him to manage a 2014 Congressional campaign."

"Who else have you met in your travels that might have some potential?"

"There is a business guy in Thousand Oaks I had the opportunity to spend some time with on my last trip home a few weeks ago. Incredibly astute businessman, very philanthropic, well-respected in the community, young, energetic, charismatic. In fact, it wouldn't surprise me if he had a hand in Rob's jobs incentive idea. He could be a great political candidate but there's an issue with him."

"He's a Democrat?"

Earl laughed out loud at that notion, exactly his when he first learned of Jon's distaste for political discourse. Neil smiled at his friend's response to what he thought was a perfectly normal and appropriate question.

"He's not a Democrat. I'm not sure what he is politically. He has the potential, but he isn't someone who would consider running for office. He hates politics. And it's too bad. I think he'd be great for the Party."

———— ≋ ————

It was a little past eleven when Earl returned to his Washington, D.C. condo from his dinner with Neil. He took off his suit and slipped into his pajamas, grabbed his cell phone, and headed for his favorite reading chair.

"Hi Earl, you're up late tonight. Everything OK?"

"Everything's fine, Rob. Just had dinner with Neil Hale and he filled me in on your idea. When were you planning to let me know about your concoction?"

Rob dismissed the question. "Well, what do you think about it?"

"Told Neil I liked it."

"Are you sure? Because if you don't like it, it wasn't my idea."

The Congressman was tired and exasperated with the whole idea of his aide talking to his biggest benefactor on his behalf and now playing a game of misdirection. "What are you talking about?"

"If you like the idea, it's mine. If you don't, it's Jon Braxton's."

"Shit, Rob, I'm tired and not in the mood for this. What are you trying to tell me?"

"Earl, it was JB's idea to set up a fund to provide incentives for out-of-state companies to bring new jobs into the county. He asked who I knew might be open to funding this and I thought of Corny and Carl. I called them, and when I discussed the idea with them, the first question they asked was if it would help your chances for reelection. Well, apparently, they came to their own conclusion it would, and they led me to believe they were strongly considering it. Did Corny give you that impression at dinner?"

Gregory closed his eyes and shook his head, resigning himself to the fact that the idea had taken root and it was now a foregone conclusion the plan would be a reality.

"Rob, you told me JB wasn't political. Why would he discuss this idea with you if he weren't? Why would he be so interested in my reelection? Does he have an expectation this will benefit Win-the-Day now that I'm on his board? He sounds highly political to me."

"If you think he crafted this idea to get you reelected, you really don't understand him."

"OK, why then is he thinking of ways to help my campaign?"

"He's not."

"No?"

"No Earl, he's thinking of local jobs without government funding.

That his idea would benefit your campaign was not in his calculation. If you want to get inside JB's head, take your political cap off and put your Ventura County resident cap on."

Fourteen

Two weeks had passed since the U.S. embassy in Yemen had been attacked and destroyed, killing all twenty-eight embassy personnel. Including the U.S. ambassador to Yemen, Charlie Carpenter. Heather Wilson-Carrington, the U.S. Secretary of State, had nominated Charlie Carpenter to the post and was feeling personally responsible for her close friend's death, given all the warnings of Al-Qaeda activity and the understanding that the embassy in Yemen was a likely target.

Nonetheless, the Obama White House and Carrington's State Department were masterful in deflecting blame. Internal State Department records detailing the terrorism warnings and the lack of responsiveness to requests from various U.S. embassies, including Yemen, had been moved to classified status and were in the process of being researched, identified, and stealthily destroyed.

Mark Parker executed Carrington's directive to protect the Obama administration at all costs and carried out the clandestine activities with skill and precision. In response to the right-wing media's constant drumbeat demanding accountability and transparency, Carrington's State Department was resisting comment, stating they were still investigating the matter and would provide information to the press once all facts had been verified. The time was also being used to build a case that the lack of embassy preparedness was directly correlated to cutbacks in State Department funding. It was an abysmal defense to an act that could clearly be tied to the department's inefficiency and, to a larger extent, the Obama administration's refusal to recognize the magnitude of the terrorist threat still growing in the wake of their decision to end military involvement in Iraq.

The death of twenty-eight Americans, including Charlie Carpenter, was weighing heavily on Heather's psyche. The political posturing taking place was putting extreme weight on her conscience. On the outside, she was functioning exactly as Sidney Rosenberg had instructed her to, but she was having increasing difficulty with an identity crisis growing within.

It was a late Wednesday afternoon when Carrington summoned Parker to her office to discuss the matter. Parker opened the Secretary's office door to find her at her desk, working on her computer. She was writing a statement to deliver to start her press conference on Friday when she would make her first public comments regarding the destruction of the embassy in Yemen. She asked Parker to meet to provide his latest summary of the intelligence State had gathered.

"Come in, Mark" she said to Parker without moving her eyes from the computer screen. "Have a seat at the conference table. I'll be with you in a minute." He moved his tall, slender, lanky frame to a round uncluttered conference table surrounded by four chairs in the corner of her office.

A moment later, she joined him. "OK Mark, where are we?"

"No new facts have come to light in the last forty-eight hours. We have firm confirmation the attack was conducted by an Al-Qaeda cell based in Sanaa. It occurred with full advance knowledge of local Yemeni police and security forces. They gave us no advance warning. They instructed all their personnel stay clear of the embassy before and during the attack. Al-Qaeda started hitting us at 03:30 local time. There were twenty Al-Qaeda fighters, and the total time to destroy the embassy was fifteen minutes. We were caught completely off guard and offered no resistance." Parker's voice trailed off. "We did not fire a single round."

"Thank you, Mark. I know this job is difficult, and you do it very well. Let staff know I'll have a copy of my statement for Friday's presser distributed by 15:00 tomorrow. Instruct everyone to read it and be prepared to comment. And do whatever you must to prevent any leaks."

She stood and extended her hand for a shake. Parker stood and reciprocated. She walked back to her desk. Parker let himself out.

―――――≈―――――

Later that evening, Heather was in her DC residence office, putting the final touches on a statement she would deliver in two days to what was certain to be an animated and thirsty press corps. And to the American people. She completed the statement at eleven. She shut down her computer, rose from her desk and headed down the hallway to her husband's study.

She paused at the study's doorway, as was her normal etiquette, knocked and waited for approval before walking in. It was an odd protocol she often thought to herself, considering that she would do no such thing for any other human being.

"Wil?"

"Come in, honey." She entered and found him lounging on the posh leather couch against the wall, fifteen feet to her right. He was reading in the prone position, his head propped up by a pillow. As Heather walked in, he turned his head in her direction and peered at her over the top of his reading glasses.

She walked to a chair that faced the couch across a three-by-five-foot contemporary coffee table and sat. The former President sat up and turned to face her, taking his glasses off.

She looked him squarely in the eye. "Do you think I would make a good president?"

He smiled. "Honey, you WILL be a GREAT president."

"What makes you think that?"

"OK Heather, what's bothering you? Is it your press conference on Friday?"

"Come on Wil, give me a break. Of course, the presser is on my mind. And poor Charlie is on my mind. And the fact that my department didn't do its job being the reason for Charlie's death is on my mind. So cut the crap and just give me your honest opinion."

"OK Mrs. Carrington, I say to you it doesn't matter what I think. It only matters what you think. You've got the experience to do the job. You've got the tenacity and bullheadedness and relentless determination to do the job. There's no question you've got the tools. But listening to you speak lately, as both Sidney and I are starting to feel, the question is whether you have the desire. This conversation shouldn't be about if you would be a great president, it should be about whether or not you really want it."

Even though it was late, and the Secretary had endured a long and trying day, she was animated. "God damnit Wil, of course I want the job. I've been around politics all my life, and all my life I've dreamed of being the country's first female president. I promised my father. I married you knowing your political ambitions. We lived in the White House for eight years. I served in the Senate for six years. I'm the god damned Secretary of State. I know everything I need to know. Do I want the job? Of course I want the job. But I need to know if I could be great at it. That's what's on my mind."

"Did you even hear a word I said?"

"Yes Wil, I heard every word". She rose and walked around the coffee table to her husband, bent over, and gave the former President a kiss on the cheek. "Go back to your book." She walked out of his office and back to hers, with more doubt than ever about her competence.

———— ≈ ————

The press briefing room at the Department of State sat fifty-six comfortably. The chairs, in rows of eight separated in the middle by a three-foot-wide aisle, faced a wooden podium with a backdrop of blue curtains framing a central oak veneer wall. The carpet was dark blue, with evenly spaced four-inch gold stars twelve inches apart. The front of the podium sported the seal of the U.S. Department of State.

It was 1642 days until Heather Carrington would have the opportunity to keep a promise she first made to her father at the age of seven—and be elected the first female President of the United States. The briefing room was full of journalists and anticipation. The Secretary of State would be addressing the media for the first time in the four weeks since the U.S. embassy in Yemen had been destroyed and twenty-eight State Department employees had been murdered.

During the previous three weeks, the left-leaning mainstream media did what it could to protect the Obama administration from taking the brunt of the criticism. Their efforts were somewhat successful, but the alternative conservative media were relentless in their effort to pin blame on the administration, and by association, the State Department.

The liberal media defenses were taking their standard positions on the matter, strategizing the passage of time would cause the memory of the tragedy to fade. They attacked the messengers instead of denying the messaging to buy time. But that strategy was weak in this case and public opinion was starting to turn. It was time for someone from the administration to come forward to set the record straight with the American people.

"Good morning, everyone," Heather Carrington said with a grim demeanor as she reached the podium from the left entrance and set her notes down where she could refer to them.

"Here's what we know. On April 15 at 03:30 local time our U.S. embassy in the Yemeni capital city of Sanaa was attacked, and twenty-eight brave American citizens lost their lives. The attack was carried out by a group of twenty well-armed Al-Qaeda fighters. They used the cover of darkness and the assistance of corrupt local Yemeni police and security forces, who were aware of the planned attack and stayed clear of the embassy while the attack was unleashed."

She looked up for a moment to take a breath and make eye contact with a few of the journalists she knew and then returned to her statement. "The fighters breached the embassy's perimeter security alarms by neutralizing the older, outdated security sensors which were targeted for replacement last year but were not due to Congressional budget cuts."

The Secretary paused and reached for the glass of water to her right. Her stomach knotted a bit as she uttered the contestable words about the sensors. She took a sip to slow her pulsing heartrate then turned to the second typewritten page of her statement.

"Once inside the embassy perimeter the fighters took up positions surrounding the compound's three buildings. Many were armed with shoulder-fired rocket propelled grenade launchers. We identified the weaponry as Russian-made RPG 29 Vampir launchers. These anti-tank RPGs easily penetrated the embassy's weakly fortified walls— walls targeted for fortification in 2011. That upgrade was also delayed due to funding limitations."

"Once the compound's walls had been breached, the fighters entered the living spaces of our staff and brutally murdered them with rifle and handgun fire. All but three members of the embassy staff were still in their sleeping quarters. The fighters knew the layout of our compound well and targeted our weapons compartment with their heaviest RPG fire at the beginning of the attack, blowing up our munitions cache and destroying our ability to respond."

The Secretary paused again. She reached for another sip of water, this time keeping her gaze on the top of the podium and turned to page three of her statement.

"In only fifteen minutes, twenty-eight Americans lost their lives, including my friend, Charlie Carpenter. The fighters looted most of the personal possessions of our staff, and all equipment that escaped destruction. We were informed of the attack by on-the-ground operatives in Sanaa at 04:30. Immediately upon gaining this information, we dispatched a twenty-member fighting force from our Al Anad airbase near the southern Yemeni city of Al Houtha. Our force reached the embassy at 05:30. They arrived to find our compound completely destroyed and deserted except for the remains of our people. Our team identified the bodies of all personnel known to be in the embassy at the time of the attack and provided the recovery for transport back to the U.S."

The Secretary, having completed the reading of her statement, with her eyes still focused on the top of the podium, straightened the three pages. She took off her glasses, folded them closed, and placed them on top of the straightened pages. She lifted her glance to look at the seated journalists all sitting in silence. She had a look of defiance.

"Ladies and gentlemen, I know you have a number of questions, and I will answer many of them before I leave. But before we start, there are a few things I must say. First, to Leila Carpenter— how deeply sorry I am for your loss, and that your loss is all our loss. Charlie Carpenter was my dear friend since our days together at Harvard Law. He, like all who died that morning, was a true patriot who bravely accepted my request to serve as our ambassador in one of the most dangerous places in the world. He did so with great courage. In the same vein, I extend my most heartfelt and sincere condolences to the families and friends of all those who lost their lives in this act of barbarism. This event was conducted by evil people, who we must commit to eliminating. As a nation, we must find the resolve to fight and destroy this evil. I also express my appreciation to my colleagues at State who have had to endure the last two weeks. They are doing a phenomenal job under very trying circumstances, and I salute them all."

"Lastly, to members of Congress, you must find it within yourselves to overcome the acrimonious spirit that endures within the halls of the House and Senate. Your inability to come together to help State protect the lives of our brave foreign-based diplomats in a manner befitting their service is a stain on our nation. Consider the deaths of our twenty-eight comrades as the catalyst to come together in a spirit of cooperation to enable this country to defend itself and its people, wherever they may be deployed. I'll now respond to your questions."

Over the next forty-five minutes, the Secretary fielded questions on all aspects of the event and handled them with grace and humility. While inside she felt the urge to be defiant at some of the more anti-administration-based questions, her better instincts took control. She never once allowed any blame or responsibility on the part of the administration to seem plausible. She had the right words to turn those questions into statements on how the inefficiency of Congress was the ultimate root cause for the loss of the American lives in Yemen.

One of the more administration-friendly journalists was selected for the last question, and she obliged with a question to allow Mrs. Carrington to go back to her relationship with Charlie Carpenter. It was the perfect question on which to end the presser, enabling Heather to leave everyone with a feeling of sympathy towards her for the loss of her close friend.

From his tenth floor Upper East Side Manhattan apartment, Sidney Rosenberg was watching on C-SPAN. The moment the presser was over, he remotely turned off his TV. He walked over to his dining room table to pick up his Blackberry to send an email to the Secretary's private email account.

"Well done, Madam President."

Fifteen

It was Congressman Gregory's number on Rob Wiley's cell phone, on Tuesday of the week before the Ventura County Economic Development Conference.

"Hello, Earl. How are things in Washington?"

"Good, Rob. How are things going with the planning for the conference next week? I'm flying home tomorrow night, will be in town all next week, and will likely head back to Washington a week from Sunday. Have you got a schedule lined up for me? It's time to get into campaign mode."

I'm way ahead of you. I'll have the schedule finalized for your time in town by our meeting Friday morning."

"Rob, there's one other thing I want you to get on my calendar. Carl and Neil Hale will both be arriving in Thousand Oaks next Monday. They are attending the conference both Thursday and Friday. I'd like to entertain them on Tuesday or Wednesday. Since they're dropping $5 million for Braxton's idea, I want to introduce them to the man. And I have another reason as well. Are you familiar with an organization called the Liberty Bell Foundation they fund in Philadelphia?"

"Can't say that I am, never heard of it."

"Do some research and get us a meeting on Tuesday with Braxton."

Wiley was puzzled and needed to confirm what he heard. "Earl, let me get this straight. You want the Hale brothers to meet JB at your direction? Are you sure you want to do this?"

"What's your hesitation, Rob?"

"You know how he can be. Given he even agrees to meet, I'm not sure he won't say something the Hales find offensive. This could come back on you, and not necessarily in a good way."

"His meeting the Hales will be good for his persona and his career, and good for Ventura County. I think Neil might really take to him. He's fed up with politicians, present company not included of course. I know he will welcome meeting Braxton. Based on some of the conversations Neil and I have had over the years, I see Jon Braxton and his perspectives being a breath of fresh air for him and Carl both. Who knows where the relationship could go?"

"Earl, you're not suggesting the Hales are going to talk to JB about a political future, are you? He'll reject it flat out and it could open up another can of worms."

"Get us the meeting. The Hales should meet the man. We'll steer the conversation towards the jobs grant incentive, Liberty Bell, and Win-the-Day. If the conversation slides off the rails and the shit hits the fan, we'll deal with it. To prep them, I'll let the Hales know Braxton is anti-political and expect to hear his views if they bring the subject up. I owe it to them to make the introduction. Actually, I'm anxious to see this meeting happen."

"OK boss, I'll take care of it. Anything else?"

"Call JB tomorrow, first thing, OK? And then let me know so I can confirm their calendars."

"Oh, now it's JB?"

"Don't give me shit, Rob. Just get us the meeting"

"Will do, but just so you know, to get anything on JB's calendar it has to be cleared by his admin."

"What?"

"His executive admin controls his calendar. Abby Martin. She's been at Spectre for about twelve years. JB trusts her implicitly. She qualifies and books all his appointments. Does some of his research, helps him prepare. They collaborate before all his meetings to make sure he's got everything he needs. It's an interesting relationship. Trust me, if he takes the meeting, he'll be ready."

"Is he sleeping with her?"

"No."

"Good. Would hate to see that skeleton in his closet."

"Jon Braxton's office. This is Abby Martin. May I help you?"

"Hey Abby, it's been way too long. It's Rob Wiley. How are you doing?"

"Well, well, well, well, well. If it isn't the mysterious Mr. Wiley. I presume you want to speak with his lordship?"

"Nope. Called to talk to you."

"Oh my, might we need to get something on the emperor's calendar?"

"Abby, I've forgotten what a pleasure it is to speak with you. We just might. By the way, do you treat JB the way you treat his callers?"

"Not at all, Mr. Wiley. His highness usually has to put up with more of my goodness than I grace his suitors with."

"Isn't he the lucky one?"

"Yes, Mr. Wiley, he most definitely is. Now what's on your mind?"

"Next Tuesday afternoon, is JB around and available?"

"Well, he's got a busy week next week, as you may know. He's giving a keynote at the Ventura County Economic Development Conference on Thursday. But I believe you know that as you were part of the lynch mob. I understand you were with the Congressman when he cut the deal. Mr. Braxton is out on Monday all day, but I believe there might be a five-minute opening on Tuesday afternoon for the right purpose."

"Abby, you're so generous. I just don't know how my boss will ever be able to repay you for the five minutes. May we ever so humbly request to reserve that time?"

"Seriously, the Congressman wants to meet with Lord Braxton here at Spectre?"

"Yup, and he's got a couple of heavy hitters he's bringing with him."

"Heavy hitters?"

"Are you familiar with Carlton and Cornelius Hale and The Hale Group?"

"Not intimately but I know their reputation and they are good hitters. Did some research on them after you suggested they might fund Jon's jobs grant incentive plan. Whew, the Congressman and the Hales coming to Spectre to meet with the king. Aren't we the special ones? You sure the Congressman wants to do this? You know Lord Braxton can be a little unpredictable when someone wants to talk politics."

Rob laughed out loud. "That was my exact reaction, but Earl said he'll prep them."

"OK Rob, what's this all about? His lordship is going to want details from me. What can I tell him?"

"JB told me not to attach his name to the jobs grant incentive idea. He left it to me to figure out how best to approach the Hales with it. So, I told the Hales it was my idea, not wanting to drag JB in, and I didn't want to attach Earl to it in case they didn't like it. If they didn't like it, they could say no without it impacting him and their relationship."

"Why, Mr. Wiley, aren't you the crafty one?"

"So, I let the Hales know it was my idea and that I had not yet discussed it with Earl. Turns out Neil Hale loved the idea. Earl and Neil had dinner together a few weeks ago and Neil told him he wanted to run with it if Earl approved. Earl had no clue I floated the idea, so when Neil started discussing it, it caught him by surprise." Rob chuckled at the thought of his boss' reaction at the moment he first realized he had contacted the Hales directly without discussing it with him first.

"Anyway, Earl calls me the same night with his muffins toasted. I calm him down, telling him my reason for not letting him know, and he settles down. Then I told him it was JB's idea, not mine. He was tired, and I could tell he was pissed off. But the next day, when I talked with him, he was fine and expressed an interest in having this meeting. And one other thing, Earl wants JB to talk about Win-the-Day. Turns out the Hales fund a similar kind of operation in Philadelphia, called the Liberty Bell Foundation. It's not doing well, and Earl thinks JB can help them."

"My, my, his holiness is certainly getting his name around these days, isn't he? How about ninety minutes starting at three on Tuesday? I'll make sure Lord Braxton is prepped on everything."

"Abby, I love you."

"Stop it, Rob. You're making my heart go pitter patter—no, wait, it's the leftover meatloaf sandwich I had for lunch. See you Tuesday at 3. Don't be late, we can't let the big dog wait."

<hr />

"Mr. Braxton, thank you for taking my call. This is Larry Morris from the county. I can't tell you how excited I was to hear from Congressman Gregory that you have agreed to give one of the keynotes at our upcoming Economic Development Conference."

"No problem, Larry. I am looking forward to it. What can I do for you?"

"I was hoping we could talk about my ideas for your speech. Are you open to collaborating with me?"

There was a long pause. Jon in no way was interested in this request. "Larry, if you have ideas for my speech, why don't you give it?" Larry laughed nervously. He realized he was treading on thin ice and if he said or did anything causing Jon to withdraw, he would pay a steep price. Morris was aware of Jon's cavalier attitude towards politically colored events and was apprehensive in approaching him. But he was still hoping to influence Jon's speech, at least to a degree. He had his own ideas how Jon could help in his recruiting new employers.

"Have you given any thought to what you're going to say?"

"I have and am working on my outline."

"Would you be willing to share the outline with me?"

"Larry, it's all in my head, so that might be a little bit of an issue." Another silent pause as Larry didn't know what to say and Jon was losing interest in the conversation. After letting Larry hang for a few seconds, he continued. "You know, Larry, I'm interested in hearing what you have in mind." Not really. Slight pause. "What are some of your ideas?"

"We'd like you to talk about yourself and your company. Talk about why you moved your business to Thousand Oaks. Talk about the success your company has enjoyed since you've been here. Describe the unique and innovative things Spectre does to help their people grow personally, professionally, and serve the community. The Spectre story is a great one, and I'm hoping you're willing to tell it."

"Larry, no worries, man. We're on the same page. I'm sorry I'm going to have to cut this short. I have a call I need to make. I'll be ready for the conference and will do you and the county proud. Don't worry. Bye, Larry." Click.

A few days later, Larry Morris called Spectre to speak with Jon again. He was not comfortable with the outcome of their first call and wanted to take another shot at getting on top of what Jon was going to say. Jon had instructed Abby if Larry happened to call again, which he fully expected, to take a detailed message. Jon had no patience for Morris' maneuvering and insecurity and preferred not speaking to him.

"Mr. Morris, Mr. Braxton is not available to take your call, but he did ask me to take a detailed message so he could reply to you in email. What would you like me to tell him?"

"Thank you, Mrs. Martin, would you tell Mr. Braxton that I need to speak with him regarding his speech next week at the conference."

"And, Mr. Morris, what in particular about the speech did you wish to discuss with Mr. Braxton?"

In a somewhat agitated tone, Morris replied "Mrs. Martin, please tell Mr. Braxton it is extremely important I have a copy of his speech within the next day or two. We're trying to coordinate all the speakers, and it's hard doing so without knowing what they plan on saying and how long they plan on speaking."

"I understand, Mr. Morris, I'll pass the message along. I'm sure Mr. Braxton will consider your request and respond. Have a good day. Goodbye."

Jon was in his office at the time, and Abby instant messaged him: *'May I have a moment, your highness?'*

'C'mon on in' appeared on her screen instantly.

Abby sprang to her feet, walked purposefully through the door to Jon's office, and took one of the chairs across his desk, facing him. "Larry Morris just called, as you predicted. He sounded upset. Asked if you could send him a copy of your speech."

Jon took an exasperated breath. "Call him back. Ask him to be here next Tuesday at 2:30. Don't tell him anything else. Just ask him to be here. If he asks you if he can pick up a copy of the speech at that time, tell him you don't know."

"OK, but remember you have the Congressman and the royal princes here at three." She didn't wait for a response. She was on her feet, on her way back to her desk before he could think of a snappy comment.

Abby waited an hour before calling Larry back. He answered the call to his direct line: "Hello, Larry Morris."

"Mr. Morris, Abby Martin here. Mr. Braxton asked me if you could meet with him here at Spectre next Tuesday at 2:30. Would that work for your schedule?"

"Mrs. Martin, did Mr. Braxton say whether I would be able to pick up a copy of his speech at that time?" Abby smiled to herself, though not surprised Jon called it.

"I'm sorry, Mr. Morris, he didn't say one way or the other. He just instructed me to have you meet with him at that time. May I confirm the appointment?"

There was a slight delay before Morris answered. He was frustrated with Jon's resistance. "Yes, you can confirm. I'll be there at 2:30 on Tuesday. Thank you, Mrs. Martin."

"You're very welcome, Mr. Morris."

———≈———

Larry Morris, fifty-three years of age in a portly, five-foot, eight-inch 220-pound frame, entered the reception area outside Jon's office. He was dressed in an untailored, department store-grade dark-blue suit. Under his suit, he wore a light-blue dress shirt with a button-down collar and a non-descript dark-blue tie with very thin yellow diagonal stripes spaced one inch apart. His wardrobe was bottomed up with scuffed, brown pull-on loafers. He looked every bit the part of a slightly uncouth, slightly unprofessional, modestly paid county government official.

Abby sensed Morris was angered, intimidated, and a bit frightened at the prospect of this meeting. With the recent dance around obtaining an advance copy of Jon's speech, Larry's emotion toward him had shifted from reverence to annoyance, and it showed.

Jon summed up the situation and wanted to meet with Larry to diffuse the tension. He was not interested in creating enemies. He felt he and Larry could come to an understanding and, as he had never met the man, felt the need for a meeting to get there. He instructed Abby to treat Larry with utmost respect and consideration, and to make him feel at home at Spectre.

"Mr. Morris, what a pleasure to meet you. I'm Abby Martin.

Welcome to Spectre. Mr. Braxton is expecting you but is on a call right now. He should be finished momentarily. I'll let him know you are here. Please have a seat." She gestured to the couch and two chairs surrounding a rectangular coffee table at the far end of the reception area. "May I offer you a bottle of water or a cup of coffee?"

Morris politely declined and took a seat on the couch.

Abby went back to her desk and instant messaged Jon. *'Larry Morris is here and looks absolutely petrified. Go easy on him, sire.'*

Within thirty seconds, Jon opened his office door and approached Morris. The stark contrast struck Abby. Her boss tall, slim, and nattily dressed in a fitted gray dress shirt, nicely tailored white wool slacks, and a pair of conservative black dress shoes—and Morris, in his thrift store outfit. *'This is not a fair fight and will end badly for Larry Morris,'* Abby concluded.

Jon walked towards Morris. "Hi Larry, how are you? Welcome to Spectre." Larry stood and they shook hands. "Let's go into my office." He glanced at his trusted assistant. "Abby, handle my calls please."

"Yes sir."

Jon gestured to Morris to enter his office and followed behind. When both were inside, Jon closed the door and motioned Larry to a seat at his office conference table. He took the seat directly across and they were now facing one another.

Jon sensed Morris' unease and spoke first. "Larry, the first thing I want you to know is that I am going to make you proud with my speech on Thursday. I've taken your input and incorporated much of it into what I'm going to talk about. I understand what you are trying to accomplish at the conference, and I am in your corner all the way."

"Thank you, Mr. Braxton. That is certainly reassuring. When you had your assistant ask me here, I wasn't sure what to expect. I thought that you might be withdrawing. Not having a copy of your address makes me nervous. I know of your disdain for politics, and we've never met, so I really don't know you. All I know is your reputation. But

Randy Boswell, who I know well, has assured me there's nothing to be concerned about. But it was important for me to hear you say you're still in. I was having doubts."

"Larry, first, please call me Jon or JB, whichever you're more comfortable with. I gave my word to Congressman Gregory that I would speak, and I would never go back on my word. Let's put that behind us. The reason I invited you over was I wanted to hear more about the conference and how it is shaping up. How many prospective out-of-state employers and in-state employers have registered? Who are some of the best prospects?"

Jon wanted to build a good relationship with Morris by showing interest how the planning of the conference was coming along and what he had accomplished so far. He succeeded in relieving Morris of all his apprehension and excited him by giving him a chance to talk about his progress.

"So far, we have forty-five companies from out of state attending and thirteen from within California. All have expressed an interest in either expanding into or relocating to Ventura County. The five out-of-state companies we feel are our best prospects are all, interestingly, from the Upper Midwest and all have listed our climate as the primary reason. The secondary reasons are labor pool diversity and proximity to Port Hueneme for shipping. The larger enterprises coming are Joy Global and Kohl's Corp from Wisconsin, Comerica Bank and Eaton Corp from Michigan, and Procter & Gamble from Ohio. We've had preliminary discussions with all five, and each has talked in the neighborhood of 300 to 600 potential jobs."

"Incredible, Larry. You're doing a phenomenal job. Convince just fifteen percent of the companies attending to move here, and you're talking 3,000 to 3,500 new jobs. I commend you on the outstanding work you've done so far."

Jon continued: "Larry, I'm looking forward to speaking, but I need to elaborate on what I told you on our call. I don't write down what

I'm going to say when I do public speaking. I put an outline together in my head, and then I speak from my instincts. That's the reason I don't have a written copy for you."

Morris was surprised by the admission. "Seriously, Jon, you don't write anything down? How do you time your talks? One of the reasons I wanted to see your speech was to make sure you were close to the thirty minutes we allocated for you. If you're either well under or over it will throw the schedule off and disrupt the flow."

"Larry, I can't explain why, but I just have a knack for this. I'll be right at thirty minutes. Don't worry, it's going to be fine." He paused for a moment to let Morris digest. "So, are we fine?"

"You're putting me in an uncomfortable position, Mr. Braxton," Morris retorted formally. "I have a lot riding on the success of this event and have been working on the planning diligently for the last twelve months. I've got a handle on everything except what you're going to say. I even have a copy of Congressman Gregory's keynote. You'll have to pardon me if I'm apprehensive about the box you're putting me into."

Jon was bothered by Larry's apprehension. He saw it as a bureaucrat's reach of control for control's sake. He stood and walked the room.

"Larry, I can understand how you feel, but I am who I am. I'm not going to write my talk down because if I do, I can't predict the outcome and I can't guarantee that I'll say what I write out. I've never spoken from a script before, and I'm not sure I want to start now. I prefer to speak from my instincts. For me, to give you my best, I have to be me. As I see it, this leaves us with two options. One, I can withdraw from the program if you wish, and I hope you don't. Or two, you can agree to let me do this my way, and I hope you do. I hope you will trust me in my promise that I will fill thirty minutes and I will represent your mission to bring jobs to Ventura County well."

Jon returned to his seat, calmly and confidently leaned back, crossing his legs, waiting for Morris' response. Morris stood and Jon followed his lead. He extended his hand. "Mr. Braxton, thank you for explaining this to me. I'm still uncomfortable, but I'm going to trust you. If I could ask you to be at the venue at 8:30 on Thursday morning for our speakers meeting. You'll be following Congressman Gregory and you'll be up from 10:30 to eleven. I'll look forward to seeing you Thursday at 8:30."

"Thank you, Larry, and I really want us to be on a first name basis from now on. I'll see you Thursday morning at 8:30 without fail."

Morris nodded to acknowledge and strode for the office door. It was now 2:55. As Morris opened the door, he was surprised by the sight of Congressman Gregory and Rob Wiley in the reception area. He also noticed two classically dressed businessmen seated to the left of Abby's desk. Gregory, upon seeing Morris, popped to his feet.

"Larry, how are you doing? You and JB cooking up some madness for Thursday?"

Larry looked at JB briefly to his left and then back to the Congressman with a nervous smile. "I guess you could say that."

"Larry, allow me introduce you to two very good friends of mine, Carlton and Cornelius Hale."

Morris looked in the direction of the Hales, who were now standing. "Carl, Neil, this is Larry Morris from the County of Ventura. Larry is the Chairman of the County's Economic Development Committee and is the primary organizer of the conference." Morris knew of the Hales. His knees started shaking.

Neil and Carl both extended their hands to Morris and they shook. "Mr. Morris, speaking for my brother, we're very pleased to meet you. Carl and I are looking forward to your show, and we have a surprise for you that we think you're going to be very happy with." As the last words were spoken, Neil Hale looked and nodded at Jon. "We'll call you later to talk about how we are going to support your efforts. You're going to love it."

Jon thought it best not to let Larry ruin the moment. "Gentleman, shall we start our meeting?"

The Congressman and Morris shook hands. "Larry, we'll definitely call you later to talk about Carl and Neil's support of the conference. It was great seeing you."

With that, the Hales, the Congressman, Rob Wiley, and Jon proceeded into Jon's office, leaving Larry Morris and Abby in the reception area. Larry was somewhat stunned at the happenings of the last two minutes and was standing where the Congressman had left him.

"Well, Mr. Morris, it's just another average day at Spectre Systems. It's amazing we build and sell anything around here, the way the celebrities come and go."

"Ms. Martin, Braxton knows the Hale brothers?" he asked, JB's legacy growing exponentially in the mind of the county government official.

"Oh yeah, the Hale boys are always looking to hang out with JB."

The five men proceeded into Jon's office and seated themselves around the conference table in the northwest corner of the twenty-by-twenty-foot, moderately but neatly appointed office of the CEO of Spectre Systems.

As was his custom, Congressman Gregory spoke first. "Jon, thank you for making the time for us this afternoon. Let me formally introduce you to my two good friends—at least I think they're still my friends. After introducing them to Larry Morris, I'm not quite sure," he said with a grin, pleased at his own attempt at clever humor to break the ice.

"Jon, Carl and Neil wanted to meet you after I informed them that the idea Rob floated to them about providing some financial incentives to companies that would move new jobs to Ventura County was actually your creation. I also spoke to them about the work you're doing with Win-the-Day. I raised Win-the-Day because Carl and Neil support a foundation in Philadelphia that is doing the same kind of work, but their results are in decline. I felt that you could provide Carl and Neil some insights, and perhaps help them in some capacity to get things back on track."

"Earl, I'm honored you thought highly enough of our work at Win-the-Day that you were open to discussing it with your distinguished friends. I'd be happy to assist in any way I can with LBF. Do you have anything specific in mind?" The fact that Jon knew the name of the organization and its acronym slipped by everyone's recognition except Rob Wiley's. *'Good girl, Abby,'.*

Neil Hale responded. "Mr. Braxton, first let me thank you for the idea you had Rob pass along to us regarding the jobs grant incentive. It's a fantastic way to support Congressman Gregory's bid for reelection this year. As you know, he's in for a tough challenge with redistricting and changing demographics."

Rob Wiley shifted uneasily in his chair. He was hoping Jon would keep his composure, now knowing that the Hales had decided to run with his idea because of its political value, and not necessarily out of any affinity for Ventura County. Jon perfectly understood the Hales motivation and was not the least bit unsettled by Neil's comment. He knew their reasons for coughing up $5 million were tied to Earl's reelection but didn't care as long as the results would benefit the community.

"I know the Congressman faces the toughest reelection campaign of his career this year. But if through his relationship with you, he can help the county bring good paying jobs in, well, that only cements his legacy of service to this community. If that happens to also assist or pull through his reelection, that's two birds with one stone in my book." The Congressman smiled and the Hales nodded approvingly. Rob was not surprised Jon hit the mark. He had seen him in awkward moments before.

Jon continued. "Mr. Hale, I've done some research on LBF and understand why you're disappointed. Let me tell you about what we do at Win-the-Day and what I feel are some of the reasons we are successful."

Jon spent the next forty-five minutes describing Win-the-Day's programs and philosophies in detail. He covered all the aspects of the organization. He talked about the core values they taught. The teaching philosophies that guided the instruction. The success measurements used to track performance. He made it a point to single out Connie McIlroy and reference her accomplishments.

Neil was grateful for Jon's insights. "Mr. Braxton, thank you for that overview. You are a most impressive young man. Your ideas and programs are very innovative. Would you be willing to start some discussions via conference call with the director of LBF as our consultant? I'm sure he would welcome your help and benefit from your perspectives. We're happy to pay you whatever you believe fair for your time."

"Mr. Hale, I will make myself available. Have your people let my assistant, Mrs. Martin, know when you want to set up the call. I look forward to getting involved. As for compensation, you decide what is fair and make an in-kind charitable contribution to WTD. Acceptable?"

"Perfectly acceptable Mr. Braxton. It's fantastic that we'll be working together on this. I look forward to it as well. However, there is something else I wanted to discuss with you if I may?" The Congressman's heart started to race a bit with anticipation. Rob Wiley again shifted uneasily in his seat, hoping the fireworks would be kept to a minimum with the upcoming conversation.

"Certainly, Mr. Hale. Please."

"First, Mr. Braxton, I'd like to shift our relationship to a first name basis. Call me Neil or Corny, as my brother does. And my distinguished brother Carlton is known as Carl to his friends. Would that be OK with you, JB?"

"Of course, Neil and Carl it is."

"Great. Now JB, tell me a little about your political philosophy. From what I've heard, you're not involved in any political organizations or causes. But I'm curious about your political beliefs and policy stances. Do you align with the left or the right?"

Jon was not expecting such a direct approach. "With all due respect to the work you and Carl do, and to the beliefs you hold, and with my huge respect for the Congressman and his body of work in Congress the last twenty-six years, I must confess that I am not aligned to the left or the right. Consider me unaligned. I don't really care for the terms 'left' and 'right' except to describe my hands and feet. I dislike using terms like that to define people. When you classify people with those definitions, politicians then cater to those mindsets and not to the true needs of the people they serve. The discourse created by these divisions moves politicians of different parties into polar opposite positions. What happens from there? The true issues become obfuscated and efforts to understand the positions of others doesn't make it out of each party's corner. To sum up my political beliefs, Carl, Neil, again with all due respect, it's more disbelief. Disbelief in how inefficient and hypocritical the business of politics is."

Jon reached for a bottle of water in front of him to let his heat-seeking missile travel through the room. Congressman Gregory frowned. Rob Wiley did everything he could to maintain a poker face, but inside he was enjoying this banter immensely. Neil Hale broke into a huge smile. He looked at Carl with satisfaction as his older brother sat motionless and emotionless.

Jon continued. "As for my policy beliefs, the cornerstone is a strong belief in free markets. I'm a big believer in the power of free enterprise. I believe the best answer to any economic, or social issue for that matter, is free market enterprise. The fact our government tries to engineer the economy and societal constructs is the root cause of most of the problems in this country. In my view, our growing government reach is bad governance which eventually leads to bad policy."

"The fundamental role of our government should be helping its citizens become better people. Better in a manner which leads people to be the best they can be. Government policy should be focused on helping its citizens maximize their opportunity for a better life. A life with health, happiness, and prosperity. Unfortunately, our political system today works against the best interests of its citizens. Building dependence on government, and overtaxing prosperity degrades the desire to achieve. This is the reason I'm not interested in political parties or interests or causes. The last thing I'll offer to sum up my beliefs—and Carl, Neil, again with all due respect to the causes you champion and your motives—I believe the presence of money and influence-peddling in government is obscene, if not criminal. The U.S. government should serve its citizens. Instead, it serves itself, those individuals who hold office, and the individuals with enough money and corrupt morals to influence individuals in office. Until the linkage between money and political office is broken, I don't have any desire to invest time or energy in any political efforts. I prefer investing my time, efforts, and capital where I can contribute to a positive outcome."

The resulting moment of silence was deafening. Jon had described exactly what the Hales were all about, in a most unflattering manner. The Congressman had been expecting a small hammer from Jon— not the nuclear bomb he just detonated. Neil was in thought for a moment. Finally, to the surprise of everyone in the room—except for Carl, who had been thinking that Jon's philosophies were in alignment with his younger brother's frustrations over the past dozen years—he flashed a huge grin.

"JB, this may shock you, but conceptually, I agree with you 100 percent. With deference to my friend Earl here, who is different from the rest of the bunch, I am sick and tired of dealing with the political shitheads in government whom Carl and I have the unfortunate experience of working with every day. And that goes right to the top on the Right. Boehner, McConnell, McCain, Graham—they're all sellouts in my estimation. They all talk a good game, but the bottom line for them is reelection and power. They'll do and say whatever it takes to get there. As a result, the best interests of the American people take a back seat to their individual interests and the interests of the lobbyists who put up the money to feed their campaigns. And the thing that sucks is my brother and I are right in the mix. I hate it because I know it's wrong, yet we still do it because it's all we know how to do to get the things we want done. Frankly, JB, this thing has been tearing me up for years, as Carl can attest. He's the only one I've expressed these feelings to, until now." Another pause.

"JB, you and I need to talk more. Would that be OK with you? Carl and I have always looked at ourselves as catalysts for change. But I'm not impressed or confident in the change agents working with us in government right now. I don't trust any of them. We need some new ideas, and I have a sense you would be a great source. Can I occasionally call you to discuss things in which we might be able to use your insights?"

"Of course, Neil. But if you're looking for me to speak to any political groups or rallies or town halls or media or anything like that, I won't. I won't be a proxy for the Hale Group or any causes you're aligned with. But I am intrigued about what your thoughts are. Let's see how our first few conversations pan out."

Neil stood and the others in the room followed suit.

"JB, that sounds like a good plan. I look forward to hearing your keynote on Thursday, and I look forward to talking with you about LBF and about how we might work together to get this country back to where we all think it should be. You're most impressive, and Earl" he turned to face the Congressman to his right, "I can't express my gratitude enough for making the introduction."

Handshakes were exchanged all around, and the five men walked out of Jon's office in single file led by Rob Wiley, who went straight over to Abby's desk. He made eye contact with her and lip-synced, '*Wow.*'

A moment later, the Hales, Rob Wiley, and the Congressman were gone. Jon moved to the sitting area adjacent to Abby's desk. He sat and looked directly ahead at a painting of a seascape on the far wall. Abby, from her desk, looked over at him, got up, walked to the sitting area, and took the seat to his left. "So?"

"I'm not exactly sure what just happened in my office, but it certainly was interesting."

"OK, your majesty, don't get uppity on us now. By the way, Larry Morris called back. Told me to tell you he already knew from Greenway about the '5 mil' from the Hales and asked me to thank you. Also, reminding you that I'm leaving early today for my karate workout with your wife."

"So, this is what you've been doing with your Tuesday afternoons lately?"

"Yes indeed. Angela and I both thought my picking up some new colored belts would help me hold you more accountable."

"Perfect, just what I need, another ninja warrior in the midst."

Abby rose to leave to meet Angela. "Shall I tell your lovely, better half who you were hobnobbing with today?"

"Good night, Mrs. Martin. See you tomorrow should you choose to come in and continue to torture me."

"Sayonara, boss man. Count on it."

Sixteen

"Good morning, everyone, and welcome to beautiful Thousand Oaks. I'm Larry Morris from the County of Ventura. Welcome to the 2012 Ventura County Economic Development Conference. To the many representatives of organizations and enterprises considering establishing a presence in our county, we are pleased to have you here. Over the next two days, we hope to inform you of the things that make our county special, and to provide you the information you need to fully consider our county for your relocation or expansion."

"I have had the pleasure of representing Ventura County in a variety of capacities for the last twelve years, and over this time have been involved with many employers who displayed the good fortune and judgment—even if I say so myself—to choose our beautiful area as their home. Over the next few days, we will introduce you to the reasons and the people who make Ventura County an extraordinary environment in which to establish roots, to build your businesses, and to prosper. In my capacities over the last twelve years, I have come to understand the needs you have in operating either a corporate headquarters or a regional division. And I hope to work with many of you going forward. My door will always be open as you consider what we have to offer and in making the critical decisions you'll be facing as you decide where in the country to invest."

"Next week, after you return home and settle back in, my office will reach out to all of you to discuss the next steps in presenting you everything we can offer your organization should you decide to consider Ventura County for your relocation or expansion. We have some very interesting incentives we will be offering, thanks to some very influential people who have offered to help us in our efforts. We're still finalizing the details, so were not ready to discuss these incentives just yet, but we're confident given all the other attributes our area has to offer, in addition to the incentives package we're working on, we can provide an attractive proposal to each of you."

"This morning, we are going to start our conference with two very special speakers. Following, we will move to the exhibit hall next door, where we'll have lunch. During our two-hour lunch break, you will be able to visit the many exhibits of our local businesses which offer services you will find valuable should you decide to locate in Ventura County. Following lunch, we'll conduct a number of various breakout sessions to provide detailed information on select topics you may find of particular interest. A list of the breakout sessions with time and location is provided in your conference program."

"For tonight, we have reserved one of the premier restaurants in our area, Mastros. We're looking forward to meeting and getting to know all of you in a more casual setting. We'll be interested to know your thoughts of today's activities and will be eager to answer your questions. The food at Mastro's is beyond compare, and we know you will find it enjoyable."

"Tomorrow morning, we will start at nine with more breakout sessions. The morning breakouts will be followed by another catered lunch in the exhibit hall, and you can continue your conversations with some of our local relocation services providers. Following lunch, we'll start our closing session featuring a panel of Ventura County leadership officials to discuss various topics that relate to our local business climate and to answer any questions. The conference will conclude at three o'clock tomorrow. We will provide transport to LAX for those who need."

"For those planning to stay the weekend, we have numerous activities lined up. One excursion will be a tour of our coveted local U.S. naval base at Point Mugu and our county-based shipping port at Port Hueneme. For the adventurists, we have reserved a charter fishing vessel to tour our beautiful Channel Islands and do some sportfishing. And for any history buffs, we have a tour bus chartered to travel all around the county to introduce you to the many landmarks and historical venues in the area."

"OK, let's get the party started. Our first guest speaker is our area's distinguished representative in the U.S. House of Representatives. This gentleman has been representing a large portion of our county in Congress for twenty-six years, and he recently announced he will be seeking a fourteenth term this November. Over the course of his career in the House, he has delivered numerous projects funded by the federal government to our county. He is a huge supporter of our naval base at Point Mugu and has close ties with many local businesses. Prior to his journey to Congress, he served as the mayor of Simi Valley, one of the larger local cities in our county. No one knows and understands our county better than this gentleman, and no one has served it better over the last twenty-six years. Ladies and gentlemen, it is my honor to introduce our local U.S Congressman, Earl Gregory."

The Congressman was seated in the front row, to the left of the podium, in front of the four-foot elevated stage of the Scherr Forum in the Thousand Oaks government center. Seated directly to Gregory's left were Carlton Hale, Cornelius Hale, Jon, and Angela.

Upon hearing his name and polite applause from the audience, the Congressman jumped to his feet and moved to the six-step stairway at the edge of the stage. He bounded up the six with an energy unexpected from a seventy-six-year-old who lived in the Washington DC wine-and-dine scene for the past twenty-six years. He arrived on stage and moved purposefully to the podium where Morris was standing and applauding.

The two exchanged a few words with the customary handshaking. Over the next thirty minutes, Earl Gregory addressed what he hoped would be many future employers for his beloved Ventura County. He described his early real estate career, local government career, and his career in Congress.

When the Congressman concluded, he was awarded a tepid and polite applause from the crowd. Larry Morris came up to rescue him. "Thank you, Congressman Gregory," said Morris in a manner meant to stoke some enthusiasm from the audience. The two shook hands and Gregory returned to his seat.

Ladies and gentlemen, it is now my pleasure to introduce you to one of our local treasures. The second-largest employer in our beautiful city relocated here from Torrance, California, thirteen years ago. Our community has not been the same since. Before moving here, Spectre Systems was fifty-five people with annual revenue of $30 million dollars. Today, Spectre employs 800 people, 600 here in Ventura County. Last year, they totaled $1.2 billion dollars in revenue. But perhaps the most impressive thing about this organization is their level of involvement in our community and their philanthropy. The support this company provides to this community's quality of life is nothing short of monumental. We've invited Spectre System's CEO and architect of their most unusual and innovative programs to join us today to tell you more about this remarkable organization. Please join me in welcoming Jonathon Braxton."

Jon stood, as did Angela. They embraced. She kissed him on the cheek. He approached the stairs to the left of the stage and started up in a much more deliberate manner than the Congressman. As he did, a loud applause started to build. Unbeknownst to Jon, thirty Spectre staffers, led by Abby Martin, had entered the Scherr Forum shortly after Congressman Gregory began his address. As Jon headed up the stairs and approached the podium, they began a loud and boisterous applause, complete with hooting and rooting. The rest of the audience felt obliged to join in. Before Jon could reach Larry Morris and his huge grin, the whole auditorium was on its feet, cheering wildly. Carl and Corny looked at each other, slightly bewildered.

Morris left Jon to the audience after a quick handshake and pat on the back. Jon stood silent for a few seconds, letting the applause subside. As he did, he looked to the back of the room and made eye contact with Abby, who was now seated. She returned the gaze with a look of utter satisfaction and a *'what else did you expect?'* grin.

"Good morning, everyone. First, let me applaud you on your outstanding judgment for considering Ventura County for your expansion or relocation. It's a choice Spectre Systems made thirteen years ago, and looking back, we were fortunate and prophetic to have done so. I truly believe our decision to locate here in 1999 was a critical factor in our evolution and subsequent success. Now, I can stand here and tell you we did a thorough investigation of all our needs and entertained proposals from numerous cities in several states before coming to our decision. Yes, I can certainly tell you that, but I won't because it's not true. We moved to Thousand Oaks because my lovely wife Angela told me she wanted to live here. Thank you, honey, it was a great call. We have had a wonderful life in this community over the last thirteen years, and if offered the chance to do it all again, we wouldn't change a thing."

"As Larry mentioned, during our time here in Thousand Oaks, Spectre has grown to 800 employees from fifty-five and to $1.2 billion in annual revenue last year from $30 million in 1999." Abby led another round of applause which started with the Spectre people, but soon spread throughout the auditorium. "And I will tell you unequivocally and without a single doubt in my mind, our growth and our success over the years can be directly linked to the quality of the people in this community. People who filled the positions in our organization needed to support our explosive growth."

"When we refer to the quality of people we've been able to attract, one of the primary factors responsible for that quality is the cultural diversity of our Ventura County workforce. This golden resource is the largest single reason I would highly recommend you consider Ventura County for your future. The cultural diversity of a workforce, and the benefits to any business that successfully harvests it, cannot be overstated. Any of you looking to build your organization should strongly consider Ventura County for its people. And as you will hear and see over the next few days, numerous other reasons as well."

Jon paused, and the audience again broke into a loud and enthusiastic round of applause, this time not instigated by Abby. Carlton and Cornelius Hale turned to look at one another. Jon looked in the direction of Larry Morris who was clapping enthusiastically.

"Ladies and gentlemen, undeniably we live and work in a global economy today. Whether the global dynamic is represented by the microcosm of our local market or by the worldwide markets our businesses support, the bottom line remains our businesses serve multiple cultures. What better way to serve multiple cultures than to have a multicultural workforce representing your organization, interacting with your customers and business partners."

"There's something else about employing multicultural teams we have learned along the way. Building multicultural teams raises the collective intelligence of those teams, the individual intelligence of those team members, and the intelligence of others in our organization who interact with those teams. The positive dynamics to an organization of multicultural teams working together towards a common objective cannot be overstated. I say this from first-hand experience."

"You know, it's a sad fact today society consists of many people intolerant of others who do not look or speak like themselves. What I've learned is intolerant people are not intolerant of others who don't look or talk like themselves. No, ladies and gentlemen, they're simply intolerant, period. And intolerance breeds dissent. Intolerance breeds inefficiency. Intolerance breeds incompetence. In contrast, multicultural teams spark tolerance and acceptance, and the performance of the resulting work environment is enhanced greatly."

"Stiff competition is a given when competing in a global economy. Your business needs every advantage it can muster to be successful. Leveraging our cultural diversity over the past thirteen years in Ventura County, has been most instrumental to the success of Spectre Systems. Our teams capitalize on the diversity of perspectives, backgrounds, and experiences. We compete effectively in our markets by maintaining better ability than our competitors to understand the dynamics of competitive situations. And this ability is correlated directly to the diversity of our workforce."

"As I understand it, most of you here today represent organizations that have put our county on your short list for potential relocation or expansion. As someone who has had an overwhelming advantage over our competitors due to the resources available here in our county, I strongly urge you to consider getting serious with Larry Morris. We are hungry for organizations like yours to help us provide more employment opportunities to support our available workforce. The people available to you to help you thrive and grow are here. They are hard-working and, as I have gratefully come to know, are incredibly industrious. I know this because I have had, and continue to have, the pleasure and honor to work with 600 of them locally every day. Spectre Systems is a true melting pot, not only of cultures, but also of ideas and principles, and we are stronger and more productive and more efficient as a result."

"When you consider our available workforce and add the many other attributes we have here in Ventura County—our climate, our local shipping port, our proximity to multiple recreational amenities, our many highly regarded school districts and universities—I challenge you to find a better home for your new offices and facilities."

Jon took a breath and reached for the bottle of water on the podium. He used the pause to frame his next words. The audience broke into another round of applause.

"I've been asked to speak with you today about some of the things we do at Spectre that are, as one might say, a little out of the box. Frankly, I'm a little uncomfortable up in front of all of you to present the things I've been asked to—uncomfortable only in the fact that I shouldn't be alone on stage taking the credit. The things we do to help the community are truly a team effort. Our efforts would not be successful if not for the dedication, love and commitment my teammates exhibit every day as they go into the community to help the less fortunate. They are the true heroes and deserve the credit."

"One of the programs we are very proud of having instituted at Spectre is our Charity Sabbatical Program. Every employee at Spectre, once they cross their one-year anniversary date has an option outside of their standard vacation time to take two weeks off each year, fully paid, to volunteer their time to work for a local charitable cause. In addition, if that Spectre employee develops an idea how to raise money or awareness for that charity, Spectre will support and fund that employee's idea when they submit an approved business plan. If the employee needs help writing a business plan, we provide the assistance. Our intent is to empower our people to go into the community and make a difference. We give our people the time they need, and if they develop a reasonable and creative approach to help a charitable cause, we provide the business skills and the necessary funding to bring their idea to reality."

"Over the last six years, an average eight percent of our employees— sixty-five people last year—take advantage of the two weeks of charity sabbatical time. Over these six years, we have worked with our people to develop and fund forty-eight distinct charity fundraising projects. These projects have generated a total of $1.6 million in charitable contributions."

The Spectre crowd in the back of the auditorium began cheering wildly, joined enthusiastically by the out-of-state and out-of-area attendees.

"If any of you would like to learn more about this program and the kinds of projects our people have formulated and constructed, please feel free to visit our website and look for the Charity Sabbatical page. Also, we have a booth in the exhibitor's hall where you will be having lunch today and tomorrow. Feel free to stop by and meet some of our people. Again, I cannot stress enough that the success of this program is 100 percent the result of the people that work for Spectre."

"When Larry Morris and I were discussing what he had in mind for me to speak with you on today, he asked me the question, 'Why are the people who work for Spectre always so positive and motivated?' 'What are you doing to create the productivity and the loyalty that's present in all the Spectre people I've met?'"

"One of the internal programs we have at Spectre that our people find motivating is our unusual 401(k) profit-sharing program— unusual because of a unique enhancement. Once Larry was informed about our program, he asked me to share it with you." Jon understood Larry Morris would be instrumental in working with these companies to bring them to Ventura County and was intentionally mentioning his name frequently.

"We affectionately refer to our internal 401(k) enhancement as the Spectre Spock Market. In the Spock Market, shares of six internal Spectre pseudo-companies are bought and sold. The six companies are Spectre Sales MLLC, Spectre Manufacturing MLLC, Spectre Marketing MLLC, Spectre Accounting MLLC, Spectre Engineering MLLC, and Spectre Warehouse Operations MLLC. MLLC as in Make-believe Limited Liability Corporation."

"At the beginning of each year, the stock price of each company in the Spock Market is set at $10. Every month, each MLLC stock price adjusts, either up or down based on how the MLLC performs against predefined metrics. For each MLLC, we use six metrics to measure performance."

"Every Spectre employee has the opportunity to buy stock in any

MLLC. Most tend to invest in the MLLC their position aligns with, as their employee performance can directly affect that MLLC's value. Stock is purchased with employee 401(k) profit-sharing contributions. For the month of January, we hold the price at $10 per share, and employees can decide how many shares they want to buy making the corresponding 401(k) contribution. We limit the amount of shares any employee can buy during a calendar year to 500. As an example, should an employee want to buy 200 shares in January, they would direct $2,000 into profit-sharing in January."

"If any of our people want to buy shares after January, they can do so at the current share price. Again, they would make their 401(k) contribution, equal to the number of shares they buy at the then current stock price. At the end of the year, we calculate the difference between the end of year share price and the price of shares employees purchased. Whatever the difference is paid to the employee as a company 401(k)-matching contribution."

"As an example, at the end of 2011, the share price for Spectre Marketing MLLC was $63. The stock had appreciated $53 over the year. For our people who had the good judgment to purchase shares in the Marketing MLLC in January 2011 for $10, they earned $53 in appreciation for the year. If someone had the good insight to purchase 300 shares in January with a $3000 pre-tax contribution, their end-of-year matching contribution was $15,900. This is on top of our baseline employer-matching contribution to our employee 401(k) accounts, which in this case would be another $3000."

"In 2011, the closing share prices for the MLLC's were as follows: Spectre Sales MLLC, $38; Spectre Manufacturing Operations MLLC, $46; Spectre Marketing MLLC, $63; Spectre Accounting MLLC, $38; Spectre Engineering MLLC, $47; and Spectre Warehouse Operations MLLC, $52."

"As you can see, any of our people who invested in the Spock Market in 2011 earned a significant end-of-year matching 401(k) contribution. Last year, seventy-eight percent of our employees invested in the Spock Market. This resulted in $6 million dollars paid out in Spock Market end-of-year matching contributions. No question, it's a large investment, but we feel it's one of the best investments we make year over year."

"We love this plan at Spectre. It's truly a win-win. Employees are motivated to contribute to their 401(k) accounts. They're motivated to perform at a high level, as job performance directly correlates to 401(k) growth and year-end company contributions. As you can imagine, Spectre enjoys extremely high employee morale and loyalty. One of the share price metrics is associated with new ideas. This leads to tremendous levels of creativity. We have so many good ideas for improving the company coming from employees we simply don't have enough time to implement them all. I encourage all of you to consider new and innovative ways to motivate and reward your people. They are your biggest asset."

Jon paused for a drink of water and a moment to frame his next words. The audience, coerced by the Spectre gang in the back, used the opportunity to break into another round of enthusiastic applause.

"Let's talk about education. We are very fortunate in Ventura County to have many distinguished and highly rated Kindergarten through grade twelve schools, especially in the East County. However, in our lower demographic West County we are not as fortunate. Excuse me for going a bit off topic here, but in case you were not aware, we have a serious education problem in this country. And it's present on our West County as well."

The left eyebrows of Carl, Neil, and Earl all rose simultaneously at the mention of Jon making a pseudo-political statement. Larry Morris shifted uneasily. *'Where's he going?'*

"Too many of our young people are not given the tools at home they need to be productive and functional members of society. They are being cast into a world for which they are not prepared, and for most, it results in a toxic lifestyle. Toxic to themselves, toxic to their families, and toxic to their communities."

"One would expect our public-school systems to be able to work with these troubled young people, many of whom—no, make that most of whom—have the capacity to be productive, functional, happy, well-adjusted members of our communities. But our public-school systems fail miserably in this endeavor." Jon paused for a moment to let the criticism take root and then continued.

"One would expect our public-school systems would understand why young people who come out of broken homes and welfare-dependent families are at such a tremendous disadvantage for living prosperous and fulfilling lives, and then create programs and curriculums that would be inclusive of the kinds of lessons these young people need to get their lives in order. But our public-school systems fail miserably in this endeavor."

The entire audience now joined Neil Hale in full study of Jon Braxton, all hanging on every word, in silence.

"One would expect our public-school systems would understand what the human spirit is all about and what fantastic things can come from a young person if that spirit is properly fed and nurtured. But our public-school systems fail miserably in this endeavor."

Jon paused for a moment, looked down at the podium devoid of any notes, gathering his thoughts. The audience waited in silence for him to continue.

"Ladies and gentlemen, I apologize to you. I apologize for imparting upon you my strong opinions on this matter. These opinions may be out of place in this setting, but I was asked today to talk to you about the things our company does in support of our community. One of the things we do directly relates to failures of our public education system, and these failures are the catalyst for one of Spectre's most successful programs."

"To me, the amount of taxpayer dollars being spent on public education in this country, relative to the results being achieved, especially for our lower-income demographic, is an unmitigated disaster. This funding, primarily benefiting teacher unions and ineffective administrators, and not our kids, in my opinion, is our nation's greatest failing. We are failing many of our children. We are failing in not providing these kids a decent chance at a decent life. By not raising them to succeed, we are essentially training our youth to fail. And if our younger generation of today fails, then tomorrow we as a nation will fail. Correcting this failing, at least at our local level, is the mission of Spectre's Win-the-Day Foundation."

A feather dropped in the silent Scherr Forum. It was heard by all.

"Our Win-the-Day foundation is, in my opinion, our greatest accomplishment at Spectre. Many will disagree with me. Many will point to our revenue growth, our employee productivity, our market share, our efficiency metrics, and so on. We are certainly proud of all these things, but the thing we are most proud of at Spectre is the difference we are making for underserved youth here in Ventura County."

"At Win-the-Day, we execute a program designed to improve the lives of these less-fortunate young people. And from the hard work, dedication, perseverance, passion, and love from our Win-the-Day staff, from the employees of Spectre who donate their time and energy, and from all the other individuals and organizations who have joined us, we are fighting and winning the day. Winning every day, leading to better lives for our local underserved young people."

"Six years ago, Spectre started the Win-the-Day Foundation in a lower socio-economic area of the county, Downtown Oxnard. We decided we would do the job our public-school systems were not doing, and the job that many mothers and fathers and other caregivers were not doing. The job of teaching young people not useless facts and irrelevant constructs, but instead lessons they needed to learn to be good human beings. We provide our students the psychological and emotional tools they need to build substantive lives for themselves. We teach our students how not to be dependent or reliant on others. We teach our students the meaning and reason for respect—respect for themselves, respect for others, respect for family, respect for their community. At WTD, we teach our students compassion, and we teach them consciousness. We teach our students how to become someone they can admire. We show them how to be their best. We guide them to develop a value system aligned with living a successful and meaningful life, and we steer them back when they stray off track."

Jon paused for a drink water. There was not a sound to be heard in the auditorium. All eyes followed the water bottle to Jon's lips and then back to the podium.

"Win-the-Day has a tremendous record of success working with very troubled young people. Our program runs nine weeks, and we have the capacity to work with one hundred new kids every cycle, totaling 500 kids per year. We are relentless in tracking our results. We review and analyze the life of each new student who comes into the program, and we track their progress and their circumstances from their first day until six months after they leave the program. It is a substantial undertaking, and I could not be prouder of the people I have the honor to work with. People who give so much of themselves to help others. The record of success we have with kids who go through the program is remarkable. Our program is now getting the attention of many local business enterprises, and we now have many new sources of volunteers and resources to enable us to expand in the near future. As I look at all of you here this morning, I am hopefully seeing many new people and enterprises to join our cause down the road."

"The success we are enjoying at Win-the-Day is most definitely the result of many people who give tremendously. But there is one individual who stands head and shoulders above the rest. The person most responsible for the day-to-day management of the program, the person most responsible for holding the organization and the concept together, the person who gives the most."

"Permit me to introduce you to the executive director of the Win-the-Day Foundation, the incredible Connie McIlroy." Jon extended his hand to the back of the room towards Abby. "Connie"—she was sitting to Abby's right— "please come up and join me." Connie was not expecting to be part of Jon's presentation. She stood, somewhat reluctantly, with a little coercion from Abby. A loud round of applause, being led by Jon, was building, with everyone turning to face the back of the room. Connie gathered herself and walked purposefully to the stage, while the auditorium continued in loud and boisterous applause. A moment later, the ovation had subsided. Connie was standing to Jon's left. He was still at the mic.

"I had the tremendously good fortune meeting this woman six years ago while my children were in elementary school here in the local Conejo Valley Unified School District. At the time, she was recently retired from the Ventura County Office of Education after a thirty-plus-year career as an elementary school teacher, principal, and county administrator. We became friends and had numerous conversations about the role and the abilities of public education. From these conversations we started formulating an idea to fill the void our underserved youth faced being educated for success. We assessed the void between what we believed these young people needed and what was being provided by their parents and the public education system. The void was huge."

"Connie worked tirelessly to come up with a curriculum and created the lesson plans, the materials, and the measurement systems. Everything used at Win-the-Day today has her fingerprints all over them."

Jon turned to look at Connie. "Connie, I can't thank you enough for everything you do, and I just wanted all these good people to know who you are." He returned his vision to the audience. "Hopefully, some of them will be moving into the community shortly and joining you to fight for our cause."

Connie moved to the mic. She wanted to speak. The look she gave Jon to give up the mic was unmistakable. He stepped back.

She gazed into the audience and took a second to compose herself. "Hello, everyone. I am a little unprepared, as I was not aware Mr. Braxton would embarrass me so. But I must politely disagree with him on a few points. Let me set the record straight. I may have my fingerprints on some of our materials, but it is Mr. Braxton's DNA which is all over this foundation. Yes, we did collaborate in forming Win-the-Day, but make no mistake, the ideas, the vision, the passion, the creativity, and the money, they all came from the genius and generosity of this man."

"It was Mr. Braxton who brought everything together, including, and most notably, the lessons and the values that form our mission. Lessons and values we would focus on to help the disadvantaged young people of Ventura County. These young people have so much to offer to themselves and to others around them, yet most of their goodness is buried so deep inside of their consciousness that without a massive excavation plan, it never sees the light of day. This is our mission at Win-the-Day. Help these young people uncover the hidden treasures they all possess and share them out."

"Personally, I feel truly blessed to have met Mr. Braxton and to have been included in this project. I spent over thirty years in public education and was so frustrated and disappointed by our inability to do the job right. I won't get into the reasons why, that's not my place. But to be a part of this effort at this stage of my life, and to be able to use my experiences in support of the mission of our foundation, is unbelievably rewarding. To see the incredible turnarounds in so many of our students is remarkable. It's nothing short of a miracle to see a young person come into our program on the verge of prison or drug addiction or suicide or gang membership and have them transform right in front of our eyes as a result of the things we do. I don't know how else to describe it other than to say they are miracles. And we owe it all to Jon."

The audience rose in unison, with a thunderous standing ovation. Jon and Connie embraced. After a moment, she pulled away, kissed him on the cheek, and headed to the stairs to the left of the podium. She was greeted at the bottom by Congressman Gregory, and they embraced before she returned to her seat.

Larry Morris looked at his watch. Jon had been on stage twenty-nine minutes and thirty seconds.

"Ladies and gentlemen, let me conclude by asking you to strongly consider our wonderful area as the choice for your expansion or relocation. Come to Ventura County to take advantage of the fantastic workforce that is available to you. Come and help us do our community service. Come and provide the good jobs we need to keep our community vibrant and prosperous. Come and take advantage of all the lifestyle-enhancing amenities our area has to offer your people and your organizations. Come and make Ventura County your home. Thank you. I hope to meet many of you tonight at Mastro's. Enjoy the rest of the conference."

Larry Morris rose and started his trip to the podium to greet Jon but couldn't get there before the audience had again risen to their feet in thunderous applause, Carlton and Cornelius Hale, Congressman Gregory, and Angela among them.

Morris made it to the podium, the crowd still applauding enthusiastically. Jon was accepting the applause gracefully. Larry approached the mic. "Ladies and gentlemen, Jonathon Braxton."

Following Jon's speech, Neil Hale asked Angela if she and Jon would join himself, Carl, and Earl for dinner the following evening after the close of the conference. She agreed and offered the Grill on the Alley in nearby Westlake Village as a place that would be suitable.

Seventeen

"Class, please take your positions. We are ready to start."

Darla Braxton was not yet a fan of karate, but her mother was insistent she follow the footsteps of her grandfather, herself, and her brother. Her Friday afternoon classes were experiences she would rather not have, but she did not have a choice in the matter.

The twelve students in Darla's class were all relative beginners. Each had achieved their entry-level white belt and were now pursuing red. They assembled per their sensei's firm command— three rows of four students each, facing a wall of mirrors and their black-belted instructor.

For all of Darla's life, she had been taught by her mother to channel her thoughts to maintain focus and discipline. When she turned six, she was entered into her first karate class to reinforce those concepts.

"Why do I have to go? I don't want to."

"How do you know you don't want to do it? You haven't tried it yet. You watched your brother. You saw what he accomplished. You saw the confidence he developed, the strength he gained. You saw how he used his training to become a better student and a better surfer, right?"

"I know, mom, but it's hard, and sometimes it hurts. And I'm scared of getting injured."

"I won't kid you, there's a chance you could get hurt as you advance. But the more you focus and concentrate on your technique, the smaller that chance becomes. And the rewards you will be paid for that focus will far outweigh any minor bumps or bruises you get along the way. I've seen you on the soccer field and I remember how well you did in gymnastics. Physically, you have what takes to be successful in karate. But mentally, I notice you often have difficulty focusing on schoolwork and your chores. Karate will help you develop skills that you will be able to use for the rest of your life. I'm grateful your grandfather insisted I learn martial arts. It made me a better person. So, I'm sorry, honey, but you are starting your white belt class next week, no ifs, ands, or buts."

The instructor started class by shouting the instruction "rei." The students and the sensei bowed.

Next, the class was led through fifteen minutes of stretching. As the class was working through their stretching regimen, the instructor walked among the students, barking words of inspiration. The class responded in kind.

"Warm-ups prepare the body for the workout, so we not only avoid injury, but also optimize performance."

"YES, SENSEI!"

"The only person you should try to be better than is the person you were yesterday."

"YES, SENSEI!"

"Maybe your body doesn't yet understand, but the pain it feels during each training session is your spirit becoming invincible."

"YES, SENSEI!"

Next, the instructor led the class through their 'kihon' to practice basic techniques—stance measurement, hip movements, footwork positioning, basic punching and kicking techniques. Again, the instructor moved amongst the students shouting words of inspiration.

"I fear not the man who has practiced 10,000 kicks, but the man who has practiced one kick 10,000 times."

"YES, SENSEI!"

"Excellence is not a skill. It is an attitude."

"YES, SENSEI!"

"Success is the sum of small efforts repeated day in and day out."

"YES, SENSEI!"

After fifteen minutes of 'kihon', the instructor commanded 'kumite'. The class separated into pairs and commenced non-contact basic punching and kicking techniques, with corresponding blocking and footwork. The instructor moved through the room and eyed each pair intently, while providing them comment and feedback on the drill.

"Pain is weakness leaving the body."

"If you are sore, you are stronger."

"You are not a product of your circumstances, but a product of your decisions."

After forty-five minutes, the session was ready to conclude. The instructor was back in front of the class. The students were again facing the mirrored wall and their sensei. "Sensei-rei." The students bowed to the instructor. "Otagai ni rei". The students bowed to each other. Class was now over. The sensei dismissed them.

Darla, sweating profusely, approached the sensei. "Mom, that was a good class."

"Thank you, sweetheart, you did well tonight. Your technique is definitely improving. Do you have all your things? Your dad will be here to pick us up in a few minutes."

"Mom, why doesn't daddy take karate?"

"Oh, I don't know. Maybe he's afraid I'll beat him up?"

Mother and daughter shared a laugh.

"Hi, guys. What's so funny?" Jon had just made his way inside the studio.

Angela responded while looking at Darla "Nothing, honey, I'll tell you later." Darla giggled. "Come on, we need to hurry. Don't want to keep your new friends waiting."

———— ≈ ————

By seven that evening, the Braxtons, the Hales, and the Congressman were seated comfortably in a circular booth at the Grill. Angela had slid into the center. Jon was on her left, and Congressman Gregory on her right. Neil took the end seat to Gregory's right by design, giving him a straight-on look at Jon. Carl Hale sat on Jon's left. Within a few moments, they were all situated with their drinks."

"Well, Mr. Braxton, that was a most impressive speech yesterday. In addition to your other talents, you are a gifted public speaker," Neil Hale said in admiration. "And you spoke without any notes. I understand you didn't write anything down. Quite impressive to speak for thirty minutes from the cuff and have it come off as if you were reading from a prompter. Quite impressive indeed."

Carlton Hale chimed in. He patted JB's left arm, which was resting on the table, caressing his club soda straight with two lime squeezes. "JB, it's clear you have some unique leadership talents and you have built quite a legacy and reputation in this community. I commend you. And of course, a great man often has a terrific woman at his side, and this is definitely one of those instances." Carl lifted his straight-up Hendrix Gin Gibson in a toast. "To JB and Angela." The Congressman and Neil lifted their glasses in unison, and Jon and Angela followed suit. Jon smiled to himself at the thought of how Abby would describe this little love fest.

At that moment, a waiter approached the table. "Mr. Braxton, this is not my station, but I saw you and I wanted to come over and say hello. I hope I'm not interrupting anything."

"Hello, Julio. It's great to see you again. And no, you're not interrupting anything very important." Earl Gregory swallowed hard. "How have you been doing?" Jon said to the young waiter he recognized as a Win-the-Day graduate.

"I'm doing very well, sir. Hello, Mrs. Braxton."

"Hi, Julio".

"Mr. Braxton, how is Mrs. McIlroy doing?"

"She's doing fine, Julio. I'll tell her we saw you and that you asked about her."

"Thank you, sir. Anyway, I just wanted to say thank you for everything you did for me. I'm not sure what would have happened if I didn't have the chance to go through the program."

"Julio, what's going on in your life right now?"

"I'll be graduating from Camarillo High this June and was offered a hardship scholarship to Cal Poly. I applied as an architecture major, and they accepted me. The admissions counselor said my graduation from Win-the-Day was a factor in being accepted. You know Mr. Braxton, before I started the program, I had no idea what I wanted to do with my life and the gangs in Oxnard were starting to close in. But Mrs. McIlroy helped me figure a lot of things out and helped me realize how much I liked architecture. And good things just started to happen from there, so, sir, thank you again."

Julio addressed the table. "I'm sorry, I didn't mean to disturb your dinner. Just wanted to say hi and thanks."

"No problem. You're more than welcome, Julio. Give Mrs. McIlroy a call. I know she would love to hear from you and hear about your college admission. Good luck down the road."

"You too, Mr. Braxton. I'll call her. See ya' around."

"See ya' around, Julio."

Julio left the tableside. Angela turned to look at her husband and winked. The Congressman dropped his eyes to the table, thinking of the interlude a few weeks ago with Jamal Peterson. Brothers Carl and Neil, sitting across from one another in the circular booth, looked directly at one another, as if rehashing everything they had witnessed the last two days. The character picture of Jonathon Braxton was coming into focus for the Hales.

"Angela," Neil broke the momentary silence. "Please tell us about yourself."

"Well, Mr. Hale, I was born in Redondo Beach, which is about forty miles south of here. My parents moved to the area from Japan in 1961. My dad was an aerospace engineer. He secured a visa and found a position with Northrup in El Segundo. I lived a normal, low-key Southern California-style childhood. Graduated from Redondo Beach High in 1991. Went on to UCLA, where on my first day in my first class, I met Mr. Braxton. Believe it or not, when we first met he had long, shaggy hair, was dressed in holey jeans and an undersized T-shirt, and had a ridiculous excuse for a beard. I'm not sure what I was thinking when I agreed to have coffee with him."

Jon interjected: ""Our friends called us Beauty and the Beast. The beast was Angela. She had two martial arts black belts by the time she was sixteen."

Angela retorted. "Mr. Braxton, you're implying you were the Beauty? Yeah, ok. Anyways, the first time we met, I thought he was a jerk—no, make that he was a jerk. But after the second time we met, I was falling for him. Not sure why, just something about him." Angela paused for a second and turned her glance from Neil to her husband. "And you saw it yesterday. He has this magnetism. People are just attracted to Jon, as was I. We started dating, and when we were juniors, he proposed, I accepted, we got married, and Jon moved into my parent's house. We spent the next three years there."

"During that time, we both graduated. I started interning with a psychologist, while considering what I wanted to do. Jon found his job at Spectre during sophomore year, and while we were seniors, he approached my dad with the idea of buying the company. It was owned by two brothers who were always feuding, and the company was floundering. Jon sensed they would be interested in an opportunity to get out and salvage something before they went under. He and my father put a package together, and they accepted. In 1994, at the tender age of twenty-two, 'Mr. Beauty' took over the company and has been piloting the rocket ship ever since. In 1999, we decided to move the company and our lives here to Thousand Oaks. I continued to work until our first child, Lucas, was born in 2001. Since then, I've been a stay-at-home mom, although the last three years I've been spending lots of time helping Connie. Our second child, Darla, was born in 2004. The two of them keep me busy. Raising two kids and keeping Mr. Braxton grounded in reality takes most of my time." She flashed a smile at Neil Hale that radiated the table.

"So, you have two children, and let's see, Lucas is now eleven and Darla is eight?"

"Yes, just had her eighth birthday in February."

"What are the kids like? Any future JB's or Angela's in the making?"

"Luke is just like Jon, same quirky mannerisms, same magnetism, same intelligence. He is without a doubt his father's son. They're extremely close. Don't get me wrong, Jon loves Darla, and they get along great, but Jon and Luke? It's hard to explain. It's almost like they're the same person. Darla seems to be her own person at this point, very smart, but seems to have more of a creative flair. But they're both healthy and happy, and to me, that's all that matters."

Now it was Carl's turn. "Earl, how did you and JB meet?"

The Congressman had both his hands cupped around his cocktail and his eyes planted squarely on the tall Bombay and tonic in front of him. He heard the question, chuckled under his breath, and looked over at the elder Hale. "Well, Carl, I don't entirely remember the occasion myself, but Rob Wiley reminded me recently that we first met at a deli not too far from here in 2008. JB and Angela were quietly enjoying their meal and each other's company when Rob and I arrived. And Rob, ever so rudely"—the Congressman recounted with a hint of sarcasm— "saw them and brought me over to their table for an introduction. As I understand it, while I had never met JB before, he starts a dialogue with me as if we knew each other well. Starts asking about Jeanine, the grandkids, what was going on in Washington. Apparently, Rob was filling JB in on what his boss was up to, so he played it out that he knew all about me and I didn't have a fucking clue who he was—sorry Angela. I was trying not to embarrass myself, so I started chatting back as if we're good friends. JB played it with such a straight face all the way through I couldn't admit I didn't know who he was." Carl and Neil joined the Congressman in laughing at the recollection. JB and Angela both smiled, enjoying the moment of humility from the Congressman.

"Mr. Hale?" Angela said looking across the table at Carl. "Jon mentioned you're involved with a foundation in Philadelphia that's similar to Win-the-Day. How long have you been working with underserved youth?"

"Neil and I crossed paths with a pastor in Philadelphia named Jeffrey Claymore about sixteen years ago. He was around fifty at the time and had a remarkable life story. Came from a typical inner-city upbringing—no father, three siblings, raised by a mother who wasn't very good at it and by grandparents who did the best they could. He lived in one of the toughest areas in North Philly, an area called Sharswood. He ended up in the penal system at seventeen, mostly minor offenses, but a few felonies in the mix for armed robbery. Spent six years in prison and, while there, found religion. When he finished his time, he went back to Sharswood and moved in with his grandparents. He joined a local Pentecostal church and, under the guidance of the church pastor, began his quest to follow his faith and studied to become a pastor himself."

"It was probably around 1978 when he took over a small parish in Sharswood, and he's been there ever since. His parish thrived early on, and he became a local hero and role model for kids. Claymore has become an icon in Philadelphia. Like you JB, he has hundreds, if not thousands of young people who owe their ability to survive the streets of Philadelphia to him."

"When our paths crossed, and we heard his story and saw his work, we wanted to get involved. It was the kind of cause we are always looking to help with. The pastor represented many of our values, and he was teaching them to kids who needed them. Over the past ten years, we've contributed around $30 million. Six years ago, we built a new teen center facility for the parish. It's known in the neighborhood as Faith Central. Today, we're still paying for a large portion of the staffing for the center. Over the years, we've tried to help the pastor scale his efforts, but administration is not one of his strong suits, and those efforts never amounted to anything."

"Two years ago, Claymore surprised us by forming a non-profit to scale his efforts. We had no idea and thought it strange he didn't consult with us. Turns out this was the beginning of a steep decline in our involvement. A Board was installed, and for the last two years, we've tried to work with them. They don't much care for us, but they do like our contributions. The pastor seems locked in the middle. We believe he wants us involved but acts otherwise. After our last contribution of 300k in April, Corny and I discussed it being our last. We revere Jeffrey, but feel his heart is no longer in it."

"About a year ago, we learned it was a former parishioner student of the pastors who was responsible for convincing him to set up the nonprofit and create the board. As we now understand, he also convinced Claymore to allow him to take over all financial and organizational management."

"My brother and I have made occasional and, frankly, only half-hearted efforts to rekindle the relationship, but Claymore has kept us at arm's length the last two years. We haven't been consulted on anything since. Corny and I take from his actions that he's discouraging us from making any more contributions. It now appears he's intentionally pushing us away. He used to be a powerful, commanding figure, but the last few times we've spoken to him, he seems dejected and defeated. Corny last met with the pastor two months ago and he barely said a word. That is most unusual for him."

Angela was intrigued. "Mr. Hale, before I heard about Liberty Bell, I was under the impression that you and your brother contributed primarily to political causes and campaigns, and that you were aligned with more conservative positions. I was surprised to hear of your involvement in inner-city Philadelphia."

"The media definitely gives Corny and I a bad rap. It's true we contribute lots of money to political organizations and candidates. But my brother and I both share the belief that our country is the greatest success story of social structure in the history of mankind, and we try to do our little part to preserve it. But things are changing. No question our country has made a lot of bad judgments over the years, but if you add everything up, you see that no country has done more to advance freedom and liberty and economic prosperity in the history of civilization. What we loved about Pastor Claymore was his focus on teaching kids about personal responsibility and integrity. So while our politics might not be aligned, we felt our values were. That's why we chose to get involved with him."

"Have you attempted to reconcile your differences with the board? It seems like that will have to happen before you can make any progress."

"We haven't tried very hard. We've been taking our cues from Claymore, and it doesn't feel like he wants us to. Corny and I have, for the most part, conceded trying to influence their activities. The only reason we have stayed remotely and financially involved is Claymore. He's a good man and has so much to offer that city, although it seems to be muted now by whatever it is that is going on there. After hearing of your success at Win-the-Day yesterday, Corny and I have been rethinking things. If there was a way to move LBF in the direction of Win-the-Day, we'd stand behind it."

At that moment, their waiter arrived at the table, described the evening specials, and took their dinner orders. After he left the table, Neil wanted to talk politics again.

"JB, something's puzzling me. You're a skilled negotiator. You wouldn't be where you are today if you weren't. In a business of your size, you must deal with government bureaucrats and politics all the time. What's behind your disdain?"

"I'm a problem-solver Neil. But you can't solve problems if you don't see them clearly. Political processes and agendas cloud problems and usually create new ones. I find everything about politics horribly inefficient. I don't have the patience to play. I don't mind debating and defending my positions, but if the only solution is a compromise which doesn't serve to solve the problem, but instead serves to satisfy an agenda or a narrative, I lose interest."

Neil pondered momentarily. "Do you ever consider the greater good in your thinking? I understand your position. But compromise is a way of life. We all compromise every day. I'm sure you and Angela don't agree on everything. There's give and take, and you make it work. And the love and the passion and the commitment stay intact even with the give and take, right? You're a man of many talents and have a lot to offer whatever cause or position you chose to stand behind. But if you draw a line for yourself not to cross just because of competing agendas standing in your way, with all due respect, I feel you're limiting yourself."

Jon replied. "I appreciate your candor but see a distinction. The give and take between two people in a personal relationship is different than between unloving parties and involving money. When Angie and I disagree on something, we end up compromising because it serves both our primary agendas—maintaining our relationship. When you're involved in a give and take where the two sides have different primary agendas, the original problem you're trying to solve takes a back seat. In this kind of situation, the problem is not best served.

Personally, I prefer to fight the battles where winning means solving the problem, not serving an agenda. Sure, I could choose to fight in other arenas and participate in these compromises but choose not to. I'm only one guy and there's only twenty-four hours in the day. I'd rather spend my time where the results of my efforts make the biggest difference. I'd much rather spend my time and energy on Win-the-Day. Plus, with Angie's two black belts, I often end up compromising as a means of survival."

Angela bit her bottom lip and playfully swatted her husband's arm.

Neil relented. "OK, we'll agree to disagree on that one. Now LBF. We both suspect their Board. If you're engaged to solve the problem, what would you do?"

"First meet with Claymore. I'd want to know how he interacts with the Board. Are their goals in alignment? I'd research their current board members. Review the board minutes for the last two years. Review all the recent large expenditures. From there I'd know what to do to turn things around."

Jon was curious. "Does LBF have a guiding principle? Our guiding principle at Win-the-Day is *Improve the future prospects of 500 young people in Ventura County each year by exposing them to principles and truths that they can use to build better lives for themselves.'* What is LBF's?"

Neil replied embarrassingly: "I'm not sure they have one. If they do, I'm not aware of it. Carl, are you?" His older brother shook his head.

Jon was not surprised. "We use our guiding principle to manage our spending. At Win-the-Day board meetings, we apply a 'smell test' to any sizable actions or expenditures. Every proposed activity or spending request over $1,000 is given the test by correlating it to our guiding principle. We have the board debate whether the activity passes the correlation test. If it doesn't, it's dropped."

"LBF needs a guiding principle, and their board must be in

alignment with it. If they're not, or if there are too many competing or personal agendas, my first recommendation would be to change the makeup of the board—and I'm assuming that wouldn't be easy."

Their dinners arrived, and they all settled in on their meal. The conversation moved to Congressman Gregory and his upcoming campaign for reelection. Carl Hale was curious to know Jon's thoughts on the matter.

"JB, I know you don't follow politics, but now that you and Earl have become comrades at Win-the-Day, do you have any thoughts on his upcoming campaign. Any chance you might want to help us?"

Jon had a suspicion this would be one of the topics of conversation when he accepted the Hales' dinner invitation. He hadn't reconciled his inclination to say no to being involved in a political campaign yet was now involved with the Congressman. And the more time he spent with Earl Gregory, the more he liked him.

"Carl, I don't do politics, but how about this. I'll publicize the Congressman has joined the board of Win-the-Day and I'll agree to host a campaign event at our complex, where the Congressman can make a speech and invite the public. Fair enough?"

"That's great, JB. Thank you. I'm sure Earl and Rob Wiley will take you up on that offer." Carl looked assuredly at the Congressman. "Now, as you may or may not know, and just between us for now, if Earl is reelected this will be his last term and he'll be announcing his retirement in 2014. Two years from now, for the first time in twenty-eight years, this District will have to offer a new Republican candidate for its House seat. It's not too early to start prospecting. Do you know anyone you'd like to see fill Earl's seat? Or better yet, might you consider the prospect? If you did, you could count on significant support from Corny and I."

"I'm flattered by your confidence, but no. I'd enjoy working to fix the country's problems, but the system is not welcoming to people like myself. I can make a better impact in non-political endeavors. I can't see myself doing the things that politicians need to do to get themselves elected and reelected. As for a potential candidate, I'd recommend Rob Wiley."

Carl and Neil moved their gaze from JB to each other and nodded what appeared to be an agreement to let JB know Rob's position.

"That's a great recommendation, but we've already talked to Rob and he said no."

Jon was puzzled. "Why not?"

"He wants you to run in 2014."

Eighteen

The Ventura County Economic Development Conference of 2012 proved a gigantic success.

The momentum following the conference led twelve out-of-state companies to sign letters of intent to locate operations in Ventura County. Four companies decided to relocate existing facilities from inside the state into Ventura County, and 2,500 new jobs were on paper to be created.

Carlton and Cornelius Hale kept their part of the grand bargain cooked up by Jon and wrote a $5 million dollar check. Larry Morris played his role expertly having new employers commit to the county. Larry and Jon collaborated as if they had known each other for years, with Jon providing innovative ideas and keen insights, and Larry executing to perfection. They were a formidable team for other geographies to compete with when pursuing a new employer. Adding Jon's and Larry's newfound and burgeoning chemistry to the money the Hales contributed to help fund new jobs, they had only one company in their crosshairs turn them down. The only reason for their one failure? The CEO had an affinity for North Carolina's golf courses.

As designed by Carl and Neil, Congressman Gregory was basking in the glory of the lucrative economic opportunities the conference sparked and the resulting sound bites and news stories. By July, with the latest polling data, it became a foregone conclusion Earl would coast to victory in November. He would serve his fourteenth term, due in no small part to the success of the conference.

The Republican Party played up Congressman Gregory's role in the County's economic expansion for the benefit of the campaign, and the Hales did nothing to diffuse that messaging. But behind closed doors, Carlton and Cornelius had other things they were discussing with their inner circle of the Republican Party's biggest donors. They were greatly concerned about the direction of the country and the Republicans' chances to win either house of Congress or the Presidency in the quickly approaching 2012 elections.

Neil Hale was correct in his assessment the Democrats had the Republican's number and that the social divide he saw them engineering was building the foundation for a long-term dynasty. His thoughts continued to strengthen his conviction the Republican Party had to significantly transform to have any chance of survival. To that end, the Hale brothers had been discussing amongst themselves they needed more time with Jon Braxton. They believed his insights and instincts would help them.

Six weeks following the Ventura County Economic Conference, Carl Hale called his little brother. "Claymore called me last night and sounded like he was getting ready to give up on LBF. He seems frustrated beyond his limits. We need to decide what we want to do. If we don't do something soon, I think he'll retire."

Carl's comment caused Neil to realize he had yet to follow up with Jon from their conversations six weeks earlier. He was about to respond to his brother, blaming their preoccupation with the election cycle for the lack of follow up, but decided that would serve no purpose. "Carl, I'll call JB tonight. I'll call you back after I speak with him."

"Hold on there little brother. Give it some thought before you approach him. And you may want to call Abby first to make sure the coast is clear."

Corny didn't always like hearing his big brother's voice of reason, but knew he was right on this. "You're right Carl, good thinking. I'll speak with Abby first."

The next morning, Abby Martin's private line rang on her office phone, with the caller ID blocked.

"Abby Martin here, how can I help?"

"Good morning, Mrs. Martin. It's so nice to hear your voice again." The younger Hale brother then paused for her reply.

"Aloha mystery caller, it is equally good to hear yours. Pray tell, with whom am I having the pleasure of playing cat and mouse this morning?"

"Mrs. Martin, the pleasure is all mine. Cornelius Hale reporting for duty."

For a few seconds, Abby was knocked off stride, having one of the most powerful and influential people in the country calling her private line. It took her two breaths to regain her composure.

"Well, well, Mr. Hale. Forgive me, I didn't recognize your voice. How are you and your esteemed brother faring these days? It was such an honor to meet you both a few weeks ago. I hope you enjoyed your visit with us."

"Mrs. Martin, Carl and I thoroughly enjoyed our time with you, JB, Angela, and the rest of your staff we had the opportunity to meet. What you and your colleagues are doing at Spectre and in the community is remarkable, and it is not lost on us for one moment the significant role you play in all of Spectre's successes. We both admire you. If JB were to ever make the catastrophic mistake of under appreciating you, we'll hire you without a second thought."

"Thank you, Mr. Hale. I shan't forget that. Now shall I see if Mr. Braxton is available?"

"Mrs. Martin, no." Cornelius again inserted a calculated pregnant pause, waiting a few seconds before continuing. "I actually called to speak with you for a few minutes. Did I interrupt anything?"

"Uh, no, sir, I'm good. What can I do for you?"

"Mrs. Martin, I'd like to approach Mr. Braxton on a matter we discussed when we were in California. By any chance are you aware of or familiar with...."

Abby interjected "…..The Liberty Bell Foundation."

"Why yes."

"Yes sir, I am. Mr. Braxton asked me to do some initial research on LBF. He mentioned you would potentially involve him in their operations."

"It's good to hear that you're familiar with LBF. Now, as far as what you can do for me? Frankly speaking, Mrs. Martin, I need some advice and guidance on how best to approach JB on the matter."

Abby regained her composure and was back in stride with her default personality. She let go of any pretense and in her most playful voice, responded. "Mr. Hale, I'm flattered by your ask. May I know, are we seeking advice and guidance to Mr. Braxton's checkbook or to his brain power?"

From anyone else, the often righteous Cornelius Hale might have been offended by the question. But Abby's voice, words, demeanor, and tone had him in a comfort zone. He had no misgivings of playing along.

"Mrs. Martin, I appreciate the offer of guidance to Mr. Braxton's checkbook, but as you might be aware, we are in pretty good shape with ours."

"Yes, of course, what was I thinking?"

Neil laughed as he started to respond. "Allow me to give you some information to consider. I did share with JB some of the issues we are having and how we would welcome his assistance given your success at Win-the-Day. But I'm uncertain if he has any interest. I'd welcome your help to coach me on how I might best approach him and convince him to help us. I hope this doesn't put you in an uncomfortable position. If it does and presents conflicts of interest for you, I will completely understand, and we can assume this conversation never happened."

Abby was aware the Hale brothers were among the wealthiest men in the USA, but since most of the outside requests Spectre and Braxton personally received were for financial contributions she didn't want to take anything for granted. "So, we really are talking brainpower?"

Neil again laughed. "Yes, I guess we are. Will you help me?"

"Mr. Hale, there is one thing you should be aware of, but this is not coming from me, OK?"

"Of course, Mrs. Martin, what is that?"

"Mr. Braxton has a huge soft spot for underprivileged kids. As you can imagine, we get numerous requests for his time and money. If the cause is not about helping kids, he usually is not interested."

"Well, that's good, since he knows that LBF is all about kids."

"From what I've read and from what I believe Mr. Braxton understands about LBF, the organization is also about politics and influence. He likes, how should I say it, uh, purity. We all put an emphasis on keeping Win-the-Day pure. From what I've researched and from what Mr. Braxton discussed with me, I'm not sure we can use the term 'pure' when describing LBF. I've known the man for almost thirteen years and have worked closely beside him for the last eight. I know what he tunes in and what he tunes out. As to helping you with LBF, I'm not sure he'll go for it. For you to have any chance to convince him, make it all about the kids."

Abby continued. "And Mr. Hale, another thought is you should have materials ready for your conversation with Mr. Braxton. If he chooses to get involved, he will want things like bank records, copies of contracts, and copies of lease agreements. And he'll want some biographical info on all the people involved with running and overseeing the nonprofit. If you can provide them quickly, you'll have a better chance. Lastly, you should know that Mr. Braxton will do two things first if he chooses to get involved—he'll follow the money and explore the people. If you have relevant data for him ready, it will go a long way for you."

Abby Martin's protection of her employer was not lost on Neil Hale. He admired her for her loyalty and was grateful for the insights she just shared. She had given him exactly what he needed to make his best case. And at the same time set the table for Jon to make an informed decision.

"Remarkable" is the term Neil used to describe Abby Martin when recapping his conversation with her to Carl, to which he replied, "They both are."

Neil needed the rest of the week to pull the information together Abby had recommended. On the following Monday, June 18, 2012, he called the main phone line for Spectre, which was answered by Spectre's receptionist.

"Thank you for calling Spectre Systems. How may I help you?"

"Good morning. Jonathon Braxton, please."

"Yes, sir, transferring you now."

The call was transferred to Jon's reception group extension. Calls to the group extension routed first to Abby. If she failed to answer, the call would forward to a subgroup of four executive assistants for Spectre's other upper management executives based in Thousand Oaks. If those four assistants failed to answer for any reason, the call would route back to Abby's voicemail. She would then determine if Jon needed to hear it.

"Mr. Braxton's office. This is Abby Martin. How can I help you?"

"Mrs. Martin, two conversations within one week. What is happening here?" Neil offered in his slow Midwestern twang, feebly trying to be cute.

She immediately recognized his voice. "Well, Mr. Hale, it sounds like we have a new member of the Abby Martin fan club in the fold. We will be sure to rush you your monogrammed T shirt and baseball cap. I'm guessing this was the reason you called?" Abby added in a slow and seductive manner to frame the silly question.

Neil couldn't resist. "Yes, that's precisely why I called. Make the T shirt a double XL and the cap should be adjustable for a large head, no pun intended."

"No pun taken, Mr. Hale. I find your head to be the perfect size. And please do your best to keep it off Mr. Braxton's chopping block." Despite speaking to one of the most influential people in the country, she couldn't help herself. "Are you ready to speak with his majesty about LBF?"

"Thanks to you, yes, as ready as I can be."

"Very well, let me see if he's available. Stand by."

Neil was placed on hold and spent fifteen brief seconds listening to Spectre's phone system on-hold messaging, playing what amounted to a commercial for some of Spectre's newest RLX system enhancements.

Abby came back on the line. "His majesty is available and will take your call. Stand by while I transfer—and go get him, Mr. Hale."

Neil didn't have time to respond as Jon came on the line within two seconds of Abby's last words of encouragement.

"Neil! It's great to hear from you. How are you and Carl?"

"Hello, JB. We're doing well, thank you. How about you and Angela?"

"We're good. Thank you for asking." Both applied their power pauses, waiting for the other to speak.

Neil went first. "JB, I called because I wanted to tell you how impressed Carl and I are with the results from the Ventura County Econ Conference. It's only been six weeks, and you've received commitments from so many companies and so many new jobs. Frankly, Carl and I were expecting a much lower level of success. We are both amazed."

"Have you had the opportunity to call Larry Morris yet and offer him your congratulations?" Jon purposefully inserted and emphasized the word 'yet'. He wanted Neil to know he expected him to and was slightly perturbed neither he nor Carl had done so.

"I have not, but I'm thinking you're suggesting I do so."

"Yes, I am suggesting. He worked tirelessly for this success for over a year. No doubt your monetary contribution was a large part of the story, but without Larry there would have been no conference, and without Larry there would not be 2,500 new jobs, and counting, coming to Ventura County. I guess you might say without Larry things would not be looking as good for Earl's reelection."

"You're absolutely right. I owe Mr. Morris a debt of gratitude. I will call him today. You have my word."

Knowing the real reason for Neil's call this morning thanks to Abby's heads-up, Jon didn't wait.

"Tell me all about Darby Robinson."

Neil was surprised to hear Jon utter Darby's name. He didn't remember mentioning it during their last dinner meeting and assumed that, even if Jon had uncovered it in his research, he would not bring it up right away. But he then recalled this was his style—up front, authentic, no BS.

"Unfortunately, I don't know much about him. He's the chairman of LBF's board, and I've only met him twice. He hasn't shown much interest in knowing Carl or I."

"Neil, in my opinion, you should get to know everything about him. I think he's a big part of your problem." Jon thought briefly about saying 'our problem'—but decided 'your problem' was more appropriate at this moment.

Neil had a calculated introduction and convincing sales pitch prepared. But the conversation had already turned in that direction. He was content letting Jon drive and put his pitch away to go along for the ride.

"What makes you think Darby is the problem?"

"Only money, politics, and power."

"I'm not sure I follow."

"Neil, if I decide to get involved with Liberty Bell, there will be two primary things I will do—one, follow the money, and two, explore the people. And I'm sensing a lot of people in Philadelphia will be somewhat, if not extremely, uncomfortable with me."

Neil heard the words *follow the money and explore the people*' and could not help but see an image of Abby lip-syncing—*'What did I tell you?'*

Neil concluded the deal was done and Jon was in. He showed his hand.

"JB, I prepared some information about LBF for you. I have their bank statements for the past three years and copies of all contracts for any expenditures over $2,500 for the last three years. I have the board minutes for the last two years, and I have some biographical information on Jeffrey Claymore and all five board members. Would it be OK for my secretary to email everything over?"

"Neil, before you send me anything, I'd like to have a phone conversation with Claymore, just he and I. Can you set it up for me? I'd like to try and get to know him without reviewing any information. I like to rely on my gut instincts for developing first impressions, and I don't want to have any information that might cloud my perception."

"I'm happy to put you two together. I'll work with Abby to get it on your calendar."

"And Neil one other thing. If I do decide to get involved, I only will do it my way. Agreed?"

"JB, knowing you now the way I now do, I wouldn't expect it any other way. Agreed."

Nineteen

The political backlash triggered by the Al-Qaeda raid on the U.S. embassy in Yemen, resulting in the deaths of twenty-eight Americans, including Heather Carrington's longtime friend Charlie Carpenter, had subsided by July of 2012.

The Secretary of State had moved past a short mourning period for her friend and put the resulting stain on her legacy in her rearview mirror. She recently related to her trusted confidant Sidney Rosenberg she was very much enjoying her State gig. She realized, for the first time in as long as she could remember, she was not involved with a current election cycle. She was not running for anything. Her campaigning was not being sought by the current administration. She had sized up the upcoming 2012 presidential election and saw no possibility of Mitt Romney defeating Obama. She was assured of being a fixture in the Executive Branch until she was ready to take the next step. A four-year election cycle was heading into the stretch run, she was not involved, and she was enjoying watching everything play out from the sidelines.

"Don't get too complacent, Heather." Sidney lectured her from his Manhattan penthouse apartment, as the two spoke on the phone one evening in late July for the first time in three weeks. "The time is coming for you to be the best candidate you've ever been. You should start getting into that mode yesterday, because four years from now will be here tomorrow,"

"C'mon, Sidney, relax. Let an old girl have some time to enjoy herself for a change. It's campaign season and I don't have anything to do. I like this."

"I'm not sure I like how that sounds. Look, you planned for your moment of glory your whole life. But you can fuck it up in a minute if you make a wrong move or say the wrong thing. You've got to stay sharp. You've got to be on your game every minute of every day. You can let your hair down in twenty-four after you have your eight-year term. Until then, or until you tell me to go away, I'm going to keep my boot up your ass. So, get comfortable with it."

"Jesus, Sidney, what dried up your vagina tonight? You sound like a frosty old maiden who hasn't been laid in a hundred years."

Heather waited for a reply. Sidney was silent with rage, and all she received was the white noise of the phone line. In the silence she sensed Sidney seething. *'Was he justified being indignant towards me at this moment?'* She had coerced him to be her primary consultant and confidant, promising him there was nothing to stop her from becoming the first female president of the United States. And he would be richly rewarded coming along for the ride.

"Sidney, I'm sorry. Listen, I need some advice from you on something." Heather waited for his reply to no avail. She decided to keep going. She would ignore for now the silent treatment he decided would be her medicine for this conversation.

"Wilton wants me to go to Philadelphia and help a family friend who's backing someone running for mayor this year. Wants me to do a campaign stump. Bring out a crowd. Fire them up."

Upon hearing this, Sidney was compelled to reengage. "Don't do it, Heather."

"For Christ's sake, is everything I say tonight going to piss you off?"

"I know the players on this one. Trust me, you don't want to go near it."

"How do you know?"

"It's my job."

"OK, you better tell me what you know, because I already agreed."

"What?" Sidney shouted in exasperation. "What is wrong with you? You want my guidance for a decision you already made? Dammit Heather, you pay me handsomely to look after your career and then you go and pull this shit? Do you want to be Madam President or not? Because if you're going to play in Hanley Michaelson's swamp, you'll get dirty and you'll get your butt kicked in Pennsylvania no matter who your idiot Republican opponent is."

"You know the answer to that, but I couldn't say no to Hanley. He was so instrumental in Wilton's '92 campaign, and he's never really asked for anything in return, until now. And what do you mean Hanley's swamp? He's been disengaged from politics since Wilton and I left the White House. We hadn't heard from him in six years until he reached out a few months ago."

Sidney dialed his frustration back a bit and went back into consult mode. "Look, Heather, first, I really don't know the answer as to whether or not you want to be the president. You've been giving off vibes for months that you're not up for a run in 2016. Only you know the answer whether you want to be back in the White House or not. Only you know if you're only playing along until you figure it out. Second, the fuck-face Michaelson is backing for mayor, Darby Robinson, is dangerous for you. My sources tell me he's got baggage. He could blow up and spray shit all over you. As for your pal, Michaelson, well he and Robinson are both lounging in that swamp, enriching themselves at the expense of labor unions throughout the state. Michaelson campaign managing Robinson for mayor has a nasty stench I can smell from here."

Heather was only half listening, not fully comprehending everything she was being told. Sidney was right to be questioning her focus. She realized her poker face wasn't working well as he had her indecision about running for president in four years pegged. She made a mental note to mask her indecision better. "OK, I screwed up, but I have to go, I'm committed. Parker set up four State business meetings for me in Philly. While I'm there, I promised Jeffrey Claymore I'd stop in and spend some time. Sidney, I'll be OK. You know how many of these things I've done. I promise I'll pull back on any direct support for this Darby Robinson loser. I'll give the crowd some good old fashion Democrat red meat. I'll make Hanley happy and stay clear of Darby. Don't worry, Sidney, we'll be fine."

"Glad you asked me for my guidance, Heather," now only a slightly agitated Sidney Rosenberg said sarcastically. "Next time check with me before you make your ill-formed decisions. When you're running for president, it's never better to beg for forgiveness than ask for permission."

"Don't worry, we'll be fine. Good night."

"Heather, one more thing you should know."

"What now?"

"Your friend Pastor Claymore is Darby Robinson's godfather. Good night."

Twenty

The early morning of a Thousand Oaks mid-July Tuesday had the promise of an exquisite day. A modest early morning breeze had filtered out the pollution and haze, often present in the early morning hours this time of year. Left behind was a deeply rich blue sky accented by twenty-something bright white puffy clouds sprinkled toward the west in the direction of the Pacific Ocean coast, only twelve crow-flown miles away. The morning was picture perfect.

Jon's mind was starting to focus on the LBF picture and why their operation had become so disappointing to LBF's largest benefactors, Carlton and Cornelius Hale. He was lightly processing the limited information Carlton Hale had offered at their dinner meeting eight weeks earlier but was reluctant to form any opinions until he had his conversation with Pastor Claymore. A conversation he was now preparing for.

At 6:30 a.m., Jon was in his office at Spectre. He was standing to the left of his desk. He had eight barroom-style darts in his hand and was lining up throws to a dartboard mounted on the wall to the right of his desk, nine feet from where he stood.

Holding all but one of the darts in his right hand, he had just moved one dart from his right hand to his left. He gently squeezed it between his left index finger and his left thumb. He brought the dart up to his left eye, leaving that eye open and closing his right. He took two slow, deliberate aiming motions with the dart pointed at the dartboard. His left arm moved the dart from in front of his left eye to a straightened position. Once, twice, bull's-eye. Almost in a trance, methodically one by one, Jon repeated the motion with all eight darts, resulting in four bull's-eyes.

With all eight darts now planted in the dartboard, he slowly and methodically walked to the board, pulled them all out with his left hand, put them into his right hand, turned around, and strode back to his launching spot. He turned to stare down the dartboard and start the ritual again.

He gave no thought to flinging and then retrieving the darts. It was automatic. The thoughts in his head were all on LBF. Was Darby Robinson corrupt? And if so, to what degree? How clueless was Jeffrey Claymore? Or was he complicit? Why were the Hale brothers so uninformed of what was happening at LBF? What was the extent of the money laundering and pilfering that may be taking place?

All these questions were on Jon's mind since his call with Neil Hale the previous week and his decision to arrange a phone call with the presumed good pastor. For ninety minutes Jon was in deep thought about the pending phone call and how to approach it. With darts in hand, the strategy was being formulated. Their next move was the only thing on his mind. Yes, 'their' next move. According to Abby, the dartboard was by association complicit whenever Jon felt the need to consult it.

It was now eight. Jon had five darts in his right hand and one in his left when the alarm on his cell phone went off. The trance was broken. He walked to a nicely appointed mahogany credenza against the west wall of his office and put the six darts away in a cigar box that was stored in the upper right-hand drawer, forgetting he had left two stuck in the dartboard.

He walked back to his desk and sat down. He assumed Abby was already at her desk with her morning coffee, reviewing emails from the East Coast. He jumped onto instant messenger and typed out a pleasantry for her screen.

'Good morning, Mrs. Martin.'

'And to you the same, your highness.'

'I've got a couple of things. Ready?'

'Does the term 'born ready' mean anything to his majesty?'

'Not really. Come on in. I need you to line up some phone calls for me.'

'So let it be written, so let it be done.'

'Nice touch. Yul Brenner in The Ten Commandments?'

'Nope, Abby Martin, in service to her lord. Don't forget your eastern region con call at nine. I just emailed you all the division forecasts, so get busy.'

'OK, we've got thirty minutes. Come in so I can tell you what I've got.'

In five seconds, Abby entered his office. Jon was already seated at the office conference table. When Abby pulled her car into the Spectre parking lot at seven, she saw Jon's car. When she walked up to her office, she saw his office door closed. She looked at her phone console and saw no activity lights. *'It's Captain Crunch dartboard time.'*

Upon entering his office, she looked directly at the dartboard and noticed two darts, both planted in the bull's-eye. She walked directly toward them, staring straight ahead. She reached the dartboard and pulled the two darts. She then walked to the credenza and opened the upper right-hand drawer. She withdrew the cigar box put the two darts in. She put the cigar box back in the drawer and closed it. She had not yet acknowledged Jon. She turned around, made eye contact, smiled warmly and walked to the table. With notepad in hand, she sat directly across from him.

"How was your meeting this morning with the captain?"

"As usual, he provided clarity, insight and perspective. Come to think of it, you know you could learn a few things from the captain. OK, do I have anything pressing on my calendar today besides the east region forecast call at nine?"

"Only if you consider your phone meeting at eleven today with the CEO of Shopify about that fifty-unit SLX-450 systems deal. I think you said something about it being four and a half mil. No big deal, right? I'll cancel it."

"You know, I should probably take that call. Let's leave it. But between now and then, I need your help getting this LBF situation dialed in. Neil Hale is setting up a call for me with Pastor Claymore. You should expect a call from him to schedule it. I haven't reviewed any data yet, but my gut tells me this Darby Robinson character is bad news. All of LBF's troubles seem to have started when he started managing the operation. What I've learned from Neil so far is that their downhill slide started when Robinson convinced, or connived, with Claymore to formalize the operation as a 501(c)(3) four years ago."

"You think Claymore is involved in the shenanigans?"

"Too soon to tell, but I should have a take after I speak with him. Line up a phone call for me as soon as possible with Congressman Gregory. And I need another call with Neil Hale. Set that up as well, ASAP."

Abby rose. "Yes, your majesty, it's an honor to serve. I'll have these calls set up for you today. You're going to have a busy afternoon, so if you had any thoughts of sneaking out and playing hooky, you can forget about it."

"Not a chance. I'd never make it past your desk."

———— ≈ ————

It was two that same afternoon. Abby buzzed Jon at his desk.

"Mr. Braxton, sir, Congressman Gregory holding for you."

"Thanks Abby. Put him through."

It had been three weeks since their last conversation, a conversation related to Win-the-Day board business. They had not yet had any conversations related to the Hales' request for Jon's assistance in examining and repairing LBF.

"Congressman, thank you for calling. How are you and the U.S. Congress getting along these days?"

"The U.S. Congress is a screwed-up hot mess. Fortunately, I'm doing somewhat better, thank you for asking. I trust you, Angela, Abby, Connie, and the rest of your banana republic are doing well. What's up?"

"I'm sure you remember our dinner after the econ conference when Neil Hale brought up the Philadelphia foundation. When he asked for my assistance at the time, I didn't really take him seriously. But apparently, he was. He reached out a week ago for my help. I asked him to send me some information on the foundation, board minutes, financial info, bios of the players, and whatnot—but not until after I spoke with Claymore. I'm having that call with him tomorrow morning. If after that call I feel Claymore is someone I can work with, I'll jump in."

"I didn't think Neil and Carl were your type. I'm surprised you're getting involved."

"Ordinarily I wouldn't, but they did put up the money to help us bring all those new jobs to the county, so I feel somewhat indebted to them. Also, underserved kids are getting screwed on this LBF situation, and I think I know by who. That's lit me up a little bit. If I jump in, it will only be because I believe we can do something to help those kids. To that end, will you help me with a couple of things?"

"Of course, JB. What do you need?"

"Pastor Jeffrey Claymore. Do you know him?"

"I've met him twice. Seems like the real deal."

"Tell me everything you know about him."

"Well, everything I know was told to me by Cornelius. Claymore must be in his late sixties. Had a rough childhood. Was in prison as a teenager and young adult. Found religion while he was incarcerated. When he was paroled, he followed on with his religious studies. Joined a local parish soon after he got out. Because of his efforts was given his own parish before he was thirty, the same parish he oversees today. Has lived his whole life in Philadelphia and is highly respected in the community. Known for his passion for helping troubled youth. Has developed some high-level connections over his career. Even became friendly with President Carrington during his first term. He became something of a spiritual advisor to both the President and his wife Heather, as I understand it. Never heard anyone say a bad word about him."

"Do you know Hanley Michaelson?"

"Not personally. From what I know about him, he's a labor union operative in Philly. Seems hard wired into that city's ugly political swamp. Mostly deal-making between local labor unions and local office holders that play ball with him. He's the guy who steers laborers to campaign events."

"Lines up contractors to do the union's business, and the like, in return for favors. Organizes labor union members for strikes. Puts together squads to scare anti-union protesters and proponents. He smells dirty but has never been indicted for anything. I'm sure he's well protected within City Hall. But as far as I know, Michaelson is not involved with LBF. I've never heard Carl or Neil ever mention anything about him."

"Sounds like someone I'll enjoy meeting should I get the opportunity," Jon responded in a tone dripping with disgust. "Back to Claymore. Do you have any reason to suspect he might be redirecting funds out of LBF for any non-foundation business?"

Gregory was stunned at the suggestion and did not immediately respond. He was insulted Jon would question the character of someone he had just a moment ago praised.

In the silence, Jon sensed Gregory's emotion. "I don't have any specific reason to believe he is but based on the conversation we had with Carl at dinner, I can't rule it out. What can you tell me about Darby Robinson?"

"Just a couple of things. I know he's Claymore's godson and that he's running for mayor of Philadelphia this year."

———— ≈ ————

It was now four. The speaker on Jon's desk phone came alive with a tone followed by Abby's voice.

"Mr. Braxton, Neil Hale holding for you."

"Thanks, Abby. Put him through."

The call was transferred over immediately and rang on Jon's desk. He picked up the handset in an instant. "Hello, Neil. Thanks for calling."

"No problem, JB. What is it? I understand your call with Claymore is confirmed for tomorrow morning."

"It is. The call is what I wanted to talk to you about. I need to understand a few relationship dynamics before I got on the phone with him. I'd like to ask a few very straightforward questions. I hope you don't mind, and I hope you won't be offended by my line of questioning."

"JB, we agreed we would do this your way, so proceed please."

"Neil, do you have any suspicion whatsoever that Pastor Claymore is doing anything inappropriate with the money that flows into LBF?"

There was a silent pause, as Neil Hale processed the question. After a few second delay, he gave an emphatic one-word answer—"No."

Jon waited for a follow-on comment and, when he realized none was coming, continued. "Tell me why."

"I've known the man for over fifteen years, and in all those years, I have never heard one person ever, ever say anything about the pastor that would lead me to believe he had the inkling, let alone the capacity, to do anything improper. I find the man above reproach. In many respects JB, he is like you—principled, decent, authentic, selfless. But unlike you, he answers to a higher power which would not allow it. So no, I do not hold any reservations whatsoever in saying to you that Pastor Claymore is not and would not be involved in any transgressions."

Jon was relieved to hear Neil Hale's passionate defense. He decided he would accept that confirmation as the default characterization of the Pastor until proven otherwise.

"Neil, Darby Robinson? I know we touched on him on our last call, and you didn't have much background on him, but I've learned a couple things that I feel if you knew, you would have shared with me. So, I believe you don't know the things I just learned, and I should fill you in as it might be important to your assessment of whether you want to continue supporting LBF."

Neil's interest was piqued, but he couldn't think of much to say except, "Go on."

"Robinson is running for mayor. And he's Claymore's godson."

Again, silence as Neil processed what he had indeed just heard for the first time. Jon was holding back, interested in Neil's first response.

"Well, this certainly spices things up a bit, doesn't it? I can understand now why you asked me about Jeffrey's ethics. Makes perfect sense. But I'm going to hold my position that the Pastor is not complicit in any potential wrongdoings or conflicts of interest on the part of Darby Robinson. If there is any funny business going on with Robinson, I must believe Jeffrey is unaware. But I think it would be appropriate for me to share your information with Carl, and for us to review our more recent conversations and interactions with Jeffrey to see if anything raises a flag for us."

"That would be helpful. Thank you. And do you feel there is any possibility that Claymore is not unaware? That, while not complicit, he is aware of some of Robinson's mis-dealings, but does not have the fortitude, as his godfather, to do anything about it?"

Before this call, Neil Hale would have responded *not possible*. But Jon's information and his line of questioning brought doubt to the forefront. Neil had the highest respect for Jeffrey Claymore. To hear his character being called into question was a bitter pill to swallow. The implication that Darby Robinson was dirty, was running for Mayor, was Jeffrey's godson, and was responsible for the decline in efficacy of LBF hit him all at once.

"I suppose it's possible."

"Neil, I'd like to know what the pastor knows about me and how you've positioned this call with him. Is he expecting I'm only connecting to offer ideas and perspectives on helping kids? Or does he know you've asked me to investigate and uncover the reasons why they're failing? And a follow-up to that—does Claymore hold a belief that things are not going well? Or is he oblivious to your concerns?"

As Jon finished his query Neil became aware he could not completely trust his fond emotions towards Pastor Claymore. "You certainly know how to peel onions, Mr. Braxton." Neil resigned himself to the notion he had to let Jon have full reign as his only chance to fully trust the pastor again.

"I asked Jeffrey to meet with you for you to share your successes at Win-the-Day. He does hold a belief, and has shared with me, that the foundation is struggling to meet their challenges and is in decline. He expressed interest meeting you for guidance on how to turn things around. He's done his own research on Win-the-Day and has expressed to us he's impressed. But he is not aware of our interest in having you dive into their operation as it relates to financial matters and the actions of their board."

"How would he feel if he was aware this was your intent?"

"At this point, I'm not sure."

Jon now had the information he wanted from this call. "I recognize this was difficult for you, and I'm sorry if I offended in any way. I'm looking forward to speaking with Claymore, but you need to understand should he and I get to the point of discussing finances and board activity, I'm not planning to pull any punches. While I trust your judgment on him, I don't believe I can do the job you want me to do unless I ask him tough questions. I'll start with the call tomorrow and if we establish a rapport, I'll set us up to meet. Is this approach OK with you?"

"We're doing it your way. I'll call Carl tonight to go over what we discussed, and if anything transpires from the call that would be pertinent, I'll let you know before your call with Jeffrey tomorrow. Anything else before we part company?"

"No. I'll let you go. Good night, and again, my apologies for any discomfort."

"Good night, JB." Click

Twenty-One

The Hanley and Associates North Philadelphia offices were located on West Liberty St. in Allentown, Pennsylvania. The building was in a nondescript office complex known as Liberty Plaza. The 3,500-square-foot office space consisted of six regulation-sized offices, an undersized conference room, and a quaint receptionist area all ringing ten smallish office cubicles.

On a late July Wednesday morning Hanley Michaelson was in his office awaiting the arrival of the man he was actively campaign-managing to be elected the next mayor of Philadelphia, Darby Robinson. They had a confirmed meeting for nine. Michaelson had several matters to discuss with Darby, one of them being the opportunity for Robinson to campaign with the former First Lady and current Secretary of State of the United States. Another agenda item was informing Robinson of his plan to launder the recent $300,000 donation to LBF from The Hale Group into Robinson's campaign.

Unbeknownst to Robinson, Michaelson had set up a campaign event for the following week, when Carrington planned to be in town. They would address a gathering at the SEIU National Headquarters on Twenty-second Street the following Thursday. Robinson would deliver a fifteen-minute speech and then introduce Heather Carrington, at which time they would embrace, providing Michaelson the photo op he wanted. He had already written Heather Carrington's speech outlining Robinson's accomplishments, praises, and prosperous vision for Philadelphia's future.

A few minutes before nine a well-sculpted, immaculately dressed six-foot, two-inch, 225-pound African American man entered the Hanley and Associates offices. He confidently approached the pretty twenty-four-year-old receptionist typing away on a desktop computer keyboard. "Good morning, Sheila. How's the most beautiful woman in Philadelphia doing this fine day?"

"Good morning, Mr. Robinson," Sheila McCrae responded. "Mr. Michaelson is expecting you, please go on in. He's waiting for you in his office."

Robinson nodded. "Thank you, Sheila. You really should reconsider going out with me," he said softly as he walked past her desk towards Hanley's office.

Michaelson stood from behind his desk as Robinson entered the room. "Ladies and gentlemen, permit me to introduce you to the next mayor of Philadelphia," he boomed. "Good morning, Darby," he continued with an amplified tone and an emphasis on Robinson's name. Taking it down a little, he went on. "Come in, sit down. We have a lot to discuss."

Hanley Michaelson was born in 1953 and raised in Philadelphia by his moderately religious Jewish mother and father. His home was a Democratic blue-collar one. His father worked as a tradesman and had been a union member all his life. Hanley grew up in the shadow of labor unions and never left. He started following his father's footsteps taking up the plumbing trade, but soon realized he was not cut out for an honest day's work. A dishonest one suited him better, and he entered the world of labor union politics at the age of twenty-nine. For the last thirty years, he had made his living on the payroll of various unions in the Philadelphia area as a 'consultant'.

Michaelson's path first crossed with Darby Robinson's in 2008. Darby, from the urging of his godfather, Pastor Jeffrey Claymore, ventured into the world of public relations. Darby joined Claymore's parish at age eight. As he matured, he exhibited strong public speaking and writing skills. At age twenty-two he was guided by Claymore to explore a career in public relations to utilize those skills.

With Claymore's endorsement, Darby was able to land an entry-level sales job with Aversa Communications, a Philadelphia PR and event management firm. His first assignment was to sell advertising in a program guide for an event the firm was directing to promote the Philadelphia city zoo. He sold out the guide in three weeks to the surprise and amazement of Aversa's managing partners.

Darby's career at Aversa, filled with strong performances and accomplishments, lasted until 2009. During the last year of Darby's tenure, he was assigned an account management role for a large and growing Aversa client, Local 332 of the Laborers' International Union of North America (LIUNA).

Darby's first meeting with his new client was held at the LIUNA Philadelphia headquarters in March of 2008, when he was introduced to LIUNA's management consultant, Hanley Michaelson.

During their first meeting, Michaelson became enamored with Darby's flashy smile, imposing physical attributes, warm demeanor, and impeccable conversational skills. From that point, Michaelson pursued Robinson as a 'business associate', believing his attributes could be utilized to further the interests of HM and Associates.

Within six months of their first meeting, Michaelson convinced Darby to leave Aversa and start his own PR firm. To that end, he promised he would bring over Local 332 as a client—for a modest ongoing consulting fee. Darby at first hesitated. This arrangement contradicted his lessons on the importance of integrity from Pastor Claymore. But Michaelson was persistent, offering additional local unions and associated businesses as potential clients—each for a modest ongoing consulting fee.

The opportunity to start his own firm and immediately acquire ten significant clients was too much temptation to resist. Darby left Aversa in August 2008 to start Darbycom Communications. Within six months, Darbycom was the lead PR firm for ten organizations within the Philadelphia metropolis, generating total average billings of $140,000 per month.

Michaelson became aware of Robinson's relationship with Jeffrey Claymore and the First Pentecostal Church of Philadelphia shortly after Darbycom was launched. Michaelson was interested in exploring Robinson's relationship with Claymore. He was aware of the pastor's popularity and reach. Michaelson had met the pastor earlier in 2006 when he rented the gymnasium at Faith Central, the brand new complex adjacent to First Pentecostal Claymore had built to provide sanctuary for at-risk youth in the Sharswood area. The complex that eventually became the shining star of the Liberty Bell Foundation. The complex that Carlton and Cornelius Hale financed with their generous donations.

After meeting Claymore in 2006 and learning of his considerable spiritual influence in Sharswood and the surrounding neighborhoods, Michaelson targeted Claymore and First Pentecostal to be clients. He saw huge opportunities for improving his legitimacy and brand by associating with the esteemed pastor. But all his efforts were rejected by Claymore. The pastor had sensed Michaelson's motives were not pure.

Michaelson and Claymore had not spoken since that time, but the opportunity to get his satellites back into the pastor's orbit was rekindled upon Michaelson learning of Darby's relationship with Claymore. From his growing relationship with Darby, he learned more about Faith Central and Claymore's relationship with the Hale Brothers. He became obsessed with somehow inserting himself. He then hatched a plan to convince Darby to convince the pastor to create a charitable, nonprofit organization to assist in raising money for the pastor's mission—monies of which he envisioned a portion always making their way to his firm in the form of a modest ongoing consulting fee.

Darby settled into one of the two chairs across the desk from

Michaelson. "Darby, I've arranged for a very special person to do some campaigning with you. Next week, you are going to be on stage with a well-known political figure who will enthusiastically endorse you—the former First Lady and current Secretary of State, Heather Carrington."

"Wow, Hanley! How did you pull that off?"

"When you've been around as long as I have, you tend to meet a lot of people and do a lot of favors. It's always good to keep track of them. They keep nicely over time and become currency you can use for future purchases. And you do realize her campaigning with you and her endorsement should be the finishing touches on your campaign putting you in the driver's seat to become the next mayor, right?"

Darby nodded, and Michaelson continued. "But I don't want to take anything for granted. I have another strategy I need your help in executing. Along the lines of favors being repaid, I need you to do something for us."

Darby, knowing Michaelson's propensity for shady, was apprehensive. Michaelson leaned to his left and reached down to a filing drawer on the lower left side of his desk. He pulled out twelve manila file folders, each with service contract paperwork. He put the folders in front of himself on the desk, then leaned back in his chair. Darby looked at the folders warily, then returned his gaze to Hanley.

"We need some additional funding for your campaign to run a number of TV, radio, and social media ads during the last four weeks. We can't take anything for granted. Carrington's endorsement is big, but it's not a lock. This is our election to win. We have to be sure not to take our eyes off the prize. Understand?"

"Yes."

"Good. Here's what we need you to do. You need to enter LBF into these service arrangements over the next three weeks and pay off these contracts in full in advance of the services being completed. Each of the service providers are offering nice discounts for advance payment. Here are the contracts. Each contract has who the checks should be written to, the dates for the work to be done, details on the advance payment discounts and the amount for the discounted payment in full. We need you to sign these contracts and checks for full payment and returned to me so I can deliver to the contractors before the end of the week. We need this done quickly so we have time to produce the ads. Make sense?"

Darby had been around Michaelson enough to know exactly what this scheme was all about. He knew Michaelson had "relationships" with these service companies and that they would all play ball with him. They would receive a check for the full amount from LBF and then write two checks—one for sixty percent to the Darby for Mayor campaign, and the other for twenty percent to Hanley Michaelson and Associates. The remaining twenty percent would stay with the contractor to cover the costs of the shoddy work they would perform for LBF to satisfy the contract. All the service providers understood they would lose money on these contracts. And all understood once Robinson was elected mayor, their participation would be rewarded handsomely. And everything would be facilitated by Hanley Michaelson—for a modest ongoing consulting fee.

Without saying anything, Darby reached over the desk and picked up the file folders. He settled back in his chair and started to review them. There was a contract for resurfacing the Faith Central gym hardwood floor for $70,000. Another for repainting the interior of Faith Central for $65,000. Another for re-carpeting all the Faith Central offices for $40,000. An annual contract for the monthly washing of all of Faith Central's windows for $35,000. And eight additional service contracts, all with highly inflated prices. All with modest discounts. All to be paid in full.

Darby closely reviewed each contract in detail. After twenty minutes he had digested the massive fraud Michaelson was proposing. He had the folders all closed and resting on his lap and was looking down at them. Slowly, he raised his head to look at Michaelson, who had returned to reviewing other paperwork on his desk. When Hanley recognized Darby was staring at him, he returned the look. "What is it, Darby?"

"Hanley, do we really need the money in the campaign this badly? I mean, this is really dirty, a lot dirtier than any of the things we've done before. I'm not comfortable with it."

"Darby, politics is a blood sport. It's eat or be eaten. You can bet Rogers"—Steve Rogers, Darby's Republican adversary in the election— "is out there doing the same thing, guaranteed. He knows he's behind, and I'm sure he's pulling out all the stops. I know his campaign manager, and she is a real ball-buster. I am sure she's shaking down all the big money conservatives in the city. I am certain they're going to hit the airwaves hard the last few weeks of the campaign. It's their only chance, and we have got to counter. We must play to win. I need you to be good with this. Once you make it to the mayor's office, you can make amends. Everyone in the city will want to curry favor with you. You can direct all kinds of support and goodwill towards LBF from the mayor's office. This is how the game is played. It's a game of winners and losers, and you certainly don't strike me as being a loser."

The meeting ended shortly thereafter, with Robinson resigned to the fact that he was going to carry out Michaelson's scheme, and he turned his attention as to how he would do it without alerting his godfather.

Twenty-two

Jon decided he would conduct his call with Claymore early in the morning from home. With the three-hour time difference, he could converse with the pastor comfortably without any potential distractions from the office, while not disturbing the pastor too early in the morning. To his relief, there was no call from Neil Hale earlier regarding any skeletons he or Carl may have found in the pastor's closet.

Jeffrey Claymore was energized and effervescent when he answered Jon's call. "Gooooood morning, Mr. Braxton. We finally connect. I've been very much looking forward to speaking with you. My friend Carlton Hale thinks the world of you, and from what he's told me, and from what I've read about the work you are doing at Win-the-Day, I'm coming along to that conclusion as well."

"The pleasure is all mine, Pastor Claymore. Thank you for making the time to speak with me."

Before Jon could utter another word, the Pastor was speaking. Jon was a bit surprised. He was expecting Claymore to be somewhat uncommunicative. "Mr. Braxton, I have a great hope you and I will become great friends, and that we will be able to help one another. I'm highly confident you will provide me tremendous insights as to how I can better operate the Liberty Bell Foundation. What I am less confident in is how I might remunerate you for your expertise, but Lord willing, I will find a way."

The pastor wasn't ready to release the floor yet. "Mr. Braxton, before we get into your questions, there are a few things I'd like to cover. Will this be OK with you?"

"Of course, Pastor Claymore."

"Splendid. Given that we are going to be great friends, I'd like to first establish how we could address one another."

Jon's first impression of the pastor upon hearing this request was one of uncertainty. *'Is he trying to handle me?'* was the uncomfortable thought that went through his head.

"Mr. Braxton, the people who like you—your friends, your associates, your confidants—how do they address you?"

"Well, I acquired a nickname about twenty years ago and it stuck. Most of my friends and colleagues call me JB."

"And the people who love you—your parents, your wife—how do they address you?"

"My parents died in an auto accident when I was very young. I don't have any memories of them. My wife calls me Jon."

"Very well, Jon it is. And it is my honor to meet you. I'm so very sorry to hear of your parents' misfortune, may God have mercy on their souls. From now on, please call me Jeffrey."

"Thank you, pastor, uh, Jeffrey."

"Jon, another thing I'd like to know, if I may, and that is do you believe in God?"

When Jon dialed Claymore's number he felt supremely prepared for this call. After Jeffrey's question he realized he was not. He needed a few seconds to conclude how to answer. He had never been asked about his spirituality before.

"Jeffrey, I can't tell you if I do or not. I don't know. I've never been asked, and I've never…"

His voice trailed off, unable to complete his thought to the pastor as he, for the first time in twenty years, thought of his parents. Jeffrey's question had invaded his consciousness. In this instant, he thought about what his life would have been like had he been raised by them, instead of growing up in the numerous foster homes that housed him during his youth. What would his mother and father have been like? How would his childhood have been different? Where in the world would he have ended up? How like or unlike his mother and father was he? How would they have taken to Angela? Would he have even met Angela? How would they have enjoyed their grandchildren?

Jonathon Braxton, for the first time he could remember, felt consumed and overwhelmed by emotion. He was grateful the pastor continued the conversation, as he was in no condition to.

Pastor Claymore sensed his pain. "Jon, something I'd like you to know about me is that I believe in God, and our Lord and Savior Jesus Christ, with every fiber of my being. I live only to serve them. I tell you this, not because I am perfect, as I am far from it. But only so you can understand me. I wanted to tell you this because I have a feeling since you have not yet partnered with God, you will have difficulty understanding me and my ways. I am certain I am not as knowledgeable nor as proficient in the ways of man as you are, and you may become frustrated with me because I only seek to be efficient in the ways of the Lord."

Jon digested Claymore's every word. He remained unable to conjure a response.

"Jon, the last thing I want you to understand before you begin your questions is that I know why our foundation is failing in its mission. And I have complete conviction you will uncover the worldly reasons for our slow demise. And once you do, you could conclude that my inaction is the reason. And you will be right." The pastor paused to gather his thoughts, and the silence further tranquilized Jon.

"I provided Carlton, per his request, numerous records of the foundation's operations and finances, records that I have not reviewed myself. I have tried to divorce myself from those matters, for better or worse. And I sense that you have not reviewed them yet either. If I know you, as I believe I do, you chose to wait until you had a chance to speak with me so you could form an opinion of me devoid of any, shall we say, paperwork. I believe you have suspicions about me, and they are justified. When you do review these records, I have a sense you will not like what you see. I have the same sense, and for a reason only the Lord knows, I have not felt the inspiration to review them. I believe the Lord has sent you to us and he wants you to take care of us. In that light, I will tell you everything you want to know."

The private sermon was over as Pastor Claymore had said everything he wanted Jon to understand up front. An awkward pause followed, both men listening to the sounds of silence for many seconds. Jon was in unchartered territory. He always knew what to say, how to respond, how to take control—until now.

Eventually he returned to the moment from the unfamiliar surroundings of self-awareness, reflection, and mortality. He was uncharacteristically humbled by the pastor's presence, despite being 3000 miles away, and felt drawn toward him. "Jeffrey, you are right about my suspicions of you and the fact I had not yet reviewed the information you supplied Mr. Hale. I had a number of questions to ask you today, but in light of what we discussed"—JB immediately realized the absurdity of that comment as he had not contributed anything to the conversation—"I'd like to revisit those questions and review the information you provided before we proceed."

"Jon, thank you for your honesty"—and, in a lighter vein— "though because of your integrity, I know you did not have a choice. Please take whatever time you want. As I said, I believe you are on a mission from the Lord. We will do this your way."

Jon chuckled to himself, recalling the same words from Neil Hale. The thought of the pastor being complicit was now the farthest thought from his mind. "Jeffrey, I'd like our next conversation to be in person. Would it be OK with you if I schedule a trip to Philadelphia to meet you?"

"I would love that."

Twenty-three

In 1577 days, Heather Carrington was expecting to be elected the first female president of the United States, allowing her to fulfill her promise to her late father. It was early evening, and she was heading down a hallway in her residence towards her husband's study. The door to the study was closed and Heather dutifully knocked before entering, this time without waiting for permission. "Wil, do you have a few minutes?"

"Of course, honey," he replied, annoyed she had already entered without his beckoning. His gaze remained on the document he had been studying.

She entered the darkened room, illuminated by two sources of contained light. On the wall to her right was a burning fireplace. Toward the wall to her left was Wil Carrington's desk, illuminated by a stylish brass desk lamp.

Heather approached the desk and sat down in one of two high-backed mahogany guest chairs, upholstered with lavish burgundy leather. Wearing a plush purple bathrobe and fluffy blue slippers, she sat back in the chair and crossed her legs.

For a few seconds, she sat in silent darkness as the light from the lamp illuminated only the desk. She waited for Wil to acknowledge her presence, which he did after a few seconds by rolling his eyes up and over his reading lenses to look at her darkened outline.

"Wil, I'm leaving for Philadelphia early on Tuesday and I wanted to see if there was anything you wanted me to do while I'm there."

"You'll be seeing both Jeffrey and Hanley?"

"Jeffrey, yes. Hanley, I'm not sure."

"I thought you we're doing a campaign stop for him. Something changed?"

"Only in my head. I'm undecided at this point."

"When were you planning to do the stop?"

"Thursday afternoon. I've got State meetings all day Tuesday and Wednesday. I'm visiting with Jeffrey on Thursday morning and then I'm supposed to make the appearance with Hanley and his candidate on Thursday afternoon."

"Do you have your speech ready?"

"Hanley wrote one for me. I've seen it. It's what you'd expect."

"Honey, I don't have anything. Give them both my best."

"Wil, Sidney gave me some information and I'm a little uncomfortable with the thought of helping Hanley. I offered to help him because of what he did for us in the '92 campaign, but I'm having a lot of second thoughts."

"What did Sidney have to say?"

"Do you know anything about this guy that Hanley is running out there for mayor?"

The former President frowned as he realized how much he had lost touch with the political landscape of 2012. As Heather was not running for anything, he had lost interest. "I don't. Is he a problem?"

"Well, I'll tell you what I've come to learn, and you tell me. This Darby Robinson, well, he's connected to Jeffrey, big time. One, he's Jeffrey's godson. Jeffrey's known him almost all his life. And second, he's the chairman of the board of Jeffrey's foundation."

"Heather, this sounds like a good thing, a good thing for you to get involved in for your run in '16. You'll need to carry Pennsylvania."

"Wil, that's not all. Apparently, Jeffrey and Hanley have a little history, and it's not good. They met some years ago when Hanley rented out the gym at Faith Central for a union meeting. Hanley learned

214

about all the good work the pastor was doing and started soliciting Jeffrey to be a client. Jeffrey ignored him. Sensed his character and motives were dubious. Four years ago, Hanley meets Darby and learns Darby is connected to Jeffrey. Hanley is still interested in attaching to Jeffrey, so he convinces Darby to convince the pastor to set up a 501c3 to raise money. And he convinces Darby to have Jeffrey authorize a board of directors and install him as chairman."

"This still sounds good. I mean the foundation is raising more money now as a legal nonprofit, and I'm sure Jeffrey is putting the funds to good use."

"Unfortunately, Wil, that does not appear to be the case. Mark Parker uncovered some additional crap for me to know, and it stinks."

The former President raised his eyebrows and took off his reading lenses as she continued.

"Mark has an Air Force buddy working at a law firm in Philly. His firm is the legal counsel for several of the labor unions Hanley consults for. Knowing our affiliation with the pastor, Mark's friend tells him the firm submitted a $60,000 retainer agreement to LBF. And there's a backside agreement that once LBF pays the firm the $60K, they write a check to the Darby for Mayor campaign for $36K and a check for $12K to Hanley Michaelson and Associates. Small print in the agreement says the retainer is for ten hours. Sixty grand for ten hours! And here's the kicker. The firm had drafted a dozen other 'service agreements' for other organizations for the same purpose."

"Honey, this is how politics is played in Philadelphia. You know this. I'm surprised you're bothered by it. You've seen much worse."

"Seriously, Wil? This is impacting Jeffrey. This could tarnish everything he's ever done. This is money that should be spent to help kids being redirected, illegally, to a political campaign. Imagine if this information gets out, the damage it could do?"

The former President quickly digested the information he was just fed. "You are right honey. You should stay away. It could hurt your 2016 chances. The risk isn't worth the reward."

———≈———

Heather's conversation with Wil bothered her all weekend. Hanley Michaelson's money laundering scheme seemed to have caused Wil only one concern. A concern it could hurt her political aspirations if the scheme became public and she were to be associated with it. Heather Carrington had, for the first time since she entered public life, started to view what were considered political norms through a different lens and what she started to see, combined with the recent loss of her good friend Charlie Carpenter, was troubling her immensely. The level of cronyism on display in Wil's office that night didn't seem to faze him at all. It was business as usual. She was thinking Sidney Rosenberg felt the same way.

———≈———

On Sunday morning, Sidney Rosenberg's cell phone buzzed with "unknown caller."

"Hello?" Rosenberg offered cautiously.

"Go Princeton."

"Beat Rutgers."

"Good morning Sidney."

"Good morning, Madam Secretary." Rosenberg went formal. He was still peeved over their last conversation.

"How are you?"

"I'm fine Heather. Can I assume the same for you?"

"No, I am not fine. I called to apologize to you. Are you accepting apologies today?"

"Only if they are sincere."

Heather ignored the comment. "Look, I'm sorry for not entrusting you with my plans regarding Michaelson, I truly am. I value your advice and your insight, I really do, and I am committing to you that I will seek them much more frequently than I have in the past. Will you forgive me? Can we move on?"

"Not bad for one who has so little experience with apologies. What's on your mind?"

"Philadelphia."

"As it should be. It's a beautiful time of the year to be there. I hope you have a successful trip."

"Goddamn it, I really don't want or need your sarcasm right now. I need your help."

"What's the deal? Are you still planning to campaign with Robinson while you're there?"

"That's what I need your help with. I don't know what I should do. If I go through with the campaign stop, we could get bloodied with what I've learned about the two of them. If I don't do it, it could put Pennsylvania at risk for us in '16."

"When are you scheduled to appear with him?"

"Thursday at two."

"Did you forget about the other meeting?"

"Shit, Sidney, what are you talking about? What other meeting?"

"The emergency foreign affairs meeting at the White House at three on Thursday."

"I don't have anything like that on my. . . . Oh, you're right, the emergency foreign affairs meeting Obama just put on my calendar. Of course, I'm so disappointed. I'll have to cancel with Hanley, and I was so much looking forward to sharing a stage with Mr. Robinson."

"Anything else, Madam Secretary?"

"No, Sidney. Thank you."

Twenty-four

A bby and Rob Wiley had been collaborating on Jon's commitment to hold a campaign event for Earl Gregory. They were discussing whether the Spectre complex in Thousand Oaks or the Win-the-Day campus in Oxnard would be the better venue. They settled on the Spectre parking lot, believing they would be able to drive more attendance.

'Good morning, sire. May I have a word?' was the instant message on Jon's monitor at eight on an early August morning.

'You may, but only a word. If you go over your limit, you have to promise to leave me alone for a week.' He typed back to her screen.

'Yes, your majesty. Don't get on the phone. I'll be in lickety-split,' appeared on Jon's screen a second later.

Within two seconds, Abby entered Jon's office and took a seat in one of the guest chairs across the desk from him. She was holding a stack of twelve manila folders, each with service contract paperwork and cleanly labeled with the name of each contractor. She set them down in the empty guest chair next to her.

"Good morning, sir."

"Good morning, Abby. What have you got?"

"I've been working with Rob on the Gregory rally. We're scheduling it for four weeks from now. Just thought I should bring you up to speed. Don't want you to stammer too badly if the Congressman or the new president of my fan club, Mr. Neil Hale, asks you for some detail. I do believe Mr. Hale will be watching closely to see how this event plays out, so I've been giving it a lot of focus. I need his majesty to look regal on this. A good showing will sit nicely on the resume."

"I had forgotten all about that commit. Why didn't you remind me?"

"Oh, uh, just thought I'd handle it. In case you forgot, you've got a billion-dollar business to run. You can't be playing around with politics, Mr. Braxton. You're lucky I let you screw around with fantasy baseball."

Jon realized it was a no-win situation to give Abby any grief.

"So, Mr. Braxton, may I fill you in?"

"If you would be so kind."

"OK, we're shooting for 3,000 attending."

"What? You've got to be kidding."

"No, your majesty, we're going big or we're staying home. We've got entertainment lined up. Food trucks. We've got Randy Boswell speaking, Larry Morris speaking. Connie will speak. Congressman Gregory, of course, will speak. At the same time, we're having a job fair for three of the companies which committed to move to the county with their 600 new jobs. Basically, we're having a freaking party. We're advertising it as such in the Chronicle and we're buying cable TV ads. Maybe 3,000 is an underestimate."

"Am I not on the speaking list?"

"No, sire. Knowing of your intolerance of politics, I didn't want to torture you any further."

"Do you know anything about the speeches?" Jon couldn't resist. "And of course, you're asking Larry Morris for three outlines and six rough drafts of his, right?"

"Well, I wasn't supposed to say anything, but Neil Hale asked Randy, since we're going to be on the Spectre campus, to talk about the company and to talk about you. And Larry Morris is going to talk about all the jobs coming to the county and giving Earl lots of credit and talk about you. Connie is going to talk about public education and Win-the-Day and you. And Earl is going to talk about what he's planning to do in Congress next term and you. And other than that, I don't know anything."

"I thought this was a campaign rally for Earl. Why are all the speakers going to talk about yours truly?"

"Well, Mr. Truly Mine, it was Neil Hale's directive—uh, I mean idea."

"Really? And Earl's OK with it?"

"Yeah, Neil mentioned something about this being an investment in your future."

"Oh really? Well, next time you talk to your new fan club head cheerleader, please tell Mr. Neil Hale that I have indeed decided to run for public office."

"I believe he will be pleased to hear that."

"And how do you think I'll perform as head dog catcher of Ventura County?"

"I know I wouldn't want to be a dog on the run if you were."

"You know Abby, this event sounds like it's going to be incredible. Was this all your doing or Rob's?" Jon asked, already knowing the answer.

"I'll let you discuss that with Rob," she added with a wink and smile. "Now, will there be anything else or can I get back to doing some Spectre work? Someone around here has to keep the choo choo chugging."

"You're the one who asked for the meeting. And by the way, you went over your word limit."

"You're right. Guess I'll have to leave you alone for a week."

"Are you taking bets on that?"

"Nope, later gator." She rose and handed Jon the file folders. "These new contracts were emailed to me by Pastor Claymore yesterday. They weren't part of the initial download. He noted these were brand new and that you might want to pay particular attention to them in prep for your meeting with him."

As she was leaving his office, Jon reminded her: "Don't forget, I'm heading out to Philadelphia on Wednesday."

Jon returned to his email, noticing a new one from Rob Wiley, the subject, *'Can I Have Some?'* It read *'Seriously, man, what do you feed Abby? She's a machine.'*

Twenty-five

The chartered plane ride from Washington to Philadelphia took less than an hour. Heather Carrington, her Chief of Staff Mark Parker, two administrative aides, and four Secret Service personnel were on board the Gulfstream G450 as it glided into Chester County Carlson Airport in Coatesville, Pennsylvania, thirty-five miles west of Downtown Philadelphia.

Upon landing, the team of eight was picked up at Carlson by two State Department black SUVs and driven directly to the U.S. Department of Defense office complex on Robbins Street, in the northeast section of the city. It was nine when Heather Carrington started the first of her five meetings planned for Tuesday and Wednesday to conduct official State Department business.

She had not yet informed Michaelson she would not be attending the Thursday afternoon rally for Robinson. Hanley would call her administrative aide six times Tuesday and Wednesday attempting to confirm, to no avail.

Heather wrapped up the last of her meetings late Wednesday afternoon. She had still not responded to Michaelson. She was exhausted and was looking forward to a quiet night in her hotel suite with room service. By five, she was headed back to the Ritz Carlton with Mark Parker. Upon arriving, she decided they should have one drink before calling it a day. They walked casually to the lobby lounge and found a discreet table. Heather ordered a whiskey sour and Parker a Guinness. As they were waiting for their drinks, Heather noticed what she considered a very handsome, but considerably younger, man sitting at the table closest to theirs. '*Where were you twenty-five years ago when I needed you?*' she fantasized.

While she was admiring him, the gentleman's cell phone rang. He retrieved it from his pocket and answered. "Jon Braxton."

———≈———

The next morning was Thursday, and Heather had still not responded to Michaelson's repeated attempts to confirm her appearance for the afternoon. At 9:45 she left the hotel with two Secret Service personnel and headed to First Pentecostal and her appointment with Jeffrey Claymore. She was very much looking forward to seeing the pastor. In the past, he had always found the right words to soothe her soul, and she never needed those words as badly as she did now. She was highly conflicted about 2016 and hoped the pastor would give her the tools she needed to construct her decision.

It was a little after ten when the black SUV pulled into the Faith Central parking lot in a neighborhood that didn't typically cater to political superstars. The two Secret Service personnel exited the vehicle first. Heather remained inside, doors and windows closed. They walked and surveyed the parking lot area and gazed at rooftops within line of sight to where the Secretary's car was parked. At that moment, a government helicopter entered the airspace around the First Pentecostal-Faith Central complex. It came in low and circled around for two minutes. The Secret Service agents on the ground were given the all-clear, and one of them opened the door for Secretary Carrington.

The two agents escorted her into the Faith Central lobby area where a receptionist greeted her and asked her to follow as she led her to the larger of the two Faith Central conference rooms. Heather made eye contact with the Secret Service agents. They would wait for her in the lobby. Upon entering the conference room, she saw her friend Pastor Claymore standing by the room's window, looking out at the agricultural area and the growing crops grounded just outside.

When their eyes met, they walked briskly towards one another and embraced. The young lady who escorted Heather left and then returned a moment later with two bottles of water, setting them at the end of the table.

"My dear Heather, it is good to see you again. I am so very glad you made time in your busy schedule to come and visit. Welcome."

"Thank you, Jeffrey. I've been looking forward to us seeing one another again."

"Yes. Please come and sit down. We have a lot to catch up on, and I have a sense that you have many things to tell me." Heather sat first on the side of the table that faced the outdoors. The pastor retrieved the two bottles of water and took a seat directly across from her.

"Please feel free to tell me or ask me anything. I am here to help you however I can."

"Oh Jeffrey, I have so many things on my mind, and some are related to you. Things are so confusing and painful. Truthfully, I feel lost these days. In the past, I always felt confident and in control, but these days, not so much. I seem to be blindsided and bewildered by events and information that comes into my view. I often don't know what to do or what to say or how to handle a situation. It's an uncomfortable feeling. I'm not used to it. And the people I turn to for help, my confidants like Wil and Sidney, give me answers and advice that seems wrong. I often feel alone in my thoughts. I don't have anyone to help me make sense of things other than you. That's why I felt the need to see you. I need your wisdom."

"Heather, I have some good news for you. There is a relatively simple answer to your problems. First, I am not sure when you prayed last, but I'd like you to pray with me right now. Will you?"

The mention of prayer brought a wave of shame over Heather, and she started to cry. She turned her gaze away from the pastor to the table, now ashamed to look at him. She realized she never said a serious prayer for Charlie or Leila Carpenter. She realized she had, as she tended to do in the heat of battle, lost track of her faith—a faith that was never strong, let alone significant to her. But a faith with remnants in her core. A faith she bottled up long ago and put away for the sake of political expediency. All these thoughts came rushing through her. Once they all landed, she raised her tear-filled eyes back to the pastor. Claymore knew, without her saying a word, exactly what she was feeling.

"Heather, take comfort in knowing that you do not have an exclusive license on shame and guilt. Those emotions belong to all of us. To live to God's standards of sanctity and morality is perhaps the most difficult task for all mankind. But thankfully God is merciful, and He forgives those who forgive themselves. And He forgives those who make the effort to find the right path and travel it. And He puts faith into men like me, to help those in need. And He has put me here for you, Heather. He has put me here for you."

"Thank you, Jeffrey. You are my best friend. You always know exactly what to say to me."

In a soft and respectful tone, the pastor worked to heal Heather's wounded soul. "Let's both say a silent prayer for Charlie and Leila Carpenter. Let's pray to Charlie in Heaven. Let's bless his soul and tell him how much we loved him while he was on Earth and how much we love him now as he rests in the shadow of God. And let's pray for Leila. Let's pray that she finds comfort in knowing Charlie's soul is in good hands and that he will live forever in the presence of the Lord."

He bowed his head. She followed his lead. They sat in silent prayer for a few minutes. Heather prayed hard. She prayed for Charlie and Leila, and she prayed for herself. She prayed she would find the right way forward as she contemplated if she truly wanted to be the President of the United States.

"I hope you feel a little better. I know how difficult it has been for you to live with Charlie's death. Take comfort in knowing that God has a plan for all of us, and he is masterful in executing His plan. As mere mortals, it is impossible for us to understand all His ways, but we do have the option of faith to help us. Please consider reconnecting with God, Heather. It's clear you have many conflicts you are dealing with. Faith is the answer you are seeking. I am here to guide you as best I can, but it starts with you and your faith." The pastor paused for Heather's reply.

"I'm having difficulty making a decision about my future. You know I have a clear path to a presidential nomination in 2016. Being the first female president of the United States has been a lifelong dream of mine. Spending eight years in the White House as the first lady gave me the knowledge and the confidence that I can do the job and that I would be an effective president. But the situation with Yemen and Charlie has me doubting myself, and I'm questioning if I really want the job. Everyone around me treats it as a foregone conclusion, and I'm simply not sure what to do or how to approach it."

"Heather, why do you want to lead the executive branch of our government?"

The question stunned her. She never considered the role of President as the pastor had just framed it. She had always considered the role, especially in light of the way her husband performed it, as more important than Claymore had just described it. It took her a moment to put into context the fact that the role of President of the United States was not set up constitutionally to be all-powerful. There were three branches of the federal government. The President was only responsible for one. Clearly the pastor was not hung up on the presidency as being the powerful office she had come to believe. He understood the concept of checks and balances and the sharing of power. These were all concepts she knew, but they had become obfuscated in her mind over the years by the thought of, and the quest for, power.

Claymore understood Heather better than she understood herself.

He knew she needed a reset to be able to come to her own conclusion whether it was the right decision to run. He knew she needed to come to an understanding different from what she currently had, to regain the will and resolve to seek the office.

He reframed the role of President for her to consider. He knew she was seeing everything through a political lens. It was only natural, given the number of years she had spent running for, and serving in, public office. He believed her doubts were the result of her distaste for campaigning, not for serving. By reframing the role as one of leadership, shared power, checks and balances, he felt he could help Heather see past the campaigning. He felt he could help her by reminding her that the job was about leadership and service, and not the campaign and power. And reminding her she would not be alone in leading the country should she be elected as the first female to hold the office. He knew she was putting too much pressure on herself to break the glass ceiling and keep her promise to her father. She had lost sight of why she entered politics in the first place.

Heather quickly understood what the pastor was conveying by his one simple question. They both sat in silence for a few minutes. The pastor was observing Heather as she processed the thoughts now running through her head.

"When you do your analysis on whether to run, answer this question for yourself. Do you deserve to be elected because of what you have done or because of what you will do?"

"As always, you ask me questions I cannot answer. But they are questions I know I must answer. And I will. I just can't right now. There is something else that's bothering me, and it has to do with you or, maybe more precisely, with LBF."

"I think I know where you're going Heather, but please, continue."

"My office has come into information that leads us to believe LBF is being used for campaign money laundering." Claymore bowed his head. She continued.

"It pains me to tell you it appears my former friend, Hanley Michaelson, is conspiring with Darby Robinson to move money from LBF into Darby's campaign and into his own pocket."

The pastor raised his head and looked directly into Heather's eyes. He had a pained look on his face, the look of one who had been terribly betrayed by a family member.

"I appreciate you telling me this, and I am not in a position to question or doubt you. I am aware there is impropriety. What I can tell you is that we are in the process of putting an end to it."

"This must be so painful for you, given everything you have done for Darby over the years. But you must be careful, Jeffrey. I wouldn't trust Hanley with your safety if he were to be discovered. Tell me how you are going about addressing this. Maybe I can help you."

"Thank you, Heather, but I have help. God, by way of Carlton and Cornelius Hale, has sent me a gentleman who I have complete faith will resolve the issues you have become aware of."

"Who? A member of the clergy or someone in the political realm?"

The pastor laughed briefly at the thought of Jon being cast in those terms. "No, Heather. He's a businessman from the West Coast, a most unusual businessman. He is the CEO of a tech company and he started and operates a foundation similar to LBF, but much more successfully so."

The pastor spent the next fifteen minutes telling Heather all about his new acquaintance and all Jon had accomplished. She was impressed. "I'd like to meet this Superman some time."

The pastor looked at his watch as it displayed 11:30. "Let's go to the lobby and I'll introduce you to him."

The pastor and the Secretary stood and hugged. "Thank you, Jeffrey. Your words were just what I needed, as usual."

The two proceeded to the lobby, where Jon was standing, engaged in an amicable conversation with Heather's Secret Service detail.

The pastor and the Secretary approached. Claymore extended his hand to Jon and introduced himself. "Hello Jon, it's great to meet you in person. Welcome to Faith Central. I'm Jeffrey Claymore, and I'd like to introduce you to my friend, Heather Carrington."

Jon recognized her as the former first lady, and she recognized him as the man she briefly fantasized about the previous evening in the cocktail lounge of the Ritz Carlton.

The Secretary and her entourage left Faith Central. When she was comfortably seated in her SUV, Heather pulled out her cell phone and dialed Hanley. "Hanley, it's Heather. I've just been called to the White House for an emergency meeting. I can't make it to the campaign event this afternoon for you. I'm so sorry. Good luck."

Twenty-six

The Secretary left Faith Central, leaving Jon and the pastor.

"Jon, come. Let me take you on a tour."

They talked while they walked. "How was your trip into Philadelphia?"

"No issues. Spent a nice night at the Ritz Carlton. How are you doing, Jeffrey?"

"Well, Jon, we have a lot to discuss on that matter."

The two left the Faith Central complex out the front door and walked thirty yards to the east. They came upon twelve concrete steps leading up to the First Pentecostal church. It was a medium-sized, nondescript house of worship. The steps led up to a pair of white paneled front doors. The doors entered into a foyer area that ran the seventy-foot width of the church and was ten feet in depth. The foyer had two sets of doors leading into the congregation area, which consisted of a six-foot-wide center aisle separating twenty rows of benches slightly angled to face the center of the pulpit area. Seating capacity was 240.

The pastor led Jon through the empty congregation area to the pulpit and then to the west side of the church which accommodated six rooms used for various purposes and three administrative offices. After the brief tour of the church, the two walked back to the street and then back to Faith Central. There the pastor showed Jon the regulation-sized basketball court and gymnasium style seating for 600. They toured the classrooms, administrative offices, and agricultural area, and then walked to the back of the property to tour the automotive and woodworking workshops. Eventually they made their way back to the same conference room where the previous meeting took place, and the two new acquaintances sat down to discuss LBF.

"Jeffrey, since we don't really know much about one another, I should share something with you. And that is, I am very direct. When I feel it appropriate to make a point, I do so. I don't do spin or dress things up to be what they are not. I'm mentioning this as I anticipate some of the things that I bring up for your consideration will be uncomfortable, given the long-standing personal relationships in play."

"I understand, and it is OK. I know my godson is a conflicted young man. He appears confident and successful, but his soul is troubled. He needs help, and sometimes that help comes in uncomfortable doses. I have been praying for Darby, and the Lord has prepared me for what is to come. I have accepted your involvement as part of God's plan for him. So, please, tell it like it is. Pull no punches. Give it to me straight. What have you learned and what do you feel we need to do?"

Jon spent the next hour doing just that, and they decided to meet again the following day in the same room with some invited guests. After leaving Faith Central, Jon phoned Neil Hale to inform him of his meeting with Jeffrey. "That sounds like a good plan. Good luck tomorrow and give my best to the pastor."

Jon arrived at Faith Central at nine the next day and met Jeffrey in the same conference room. They were expecting Hanley and Darby at ten. The pastor called Darby after his meeting with Jon and asked him to bring Hanley to meet with him at that time. Darby was concerned about the request and tried to pry the reason from the pastor but could not. He and Hanley strategized how to respond to any questions from the pastor about the bogus service contracts. They felt they could continue to deceive Claymore and were not expecting anyone else to be in the meeting. They were surprised to see an unknown gentleman in the conference room when they arrived.

Jon stood up, and they viewed him warily.

"Hanley, Darby, allow me to introduce you to Jon Braxton. Jon works for the Hale brothers, and he is here to do some accounting of the contributions the Hales so generously donate to LBF."

Jon approached both and extended his hand, looking both squarely in the eyes. They shunned eye contact, shook, and sat down.

"Gentlemen, Carl and Cornelius Hale have asked me to do some due diligence accounting work relative to the funding they provide this organization. The reason we have asked you both here today is that we have uncovered a few irregularities and are hoping with your assistance we can get things squared away."

Robinson and Michaelson looked at one another, unsure of what was coming, and then looked back to Jon, who continued.

"As you are both aware, the Hales feel a kinship to this organization. They were primarily responsible for the funding to build this complex, and they have a keen interest in the work that is done here to help disadvantaged youth gain opportunities to excel and succeed. The reason I am here is that it has come to the Hales' attention that the foundation has not been living up to its previous standards over the past two years and I am here to assist in getting things restored. Now, Mr. Robinson, I understand you are the chairman of LBF's board of directors. Is that correct?"

Before Darby could answer, Hanley interrupted: "Excuse me, Mr. Braxton, as I am not affiliated with LBF, I don't understand why I am here."

"Mr. Michaelson, I believe you know exactly why you are here, and I will get to that in a moment."

"I'm sorry, Mr. Braxton, I am a busy man and I do not have time for this. You will have to excuse me." He stood and started to leave the room. Darby's eyes were following him. A sense of anger and betrayal was building.

As Hanley approached the door Jon caused him to stop. "Mr. Michaelson, if you enjoy your life as a free man and would like to continue to live your life as a free man, I suggest you sit down."

Michaelson, unsure of who was delivering this threat, but aware of the immense influence of the Hale brothers, reversed course and returned to his seat.

Jon continued. "Gentlemen, I have some information I need to share with you." With that he reached into his shoulder bag, pulled out the twelve manila folders Abby had prepared for him earlier in the week, and placed them on the table in front of him.

"Mr. Robinson, you recently entered LBF into twelve contracts for a variety of services. Is that correct?"

"Yes, they were all for services that the foundation needs to maintain its personnel and its facilities."

"Did you seek competitive bids for these services? And if so, can you provide me with copies of those bids?"

Darby knew how to handle this. "Yes, we did go out for competitive bids, but I do not have them with me. I'll have to forward those to you when I have access to them."

"Very good, Mr. Robinson. Thank you. Can you tell me if these twelve contracts you approved were the low bids?"

"No, Mr. Braxton, not in all cases. We tried to choose the contractors that offered the best value. Sometimes those are not the lowest price."

"I see. Can you give me an example of one of the contracts that was not the low bid, but was selected based on value?"

"Uh, let's see. Um, you know, I would have to review the data. I can't answer that off the top of my head."

"I see. Now of these twelve contractors, did any of them have any prior business transactions with LBF?"

"I'm not sure. It's possible."

Jon ignored the last answer and continued, rapid-fire. "Since some or all of these contractors were new to doing business with LBF, did you ask for and check any of their references?"

"Uh, I think so. I don't recall."

Jon again ignored Darby's non-answer. "Can you give me the names of any of the representatives of any of these contractors you negotiated with?"

"Uh, I'd have to check my notes for that information."

"Did you do any price negotiation on any of these contracts?"

Michaelson, seeing his young protégé besieged by Jon's relentless questioning, intervened. "Mr. Braxton, good god." The pastor raised an eyebrow in Hanley's direction. "What are you trying to do here? It's clear you have a preconceived notion about these contracts. It would be only fair to allow Mr. Robinson to gather his thoughts so he can answer your questions thoughtfully and intelligently."

"Mr. Michaelson, you're right. Allow me to apologize. I have just one more question for Mr. Robinson. May I?"

"Of course."

Jeffrey knew what was coming. He bowed his head and clasped his hands in prayer.

"Mr. Robinson, were you aware of the shadow agreements attached to these contracts, ones that had these contractors agreeing to pay a large portion of the proceeds back to your mayoral campaign and to Mr. Michaelson's firm?"

Both Michaelson and Robinson were stunned Jon had become aware of the side deals—having done so thanks to Carlton Hale's relationship with one of the partners at the law firm Michaelson used. Michaelson thought Jon might be bluffing or, at least, could not prove his claim.

"That's preposterous, Mr. Braxton. How dare you make that allegation."

Jon was growing tired of the charade and decided to end it. "Mr. Michaelson, Mr. Robinson, I have a proposition for you." Jon pulled one of the written side agreements from one of the manila folders and slid it across the table to Hanley. "Are you open to one?"

Robinson, now frozen in panic, was unable to do anything but sit still and silent. Michaelson, an old war horse having been involved in numerous shady transactions over the course of his dubious career, was not. He reviewed the signed side agreement implicating him in the kickback scheme, and knew it was time to capitulate and limit the damage.

"What do you have in mind, Mr. Braxton?"

"The pastor is willing to disregard this malfeasance under the following conditions. First, all contractors will provide recession letters offering LBF out of the contracts with no liability. Second, all contractors will remit a charitable tax-deductible contribution to LBF in the amount of the donation they were going to make to Darby's campaign fund under your scheme. Third, Hanley Michaelson and Associates will make a $30,000 charitable tax-deductible contribution to LBF. And fourth, Darby, you will submit your letter of resignation from the LBF board effective immediately. Gentlemen, as time is of the essence on these matters, all recession letters and contribution checks must be delivered to Faith Central within two weeks from today. If this is taken care of, neither the pastor nor I nor the Hales will ever discuss this matter with anyone outside this room. If you are, for whatever reason, unable to accommodate us, then these contracts and side agreements will be shared with the Rogers' campaign, the media, and the city district attorney. Do we have an understanding?"

"You drive a hard bargain, Mr. Braxton. We should negotiate these terms. I feel they are unreasonable."

"I'm sorry, Mr. Michaelson. The only thing unreasonable is the fact you were attempting to deceitfully redirect funds contributed to this organization to serve the needs of this community into your own pocket. We are not negotiable. You have two weeks. Good luck."

Jon gathered the manila folders and put them back in his shoulder bag. It was clear he was finished discussing the matter. He hoped Michaelson would deliver the recession letters and the checks. If not, Jon would share the information, ruining Darby Robinson's career in politics and staining the reputations of Michaelson and his crony contractors. And likely sending Michaelson, and perhaps Darby Robinson, to prison.

Michaelson realized it was 'checkmate' and moved towards the conference room door. Robinson was still sitting, eyes fixed on the table. "Darby, are you coming?"

"No."

After Michaelson left, Darby asked the pastor to forgive him. He promised to resign from the board immediately. He decided on the spot he would drop out of the mayor's race and cut all ties with Hanley Michaelson. Darby realized his PR business would suffer losing Michaelson's association, but felt it was a small price to pay to win the pastor's trust back. Darby offered apologies to Jon and committed to providing him any information he requested about any of his previous LBF transgressions. The apology was accepted.

Darby left shortly thereafter, leaving Jon and the Pastor alone in the conference room.

"Thank you, Jon, for everything. I believe God made the right choice to bring you here. On top of everything else, you found a way to help Darby see some light. You have amazing talents. God, I'm certain, has big things in store for you."

"You're welcome, Jeffrey. I know this was trying for you. I regret we didn't even have much chance to discuss your programs and how you work with your kids. We need to do that soon. I'd like you to come visit our facility and meet Connie McIlroy. She's the executive director at Win-the-Day, and you two will have a lot to talk about. By the way, when you talk to Carl Hale, you can use this meeting as another reason I hate politics."

"Noted. What time is your flight back to Los Angeles?"

"Six."

"We have a couple of hours. Let's go back to my office and chat."

Jeffrey and Jon made their way from the conference room at Faith Central back to Jeffrey's office at First Pentecostal. The windowless office was small, dark, and musty, with thirty-year-old navy-blue shag carpeting. The room barely had space for the pastor's old walnut-stained desk, the bookshelves behind it, and the two un-upholstered wooden guest chairs in front. In the corner of the room was a floor standing brass lamp that provided only moderate illumination. The desk was completely covered in books and papers, some stacks approaching six inches in height.

The pastor led the way by unlocking his office door and walking in. Jon followed.

Jeffrey extended a hand towards one of the guest chairs as he navigated the cluttered office to his chair, also lacking upholstery but not four squeaking roller wheels, which moaned when the pastor loaded his large frame onto the seat. "Please excuse my mess. I hope you won't judge me by the lack of organization of my desk. I tend to focus more on organizing my thoughts. I trust your desk looks nothing like mine."

"Thanks only to my executive assistant."

"Yes Mrs. Martin. She was a pleasure to work with. Jon, I wanted to take this time with you to revisit the call you and I had last week. Specifically, I want to ask you about your parents. I sense unresolved conflict related to their premature death and your subsequent upbringing. These conflicts, stemming from incidents early in life, often lead to emotional distress and difficulty in later years. But they can also serve as motivation for great accomplishment and personal growth, which I believe to be the case with you. For you to continue your life's work, I believe you must come to an understanding how your life's experiences have molded you. I don't believe you have that understanding. I would very much enjoy discussing your feelings and experiences and learning more about your personal journey through time. I realize for you, as a man who has not had much exposure to spirituality, this may seem somewhat, shall we say, abstract. But it is my job to do this kind of work for people whom the Lord brings me into contact with. Are you open to letting me work?"

"I'd be a hypocrite to say no, considering you stood aside to let me do my work this morning with Michaelson. But you're right, this is abstract to me. I've never given much thought about my childhood or how it influenced me. I've never been one to reflect. I'm driven by action and results, and that focus forces me to look forward. Any thoughts I give you about my past will not be well formed."

"Fair enough, and that's fine. We must start somewhere. You mentioned your parents were killed when you were a young age. Tell me more about that and what happened to you after."

"I did not know the truth about what happened to them until I was eight. I was only four when they died. They were killed on a highway outside of L.A. by a drunk driver. I was home with a babysitter when it happened. A few hours after the accident, someone from the L.A. Department of Child Services picked me up. I spent a few days in their custody and then was placed in a foster care home in an area of L.A. called Sylmar. I lived there for three years and had to move because the custodian, Mary Shannon, contracted cancer and retired. From there until I was sixteen, I lived in three other foster homes."

"Is Mary Shannon still alive and do you have any contact with her?"

"No, she passed shortly after she closed her home."

"Your parents were killed when you were four, and you were placed in a strange house with people you had never met before. What were you told about what happened?"

"I was told my parents had to go away for a while, and they would come back one day to pick me up."

"When did you learn the truth?"

"I was eight and living in a foster home in Van Nuys with four other boys, all older. The foster mother was Teresa McBride. One day she took me to an office building, where we had an appointment with a counselor. It was a woman, and in that meeting, she told me my parents were no longer living and that I would be living with McBride for the foreseeable future. That's all I remember from that conversation."

"What a horrible burden for an eight-year-old to carry. Do you remember anything about your feelings or emotions when you learned this?"

"No. In fact, I had not thought of my parents for almost twenty years until you mentioned them on our call. Angela asked me about them when we were dating, and I shut her down. I told her they died when I was four and I had no memories of them. It was not something I wanted to talk about."

"Does she ever ask you about your childhood or adolescence?"

"She brings it up occasionally, but I always change the subject."

"And she never presses you?"

"She does, but I resist."

"When you had the meeting with the counselor and she told you your parents were gone, did she say when? Did you learn it had happened four years before?"

Jon had never made the connection that, from the time of the accident when he was four until he was eight, he maintained hope his parents would return for him and that he had lived with that combination of hope and disappointment every day for four years. Memories that he had completely erased now came rushing back. Jon had been looking at the pastor when these newfound memories came into focus. He bowed his head.

———≈———

It's wintertime and the house is cold. Frigid air flows through the poorly flashed door sills and porous window frames unabated. I'm almost awake, but not quite. I haven't yet had my early morning visit from Monty. I know he's coming. He always does. First, I see his face and then I see his fate. Suddenly, I'm awake, shivering. The cold outside air has formed a cloud inside, which has now enshrouded me. My six-year-old body is frozen, frozen in fear, frozen with remorse, frozen from uncertainty. My memories of warmth and comfort are distant and fleeting. Where are my parents? Why haven't they come for me? Are they mad at me for what happened to Monty? They couldn't be. They didn't know Monty. Or did they? That must be it. Why else would they not come?

———≈———

"Take me all the way through from the point you were told they were gone until you met Angela."

Jon raised his head to return his moistened eyes to Jeffrey's. "I was taken out of McBride's house shortly after that appointment. I started fighting a lot with the other boys I was living with. Sometimes the fights would get pretty bad. I was getting hurt, and the house was taking a beating. From there, I moved to another foster care home back in Sylmar but wasn't there long. Couldn't get along with the other kids."

"You moved back to Sylmar when you were nine. You were enraged at having been deceived by DCS that your parents were alive between the ages of four and eight. What do you remember about your time back in Sylmar?"

"I had the same problems. Always fighting. I didn't have any friends, was alone most of the time. I don't really have any memories of that time back in Sylmar other than those."

"You mentioned you lived in four foster care homes. What do you remember about the fourth?"

"I was thirteen when DCS moved me again. This time to North Hollywood. It was a little better because I was the oldest. When I was fourteen, an old friend of my father's showed up. His name was Henry Hairston. He told me he knew both my mom and dad for about eight years before they died. He told me my dad was a litigator in a law firm in downtown L.A. and that he met my mother in Honolulu when he was there on business. She was native Hawaiian and was working as a psychologist in the Honolulu school district. He said he had a recent dream about my dad, which had inspired him to find me and see how I was doing."

"Your father was a litigator. That certainly explains your negotiating skills."

"And my mother was Hawaiian and a psychologist."

"Why do you mention that? Is there any significance?"

Jon was struck by his realization. He squinted, swiveled his head slightly and responded as if perplexed: "Angie, her parents are Japanese, and she was starting to study psychology at UCLA when we met."

"What about Henry Hairston stands out for you?"

"For three years, before he moved to the East Coast to care for his elderly parents, he was a father figure to me. When I was sixteen, he was able to have DCS release me into his custody. I lived with him and his wife for a little over a year before they moved to the east coast to take care of Henry's father. After that, I lived with a high school friend and his mother until I graduated."

"What do you recall about your relationship with Henry from the point when you first met him?"

"We did a lot of fishing. He taught me how to drive. He made sure I had decent clothes to wear. He shared his love of baseball with me. He bought me my first car and my first computer, an IBM PC/XT, which I spent hundreds of hours learning how to use and repair. He taught me things I had never considered. He urged me to take school more seriously. But the thing I remember most about Henry is a book he made me read."

"I take it was not the Bible." The two shared a smile.

"It was a book about the subconscious mind. After I finished reading it, everything seemed to change. Up until that time, life seemed so random, so disjointed. It was hard to hope, hard to think positively. But what I read in this book resonated with me. I started to put the recommendations into practice. I developed a positive mental outlook. I started to do well in high school. I made friends, attracted a couple of girlfriends, started playing baseball and surfing. My whole outlook on life changed. I stopped being angry and started to enjoy living. I came to the realization that I was able to make myself whatever I wanted to be." Jon stopped abruptly and again swiveled his head as if confused.

"What are you thinking, Jon?"

"I never thought about or considered what I learned from Henry when I came up with the concept for Win-the-Day." Jeffrey closed his eyes and nodded in Jon's direction.

"What was your path to UCLA and Angela?"

"Henry lived in an area of L.A. called Woodland Hills. When I went to live with him, he enrolled me into Taft High School. Everything started jelling. My grades were all As and Bs. I played two years of varsity baseball, got more involved with computer technology, which was just starting to move into the mainstream. I realized I liked journalism and was the editor of the school newspaper my senior year. I was always focused on my grades and ended up with a full-ride journalism scholarship to UCLA. My first day there, I met Angela."

"How much of this does Angela know?"

"Not much," Jon uttered as he processed his internal confusion and disappointment of why he never shared with Angela much of what he had just recounted for Jeffrey. "I've never been comfortable talking to her about my past. I've always felt ashamed about my upbringing."

"Jon, I'd like you to go back and revisit your experiences again, and this time reflect on how these experiences have shaped your life. Will you do that for me?"

"One of my earliest memories was when I was four and living in Mary Shannon's house with four older girls. One day, a new boy came to live with us. He was six months younger than I and we became friends. Monty. Four months after that, he was killed by a car in the street in front of our house. He was chasing a ball I had accidentally kicked that made it out to the street. I always felt responsible. Thirty years later, I start having dreams about Monty and decide to find out about his family. I'm not sure what drove me, but it led me to find he had a nephew who they named after him, middle name. His nephew, Jamal Montgomery Peterson, was living not too far from where we did. He was a troubled kid, tough neighborhood, unfit parents, gangs, drugs—who you work with every day. I met his grandfather and he told me Jamal's story. Six months later, I am starting Win-the-Day with the intent of having Jamal as our first student."

"When you were fourteen, someone from your past, Henry, sought you out. He was motivated by something to help you. Is there a correlation between that and your inspiration to find and help Jamal?"

Jon nodded with realization. All at once he recognized how his past was linked to his present.

"You said Henry taught you fishing. Do you still like to?"

"Angie, Luke, Darla, and I go at least every other month."

"What else comes to mind, Jon?"

"If Henry hadn't bought me a computer, I'd probably be washing dishes?"

"Well, I don't really see you as a dishwasher, but the fact that you started learning computer technology when you did is a large contributing factor to where you are now. What else?"

"I don't drink alcohol. Guess that's what happens when your parents are killed by a drunk driver."

"Jon, the reason I wanted you to go down this road with me is because you are doing important work, and for you to do your best work, you must be closely in touch with your soul. From what little interaction I've had with you, I feel like you have not yet made your connections. And that is what you should do with your life starting now. Connect. Connect with your innermost being. To do that you must realize how and why you are the person you are now. Connect to what has molded you. Connect to what has influenced and shaped you. It is the way for you to better understand yourself, and from there you can better understand others. Lord knows, since there are so few people like you, it's important for you to always improve your leadership qualities."

Jon was again reflecting. "It's exactly what we teach at Win-The-Day, but I had never considered the lessons for myself."

"Subconsciously, you built the content as if it were for your fourteen-year-old self. And only once you were satisfied it was good enough for you, did you decide it was good enough for others. And you then launched the foundation."

Claymore looked at his watch. "Where did the time go? We better wrap up. You need to start for the airport. Come, I'll walk out with you." He pulled his huge frame up from his chair, and Jon followed. The two walked out of the church and started for the Faith Central parking lot and Jon's rental car.

"Jon, promise me you will share your story. Share it with Angela, share it with your children, share it with WTD. There are so many important life lessons you have to offer. Will you promise to do this?"

"I will, if you promise me something Jeffrey."

"And what is that Mr. Litigator?"

"Consider never again saying you are not wise in the ways of man."

Twenty-seven

Jon took the day off on Monday. Abby Martin did not. Jon tasked her to provide him an update on how the second quarter for Spectre was looking and to fill him in on any minutiae that transpired since he left for Philadelphia the previous Wednesday. She spent an hour on Monday pulling together everything she knew her boss would like to know. They met at ten on Tuesday.

"OK, Mrs. Martin, what's going on I need to know?"

"Well, your highness, it's been rather dull and boring around here lately. Let's see. The $4.5 million Shopify purchase order came in on Friday. Sales projections for the second quarter in all regions are on a run rate of 120 percent of plan. The Spock market is up forty-two percent for the year. Lloyd and Jamie resolved their differences in the warehouse and are friends again. Miranda said Lloyd is executing well on his success plan. Larry Morris closed three more companies last week to move here and bring 800 more jobs with them. According to Rob, Earl is revitalized and is putting pedal to the metal on campaigning. The Gregory campaign event which is coming up in three weeks is getting tons of attention from the media, people wanting tickets, and vendors hoping to sell their wares. Connie weighed in and said this session's in-out assessment metrics would be their best since WTD started. Three of our people submitted Charity Sabbatical business plans last week. News of your efforts in Philadelphia last week made it to the Hales and they wired $200K to WTD. Pastor Claymore reached out to me yesterday to schedule a trip to meet with you out here. And

I took a prank call from Washington, D.C. yesterday, supposedly from the State Department. Imagine that. Pranked me about wanting to set up a call for you. Other than that, not much going on around here, your lordship. Like I said, kinda boring."

"The State Department? Well I did briefly meet Heather Carrington while I was in Philadelphia."

"Holy Schnikees, Batman. The Congressman, the Hale brothers, and now the former First Lady? My, my, my, we certainly know faces in high places now. Don't we?"

"I know, right? It's crazy. Go ahead and schedule a call for me with the Secretary."

———≈———

"Mom, I don't feel good."

Lucas Braxton was standing at the edge of his parents' bed as he tried to quietly wake Angela by shaking her arm. It was three in the morning. Angela awoke slowly and sleepily. "What's the matter, Luke?"

"I don't feel good. I can't sleep. I've been really thirsty the last few days and dizzy and I keep having to pee. I think I pee'd in my bed a few minutes ago, and my vision is real blurry."

Angela woke herself, sat up in bed, and moved her feet to the floor. She looked over at her husband, still sound asleep, and decided to not to wake him.

"C'mon, honey, let's go downstairs."

On the way, Angela checked Luke's bed and it was wet. A first. She quickly removed the sheets and helped him change clothes before they descended. She poured Luke a glass of water, and they went into the family room to sit down on the couch.

"OK, honey, tell me what's going on with you. When did you first notice these changes?"

"About four days ago, I think. I started getting real thirsty and tired. I started having to drink lots of water. When I would stand up, I would get dizzy. I always have to pee. Sometimes I can't control it. And I just don't feel good."

"Why didn't you tell me sooner honey?"

"I thought it would go away."

Angela got up and retrieved her laptop computer from the kitchen nook and came back to sit next to Luke. She told him to lay down next to her and try to go to sleep. She turned on her laptop and went online in search of answers. After fifteen minutes, she shut it down and had Luke, still awake, put his head in her lap. She stared into the future, tears forming.

Luke fell asleep after a few minutes and she let him sleep peacefully in her lap until five, when she woke him and took him back to his bedroom. She put new sheets on the bed and tucked him in. She then went downstairs and called their family doctor's answering service requesting an appointment. She stayed downstairs until six when she went upstairs to wake Jon. She described to him in detail her encounter with Luke three hours earlier and what she had discovered about Luke's symptoms. They went downstairs together and waited for the return call at the kitchen table.

The call from the doctor came at seven. Angela described all to Dr. Eleanor Crane, their family doctor since they moved to the area in 1999. "Bring Luke over to my office now. I'll meet you there at eight. I'll have my team to take blood and check his vitals when you get there. Not to alarm you, but we need to diagnose immediately. See you soon."

———— ≈ ————

At eleven Dr. Crane came out to the waiting area to speak with Jon and Angela. She sat down in a chair directly facing them, with a grim but professional expression.

"Angela, Jon, we're preliminarily diagnosing Luke with having contracted Type one diabetes."

The memory of his first meeting Monty and seeing him injected with insulin rushed into Jon's head.

"We'll wait for the results from his blood work to positively confirm, but we are quite certain of this diagnosis. Understand Type 1 is treatable, and Luke can live a long, mostly normal life. There are tremendous advancements in the medical community for better therapeutics and a cure. The science is advancing rapidly. It's possible we'll see a cure in Luke's lifetime. But you need to know that T1D is a life-threatening disease, and there currently is no cure. Read the material I'm going to give you. It's imperative you take time to fully understand this disease. The other thing to understand is effectively treating the disease will require tremendous discipline on your part. And Luke's as well. Blood sugar levels change quickly. It's critical you be ready to administer insulin when it's called for. Twenty-four by seven by 365. T1D does not take days off. It will also be critical to control Luke's carbohydrate intake. Luke's condition is preventing his body from efficiently converting carbohydrates into glucose. His pancreas is under attack from his immune system, and the cells produced by his pancreas to perform the glucose conversion are compromised. Unconverted sugar released into the bloodstream puts tremendous strain on the body's organs. Now it is up to you, and Luke, to take over the work of his pancreas. There is no other way to say this. Your lives will never be the same. I am so sorry. I need you to stay for a few hours. We're going to train you to monitor his blood sugar levels and when and how to administer insulin."

Luke, Angela, and Jon left Dr. Crane's office at four and headed home, with Luke's positively confirmed diagnosis. Luke was feeling better after having his first insulin treatment. After a conversation with Dr. Crane and his parents about his condition, he had a superficial awareness of what was happening and what he was facing.

The next few weeks in the Braxton household were chaotic. Everyone was getting used to new protocols around eating, drinking, poking, and injecting. Finger pricking, blood testing, and administering insulin shots became regularities. As did moments of fear, uncertainty, and anger.

Luke had the good fortune of having two strong-willed parents, and as a family unit they developed a rhythm that allowed them to quickly come to grips with their new reality. Luke with the resoluteness of his parents, quickly learned to perform his new tasks responsibly. He accepted the routine of pricking his finger and checking his blood levels every two hours, and he learned how to self-administer his insulin shots when needed.

Jon and Angela were both experiencing unsynchronized moments of despair and frustration, but they leaned on one another for support when these moments became protracted. One evening at home two weeks after Luke's diagnosis, Jon and Angela were in their family room after Luke and Darla had gone to bed. "Honey, I'd like to tell you about my time with Pastor Claymore in Philadelphia a few weeks ago." He hadn't shared much about his trip, as Luke's situation consumed them shortly after he returned.

"Something about that man has been on my mind. Some of the things he asked me and said to me knocked me back on my heels. Before we could talk business, he wanted to know about my faith. And the way he brought it up made me think of my parents and how they died, and it made me think about a lot of what-ifs. It also made me think of you and I, and what we believe, why we are here, and why we do the things we do. Now, with Luke, I've been thinking a lot about the pastor again. I really would like for us to talk to Claymore together. Would you be OK with that?"

"Of course, Jon. If he can bring you comfort and understanding, then of course."

"Hopefully bring 'us.'"

———≈———

The next morning, Jon headed for the office for the first time in the fourteen days since Luke's diagnosis. When he walked into the Spectre executive office reception area, his eyes met with Abby's and she jumped out of her chair, approaching him with her arms open. They embraced for a few seconds and then released. "Welcome back. I'm so sorry, Jon. How is Luke? How are you and Angie doing?"

"We're coping. Doing our best. This type 1 diabetes is a monster. And it seems to mostly go after young kids. So far, Luke's resolve is holding. He's managing finger pricks and insulin shots as well as any twelve-year-old could. Unfortunately, there is no cure for Type 1, but he's optimistic about the future. Though I'm not sure why."

"JB Jr., I'd say", Abby responded, trying to lift the mood. "Jon, I did something you may be upset with, but I hope not. Pastor Claymore happened to call in for you and I ended up in a conversation with him about Luke's situation. He is moving his trip up out here to next week. He wants to meet your family. I hope you're OK with it."

"Perfectly OK, Abby. Thank you. He's been on my mind, and I had the thought of asking him to come out soon. As usual, you're one step ahead of me."

———≈———

The following Wednesday afternoon, Jeffrey Claymore landed at LAX. Per Jon's insistence, he and Angela picked him up. They were waiting in the baggage area when Claymore arrived. When the pastor saw Jon, he smiled and approached him. The two men hugged for what seemed like an eternity. Angela watched, thinking she had never seen Jon react in such a manner to anyone outside of her and the kids. As she watched the two of them, she couldn't help but think her husband's soul had been touched by this man of faith. The two of them finally stepped back and the pastor turned to Angela. Without saying a word, he moved to embrace her, which she accepted gratefully. In his embrace, she felt his spiritual presence as well.

The three of them made their way to the parking structure and then began the two-hour drive—thanks to L.A. traffic—back to Thousand Oaks. The pastor had decided to reserve his consoling words for Jon and Angela until they were back in the Braxton home, and he had the opportunity to meet the family. He was especially looking forward to meeting and speaking with Luke. During the drive, the conversation was mostly about Jon and Angela's story, pre-diabetes.

They shared all their highlights as a couple with the pastor. He asked leading questions and made observations that had Jon and Angela laughing for the first time since Luke's diagnosis—a fact both Jon and Angela acknowledged afterward as the first installment of the comfort package the pastor had brought for them.

As Jon had been preoccupied the last two weeks, he had not yet asked the pastor what eventually happened with the Hanley and Darby situation. "Well, Jon, thanks to you, Liberty Bell has received some sizable donations from a lot of organizations that had never supported us before—and without the need for any quid pro quo! My godson seems to have become a new man, rededicating himself to the church and becoming active again with our kids. So, I guess you might say mission accomplished." He turned to face Angela, riding in the back seat. "Angela, your husband is somewhat of a miracle man."

"He has the same thoughts of you."

The three of them arrived back at the Braxton household. Jon had insisted the pastor stay with them during his visit as they had a spare bedroom and plenty of space. Claymore gratefully accepted the offer.

Once they were settled and finished with dinner, Jeffrey asked Jon and Angela if he could have some time alone with Luke. During dinner, the pastor avoided any mention of Luke's condition and the conversation stayed on the lighter side. As during the ride from the airport, the pastor asked both Luke and Darla about their lives, without introducing any discussion about diabetes. Luke had brought it up briefly in passing, and the pastor, to redirect the conversation, responded that they had plenty of time to discuss that later. But now, he was more interested in the other aspects of Luke's life.

It was an intentional redirection, designed to minimize the importance of the diagnosis in Luke's mind. The pastor attempted to make that point by not discussing it at the table with all present. The words Jeffrey had in mind for Luke would be best delivered when the two of them were alone, after he opened Luke's heart to pour his wisdom in. Jon and Angela, listening and watching Jeffrey in action, understood perfectly.

A few minutes later, he had that opportunity, as Luke and the pastor retired to Luke's room.

"I like your room, Luke, and I really love your mom and dad. They're very special people, and you are very lucky to have them as parents. And you are lucky to have a little sister who adores you. You know she does, right?"

"Yeah."

"Has your dad told you much about me?"

"Only a little. He said you live in a very poor area in Philadelphia, and you do a lot of stuff kinda like my dad does with Win-the-Day."

"That's right. And tell me, do you know much about Win-the-Day?"

"A little. I know he works with kids that grow up poor and without a mom or a dad or both."

"That's right. He does tremendous work. There are many people who think your dad is a rock star, myself included." Luke smiled.

"Luke, do you ever think about the universe?"

"Sometimes. I like looking at the stars."

"Do you ever think about where all the stars come from? Where the Earth we live on comes from? Who made it? How did it get here?"

"Sometimes. I know my dad's foundation asks the same kinds of questions. But I haven't thought too much about it."

"I think you should start to think more about it, because I know in your mind you have lots of questions about diabetes, questions that are really hard to answer. Questions like, why do I have it? How did I get it? Why do other kids at random get this? Why are some kids sick, while some are not? I know you have these kinds of questions, and when you talk to your mom or your dad or to the doctors, they are not going to have the answers for you. I can't even give you the answers, and I talk to God all the time."

"What do you say when you talk to God?"

"Well, I always thank him. I thank him for all our blessings. And I always ask him to watch over people, particularly the people I know who need help. And by help, I mean help in understanding life. I ask him to make people happy and comfortable in their own skin. Do you understand what I mean by that?"

"Kinda. I think it's like liking yourself?"

"Exactly right, Luke. Happiness and love—and I'll throw spirituality in there as well—are the keys to a life well-lived. And I think that is what we as people should strive for. For you to love others you must love yourself. To love yourself, you must accept and embrace who you are and always strive to be the best person you can be. Do you ever notice in the world there are people who have no material things, people who are very poor, yet are very happy? And then do you notice there are some people who have many material things and are always unhappy? Can you think of anyone you know that fits those descriptions?"

"Yeah."

"Will you believe me when I tell you that happiness comes from within? Your happiness is not determined by what happens to you, it comes from how you feel about what happens to you. And since you can control how you feel, even though you cannot control what happens, you have the power to be happy, to love and to feel fulfilled inside you. All people have this tremendous power inside. Does that make sense?"

"I think so."

"Luke, I'd like you to do something for me, and I am going to do something for you. OK?"

"OK."

"What I'd like you to do for me is to think about what we talked about as often as you can. Think about how big the universe is. Think about how it started and how well it operates, things like the sun rising and setting every day. Things like being part of a loving family and how that allows kids like you to grow up and reach their goals. And try to think about these kinds of things whenever you start to feel mad or sad about diabetes. Think about all your blessings. Always think of your mom and your dad. They are going to feed off your strength. I know this situation is tough for you, but it is even tougher for them. Please believe that. You know how you feel, but they truly don't. They are in the dark, and their only light is your attitude. Whenever you get mad or sad, think of them and how you can help them feel better by showing them even though diabetes is hard to live with, you can handle it because you are strong, and you are smart, and you know that feeling sorry for yourself or sad or mad doesn't help anyone. I like to call this thinking big. Always try to think big. The best way to do that is to not think about yourself or your situation. Always think about helping others. Always think about how you can make your dad and mom feel better. And this will always make you feel better. Always believe that you are in control and the way you exercise your control is through your thoughts. Always try to think good thoughts."

"Is that what my dad means when he talks about being selfless?"

"One hundred percent. That's exactly what it means. By being selfless, you are free to help others. And when you help others, you will know no greater happiness for yourself. Make sense?"

"Yeah."

"And as for what I am going to do for you, Luke, I am going to talk to God about you. I am going to ask him to give you the courage and strength fight diabetes by using your thoughts, and to always have the mental toughness to take control of your thoughts and to make sure you show the people who love you that you are going to be fine. Is it OK for me to do that for you?"

"Yeah."

"Good. Well, I'm going to excuse myself now and go to sleep. I had to get up early this morning to catch the airplane, and your dad has a full day for me tomorrow. Good night, Luke, and may God bless you."

"Good night, pastor. Thank you."

The next morning at nine a large limousine carrying Carlton and Cornelius Hale, and Congressman Gregory, unexpectedly pulled into the Braxton's driveway. The Hales were in Thousand Oaks for the Gregory rally, and when they heard that Jeffrey would be in Thousand Oaks at the same time, they moved their trip up. When they learned Jon was taking the pastor to Win-the-Day to learn more about the operation and meet Connie, they invited themselves along, offering to supply the limo and driver to transport the five of them comfortably. They also saw the opportunity to express their best wishes to Jon and Angela in light of Luke's diagnosis.

Within a few minutes Jon, the pastor, the Congressman and the Hales embarked on the thirty-five-minute trip to Oxnard. The Hales wanted to hear from Jon about the showdown with Michaelson and Robinson, and to express their gratitude for the successful resolution of the matter concerning the attempted laundering of their contribution. Jon expressed his gratitude to the Hales for the $200k WTD contribution and suggested they be the ones to tell Connie, as she was not yet aware.

The five of them were in Oxnard the entire day. Connie described to Jeffrey all WTDs metrics, processes, and procedures. Connie and the pastor hit it off immediately, and Jon learned for the first time her fondness for her Protestant faith. Her training in public education had successfully suppressed her spirituality when it came to teaching and administering, and she had brought that secular inclination to WTD. Jon could sense through her exchanges with the pastor, she was interested in bringing more spirituality to the program, and fully expected she would soon approach him on the matter. He imagined he wouldn't object.

Jeffrey asked numerous probing questions, and between him, Connie, and Jon, the information exchange was plentiful, insightful, and productive.

On the ride back to Thousand Oaks, the Hales, and Congressman Gregory shared some light-hearted moments with the pastor. All three shared how their lives had intersected with Jonathon Braxton over the last three months. The pastor shared his meeting with Jon, Darby and Hanley, and his introduction of Jon to the former First Lady.

At a pause point in the conversation, Jon brought up something which had been bothering him the last few days. "Earl, I have a question for you."

"Fire away."

"I'm reading that Congress has an affinity for funding diabetes research. Over the past many years, the U.S. government has invested hundreds of millions, and yet the medical research community still has no plausible theories on what causes Type 1. No preventatives on the market. And no cures on the horizon. Also, I've done some research on embryonic stem cell therapy. Preliminary studies are promising, yet there doesn't seem to be any effort in Congress to fund this specific research as a pathway to a cure for Type 1. Or as a cure for many other conditions it could apply to. Why is that?"

Earl frowned, knowing the answer would not satisfy Jon, but

proceeded. "It's a sensitive subject, as you might imagine. Harvesting embryonic material for scientific research challenges many on the basis that embryos are considered human life. It presents a moral dilemma on both sides of the aisle, and no Congressman or woman has had the inclination or the motivation to take it on. Congress has held many hearings over the years and we have heard compelling arguments for and against from both the medical community and the Evangelicals, but the subject is simply too delicate. Bush 43 used his first veto to veto a measure put on his desk to ease the restriction on federal funding for embryonic stem cell research and instead instituted a restrictive federal funding ban."

"Congress tried again in 2007, passing a bill that would permit federal funding for research, but only on donated surplus embryonic stem cells from fertility clinics. In other words, no harvesting specifically for research and only on artificially inseminated embryos that were going to be discarded anyway. Bush vetoed that one as well."

"Obama had a completely different viewpoint. In 2009, he signed an executive order overturning Bush's ban and restoring embryonic stem cell funding with limitations. But no one is comfortable giving a full-throttled go-ahead, and funding from Congress specific to embryonic stem cell research has been sparse. Jeffrey, care to offer your perspective on the moral dilemma?"

"Jon, it comes down to the question when does human life begin. Is it at the time of conception? If that is the case, then does the clump of cells in the petri dish from which you'd extract the stem cells constitute a human life? If it does, the question of whether that life is being taken for the purpose of genetic material harvesting arises. To people of faith, the process constitutes a mortal sin. However, there are those who feel the state of those cells in the petri dish does not constitute a human life. There are arguments that the genetic constitution of these cells is not an embryo. If produced by artificial insemination and not yet implanted into a woman's uterus, are these cells a human life given, at their earliest stage of development, there are no recognizable human features. While the church considers this a human life, there are many in my community who have an opposing viewpoint."

"Over the years, I've had many conversations on this matter with members of my parish. We have many families impacted by Type 1 diabetes in Sharswood. It affects the black community hard. I have an internal conflict on the matter, and I am not certain that this type of research, for this purpose, should be considered sinful."

Neil jumped in. "Where is your question coming from, JB?"

"I'm frustrated there is no cure for Type 1 on the horizon, despite hundreds of millions having been invested in the U.S. And who knows how much abroad. Seems like the medical research community could use some assistance. Have you ever done any reading about pluripotent stem cells?"

Neil was intrigued. "I can't say I have. What have you learned?"

"There's a belief in the research community that pluripotent stem cells are the best avenue to a cure. I've been studying this since Luke's diagnosis. Pluripotent stem cells have the elasticity to evolve into multiple cell types based on signaling, among them, pancreatic cells. These cells can also reproduce themselves indefinitely. Studies have been started to test the hypothesis, but they're not well funded. On paper, these cells have great potential. I'm looking into avenues for driving more research."

The next morning was the day of Earl Gregory's campaign event in the Spectre parking lot. Abby and Rob had everything ready to go. At eight Jon, not planning to go to the rally, took a call from Neil Hale. "JB, can Carl, Earl, and I stop by this morning? Wanted to run something by you. Was hoping Angela and Pastor Claymore would join us as well. Would you have an hour for us?"

"Sure, Neil. Come on by."

Thirty minutes later, the Hale's Town Car pulled into Jon's driveway. Neil, Carl, and Earl exited, headed to the front door, and rang the doorbell. A moment later, the six of them were seated comfortably in the Braxtons' family room.

Neil started. "JB, last night Carl and I came up with an idea to share with you. It involved the conversation we had in the car yesterday, and we ran it by Earl to get his opinion. The three of us like it, and we're hoping you will as well. From what you told us yesterday, it appears you have created a new mission for yourself. We have tremendous confidence in your abilities, and the three of us believe you will accomplish whatever you choose to set your mind to. You advised us you want to help the medical research community in the U.S. find a cure for Type 1 diabetes. I'm sure you have determined that researching and finding a cure will require huge sums of money. Where's the best place to find that kind of money? It's where the printing presses are, the U.S. government. Typically, the way to squeeze money like this out of the government is to lobby. But lobbying is slow and it's dirty and it's political. And, we know, against your nature. However, there is another way. It's faster and more palatable."

Jon was intrigued. "Go on."

"In eight weeks, the Republican National Committee is holding its convention to formally nominate Mitt Romney as our party candidate for president. If you would be interested, Carl and I will pull some strings to get you a speaking slot at the convention. You will be able to make your case to increase federal government funding for diabetes research to all the delegates and the party apparatchik. If you make the right impression, along with some assistance from Mr. Gregory, you'd likely get a chance to attend a congressional hearing to make your arguments before the people that run the presses, cutting through the normal lobbying BS. From what we've seen of your speaking abilities, and knowing how important this matter is for you, well, we all know you'd do very well."

Congressman Gregory chimed in. "I've been in lots of hearings over the years and listened to hundreds of advocates. The right message from the right advocate can move Congress to do some crazy things. Speaking at the convention would put you into prime position to get a hearing. I'm on the right committee. I can make it happen for you."

Pastor Claymore, having heard the Hales idea for the first time, was inspired to add his sentiment. "Jon, you are a good man, and your heart is in the right place. You may or may not be successful in solving the moral dilemma for members of Congress, but you should take this opportunity. Advocate for what you believe is right. Your goal is to help people and to relieve suffering. It is a noble pursuit. If the method to be funded happens to be a sin in the eyes of God, what He will also see is one of His creations trying to help humanity. And perhaps God Himself will provide you the guidance to find the cure in a manner which He can and will give His blessing. Take the opportunity Jon. I believe it is your calling."

Jon looked to Angela sitting on his right for her reaction and got a nod of approval. At that moment, Luke came bouncing down the stairs heading to the kitchen. The sight of Luke at that instant settled it. Jon Braxton was going to Tampa to speak to the convention. And to the nation.

Twenty-eight

The Earl Gregory campaign rally held in the Spectre parking lot was a rousing success. All the speakers and exhibitors performed their tasks flawlessly, culminating with Congressman Gregory delivering an impassioned speech highlighting his years of service and his plans for his next term. He didn't make any mention of it being his last.

Jon was not physically in attendance, but he was part of the affair, as Larry Morris, Randy Boswell, and the Congressman all featured him and his contributions to the city's prosperity. Abby also joined the parade. She introduced Congressman Gregory to the stage, but not before some impassioned words of praise for her conspicuously missing boss, who was sportfishing in the Channel Islands with Luke and Jeffrey.

The Hale brothers enjoyed themselves immensely. They left the rally after the Congressman finished his remarks, having their driver whisk them to LAX for a flight to Atlanta. The flight they were on together before separating and connecting home. Heading to Atlanta, the conversation between the two power brokers was all about Jon and the convention.

They decided that they would work to build an aura of mystery around him, so when it was his time to speak, the crowd of delegates, and operatives on the floor would *sit down, shut up and listen*. They decided they would do whatever they could to position Jon in the right light both for his purposes and their own.

———≈———

The following day was Saturday. The pastor was flying home, and Jon drove him to LAX. During their drive, the conversation centered mostly on LBF and how the pastor, and Darby, could use some of WTD's methods to further improve the lives of the kids the pastor was mentoring. Jeffrey had some words of inspiration in mind for Jon but was reserving them until they were closer to the airport. He wanted to leave Jon with his own thoughts after he delivered them. When they were ten minutes away, Jeffrey changed the course of their conversation.

"Jon, I've been thinking a lot about the journey you have been on the last few months. Have you given much thought about it?"

"You know, Jeffrey, in the past, I wouldn't have. I've never been one to look backwards. If anything, I think the last few months, especially with our conversation in your office and now with Luke's situation, has made me more reflective. So yes, I have been thinking about things differently recently."

"Good. That is good for your soul. I have some perspectives on your journey. May I share them with you?"

"Yes, but please be gentle." The two shared a smile.

"Jon, the Lord works in mysterious ways. Given the situation with Luke, I know you might be questioning His ways. For the record, I never do. In my profession, we call this faith. Regarding Luke, here are my thoughts. Luke's contracting Type 1 is not random, and it is not coincidental. It is God's plan. I believe his plan includes the two of you to carry out His will and let us pray His will includes the world finding a cure for the disease."

"Jon, you are a remarkable human being. A gift to humanity. Now it is time for you to take your wisdom and your talents to another level. And Luke will help you. He will help you through his courage to accept and respond to his condition in such a manner that you will feel inspired to do the work you have set out to do. I am not enlightened enough to take a position on the type of medical research you will be fighting for. But I have faith. I have faith that God will show you the way. He would not have placed you on this path otherwise. And when you do your reflecting, and feel free to call it praying, I hope you will come to embrace and accept his plan. Oh, and one other thing: You have my permission to use the letters 'LBF'."

"What?"

"For the Lucas Braxton Foundation."

At that very moment, Jon had pulled up to the curbside, where he and the pastor would part company. The pastor had, as he had done at the close of their first meeting, left Jon speechless. He was only able to process Jeffrey's reflections and silently watch him amble out the car and grab his bag from the back seat.

Claymore closed the car door, leaned down to the open passenger-side car window, and placed his forearms on the door. The two made eye contact. "Find your faith, Jon. And then hold it dearly and never let it go. May God bless you."

Twenty-nine

The following Monday, Jon arrived at the office early. He wanted to catch up on Spectre business, which included making calls to the sales management and operations staff on the East Coast. He also wanted to sit down with Abby early in the day to get caught up on what she felt he needed to know. The last few days with Jeffery had taken him out of his comfort zone and he felt an urge to dive back in. A recap meeting with Abby was the ticket.

The usual banter between Jon and Abby had taken on a muted tone since Luke's diagnosis. Given the seriousness of Luke's condition, she felt it inappropriate to stick with the routine.

There was a knock at his office door. It was Abby with a freshly brewed café mocha in hand for her boss. When she pulled into the parking lot at 7:30 and saw Jon's car, she shifted her plans for the morning. She was not aware he was coming in and had planned her day as such. But she quickly changed course, the hot café mocha being the first shift. "I'm ready to meet when you are." She shuffled in and put the coffee on his desk.

"Thanks, Abby. Give me twenty minutes and then come in."

"You got it."

Their meeting started on time, and Abby spent the next thirty minutes filling Jon in on all the company happenings over the last few days, including a detailed recap of the Gregory rally. She asked Jon how Luke, Darla, and Angela were doing. As she was getting ready to wrap up, she brought up the pending call from the State Department.

"One last thing, I heard from Secretary Carrington's office. They asked if you'd be available for a fifteen-minute call Wednesday morning."

"Put it on my calendar. Also, show me as out of the office the week of August 26."

"Dare I ask where you'll be?"

"Speaking at the Republican National Convention in Tampa."

"Of course, I should have known."

———— ≈ ————

The conversations over the last few days with Jeffrey were sticking to Jon's consciousness. He replayed them in his head, over and over. The pastor had successfully inserted himself and his spirituality into Jon's thoughts as he was digesting the magnitude of the events that would soon be unfolding. He recognized the serious firepower now attached to his mission. The events looming were large, and Luke's health and well-being were connected. At times, Jon felt overwhelmed, an unfamiliar emotion, until the pastor's words of inevitability and spiritual guidance helped center him.

Another source of motivation for Jon was he and Angela meeting many other Type 1 families. Since Luke's diagnosis, they had been participating in the many support groups around Los Angeles. The stories he and Angela heard from other parents living the reality they were now facing proved emotional on many fronts. Inspiring, gut-wrenching, heartbreaking, frightful, and keenly motivational for Jon's new mission. A mission of advocating for the entire worldwide population of people impacted by Type 1 diabetes. He would soon be on a very big stage.

It was the summer of 2012 and Type 1 diabetes had no cure—but it had not yet faced off with Jonathon Braxton.

———— ≈ ————

The call from Washington, DC came at 8:30 a.m., Pacific time. Abby had given Marcie James, a member of Heather Carrington's senior staff, her direct number.

"Spectre Systems."

"Good morning, Mrs. Martin. It's Marcie James from Secretary Carrington's office."

"Good morning, Marcie. How are things in our nation's capital?"

"About what you'd expect. I have Secretary Carrington standing by to speak with Mr. Braxton. Can you patch him to me, and I'll relay the call?"

'Well then, all business'. "Certainly, stand by."

Abby put Marcie on hold and decided to let her hold a while. *'We have important business too,'* she thought. She took another line and called Jon. "Ready to help the State Department get their act in order?"

"Put Secretary Carrington through."

"Well, Mr. Braxton, it doesn't quite work that way. You have to talk to her admin first."

"OK, then put him or her through."

"It's a her. Marcie James. Stand by."

Abby bridged the three of them together, introduced Jon to Marcie, and dropped off the line.

"Good morning, Mr. Braxton. I'm Marcie James, senior administrative aide to Secretary Carrington. Please stand by while I bridge her on the line for you."

"Thank you, Ms. James."

"Mr. Braxton, good morning. This is Heather Carrington."

"Good morning, Madam Secretary."

"Mr. Braxton, it was good meeting you in Philadelphia a few weeks ago. I'm sure you're wondering why I was interested in speaking to you. The reason has nothing to do with official business, so please do not have any concern. My reason is purely personal. I've known Jeffrey Claymore for more than twenty years and am very fond of him, and he seems to be very fond of you. I don't know if you were aware, but it was I—unfortunately—who made the introduction of Hanley Michaelson to Jeffrey many years ago. Before you spoke with him about Hanley, I had become aware of his scheme and offered to help Jeffrey deal with it. He told me there was no need because he already had someone to take care of things, referring to you."

"I spoke with Jeffrey soon after your visit, and he advised me you had efficiently taken care of everything and even managed to turn things around where LBF was receiving contributions from the organizations which were planning the extorting. From lemons to lemonade is how he characterized it. And knowing how slimy Michaelson is, well, I just had to call you and thank you for helping my friend. Jeffrey has been telling me about your business, your philanthropic efforts, and your assistance with Jeffrey's foundation. You sound like quite a guy, Mr. Braxton. Jeffrey is very important to me, and I'm grateful you have come into his life. Between you and I, he's been my spiritual advisor, and that's a big task as I'm not sure I have a spiritual bone in my body. I would very much like to get to know you better. If you're ever in DC, please get in touch with Marcie. Maybe we can grab coffee sometime. Oh, and now I'm late for a call with the British Prime Minister. Very nice talking to you, Mr. Braxton. Stay well." Click.

"Nice speaking with you, Madam," Jon muttered into the handset, with no one on the receiving end.

Abby saw Jon's phone line go dark, got up from her desk approached his closed office door. She, knocked twice, opened the door twelve inches, and popped her head in. "Well?"

"She wants to buy me a Starbucks."

"Hello and thank you for calling the RNC," answered the phone operator for the Republican National Committee in Washington DC.

"This is Carlton Hale calling for Lance Reibus." The senior Hale had the stronger relationship with the Chairman of the RNC, so the brothers decided Carl would make the call.

"Yes, Mr. Hale. I know he'll want to speak with you. Stand by."

Reibus had been the chairman of the RNC for many years. The upcoming convention was his show. Lance was eager to speak with Carl. The Hale brothers were good for at least a million every four years to help fund it. They hadn't yet sent in this year's contribution.

"Carl. Good to hear from you. How are you and your esteemed younger brother?"

"We're fine, Lance, thank you. How are the preparations coming along for the convention?"

"Everything is moving forward. Slower than we'd like, but fast enough to keep us from panicking. What can I do for you?"

"I've got an ask, and it's a big one."

"OK, shoot."

"I need a speaking slot at the convention."

"Not for you or Neil I'm guessing."

"No. For someone we want to showcase to the party. And to the country."

"I always appreciate your support for the committee. But that's a little beyond what we can do this year."

"Lance, I'm sure you know we have not yet sent you our customary convention contribution."

"I was hoping you'd bring it up. I was getting concerned. I know you don't like Romney's chances."

"You're right. I don't like Romney and we need a speaking slot."

"Are you saying what I think you're saying."

"Yes."

"The only slot I have open is Monday at two."

"Wednesday in prime time would be perfect. Thank you, Lance."

"You're joking, right? Ryan is accepting for VP on Wednesday. Do you realize how many eyeballs will be on your guy?"

"Probably not enough. His name is Jonathon Braxton. I'll expect to see a conference schedule with his name on it for Wednesday during prime time. It's worth two mil."

"What's he going to speak on?"

"If I remember correctly, you have a young niece with Type 1 diabetes."

"What's that got to do with anything?"

"You'll have to trust me. And you can thank me after you hear Braxton. And one other thing. He doesn't use a prompter."

"You're shitting me."

Thirty

I t was the Friday of the week prior to the convention, fifty-three days since Luke's T1D diagnosis. State delegates, Republican Party operatives, media, and other political figures began checking into their hotel rooms in and around the Tampa Convention Center. Many arrived early to prepare for the official conference opening ceremonies the following Monday. Others arrived early to vacation and party.

All the state delegates and other members of the party granted access to the show floor had a package from Lance Reibus awaiting them in their hotel rooms. The package included numerous items to be expected—toiletries, party swag, collector items, show agendas, specific instructions by state delegation and—an elegant 9" x 12" framed picture, courtesy of Carl and Neil Hale.

Over the following days the delegates and party operatives began to socialize, and a strong buzz emerged. "Who is this 'JB' character speaking on Wednesday?" "Is it a guy or a gal?" "What's her story?" "Never heard of him." "What's she going to talk about?" "Who the hell is he?"

Those who took the trouble to look more closely at the conference agenda noticed a very brief small-print bio. It listed *'Jonathon Braxton, Southern California Business Executive, Tech Sector.'* There was no other mention than that, adding to the intrigue spreading amongst the convention delegates, the media and the Republican party operatives in Tampa for the big event.

Jon, Angela, and Luke arrived in Tampa on Tuesday. Neil Hale had reserved them the Bayview Luxury Suite at the Grand Hyatt Hotel. He also arranged a limo to bring them to the hotel from the airport. The Braxtons checked into their suite at six and settled in. Jon would work on his speech's finishing touches on Wednesday morning. Angela and Luke were going to sightsee, purposely staying away from the suite to allow Jon to sharpen his thoughts.

As was his custom, Jon constructed his speech using a mental outline. Lance Reibus had asked Carl Hale for a transcript to review.

"No can do, Lance. The man writes his speeches in his head. Just sit back and enjoy the journey."

This only added to Reibus' stress: "You're shoving an unknown speaker down my throat, in prime time no less, and you can't give me a fucking clue what he's going to say. I'm not sure the $2 mil is worth it."

"Lance, relax."

———≈———

Angela and Luke made it back to the suite by two. Jon was in the shower. Angela had Luke check his blood sugar levels. His readings were high, and Angela administered an insulin shot.

The pastor's words came to Luke's mind as Angela injected insulin into his stomach. He could see and feel her fear. "Mom, I want you to know that I'm fine and I'm going to fight diabetes until dad finds the cure. I won't let it make me sad. Please don't let it make you sad."

Angela finished the injection. She looked at Luke, smiled faintly, and gave a brief nod. "I know, honey. You're a tough young man, and you're going to be just like your dad. I am so proud of you and the way you are handling things. I want to be strong like you. Keep reminding me, OK? Now let's start getting ready to go watch your dad light things up."

At that very moment, Jon emerged from the master bedroom, dressed and ready to go. He saw his wife and his son embracing, giving him an extra boost to the high level of resolve he had already mustered for his performance.

He kissed them both and left to meet Neil Hale downstairs in the lobby bar with nothing in hand but a cellphone before their ride together to the convention center. Neil arranged another limo for Luke and Angela to leave an hour later, with their gallery convention passes in hand.

The Convention floor was packed and the noises from the floor were loud and distracting. The delegates and party operatives were but bees in the hive. Buzzing around, seemingly directionless. The scene was noisy and boisterous. Tonight, Paul Ryan was the headline speaker and would be accepting the party's nomination for Vice President. There also was anticipation about the mysterious individual addressing the conference within the next sixty minutes.

Neil and Jon arrived at the Convention Center at 4:30. Neil had arranged to introduce Jon to Lance Reibus. Despite having more demands on his time than he could possibly accommodate, Lance requested five minutes to meet the man who could very likely end his career working for the Republican Party. The three of them met in a small meeting room near the convention center stage backdrop, fifty steps from the podium.

"Mr. Braxton, I'm Lance Reibus. Welcome to my show."

"Thank you, Mr Reibus. It's good to be here. Thank you for the opportunity."

"No need to thank me, Mr. Braxton. You can thank Carl and Neil. Truthfully, having you on stage tonight scares the shit out of me. They have assured me you are a capable public speaker and have an important message to deliver. But I don't know you and I don't know anything about what you will be saying. So, at this point my future with the Party could very well be resting in your hands. You're only here because I'm trusting Carl's and Neil's judgment. This is an important night for the Party. Paul Ryan will be speaking about an hour after you, so there will be lots of people watching and listening when you're on stage. I hope you understand."

"Mr. Reibus, what I understand is you have a nine-year-old niece who was diagnosed with Type 1 diabetes when she was three."

"I do."

"Is she your brother's or your sister's daughter?"

"My sister's."

"Where do they live?"

"Milwaukee."

"How often do you see your sister and your niece?"

"Not very often. My job keeps me on the road most of the time and busy twenty-four seven."

"Being the parent of a young child with Type 1 is not much fun. You should support your sister."

Reibus stayed silent, anger starting to build.

Jon continued. "What will you be doing while I'm speaking?"

Now indignant. "I'll be working with my team to make sure convention business gets done."

"You should trust the convention business to your team and listen for the sake of your sister and your niece. And please call your sister and ask her to watch."

———— ≋ ————

"Please welcome to the podium, Jonathon Braxton."

With that announcement from the public address system, the noise on the floor started to abate. There was no applause, only silent intrigue. The attendees had been asking lots of questions for days about the mysterious Wednesday prime-time speaker, and now here he was. Jon came out from the backdrop and walked confidently to the podium. The teleprompters were off. He was dressed in a conservative gray pinstriped suit, white dress shirt, and red striped tie. He gathered himself and looked out on the expanse of the crowd. The delegates stared back. Only a few pockets of convention floor buzz remained. He grasped both sides of the podium with his hands and stood upright.

"Good evening, ladies and gentlemen. I recognize that you have a lot of questions about who I am and why I'm here. I will answer them shortly. But first, I have two questions to ask you. With all due respect, I'd like to ask you why you are here?" Any remnants of noise dissipated. "And what are you hoping to accomplish while you are here? What is your why? And why is your what?"

"As to why you are here, I'm curious what the primary reason is. Or asked another way, what is the deal-breaker for you not to be here? Is it the parties, the food, the booze, the socializing with old friends, the excuse to vacation that has brought you to Tampa? Or is the primary reason you are here the chance to make a positive difference in the way our government operates? I hope this is your why."

"And what is it you hope to accomplish while you're here? Is your primary what to simply enjoy the experience, do your convention business, then go back home and return to the status quo? Or is your primary what to bring something home that inspires you to do things that make a difference? My hope is your what is to go home and be inspired to act. And my what for being on this stage this evening is to attempt to provide you that inspiration."

"Along the way, I may offend you. Perhaps I already have. If so, I apologize, for that is not my intent. I promised to answer your questions about me and here goes. First, I am not a politician nor a political operative. You should not expect the kind of speech from me to which you are accustomed. I will be direct and to the point and totally honest with you. Probably to a fault."

"There is a why and a what for my being here with you tonight. My why is I am the father of a twelve-year-old young man who was recently diagnosed with Type 1 diabetes." Jon paused for a few seconds, seemingly making direct eye contact with all 4500 people on the floor and in the gallery. "I am here tonight to share with you my passion for finding a cure for this insidious disease. Despite the hundreds of millions of dollars in U.S. government funding over the last twelve years, currently there is no cure for Type 1 diabetes. Nor is there one on the horizon."

"Why am I here? I am here because I love my son and because I have learned more about this disease over the last two months than anyone should ever care to know. And I am here because I am on a mission to do everything in my power to find the cure."

"What am I going to do while I'm here? My what is that I, hopefully with your understanding and support, am going to chart a path that we can follow together, you and I if you're willing, to lead the effort to develop a cure."

"Now allow me to tell you who and what I am not." The convention floor was silent.

"As I stated a moment ago, I am not a politician, and I am not a political operative. I belong to no campaigns. I belong to no political parties. I am not a doctor. I do not have any medical affiliations. I am not a lobbyist. I have nothing to do with big pharma. I am not being paid by anyone to be here. And to Lance Reibus if you are listening, perhaps you should cover your ears, I despise politics. But I am here nonetheless." Jon paused and looked to the gallery high above to the left and met eyes with Luke's. He turned back to the silent and mesmerized convention delegates.

"I expect there are many of you who are not familiar with this disease. But I would venture to say many of you know, or know of, someone with a young child or adolescent who lives with Type 1 diabetes. A family member, a family friend, a coworker, a celebrity, a sports personality, someone from your church, someone you play softball with or bingo. Someone."

"I say young child because Type 1 tends to first attack people when they are young, starting as early as age two. And when Type 1 is contracted, it is unrelenting. Fighting this condition becomes a twenty-four by seven by 365 confrontation. Type 1 does not take a day off, and it does not follow a schedule. It is a brutal disease. It's brutal on the afflicted and brutal on those care about and care for the afflicted."

Another pause. Jon again scanned the convention floor for his eyes to make their point.

"I ask any of you who know anyone, or of anyone, with this condition to raise your hand."

He gave the crowd a chance to respond. Hands started to raise, slowly but steadily increasing. Ten percent, twenty percent, forty percent, fifty percent, sixty percent. A few seconds later, seventy-five percent of the delegates acknowledged knowing someone with Type 1. They looked around, amazed at the sea of raised hands. The delegates held their hands up for a moment and once the magnitude of the response was realized, they started to lower.

Lance Reibus was watching on a TV monitor in the small meeting room where they met forty-five minutes earlier. Thoughts of the stresses of running the show abated. Thoughts of his niece and his sister replaced them. Neil was in the room as well, watching Jon tame the crowd. He was grinning at the thought of what must be going through the heads of the Republican Party elite at this moment. As the crowd was raising their hands, Lance and Neil were joined by Paul Ryan, who was staring at the monitor as he walked in. He sat down slowly next to Neil without taking his eyes off Jon.

Angela and Luke were seated in the gallery high above the left side of the stage. She had her right arm around Luke's shoulders and was, somewhat unsuccessfully, trying to hold back her tears. Luke was smiling proudly.

"It appears some seventy-five percent of you know someone afflicted with Type 1. I am now going to ask all of you who do to close your eyes." The delegates willfully complied.

"Now, those with your eyes closed, picture that person you know with Type 1 diabetes. Picture that person's caregivers, likely their parents, likely people you know. With your eyes still closed, imagine now you are that person's caregiver, that Type 1 diabetic's parent. Everyone have that picture in mind? Keep your eyes closed and allow me now to take you on a little journey. Lance Reibus, I hope your eyes are closed and you are joining us."

"Now as you are picturing yourself as the primary caregiver for the someone you know diagnosed with this condition, we're going back in time to the moment you first learned your loved one was a Type 1 diabetic. I'll help you visualize by telling our story. The story of Luke and Angela and I. This will not be pleasant, but it is the reality for people who learn a loved one is now living with this disease."

"The person you know with this condition did not always have it. Until the time they started to feel the effects and were subsequently diagnosed, their pancreas and autoimmune system were functioning normally. And then for reasons we still don't know, out of nowhere, they become compromised. The pancreas, as if having a switch flipped, stops production of insulin-producing cells."

"Your loved one comes to you and tells you they don't feel well. They're always thirsty. They're tired and listless. They're losing weight. They're urinating constantly and often uncontrollably. They're shaking and often dizzy or light-headed. Their pajamas and bed sheets are soaked with perspiration."

"You're scared, and you take your loved one to the doctor. They run tests while you fear the uncertainty, and then you receive the news. Your loved one's autoimmune system has begun attacking their pancreas. You don't understand what this means so your doctor explains yours and your loved one's new reality."

Jon pauses. The convention floor remains silent and motionless.

"You learn your loved one's autoimmune system is now working to harm them. As human beings, our bodies need glucose. You learn that without insulin produced by the pancreas, your loved one's body is unable to convert the sugar from ingested carbohydrates into glucose, and these unconverted sugars are now roaming their circulatory system. Glucose is the fuel our body uses to keep its organs functioning. You learn that without insulin, your loved one's organs become energy-deficient and will begin to fail. Your loved one is now diagnosed with a condition which if left untreated will cause them to live uncomfortably and prematurely die an unpleasant death."

"When your loved one's body recognizes it is deficient in glucose, it attempts to compensate by releasing fat stored in the liver, also known as ketones. To fill the energy void, these ketones are released into the bloodstream, but in volume they are toxic and can be life threatening. There are a number of reactions by the body as the result of repeated insulin deficiency over time, including heart disease, circulatory issues leading to amputations, and blindness."

"You hear this news and have no idea what to think or how to process. All you think about is your precious loved one and what their life is now reduced to. Your doctor tells you, while there is no cure and the cause of the condition is unknown, there is reason to hope. The condition is treatable. The treatment is administering insulin when the body needs it. And when the injected insulin overcompensates and creates a low blood sugar condition—not uncommon—immediate sugar ingestion is called for. With efficient insulin management and blood sugar control, your loved one can live a somewhat normal life, albeit a different life. And it's a confusing life. Your loved one's blood sugar level bounces up and down—seemingly randomly—and you always have to be ready to respond."

"You learn for the rest of your loved one's life, until such time as a cure is discovered, some one or some thing will have to monitor their blood sugar levels. This monitoring must be done multiple times a day, every day. Weekends and holidays included. In the Braxton household, it's done by pricking Luke's finger, placing blood droplets on a test strip, and then placing the strip in a glucose meter."

"When blood sugar level readings are too low, because of injected insulin working too aggressively, it's dangerous. Something high in sugar content should be ingested immediately. In the Braxton household, this is typically orange juice. When the levels are too high, insulin must be administered immediately. In the Braxton household, that is a shot of insulin into Luke's abdomen."

"You are now aware that your loved one has a life-threatening condition that must be monitored and managed each and every day. No exceptions. You are now armed with knowledge and treatments. Now it's time to go back to life. But it is not the same life for your loved one or for you. The pressure on you is immense. Your loved one is in peril, and it is up to you to keep them safe. It is a role unlike any you have experienced before. Your loved one's survival is in your hands. Your opponent is their immune system. There is no preparation for this opponent and this war. You are in unfamiliar territory, and danger is always lurking."

"You need a battle plan and a strategy designed to keep your loved one's blood sugar levels within an acceptable range. Your loved one's diet becomes a primary area of focus. Since their body is now challenged to process carbohydrates, it is desirable to minimize, to the largest degree possible, their carbohydrate intake. You and your loved one are now faced with making constant decisions about what to eat and drink. Food's high in carbohydrates are ones that are difficult to resist but resist you must. The quality and longevity of your loved one's life is directly correlated to these choices. The phrases 'low-carb' and 'no-carb' become foundational in your lexicon."

"The social life of your loved one is also part of the battle plan. Many social situations and events are difficult for your loved one. Events where food and drink rich in carbs are abundant challenge the battle plan. You're again faced with tough choices, quality of life choices. You sometimes think it's OK to cheat a little bit. Your loved one shouldn't be denied going to their friend's birthday party. You make an exception. Now what about the next time? And the next? You want so much for your loved one to be happy, yet you are constantly forced to make decisions that do the opposite. They question your love. You question your decisions and your ability to make the correct ones."

"There are times when you're doing everything right, and yet things do not work out. It could be your loved one's body did not like the last insulin injection and over absorbs, creating a condition known as insulin shock. Your loved one faints in front of you. If not treated quickly, the excess insulin condition can cause seizures, severe headaches, dizziness."

"What did you do wrong? Nothing. You did everything right, yet you still lost this skirmish. You wonder if you can develop the mental toughness to deal with these challenges. You question if you can be an effective primary caregiver. Speaking for Angela and myself, it is the most difficult challenge we have ever faced in our lives. Thankfully, our son Luke is a rock. It has taken some time, but he has now taken primary responsibility for his health. He understands the reasons for the sacrifices he must make, and he makes them. He doesn't like them.

Angela and I don't like them. But sacrifice becomes a critical element of the battle plan. Such is the life of a Type 1 diabetic and those who care for them."

Five seconds of silence more deafening than the last.

"Ladies and gentlemen, please open your eyes. And then open your mind to the fact the U.S. government is the single biggest contributor in the world to diabetes medical research. Yet for all the millions of dollars they have allocated, we have no cure. Thankfully, as a result of the work of the medical research community and the tremendous efforts of advocacy groups, there have been significant advancements made in the areas of treatment for Type 1. There are many who deserve to be recognized and commended for these efforts. But should we be satisfied with the return on our investment? Should we consider these investments a success?"

"As you may have gathered, I am a businessman. As such, I tend to look at things through a lens shaped to focus on results and return on investment. The U.S. government has spent hundreds of millions of dollars on diabetes research, and we still do not know the cause nor have a cure for Type 1. And at this point, there is only one pathway on the horizon that holds promise, but that pathway has funding obstacles."

"To my point of view, and without questioning the efficacy of current efforts being made in research, the government's investment is underperforming. It's clear and unfortunate that this has little bearing on government decision making. As a businessman, now focused on diabetes medical research, I am here to advocate for a change in philosophy and a change in direction."

"I mentioned a moment ago that there is a pathway that holds the promise of a cure for Type 1. But not only for Type 1. This pathway holds promise for many other conditions and diseases, but this pathway presents a moral dilemma for many. I'd like to explore this dilemma with you."

"I realize what I'm about to discuss will be uncomfortable for many who hold strong religious beliefs. You should know that I do not, but I have become a more spiritual person in the last few months, thanks to an enlightened new friend. When you have a child indiscriminately chosen to have his own immune system start attacking life-enabling cells in his own body, it's impossible not to question one's faith. In my case, I did not have a faith to question. Over the last few months, considering what has transpired, when many would run from their faith, I have come to discover mine."

"Over the last few months, I have been studying the miracle of what are referred to in the medical research community as pluripotent stem cells. These are cells that are produced by what we might agree on as a miracle. They are formed within four to five days following the insemination of a human egg with human sperm. This formation can occur in the lab as well as within the female body. In the case of the lab instance, the characteristics of these cells at this stage have tremendous promise to ease human suffering."

"What makes these cells so promising as a cure for diabetes, heart disease, Parkinson's disease, spinal cord injuries, and many others? Simply stated, these cells developed at the earliest stage of cellular development, have the ability, if properly cultured at the right time, to be converted into virtually any cell type in the body. In the case of a Type 1 diabetic, into functioning pancreatic cells. And these pluripotent cells have the capacity to replicate themselves indefinitely."

"Now for the moral dilemma. Our dilemma is centered on the question of when human life begins. In fertility labs across the planet, artificial insemination is taking place. On a successfully inseminated human egg, pluripotent cell extraction would take place in the following four to five days. At that point following insemination, a cluster of 200 cells have formed. In the lab, this cluster is referred to as a blastocyst, technically not yet an embryo. It has no recognizable features, no human form, is barely visible to the naked eye."

"Should we consider this 200-cell formation human life? I know many of you will say yes. You say human life begins at conception. You believe the insemination process, artificial or not, is the miracle of life. And I agree, it is a miracle."

"Pluripotent cells in themselves are also a miracle. They hold tremendous promise to end much human suffering. If the thought of extracting these cells causes you pain and grief because you hold it is equivalent to ending a human life, I ask you to consider another thought. And that is, if God is providing us the genetic material to end so much human suffering, would he not want us to use it?"

"For the first time in my life, allow me to quote scripture. From John 3:17: 'But if anyone has the world's goods and sees his brother in need, yet closes his heart against him, how does God's love abide in him?'"

"Could it be possible that God expects us to do what we can to end human suffering and he has made this material available to us for this purpose? In the evolutionary process of these cells, this material is only in a state where it is functional for our purposes for a few days. After this four-to-five-day time period, pluripotent cells begin to take on the characteristics of their eventual cell formation. Is it conceivable to consider that human life begins when the cells of the blastocyst take on human characteristics? And that extracting them before they do for the purpose of easing human suffering is noble and not a sin?"

"Ladies and gentlemen, I know my arguments will not convince many of you. I just ask that you consider them. Look into your hearts. Consider the good that advancing our understanding of these miracle pluripotent cells can bring. Consider perhaps God made this material, and its evolutionary process, available to us for this purpose. Consider this extraction process cannot take place within the blastocyst in the human body. Consider that aborting a child in the womb does not produce pluripotent cells. They have already evolved past the point of their use in this research. They can only be extracted in a lab environment shortly after artificial insemination."

"I mentioned to you that I am not a religious person, but I do have a spiritual counselor. I knew I would travel into choppy waters with many of you tonight and I asked him for guidance. I shared with him my 'what' which I shared with you earlier, knowing that many, and perhaps he himself, would be troubled by the research I'm advocating. His advice for me was to not stop. It was to push forward. He said if what I was advocating was sinful, then God would let me know along the way. He told me God would consider our efforts to ease human suffering righteous, and if our method was not, he would advise."

"I am here tonight to let you know I am pushing forward until I am convinced from a moral or a spiritual argument to stop. I am pushing forward to advocate for this research and to control any potential abuses. I am pushing forward by announcing the formation of the Lucas Braxton Foundation, in honor of my son. I am pushing forward by focusing our foundation to end human suffering to the degree we can, while remaining respectful of the miracle of human life, through pluripotent cell research. I am pushing forward to advocate for the millions of people around the world suffering from diseases and conditions that potentially could be treated or cured by advancements in this field."

"The Lucas Braxton Foundation will be advocating to the U.S. Congress to increase the size of diabetes research by a factor of ten. And we will advocate earmarking a sizable portion of that funding to pluripotent cell research. In parallel, we will be communicating with medical research entities to join us in our advocacy. We will work to educate the people of this country and around the world about the science. And we will work towards diminishing the stigma attached to this research. Hopefully, this evening, we have successfully begun these efforts."

"I ask you all to look into your hearts. Recognize the amount of human suffering for which this research holds promise. I know this ask presents moral and spiritual challenges for many. Hopefully, you will find room in your heart and soul to consider supporting us."

"Ladies and gentlemen, thank you all again for your time and attention. Enjoy the remainder of your conference. Good night."

Renee Jacobs, a forty-seven-year-old housewife in Columbus, Ohio, the aunt of Lauren Woods, a Type 1 diabetic diagnosed at age four, and the wife of the current governor of Ohio, was riveted on every word. As were Lance Reibus and his sister in Milwaukee.

Jon left the podium and walked off the stage to a loud and thunderous applause. Lance Reibus was just offstage to greet him. He extended his right hand, and they shook. "Thank you, Mr. Braxton."

Next to Lance was Paul Ryan, the party's candidate for vice president. He also extended his hand. "Mr. Braxton, I'm Paul Ryan. Congressman Gregory has been telling me about you. That was a terrific speech. And no prompter! Congratulations. I imagine we'll be seeing you in committee soon."

Thirty-one

The next day the Braxton's were still in Tampa, off for a day of sportfishing in the gulf. Jon turned off his cell phone early in the morning and left it at the hotel. When they returned Thursday evening, he found a full voicemail box and 300 new emails.

He started going through his voicemails, which included one from Abby at three Pacific time. He listened to it and then had Angela and Luke listen as well.

'OMG, Jon. OMG, OMG, OMG. This place is going crazy. The number of people calling and emailing, it's absolutely nuts. Important people calling and writing to congratulate you and wanting to know how to donate to the foundation. You have no idea what you started. OK, maybe you do. But hurry up and get your butt back here. We've got a lot of things to get done, and I need you here. By the way, Darla's doing fine. She asked me to ask you if she could spend a few more nights with us. It's cool, right? OK, give my best to Luke and Angie, and get home safe. Love you guys. OMG. Bye.'

The flight home on Friday was uneventful, and the Braxton's were back home at seven. On Saturday, Jon dove into all the communications that had come his way since he delivered his address on Wednesday. One call was from Lance Reibus, asking Jon to call him back as soon as possible.

"Lance Reibus."

"Good morning, Lance. It's Jon Braxton."

"Jon, I'm so glad you called. I trust you and the family made it home safely."

"We did, thank you. What can I do for you, Lance?"

"Jon, are you familiar with Wallis Kriss? He anchors a Sunday morning cable news talk show from DC on the Big News Channel."

"I'm familiar with the name, but I don't watch him."

"Watch him tomorrow. He's dialed in to the buzz you created. Called me yesterday to ask a lot of questions about you. He'll be doing a segment tomorrow about you as part of his convention recap. He wants to interview you on his show next week. Any chance you'll be in the DC area next Sunday?"

"I wasn't planning on it, and I'm not sure it's something I'd want to do. I don't really do politics."

"Jon, with all due respect to your position on politics, this is a great opportunity to promote your cause and your foundation. A lot of the people you'll be meeting soon who can help you watch his show religiously. Including many who might not have tuned in on Wednesday. Since you created quite a commotion, I'm sure those who missed you on Wednesday will make it a point to watch him if they know you're on."

"Can you guarantee the interview will not go into politics and will stick to the cause?"

"I can't guarantee it, but I can make the request."

"Get me a guarantee and I'll do it. One more thing, did your sister watch on Wednesday?"

"She did and made me swear on our mother's grave to introduce you."

———≈———

"Rob Wiley."

"Hey Rob, it's Jon returning your call. How you doing?"

"JB, my man. Holy crap, do you know what's going on since your performance?"

"I'm starting to get the picture."

"Listen, I only have a minute. Earl wants you in DC a week from Tuesday. You've got to make it. You'll have a chance to discuss your foundation and research in front of the House Health and Human Services Committee. Can't believe it happened this fast. You need to be there."

"How would I prepare? What would I need to do?"

"No problema. I'll drop by your office with a playbook. Can I let Earl know you'll be there?"

"Go ahead."

"Marcie James."

"Good morning Ms. James, this is Jon Braxton returning your call."

"Hello Mr. Braxton, I'm calling for Secretary Carrington. She would like to speak to you. Would you have time at one Pacific today? Oh wait, she's calling me on the other line, please hold for a moment. Mr. Braxton, are you available now? The Secretary is available."

"Yes. Put her through."

"Mr. Braxton, congratulations. What a terrific speech you gave on Wednesday. I imagine you are being swamped with well-wishers. I have a few things to discuss with you. Do you have a few minutes?"

"Thank you, Madam Secretary. I do. What can I do for you?"

"First, let me wish you the very best for Luke. I had no idea of his condition when we last spoke. Please give him my best. Second, I heard through the grapevine that Wallis Kriss is looking to interview you. Have his people reached out to you?"

"Yes, through Lance Reibus, and I've agreed to go on."

"May I give you a few words of advice?"

"Of course."

"Wallis can be a real asshole. Be ready for him. He will say and do anything to get people he wants on his show. If he makes a commitment to you, rest assured he will break it. He'll try to corner you into saying something you don't want to. I imagine you only want to talk about your cause, and he will push to dive into your politics. He's on a conservative network, but he leans left and if he senses he can flush out Republican hypocrisy, he'll go for it."

"Thank you, Madam Secretary. That's great advice. Why are you telling me this? I assume your politics are aligned with his."

"Jeffrey Claymore would insist." She laughed. "And one more thing: Since you're coming to DC we're having coffee together. I'll send a car to your hotel to pick you up Monday at nine. Let Marcie know where you're staying. I look forward to getting to know you."

———— ≈ ————

"Jon, thank you for calling me back. How are you? How's Luke, Angie, and Darla?"

"We're all fine, Jeffrey. Just made it back home last night. Did you watch?"

"I did and am so proud of you. The way you inspired everyone to see your mission. The way you framed the dilemma and made your case. The way you included God. You are a special man, Jon Braxton. If there's anyone on the planet that can move the needle to find a cure for Type 1, I believe God chose well. I know you likely have much to attend to today, so I'll be brief. Just wanted you to know that I am available to help you with your LBF, as you helped me with mine. If I can ever assist you, please know you can count on me."

"Thank you, Jeffrey. I have a feeling this will be the case."

"And Jon, another thing, I had the occasion to speak with Heather

Carrington. I have a feeling she will be reaching out to you. She is struggling with some career indecision, and she has shared with me that she feels you may be able to give her some perspectives from outside her inner circle. She's looking for answers and feels you can help her find them. Just between you and I."

———— ≋ ————

"Andy Whitaker."

"Andy, Jon Braxton."

"Jon, congratulations. You nailed it on Wednesday. Are you back home?"

"Yes, Andy, we're back and swamped. We need to get the charter and by laws for the foundation on the front burner. Can I have them sometime this week?"

"We can, but I'll need two hours with you. Can we get together Monday afternoon?"

"Let's meet in my office if you don't mind. Two o'clock, OK?"

"Sure thing. See you Monday at two."

———— ≋ ————

"Jon, thanks for calling. Oh my god, you have no idea what's been happening since you spoke. By the way, Darla's fine. It's unbelievable. There has been so much outreach to you since Thursday. We need to hire a PR firm quickly to deal with all the communications. It's going to be too much for us with everything else we have going on. Glad you're back, by the way."

"Good to be back, Abby. You're right about hiring a PR firm. I'll get on that. I'll be in the office first thing Monday. OK, if I come over to pick up Darla tomorrow at three?"

———— ≋ ————

"Jonathon Braxton."

"Jon, Lance Reibus. Just called to tell you that I worked it out with Wallis Kriss to stay away from your politics and keep the interview on your story, your cause, and the foundation."

"Can I trust him?"

"Truthfully, no. So be ready."

———— ≈ ————

Abby was in at seven Monday morning, beating Jon to the office by thirty minutes. They met in the executive conference room at eight.

"Well, your highness. I imagine I should fill you in on what it was like here last Thursday and Friday while you were fishing in the gulf."

"We only fished on Thursday."

"How nice to hear a few more tuna will live to see another day. Anyway, it was an absolute nuthouse last week. People from everywhere calling in. Local government, media, customers, vendors, business partners. Everyone wants to know when the foundation website will be up. Can we mail some information? Will the foundation be a 501c3? Where do we send contributions? Are you available for speaking engagements? It was the first most heard about Luke, and the offers to help were overwhelming."

"I know the brunt of this fell on you. Thank you for everything you do. I'm not sure what I would do without you. By the way, show me out of office next Monday through Wednesday."

"Oh?"

"I'm in DC. Wallis Kriss show Sunday. Meeting with Secretary Carrington Monday. On Capitol Hill Tuesday. Committee hearing."

"That's it. No meeting with Obama?"

Thirty-two

"Good morning from Washington DC. It's Sunday, September 9. I'm Wallis Kriss, and welcome to Big News Sunday."

"Ten days ago, the Republican Party wrapped up its national convention in Tampa, Florida, nominating Mitt Romney to represent the party in the upcoming presidential election. Representative Paul Ryan will be joining him on the ticket as the vice-presidential nominee. Mr. Romney will be joining us live on our second segment to lay out his party's agenda for his first term, if elected."

"But first, mention of the convention would not be complete without covering a couple of surprises that took place. One was the appearance of Clint Eastwood giving an emotional endorsement speech for Romney. The other an appearance of an unknown on stage during prime time on Wednesday night, a highly coveted speaking time slot. Jonathon Braxton, a businessman from Southern California, was given the floor and became the darling of the night with his passionate advocacy for embryonic stem cell research. It was an apolitical speech on a topic that likely rankled many Republicans. We're curious as to why and how Mr. Braxton made it into prime time with that message. And Mr. Braxton is here to tell us."

The camera on Kriss panned out to show Jon sitting across from him, at a forty-five-degree angle. Jon was at ease, leaning back in his chair a bit, his legs crossed, and his hands interlocked on his lap.

"On last week's show, we mentioned your surprise appearance at the Republican National Convention in Tampa the week before last. Being a Southern California technology company CEO, you were unknown in Washington DC and in political circles, yet were given a coveted Wednesday evening prime time speaking slot. We learned your twelve-year-old son Lucas had recently been diagnosed with Type 1 diabetes, a disease for which currently there is no cure. You delivered a powerful address to the convention, advocating for expanding research into a pathway that offers promise for a potential cure. However, that research would involve utilizing embryonic stem cells, which has always been controversial to a large majority of Republicans. And here you are. We were curious to understand more of your story. So welcome, Mr. Braxton, to Washington, and to Big News Sunday."

"Thank you, Wallis. Nice to be here."

"Mr. Braxton, your appearance at the Republican National Convention was a surprise in many respects and also a big hit. Can you tell us some of the story as to how you made it to the national stage in prime time?"

"Well, Wallis, the last few months have been somewhat of a tornado for my family. My son fell ill sixty-seven days ago and was diagnosed with an autoimmune disorder. A nasty disorder that impacts mostly young people, Type 1 diabetes. This disorder turns the body's immune system against itself and begins attacking the cells in the body that produce insulin."

"I'm a research guy, so I started studying the disease. Early on, I learned a few things that bothered me. First was the fact the medical community does not yet know what causes this disease and, as a result, they don't know how to cure it. What also bothered me was the U.S. government invests millions of dollars every year with the medical research community for this purpose, yet the research community has only developed treatments. Bottom line, despite the huge investments, we have little understanding of what causes the condition, no preventions and no cures."

"OK, Mr. Braxton, you're a businessman in Southern California with no ties to the Republican Party, and next thing we know, Lance Reibus is putting you on stage in prime time, right in front of Paul Ryan. How did that happen?"

"I won the coin flip with Clint Eastwood."

Kriss laughed nervously. "Seriously, Mr. Braxton, our audience would like to know."

"Wallis, I'm not sure how much time we have, but I would like to tell your audience about our foundation and the work we are setting out to do."

"Mr. Braxton, I'm sure they are interested in that, but they will be much more engaged if they knew more about you and how you advanced so quickly into the Republican Party limelight."

"Wallis, perhaps I should let your audience know that I do not belong to the Republican Party, nor the Democrat, nor the Libertarian nor the Green nor any other. I'd like to take the few minutes we have remaining to discuss our foundation." Kriss tried to get a word in, but Jon resisted.

"The Lucas Braxton Foundation is focused on developing treatments and cures that can reduce human suffering from conditions and diseases where targeted cell transplants offer promise. Wallis, you used the term embryonic stem cell research to describe our mission. That was slightly incorrect. Technically the cells we will be researching are so early in the evolutionary process that they have not yet taken on the characteristics of a human embryo. In the medical community, these cells are referred to as pluripotent cells, and they can be cultured to evolve into specific cell types. This is what holds their promise. Not only for Type 1, but for numerous other diseases and conditions where the infusion of specific cell types can be effective. Other information your audience may be interested in can be found on our websites, lucasbraxtonfoundation.org and curetype1.org. The websites are still in early stages of development and the information is not up yet, but your viewers can leave us their email addresses and we'll stay in touch as we get our information published. The point to keep in mind is this research offers the promise of reducing the suffering of millions of people around the globe suffering from a variety of maladies."

"Mr. Braxton, the fact that you were able to present your cause to the convention in prime time, a cause that would be against the morals of many in the Republican Party, is curious. Can you give our audience an explanation how you were able to do so, considering the speaking slots in prime time are normally reserved for the party elite or upcoming stars the party wants to showcase?"

"Wallis, I think that question could best be answered by Lance Reibus. He is the one that offered the slot to us. Maybe the fact he has a nine-year-old niece suffering from this disease since the age of three had something to do with it."

———— ≈ ————

The State Department vehicle pulled into the Washington DC Fairmont Hotel at nine. Jon was waiting in the lobby. The driver came in, they met eyes, and Jon followed him out the front entrance to a black GMC Yukon SUV. The rear door was opened for him.

In ten minutes, they entered the private State Department parking garage. Mark Parker was waiting by the bank of elevators that led from the parking garage to the upper floors of State. "Mr. Braxton, I'm Mark Parker, Secretary Carrington's Chief of Staff. Welcome."

"Thank you, Mr. Parker. What have you got in store for me?"

"We're going to the Starbucks on the mezzanine level. The Secretary is waiting for you."

"Mr. Braxton, welcome to State." Heather rose as Mark and Jon approached her table off to one end of the coffee hut. Strategically, all the tables near hers had been moved. They were twenty feet away from the next nearest patron. Parker bid Jon goodbye and left the two of them.

"Hello, Madam Secretary. Nice to see you again."

"You didn't get the memo to call me Heather? I got yours to call you Jon."

"I must have overlooked it. Sorry about that. I've been inundated since the convention."

"Washington loves speeches like the one you delivered. You are a new light, and the people here are mostly old moths attracted to shiny new objects. Unfortunately, that light somewhat blinds them and they won't be able to see nor appreciate the magnitude of your accomplishments. But I do."

"Thank you, Heather. You are somewhat accomplished yourself, although I don't pay much attention to politics, so I'm not familiar with your career."

"That's OK, Jon. I'm more interested talking to you about the future than the past. I'm interested in understanding your viewpoints and perspectives about our country. As you may know, I'm in position to contend for the presidency in 2016 and frankly, am concerned about our chances. It's customary for one party to be in office for eight years and then for the other party to take over. To reverse this trend in '16, we must expand our base. Debbie Schultz and Donna Brazile have that job, but they would not value your insights as I would. We need new perspectives."

"What would you like from me?"

"Jon, there are millions of people in the country like you. People who have decided to ignore the political process. I'd like to understand why and perhaps learn how to change their perception of government so people like you would want to be involved. I know you have no interest in politics, and I'm not here to change your thinking. I just want to understand it. Better political processes can lead to better outcomes. I've grown up in government and have difficulty, like Debbie and Donna, seeing through the fog. I believe you can help me see things more clearly. Will you?"

"I'm not sure what you're asking for. Do you have any specific questions you want to ask? Or are you looking for me to write something out?"

"Can we start with me asking a few questions? I don't have a lot of time this morning, and I hope we can have many more conversations over the next few years. But I do have a few top-of-mind things I'd like to ask."

"Of course, Heather. Fire away. But understand, I don't spend any time thinking about how to improve the workings of politics. It's just not my thing."

"I understand, but I'm still interested in your thoughts. I'll consider they're not well-baked."

"OK, go ahead."

"Is there anything specific that you experienced which caused you to form your current opinion of politics?"

"There was. Until I met Fred Berman, I really had no opinion of politics, just disinterest. After my interaction with him I formed an opinion, and it wasn't very good."

"I know Fred. He's a swamp rat. What happened?"

"In 2004, Berman was our congressman. A team of engineers in Israel had developed a systems architecture I wanted to invest in. I applied for their visas to come to the U.S. and work with us but had no success getting them issued. After six months I called Berman. He said he could help and asked to meet me at Spectre. He said a $50k check would take care of it. I threw him out."

"Shit, sorry to hear that. I can understand why you feel as you do. This seems to happen a lot. I'm sorry. OK, next question. In your opinion, what is the fundamental problem with our political system in your eyes. The one primary problem which causes people to avoid involvement? What's the one thing in your estimation is the root cause of the reason why so many in the country tune out?"

"Without parsing through everything, I'd say too much money

and not enough accountability. Money in politics leads to the wrong kind of people running, and for the wrong reasons. With the wrong people in office for the wrong reasons, wrong decisions are the norm, and the will of the people takes a backseat. Good people running for the right reasons, real problem solvers, don't seek office because of this."

"People like Jon Braxton?"

Jon was going to answer but paused. For the first time he harbored a thought of occupying public office. Could he do more for Luke by being in office, rather than advocacy? Could being in public office give him a better platform to fight for the Lucas Braxton Foundation's cause? Could he function, let alone survive, being in public office given the hypocrisy, the inefficiency, and the dishonesty?

"Yes, Heather, people like me."

"What would you change to attract the right people to run and to energize more people to get involved in the process?"

"I'd start with term limits. In line with that, campaign finance reform. It's never made sense to me why a candidate who happens to be more proficient in fundraising should have an advantage. All campaigns should be publicly funded. Each candidate allocated a set amount for their campaign based on the office they're seeking. They then decide how to spend those limited funds. Anyone violating campaign finance rules would be disqualified. If impropriety were discovered after they were elected, they would be impeached. We only have two viable political parties because of money. As a result, realistically, we only have binary choices. The two-party system doesn't serve the people. It only serves the two parties and their ability to fundraise and attract dirty money. Allowing someone the opportunity to run without having to answer to only one of two parties would expand the field and attract more principled candidates. Am I making any sense to you? Can you understand why I find politics disgusting?"

"Yes, I can."

"Don't you?"

"Jon, I can't answer that without being hypocritical."

"No, I guess you can't. May I ask you a question?"

"OK, but I've only got a minute or two."

"Are you good with what you do?"

She laughed nervously. "What do you mean?"

"You seem uncomfortable. You seem to have doubts about yourself and your profession. I get a sense that you're not happy nor satisfied with the work you're doing."

"Very observant, Jon."

"Another perspective for you Madam Secretary?"

"OK."

"Spend more time with Jeffrey."

Heather's cell phone buzzed. She answered it, thanked Jon for his time, and headed back upstairs, along the way asking Mark Parker to arrange Jon a ride back to his hotel.

Tuesday was Capitol Hill Day for the newest curiosity of the U.S. Congress, Jonathon Braxton.

He arrived on the Hill at nine and was greeted by Earl Gregory. He and Earl spent some time in Gregory's office, discussing the day ahead. Earl asked Jon if he was prepared. He said he was.

Jon was scheduled to appear before the House Health and Human Services Subcommittee at eleven, but procedural bureaucracy took his appearance past lunch. He was finally seated at two. While fully prepared, Jon never got the opportunity to lay out his vision. A few of the Republican Congress people on the committee, ignorant of Jon's arguments and making assumptions his agenda would alienate some of their constituents, pontificated and badgered. Jon maintained his composure and got a few blows in, but when the session was adjourned at four, he was thoroughly frustrated. Back in his hotel, he took a call from Abby, delivering some Spectre business news. She asked how his three-day tour of DC was.

"I need a long scrub shower to get all the dirt and slime off."

———≈———

Jon returned home on Thursday afternoon and, in the evening took a call from Jeffrey.

"How was your visit to Washington? I certainly enjoyed watching you dance with Wallis Kriss."

"It was a great reminder of why I hate politics. What's new with you Jeffrey?"

"Heather Carrington called me the evening after your meeting with her. Seems she enjoyed getting to know you. How did you two get along?"

"I think fine, though I may have made her a bit uncomfortable with some of my observations. You were right, she certainly seems conflicted. And to be candid with you, so am I."

"Oh. What's on your mind?"

"Our only avenue to raise the amount of money needed to fund pluripotent cell research is the federal government. All the other efforts we can make are noble, but they will never be enough. Our projected needs are a billion a year for three to five years to do the research effectively. As much as I despise politics, running for Earl's seat in 2014, getting into Congress and onto the right committees might be our only shot."

"That's going to be sweet music to a lot of influential people. Have you shared this with Neil, or Angela or anyone else?"

"I'm not sure I've shared it with myself yet. Everything seems a bit surreal right now. From my conversation with Heather, the thought that keeps running through my head is of two battleships crossing in the night. One heading out for battle and the other heading into dry dock."

Thirty-three

The 2012 election cycle completed with relatively few surprises. Barack Obama was reelected to the presidency and Earl Gregory cruised to reelection in California's twenty-sixth. The Republicans lost eight seats in the House but maintained a 234-201 majority. In the Senate there were thirty-three seats up for election. Twenty-three held by Democrats. They needed win only twenty-one of those to retain the majority. They held several more, increasing their majority from four seats to eight.

All in all, election night 2012 was a tough one for Republicans. Carlton and Cornelius Hale were disappointed, but not surprised, as they started to turn their thoughts to the 2014 midterms.

In Thousand Oaks, Jon Braxton was spending most of his time and energy on his family and the Lucas Braxton Foundation. To devote more time to those pursuits, he formally promoted Abby Martin to the job she had been performing as a proxy with supreme efficiency for the past many years, Chief Operations Officer. She was now officially managing all day-to-day operations of Spectre, occupying Jon's old office.

The Lucas Braxton Foundation was up, operating, and successfully raising money while identifying research organizations to begin targeted pluripotent cell research. Jon was speaking all over the country and working with Earl Gregory and the Health and Human Services subcommittee in Congress, to advocate for more diabetes research funding. Progress was slow, and he was only able to gain a ten percent increase in Congressional funding for diabetes research in the next budget allocation to be distributed starting July 1, 2013. Jon considered his results unacceptable and vowed to himself—and to Luke—to work harder.

Lucas Braxton was back in school and had adapted to living life with Type 1 diabetes. He had sacrificed many of the things he used to do with friends, especially around diet. His metabolism was not always accepting his injected insulin gracefully and his blood sugar readings were bouncing around unpredictably. On two occasions, he had lapsed into hypoglycemic shock when his blood sugar readings plummeted. Both times, he was home with mom and dad, and they took the appropriate measures to regulate him. Life in the Braxton home was stressful, and Jon had no shortage of motivation continuing his journey to find a cure.

Jon took a call from Rob Wiley, 253 days following Luke's T1D diagnosis,

"Are you sitting down?"

"Hi Rob, what is it?"

"It's Earl. He suffered a stroke a few hours ago. He's at John Hopkins in DC. From what I hear, it's pretty bad."

"That's terrible Rob. Anything I can do?"

"At this point, I'm not sure. Still coming to grips with everything. I'll call you back when I have more info. Just wanted you to hear it from me and not the press."

"OK thanks. Give our best to his family. Let me know how I can help, please."

It had been a week since Earl's stroke. His condition had stabilized, and he regained many of his motor functions. His speech was somewhat slurred, his left leg was immobile, and he was minimally impaired cognitively. The prognosis was he would continue to improve, but at his age, would be debilitated to some degree. As each day passed, it became clearer it would be unlikely Gregory would return to a state of health enabling him to perform his congressional responsibilities.

Conversations within the Republican caucus in the House were starting on replacing the fourteen-term Congressman. House Speaker John Boehner and House Majority Leader Paul Ryan were spearheading them.

Rob Wiley's name was consistently being raised. California law required during the first year of the two-year House election cycle, the governor call a special election to fill a vacant seat. Given the popularity of Earl Gregory in his district, and the large margin of victory he enjoyed just a few months earlier, it was a foregone conclusion whoever the Republican party endorsed in the special election would be successful in succeeding him.

People outside the beltway were also being consulted. Majority Leader Ryan called Neil Hale to get his opinion of Wiley. "Rob would do a great job and hit the ground running. He knows Earl like the back of his hand and would be square with his agenda. But you should you make sure he wants it before going too far down that road."

"Great. Thanks, Neil. Hey, one last thing—Braxton? Has he shared any political ambitions with you?"

"Paul, trust me, you wouldn't want JB in your caucus. You couldn't control him. But if he wanted the job, which he doesn't, he'd be just what our party needed. And, in a humbler opinion, just what the country needed."

———≈———

Despite his lackluster interest for serving in Congress, Rob Wiley was still on the top of the Republican's House leadership list to run in the special election and succeed his longtime mentor should Earl Gregory decide to retire. All the right people in the House had signed off on him and had asked him to confirm his interest.

"Rob, it's Paul Ryan. Did I catch you at a good time?"

"Hello, Paul. Yes, I'm good. What did you need?"

"The leadership needs your decision quickly. It's getting down to the wire. Where's your head?"

"Paul, I need a little more time. Can you give me forty-eight hours?"

Wiley's uncertainty concerned Ryan. "Forty-eight hours and no longer. If we don't have your answer by then, we'll assume you're out and we'll move on."

"Rob, good to hear from you. How are you holding up? What's the latest on Earl's condition?"

"I'm good, JB. And Earl's feeling better. He's being released from Hopkins tomorrow and will be home in a few days. He's got a long road ahead with physical therapy, and it's not certain if he'll walk unassisted again. Doctors give him a fifty percent chance. But his spirits are up and he's looking forward to seeing his grandkids again."

"Tell Earl when you talk, that everyone at Spectre and Win-the-Day very much look forward to seeing him. We've got a lot of people around here who will be onboard to help him out. Please let him know he can expect a lot of support."

"I will and I'm sure he'll be grateful to hear that. I wanted to talk to you about a conversation he and I had yesterday. Do you have a few minutes?"

"Of course."

"JB, Earl's feeling much better and he's expected to make a

significant recovery. How significant is unknown. And with the uncertainty, he's going to announce his retirement after he gets home."

"I'm sorry to hear that. What does this mean for you?"

"This is what I need to talk to you about. Paul Ryan offered me the House leadership's endorsement to fill Earl's seat."

"Congratulations Rob. I'm sure you'll do great."

"I spoke with Earl yesterday to let him know I don't want it. I don't want commute to DC and truth be told, I'm not sure I'd be good at it. And the thought of campaigning scares the shit of me. He asked me to talk to you."

"Go on."

"Earl has been grooming me for many years for a run when he was done. It was difficult to tell him I just don't have it in me. He said he understood. Look JB, I know this is the last thing on your mind right now. I know you need to focus on the Foundation and Luke. But think about how much influence you would have to push your cause if you were in the House. Boehner, Ryan and McCarthy all asked Earl about you. You would get huge support from some powerful people. Think about it. Think about Luke and everyone else you could help in that role. And I'll be your Chief of Staff any day of the week and twice on Sunday if you want me." (pause) "At the risk of pissing you off, I already talked to Angela about it."

"You talked to Angela? What did she say?"

"She said OK."

"She said OK?"

"She said OK."

"OK!"

"OK, what?"

"OK, let's do this"

Thirty-four

A lot of powerful and influential people in and around government were surprised when they learned Jonathon Braxton, a political unknown, and a man who abhorred the sport, decided to run in the special election to fill the House of Representatives seat recently vacated by Earl Gregory. Many very pleasantly surprised.

Numerous conversations were activated in Washington, Philadelphia and Thousand Oaks by this most unexpected and, in many circles, welcomed development.

Lance Reibus to his sister—"You won't believe the news I have for you."

Wallis Kriss to his producer—"Book him for the show again, quick, before he gets buried with requests."

Cornelius Hale to Carlton Hale—"Well big brother, somehow we got our man."

Jeffrey Claymore to Heather Carrington—"Well, Heather, not sure if you had anything to do with this but, if you did, well done!"

Heather Carrington to Jeffrey Claymore—"I'm not sure how this happened, and I sure wouldn't want to be the poor schmuck who has to run against him."

Hanley Michaelson to himself—"Son of a bitch!"

Darby Robinson to Jeffrey Claymore—"Son of a gun!"

John Boehner to Paul Ryan—"Well, Paul, I heard you might have your hands full shortly."

Earl Gregory to Rob Wiley—"Rob, I hope you can serve JB half as well as you served me. I can't thank you enough."

Abby Martin to Angela Braxton—"No freaking way. Seriously? Oh my god, as if Spectre isn't enough of a three-ring circus already."

Cornelius Hale to Jon—"Well, Congressman, ready to take the JB show to DC? Carl and I have your back all the way. Anything you need. Anything."

Connie McIlroy to Rob Wiley—"I couldn't be happier."

Abby Martin to Jonathon Braxton—"Well, your highness—I mean Congressman—so much for hating politics."

Lucas Braxton to Jonathon Braxton—"I love you, dad."

Angela Braxton to Jonathon Braxton—"Me too."

———— ≈ ————

"Good morning from Washington, DC. It's Sunday March 31. I'm Wallis Kriss, and welcome to Big News Sunday. In September of last year, we interviewed Jonathon Braxton, a tech sector CEO from Southern California, after he made an impressive appearance at the Republican National Convention. He had delivered an impassioned address advocating not for embryonic stem cell research, but pluripotent cell research—I hope I have that correct—as a potential cure for numerous health issues. During his appearance, Braxton stated he had no political associations or ambitions and was solely advocating for his cause. We have now learned he has announced he will seek to fill Congressman Earl Gregory's seat in a special election in California. We invited Mr. Braxton to tell us why he is now running for public office after telling us he had no intention of doing so. He is here in studio to speak with us. Thank you for joining us, Mr. Braxton. Welcome back to Big News Sunday."

"Thank you, Wallis. Nice to be back. And thank you for making the distinction between embryonic stem cells and pluripotent cells. It's important not to mislead our viewers so they can form their opinions based on the facts."

The veins in Kriss' neck started to rise, as well as his blood pressure. While planning for a non-confrontational discussion, he was now not sure where Jon wanted this interview to go. Kriss concluded he needed to quickly regain control and the best way was to bring some heat.

Jon was ready. He realized going to Congress as the ultimate outsider would be akin to hand-to-hand combat, and he was anxious to sharpen his skills. He calculated he'd likely not be invited back to Kriss' show after delivering what he had planned and couldn't care less.

"Mr. Braxton, you told our audience last September you had no political affiliations or ambitions. Today you appear to be the darling of the Republican Party and are running for office. So, who is doing the misleading here?"

"When I told you and your audience about my positions at that time, they were 100 percent true. Since then, many things have occurred which changed my thinking. I'm sure, Wallis, you change your thinking on occasion. You learn new details, hear different perspectives, you change your mind. You can't tell me you never have. No one can say they never have."

"Very well, sir. Now that you are running for office, your potential constituents will be basing their decision to vote for you on what you say. Considering you changed your mind about running, how will they be able to trust what you say is what you believe and what you will do? Politics is a slippery slope, Mr. Braxton. People judge you on your words."

"That's unfortunate isn't it. Words don't solve problems. They often create them. It's action that gets the job done. Let me tell you why I changed my mind. Then let's leave it to your viewers to decide how to judge me." Beads of sweat formed on Kriss' forehead. His facial expressions clearly displayed the anger he was feeling at this moment towards Jon. This was his show. How dare this guest question his authority to render judgment.

"As you know, I spoke at the convention last August to announce the formation of a foundation to advocate for a specific area of medical research. It was personal for me because this research holds promise as a pathway to a cure for Type 1 diabetes which afflicts my son. Following the convention, I began investigating what the necessary level of funding which would enable us to accomplish our objectives. With help from many in the research community, we concluded we would need at least $1 billion dollars a year for three to five years to enable us to fully research our hypothesis that pluripotent cells, curated in the proper manner, hold the promise of curing numerous maladies. Are you with me so far?"

Kriss gritted his teeth but couldn't think of a rebuttal that wouldn't sound petty. "Go on, sir."

"Annual funding over the last six years for diabetes research and development from the U.S. Congress has averaged around $150 million a year. Monies raised from other advocacy groups, walks, galas, fundraisers, bake sales, silent auctions, and the like, total around $40 million a year. That's a huge gap. It's clear our only realistic possibility to achieve our objectives in a timely manner is the U.S. Congress substantially increasing their funding. Agreed?"

Kriss shifted in his seat uncomfortably. His anger and tension abated a bit. "Go on Mr. Braxton."

"After the convention, I was invited to Capitol Hill to discuss our positions with the House Subcommittee on Health and Human Services. I was also granted a meeting with Kathleen Sebelius, the Secretary of Health and Human Services. From our efforts thus far, we have only secured a ten percent increase in diabetes research funding. Nowhere close to where we need to be. I was working on improving our fundraising performance when Earl Gregory suffered his stroke. The opportunity to enter the special election was offered. My thinking was we could be more effective in our mission if I were on Capitol Hill. This is the only reason I changed my mind. I'm still not a member of the Republican Party, and my political aspirations are only related to finding a cure for Type 1 diabetes. If I'm elected and we generate enough awareness to raise the required funding for our cause during my tenure as a congressman, in one or two terms, I'll retire at that time."

"And if you can't get the funding needed while in Congress, would you seek a higher office or a cabinet post?"

"We'll cross that bridge if it's along our path.".

Carlton and Cornelius Hale, Lance Reibus, Rob Wiley, Heather Carrington, John Boehner, Paul Ryan, and Kevin McCarthy were all watching—and all took note.

———≈———

"Good morning, America. I'm Todd Chuckman and welcome to NBC's Greet the Press. Today, our first guest hails from Southern California. Jonathon Braxton is running as a Republican to fill California's twenty-sixth district House seat, recently vacated by the retiring Earl Gregory."

"Braxton is very much an unknown in political circles. He's never run for public office and has been characterized as having an outspoken distaste for politics and politicians. Yet he has thrown his hat into the ring for the open seat in his home Congressional district. Mr. Braxton, welcome to Greet the Press."

"Thank you, Todd. I have a question for you if I may."

"OK, Mr. Braxton, get one in," Chuckman replied nervously, He had watched Jon handle Wallis Kriss and suspected this interview could be a challenge. He didn't want to start off on the wrong foot. "But remember who is the interviewer. And who is the interviewee."

"I've been thinking about this a lot and hoping you might answer it for me. Is one running for or holding political office necessarily a politician?"

"Well, there are other defining characteristics of what a politician is."

"What would you define those other characteristics to be?"

Chuckman realized he best not answer. "Mr. Braxton, I have a feeling you'll soon be finding out."

"I'm sure you're right. You've been in the game much longer than I, but don't be surprised if I choose not to take on those characteristics."

"Very good, Mr. Braxton. Let's talk policy. The voters in your district will be expecting representation from you on numerous issues. We don't know much about your positions. I'd like to explore a couple."

"Sure, Todd. What would you like to cover first?"

"Health care is on everyone's mind these days. Can you give us your perspectives on Obamacare?"

"I don't view the Affordable Care Act as legislation that improves health care. There's nothing in the legislation which serves to improve the quality or availability of services. It's primarily focused on how goods and services are paid for. The ACA does not address assuring those goods and services are abundant, of high quality and low in cost. I'm not a fan."

Chuckman smirked and nodded, feeling as if he had struck the first blow by exposing Jon's conservative tendencies. He looked at his producer who, out of Jon's view, gave him a thumbs up. Chuckman tried to get in a response, but Jon was not yet ready for it.

"I don't believe government should be legislating the delivery of health care. Quality is best delivered through a personal connection between a patient and a doctor who they trust. The best activity for government to assure quality health care for its citizens is to strengthen these associations. Secondarily, assure the underlying products and services prescribed by doctors are abundantly available, of high quality and affordable. These tasks are best performed by free markets, not government intervention."

"But, Mr. Braxton, there is large inequality in this country. Health care costs are expensive, and out of reach for many. If people don't have good insurance, they can lose their life savings if they get sick. Shouldn't the less fortunate have access to health care which is now only available to the more fortunate? This is the promise of Obamacare."

"Todd, you are right about the costs of health care services and health care insurance. As an employer of 800 people, and the provider of their access to health care insurance, I know first-hand how rapidly costs have risen. Where you and I differ is how to lower those costs. The ACA is not an efficient solution. I'm a big free market advocate. I see the ACA restricting free markets and negatively impacting the availability, quality, and cost of health care services for the majority of Americans. To assure quality medical goods and services are abundantly available at the lowest cost, policies I would support must focus on aligning government action with protecting free markets and competition. Protecting both the manufacturers of medicines and medical equipment, and the medical care professionals who deliver services into the market, from burdensome overregulation, excess taxation and unnecessary constraints, assures the market of efficiency."

Chuckman tried to fire a response, but Jon would not have it.

"To lower costs let's understand why they are high. They are high because there are barriers to competition and many market inefficiencies. If we restore free market competition and increase efficiency, costs for medical goods, services and insurance would drop significantly."

Chuckman wasn't buying it. "Sadly Mr. Braxton you seem oblivious to the plight of many Americans. Health care is simply unaffordable to those less fortunate."

"Agreed, but my view of the solution is to make these services not only less expensive, but of high quality and abundance as well. If we subsidize health care costs for the less fortunate, but in doing so, reduce quality and availability for all Americans, are we doing a good job? Can you show me one case where the government is active in engineering a marketplace where the end result is low cost, quality and abundance?"

"Mr. Braxton, everyone deserves the basic necessities of life, and those with wealth should pay their fair share in taxes so that these necessities can be affordable for the less fortunate."

"OK, taxes. Fair share? Please define that for me. If I voted in Congress to raise your federal income tax rate to 60 percent of your income would that be fair? Would you vote to reelect me? That's what we'll need from you to insert the government into this marketplace to deliver the poor quality and hard-to-find services you want provided."

"Mr. Braxton, that is not I want to provide. And it is not the point."

"Then what is the point?"

"I am talking about providing access to health care for people who cannot afford it."

"OK, back to health care. Let's discuss the reason many cannot afford health care, shall we? Could it be because of ineffective government engineering of the marketplace? Engineering being driven by companies and industries lobbying legislation to limit competition? It's been proven throughout history the only way to reduce costs without destroying quality and availability are unencumbered free markets."

"You sound like a good old-fashioned Republican to me."

"Sorry to disappoint you. Would you still think that if I accepted zero campaign money from the medical and big pharma lobbies as many members of Congress from both parties do?"

Chuckman's attitude shifted from confident interrogator to unsure debater. His recognized his arguments were weak against Jon's positions. He resorted to attacking Jon's character. "It's clear you have little interest in helping the less fortunate among us. You seem a heartless soul. Now let's discuss those income tax rates. Many people in this country pay very little in income tax relative to their incomes thanks to loopholes and shelters. What is your position on income tax rates?"

Jon was ready to respond to Chuckman's attempt to assassinate his character but decided to hold his fire—for now.

"OK, back to tax rates. Todd, I happen to agree with you here if your point is the federal tax code needs overhauling. The loopholes and shelters you refer to—I agree should be eliminated to create a fairer taxation system. But raising tax rates is not the answer. My solution is a single-rate, flat income tax with no more than five eligible deductions—home mortgage interest, charitable contributions, excessive health care expenses, and higher education expenses, being among them."

"Surely, you're not advocating high-income earners pay lower tax rates, are you?"

"Surely, I am, with a focus on the bottom line. Eliminate superfluous deductions, shelters, and loopholes, and wealthy people will pay significantly more income tax. If the goal is to have wealthy people pay more without hampering motivation to earn and produce, then a flat-rate income tax is the most efficient solution. The U.S. federal income tax code is an abomination. Every deduction is in place to benefit a special interest. My vision is everyone paying seventeen percent of their income, with a few eligible deductions capped at fifteen percent of their tax liability. This scenario collects the Treasury significantly more revenue than is collected today. That is the ultimate goal, correct? People with higher incomes pay more. Seventeen percent of $200,000 is more than seventeen percent of $50,000. That's fair, Todd, right?"

"You can't be serious advocating someone earning $200k a year pay the same tax rate as someone earning $50k."

"You're not seeing this clearly. Under a seventeen percent flat tax, assuming allowed deductions were capped at fifteen percent of tax liability, the person earning $200k a year, taking maximum deductions, would pay $28,900 in federal income tax. The person earning $50k a year, taking maximum deductions, would pay $7,225. The entire economy would benefit. Less capital would be wasted harvesting tax returns and feeding special interests. More revenue would flow into the Treasury. Productivity would not be encumbered. Eliminating unworthy deductions and loopholes would ensure that spending decisions on the part of individuals are based on the quality of the decision—not tax implications. The deductions we would keep would be those that align with supporting a better quality of life, such as home ownership, and charitable giving."

"The deductions and loopholes in the current tax code incentivize spending for favorable tax outcomes. Unfortunately, these expenditures are not necessarily wise. They often lead to taking on large debt and would be considered wasteful or superfluous when tax implications were not considered."

Chuckman tried to interject. Jon refused him the opening.

"I realize this is not popular on Capitol Hill. I've likely now made a few more enemies. But the current system clearly favors special interests and the wealthy. A flat-rate income tax would lessen this inequity. Our discussion should not be about the rate. It should be about efficiency and bottom-line impact. Todd you'd agree with me, I'm sure, that the current tax code could not be more inefficient."

Before Chuckman could answer, Jon continued. "And just one more thing. Actions are the better judge of one's character than words taken out of context. Before you judge me do your homework. If you research our company and our learning academy you will learn of our deeds in support of the less fortunate. Do your research. Then we can discuss my character."

Chuckman turned his eyes from Jon to the camera. "We'll be right back after a word from our sponsors."

Chuckman took off his earpiece, got up, ignored Jon, and stormed offstage, directly to the show's producer. "This interview is over, and he's never coming back."

Thirty-five

It was 346 days following Luke's T1D diagnosis when Jonathon Braxton, running unopposed, was victorious in a special election to represent California's twenty-sixth district in the U.S. House of Representatives. Two Democrat challengers filed to run, but shortly thereafter better understood the political landscape and realized they had no chance. Both dropped out within a week of filing.

That evening, a victory party was in progress at Spectre. Angela and Abby planned the affair. It was perfectly understated, reflecting the blend of emotions in play. There was excitement in the air, but also a soberness reflecting the mission of this campaign. The muted celebration was being held in the Spectre component warehouse, reflecting the no-frills theme. Many from the Type 1 community Jon and Angela met in the months following Luke's diagnosis were in attendance. The food and drink were modest and non-alcoholic. Sweets and carbohydrates were nowhere to be found, but optimism was in abundance. Jon was the one physically going to Washington, but there were many thousands going with him in spirit.

Earl Gregory had made an unexpectedly fast recovery from his stroke and was able to attend with Jeannine, walking with a cane under his own power. He also regained the ability to speak clearly. Also in attendance were the Hale brothers and Rob Wiley, as well as employees from Spectre, Win-the-Day and City Hall. Jon had invited Jeffrey Claymore to come to Thousand Oaks for the event, though when Jeffrey arrived a little late, he was surprised to see Heather Carrington

317

had joined him. When he saw her, he smiled and wondered why she made the trek.

The crowd was anxious to hear Jon speak. Rob sensed it and asked Earl to say a few words to warm things up. There was a makeshift podium set up at the west end of the warehouse. Earl was no stranger to a microphone or to public speaking and was comfortable and confident as he surveyed the crowd, microphone in hand.

"Ladies and gentlemen, thank you all for being here to share this special moment. Despite what you might think, this is not a moment for Jon and the rest of us to celebrate this victory, and Jon would be the second one to tell you that." Earl paused momentarily hoping the levity of his comment would be recognized. It wasn't. "This is only a first step, but this is a moment of hope and promise for all of us. It is a moment for us to recognize how fortunate we are to have this man to fight for us. It's a moment for us to come together and to let this man know he will not be alone when he goes to Washington. Trust me, I know from personal experience how difficult his road will be. It will be difficult because he is an outsider and outsiders are not welcome in the swamp. It will be difficult because he will be advocating a cause that will be scorned and ridiculed by many, even from within his own caucus. It will be difficult because of who and what he is. We all know he is not a politician and that he is not interested in playing ball. We will have to continuously remind him what is important, because in DC, it's almost impossible to remember. We must be there to pick him up when he gets down, and trust me, he will be knocked down more times than he will care to recount."

"Despite the deck being stacked against him, I am overwhelmingly optimistic Jon will be successful in whatever endeavor he sets his mind to in Washington. For all my years in Congress, I can confidently say no one I met had the character and the tenacity to take on Washington better than Jon. We have good reason to hope. It's a big job which needs to get done, but we have the right man. Jon, all the best to you.

Shake things up and move mountains. And rest-assured, when you need us, we'll be here."

There was no applause, only silent recognition of the magnitude of the sacrifice Jon was making. Rob Wiley came to the podium to take the mic from Earl. "Pastor Claymore, will you say a few words for us?"

The pastor was standing next to Luke, He squeezed his shoulder with affection then strode slowly to the podium. Rob handed him the mic.

"Hello, everyone. I'm Jeffrey Claymore, and I'm from Philadelphia. The first interaction I had with Jon was one year ago over the telephone. We were ready to engage in what you might call a business discussion. Before we got started with the business at hand, I asked Jon a question. It's a question I often ask when meeting someone new. I asked Jon if he believed in God. He was candid and honest in his response, which I have come to learn is his trademark. He said he wasn't sure. And after he shared with me his upbringing, I understood his uncertainty. Jon did not have the benefit of loving parents or a community that could share God with him as a child. It's difficult, though not impossible, for one to develop a belief in God with no one to show the way."

"And while Jon still has uncertainty about his faith, I'll tell you one thing I know for sure. Without question, God believes in him. I know this for a fact because God tells me. Not in words. God communicates in other ways. Every time I see Jon or talk to him or hear about one of his incredible ideas, I'm reminded how much God believes in him.

Now Jon is going to Washington. Not one of God's favorite places, but there is a job to be done. It's an important job, and God is sending His best. The job calls for making men and women rethink priorities in the face of enormous distractions. Distractions of money and power. Not an easy job whatsoever. This job requires a man of great persuasion. Of great passion. Of great enthusiasm. Of great intellect. And of selfless character. The job requires Jonathon Braxton, and he has accepted the call. Jon may God look after you each and every day and give you the strength to carry on. And may God bless you."

Rob Wiley came for the mic amidst a muted chorus of "amens." He looked at Jon, off to the left of the podium. He was standing with Angela and Abby, struggling to keep his emotions in check. His thoughts were with Luke. Rob pointed the mic at him, as if to say— *'it's your turn, man.'*

Jon came for the mic clutching Angela, not letting her hang back. With his arm still around her shoulders, he took the mic and pursed his lips. The warehouse was silent, except for the distant, mischievous laughter and movement of some of the younger kids, rampaging around the far reaches of the warehouse.

"Luke, Darla, will you come up here and join mom and I?" He was now surrounded by his family. "To Congressman Gregory and Pastor Claymore, thank you for the kind words and encouragement. Wish I could say I won't be needing them, but I have a feeling I will. I also have a feeling this is not going to be one of my better speaking moments."

There were a few half-hearted laughs. Jon cleared his throat, trying to center his thoughts and emotions. He was struggling. "Your confidence and kind wishes are humbling and overwhelming. I'm having trouble finding the right words to express our gratitude. The four of us feel truly blessed to have friends like you, and I sincerely hope that I can live up to your expectations in the important months and, perhaps, years ahead. Let's all put our faith in Pastor Claymore that I am the right guy for the job. Sometimes I feel it and sometimes frankly I don't. Since Luke's diagnosis, my confidence and self-assuredness has taken some lumps. I can only imagine what it has been like for Angela, yet she has remained steady while I've wobbled. She is the strongest, most resolute woman I know. She has been my stabilizer, and I could not have chosen this path for us without her strength."

"I want to share some words for my family. I consider you all my family now, but these words are for Angela, Luke, and Darla. Guys,

I want to tell you how much I love you. I think you already know I'm not going to be home much of the time over the next few years. I know we will miss each other, and it will be hard. Angie, I know it will be especially hard for you to be alone raising our kids. As much of a sacrifice as this might seem to be for your husband, you are making the much greater one. And I could not respect you more. So, Luke, Darla, you need to respect your mom as I do and make this as easy on her as you can."

"And to all of you,"—Jon turned his attention back to the throng of about three hundred— "I pledge to work for you every day. And I pledge to further the objectives of our Lucas Braxton Foundation. As you know, this is the primary reason for putting my family through what they are about to go through, but please don't doubt me for a moment. I do this with conviction. I do this not only for Luke, but also for every family that has Type 1 diabetes in their lives."

"I'm sorry I could not be more eloquent but thank you all for coming. Thank you all for your kind words and offers of support. Feel free to hang around as long as you'd like."

As Jon wrapped up, everyone in the room converged toward him to shake his hand, give him a hug, or pat him on the back. After several minutes, the well-wishers began dispersing. As Jon was accepting the congratulations and words of encouragement from a large group that had gathered around him, he looked to his left and noticed Heather, Carl, and Neil walking toward Abby, who was standing alone.

"Hello, Mrs. Martin. It's a pleasure to see you again. You know my brother Carl, of course, and I wanted to introduce you to our friend, Mrs. Heather Carrington."

"Mr. Neil Hale, the pleasure is all mine. Mr. Carl Hale, it's so nice to see you again. Mrs. Carrington, it's an honor to meet you."

"Mrs. Martin, I've heard quite a bit about you and the terrific work you do for Spectre and all its associated interests. You are a remarkable woman, and I was so looking forward to meeting you."

"I'm glad we have now met, Mrs. Carrington. Since you're here, there's a few things we should discuss."

"Oh?"

"Yes. May I call you Heather?"

"Uh, you may. Abby. What's on your mind?"

"OK, Heather here's the deal—I need you to be my proxy when Mr. Braxton is in Washington."

"What?"

"Yes, he needs someone close by to give him crap, but in a friendly way. He thrives on it. It's what gets his juices flowing. And if you haven't yet noticed, when he gets juiced up, well, amazing things start to happen. So, you must promise me you will watch over him, call him often, and give him lots of friendly crap. OK?"

"OK Abby. I promise."

Neil Hale, continuing to be amused by Abby, could not help but flash a huge grin. Carl acted as if he hadn't heard a word. Heather noticed the crowd around Jon was thinning and excused herself to speak with him.

"Well, Jon, you've been busy in the many months since our last conversation. Given what we talked about in Washington, I couldn't quite believe it when I heard you were running for Earl's seat. Congratulations on being elected to Congress."

"Hello Heather. Thank you coming but we really should stop meeting like this. After all, we're now officially across the aisle."

"Sorry Jon, not going to happen. Abby has something else in mind for me, and I'm now taking my orders from her."

Thirty-six

Jon Braxton officially began his political career upon arriving in Washington, 374 days following Luke's T1D diagnosis. He was sworn into office the following day. Rob Wiley travelled with him, and Jon was introduced to Earl Gregory's Washington Office Chief of Staff, Brandon McKay, whom he also retained. The three had numerous conversations over the next few weeks, setting Jon's agenda upon his arrival until the traditional August recess, six weeks away.

Jon spent much of his time during his first weeks in Washington on two tracks. The first was learning the ins and outs of being a congressman. He studied and researched legislation on the docket for Congress' return to session after Labor Day. He studied and researched Congress' committee and subcommittee structure. He studied the protocols of working the halls of the Capitol, shaking his head in disbelief at most of them. He made a point to introduce himself to as many members of the House as he could, leading to a few awkward moments. Jon's reputation as a maverick and outspoken outsider had preceded him. Many of the old guard in the House were standoffish and dismissed him as a likely one-term wonder. The awkward interactions had been kept to a minimum thanks to Majority Whip McCarthy taking a liking to Jon and clearing lots of paths for him. The relationship between them was growing closer by the moment.

McCarthy was taken aside by many in his caucus to ask about Jon's philosophies. It was no secret—thanks to his appearances on Sunday DC beltway TV with Wallis Kriss and Todd Chuckman—Jon disliked politics and politicians. Many within the Republican House caucus expressed their concerns. McCarthy was only moderately successful addressing them.

The second track occupying Jon's attention was centered on federal budget processes. How revenues were collected, and allocations appropriated. As he learned during his minimally successful advocacy activities, there were significant competitors for the budgeted monies Congress would make available for medical research grants. To pursue those highly contested funds more successfully, he decided it best to learn the rules of the road before getting back into the car.

The six weeks flew by, and Jon returned to Thousand Oaks in early August. The time in Washington had both strengthened his resolve and reinforced his dislike of politics. While home, he called Neil Hale.

"Congressman! Good to hear your voice. I'm guessing your home for the Labor Day break. How are they treating you on the Hill?"

"Like I have the plague. But McCarthy and I are getting along well and he's working to get me into the boy's club. Just don't think I'll be spending much time in the clubhouse. Square peg, round hole."

"I told Carl this would be the case, but don't worry. Keep your focus on what you want to accomplish. Those old bastards will move out of your way if you don't back down."

"Thanks Neil. I've got a couple of questions. Do you have a few minutes?"

"Shoot."

"I want to author some education legislation."

"Well, it seems like you've settled right in. But didn't Congress just pass an education bill a few weeks ago?"

"Yes. The Student Success Act. It's weak and it won't work. I know where the flaws in public education are and have ideas how to improve things."

"Bills and resolutions written by first-term Congressmen are not usually given much consideration, and I've heard through the grapevine you're not the most popular girl at the dance. You might want to reconsider and spend your time building some bridges."

"If you really know me, you know I can't do that. What if I had McCarthy and Ryan as cosponsors?"

"Do you?"

"McCarthy yes and Ryan's close."

"That would certainly change things."

———— ≋ ————

Jeffrey was at his desk at First Pentecostal when the call from Thousand Oaks came in.

"Hello, Jon. It's good to hear from you. How is Washington treating you? And how is my main man, Luke?"

"Luke is doing well thanks to you. Your talks have helped immensely. I'm grateful for your influence. I don't know how to thank you."

"As I see it, you already have. What about Luke's blood sugar? Are you able to keep it under control?"

"It's proving difficult. His body reacts randomly to the insulin injections. He's had a couple of scary episodes but we're going in the right direction."

"Keep the faith, Jon. Stay on the path. You are doing the right things. His body will acclimate."

"I will. I think I need your help on something. Do you have a few minutes?"

"Of course, anything."

"I'm writing new education legislation. Bush's No Child Left Behind Act and the recent Student Success Act are incredibly flawed. I'm going to introduce some ideas which can make more of an impact on kids in this country, particularly the underserved. I plan to take the work we do at Win-the-Day and shape it to be delivered in a public-school setting nationwide by adding our curriculum into the 5ᵗʰ grade in public schools."

"It's a great idea, Jon. How can I help?"

"I want this to be bipartisan. I want to introduce it as joint legislation and I need a Democrat senator to cosponsor."

"Understood. I'll make the call.

———≈———

Jon's cell phone rings. It's direct from the Secretary of State.

"Hello, Jon. It's Heather Carrington.

"Hello, Madam Secretary."

"Thought we agreed to dispense with those titles." She laughed. "Jeffrey Claymore insisted I help you with some legislation. What are you up to?"

"I need a Democrat senator I can work with on education reform."

"And?"

"I want to make a name for myself quickly to gain credibility for my primary agenda item, diabetes research. I have ideas how to improve public education. I know they will be successful if implemented properly because I've done it in the private sector. I'm writing legislation to amend the Student Success Act Congress passed a few weeks ago and I want to bring it to the floor as bipartisan joint legislation. I need a Democrat Senator as a co-sponsor."

"You're out of your fucking mind. Sponsoring a bipartisan joint resolution after only six weeks in office? Not going to happen."

"McCarthy is co-sponsoring, and I expect Ryan on board soon."

"What? After only six weeks in your seat? They're behind you on this? Wow. It must be something special. Tom Harkin might be interested. Tell me more."

———≈———

Jon hadn't spoken with Abby for two weeks and being home knew he needed to pay her a visit. He entered the Spectre executive office lobby. Roberta was sitting at Abby's old desk. Abby had occupied Jon's office. Her door was closed.

"Hi Roberta."

"Mr. Braxton, what a surprise. How good to see you."

"Great to see you as well. You look very comfortable at that desk."

"Thank you. I may look comfortable, but inside I'm a nervous wreck. I can't believe all the work Mrs. Martin did in this position. It's overwhelming to keep up with everything."

"I'm sure you'll settle in. Speaking of Mrs. Martin is she busy?"

"Not that busy. I'll let her know you're here."

———— ≈ ————

They met in Abby's new office. "Well, well, Congressman Braxton, thank you for blessing us with your presence this fine day. Thought perhaps you had forgotten about your little old COO."

"You are not little, and you are definitely not old. But you are the COO, and I'm way late on checking in. I hope you interpret the expanding spaces between our conversations as representative of the complete confidence I have in you."

Abby looks to the dartboard on the wall to her left. "I am certainly OK, but I cannot say the same for Captain Crunch. He misses you."

"Ah, the Captain, I could certainly use him in DC. Some of the decisions I have to make in the ebb and flow of the swamp are mind-numbing. I could use the Captain's clarity."

"Shall I get the Captain a plane ticket and send him off to the quagmire?"

"Not yet. He's an old friend and I can't see throwing him into the swamp yet. Let me get my sea legs first."

"Well, your highness. What brings you here today?"

"Wanted you to know I'm working on my first legislation. We're going to take the lessons from WTD and teach them in the 5th grade across the country."

"My, my. So ambitious, though I expect nothing less. Is Heather Carrington making any contributions to your efforts?"

"She is. And I've been meaning to ask about the conversation you had with her at the victory party."

"Sorry, Mr. Congressman. That was off-the-record girl talk. Now tell me, what personality style are you using to cross the aisle?"

"Style? Style...Thanks, Abby."

———≈———

The first session of the 2013-14 Congress resumed in Washington the Tuesday after Labor Day, 429 days following Luke's Type 1 diagnosis. Jon made it a point to get on Leader Ryan's calendar first thing back. Ryan's admin got him fifteen minutes on Thursday.

"Paul, I wanted to follow up with you a little more on the idea I briefly shared before the recess. I know Congress just passed the Student Success Act before the recess to fill gaps in No Child Left Behind. I get it, but these efforts aren't going to make a significant difference in the lives and education for most of the kids in the country. Raising standards for teaching traditional subjects is noble, but without the right foundation, our kids are not going to be able to absorb the education you want to give them. They need to supplement a different kind of education, an education that teaches them how they build the right foundation for themselves where they will want to learn. Until kids develop that foundation for learning, raising teaching standards won't make a significant difference in their lives."

Ryan had his secretary cancel his next appointment and spent the next hour with Jon as he described his idea in more detail. Jon shared his experiences and successes from Win-the-Day. He argued for proposing this resolution to lead to a joint bipartisan exploratory commission. He described his proposed curriculum to be taught to all fifth graders in the United States. He went into the reasons why each of the tracks would lead to better outcomes in educating fifth graders.

"All very commendable JB, but you realize this is going to alienate a lot of your colleagues who endorsed and promoted the SSA."

"I realize that, but I'm not here to play along. I see a problem and I know the solution. And I have few updates. Most importantly, Tom Harkin has agreed to co-sponsor and bring to the floor in the Senate."

"We're bipartisan now? Wow. How did you pull that off?"

"I get by with a little help from my friends."

———— ≈ ————

Wallis Kriss was working in his office when his administrative assistant buzzed him on the intercom. "Yes, Diane?"

"Mr. Kriss, Secretary Carrington's office has called in, and the Secretary is asking to speak with you. Are you available?"

"Yes, Diane, put her through. ... Wallis Kriss."

"Well, well, Wallis Kriss, it's Heather Carrington. Long time no talk."

"Hello, Madam Secretary. It certainly has been. Not since the 2008 campaign, I believe."

"You're right, Wallis, 2008. Oh, how I've missed you."

"Something tells me you might be pulling my chain, Madam Secretary. As I recall, our last interview did not go particularly well."

"And I recall it the same way, Wallis. After everything we went through together when I was in the White House, for you to favor Barack in 2008, well, let's just say that was a bit tough to swallow."

"Yes, Madam Secretary, I can see that. Yet you called. Why?"

"Well, Wallis, I feel you owe me, and I'd like to collect if OK with you."

"I'll do my best. What do you have in mind?"

"I have a scoop for you, and I'd like you to use that scoop to help a friend."

"OK. What have you got?"

"I have a friend in Congress whom you know. I don't think you particularly like him, but I'd like you to put that aside. My friend is making a bit of history in Congress this week. I'd like to tell you about it, and I'd like you to invite him back to your show and give him a platform."

"And your mystery friend is?"

"Jonathon Braxton."

Kriss was surprised. "Jonathon Braxton is your friend?"

"Yes, he is. And he is introducing a joint bipartisan resolution in Congress for some education reform. It's a terrific plan, and his cosponsors are Paul Ryan, Kevin McCarthy, and Tom Harkin."

"Wait, what? He has a Democrat Senator as a cosponsor? Harkin's the Health and Education Chair in the Senate, right? And Paul Ryan is putting his ass on the line too? Wow. This may be unprecedented for a first-term Congressman."

"JB seems to make it a habit of doing things that are unprecedented."

"Oh, and were calling him JB now?"

"That's right."

"The chair recognizes Representative Jonathon Braxton from California to present and introduce for consideration H.J. Res. 1641, the Success Training and Youth Life Lessons Education Resolution. The STYLE's resolution sponsor is Representative Jonathon Braxton and cosponsors are Majority Leader Ryan, Majority Whip McCarthy, and Senator Tom Harkin."

The house was a bit stunned with the announcement of the

cosponsors, as Jon left his desk and approached the Speaker's podium. He had nothing in hand but a government-issued Blackberry. The teleprompters were switched off.

"Thank you, Mr. Speaker. Dear esteemed colleagues, thank you for this opportunity. As I am new to Congress, I have not had the opportunity to meet many of you personally. To give you some background relating to the joint resolution we are proposing, you should know what I am proposing I have successfully implemented in the private sector. For the past six years, I have had the great fortune to oversee a private foundation I co-founded in Oxnard, California, a low-income, heavily minority-populated city in Southern California. Oxnard is a gritty community, where the predominant economic activity is farm labor. Its racial demographic is heavily Latino and African American. Most kids growing up in Oxnard face many challenges. Many grow up without fathers and, in many cases, without mothers as well. Many grow up in gang-infested neighborhoods. Crime, drug use, and drug-dealing are always present. Many kids in the community grow into lives of gang affiliation, crime, drug abuse, prison, and premature death."

"Six years ago, I had the opportunity to meet with a retired teacher and administrator from the area. A veteran of thirty years in public education. She counseled me on her frustrations with the public school system and its deficiencies. I was interested in her input, as I had a young son in the third grade within that system. As a result of numerous conversations, she and I formed an idea to provide troubled youth with the education we felt they needed to break out of the chain of failure that young people in the Oxnard community faced. Our objective was to provide these young people the tools they need to break out of systemic poverty and give them the confidence they need to carve out better lives for themselves."

"Many of you are thinking Congress recently passed the Student Success Act to fill the gaps in No Child Left Behind. We do not need another education bill at this time. I'm sorry, but I must disagree for the simple reason that neither of those acts address the core education needs of many kids growing up in today's America. When I say core education needs, I'm not referring to math or English or social studies or science or history. This is not to say those subjects are not important. They are. But NCLB and SSA do not address the root cause of the failures in public education. Addressing the systemic high failing and dropout rates that exist in public education requires a different kind of curriculum. A curriculum that has proven successful in Oxnard and can be shaped to be delivered in a public education environment."

"The focus of our resolution is to bring to light the fact that kids have difficulty learning information if they have difficulty understanding why they need to learn that information. Kids need a reason to learn. Many kids in our society unfortunately do not comprehend the importance of education. In their minds they do not link a quality education with a quality life. They do not understand the real world as adults do, and unfortunately, many adults do not have the tools to teach their kids why they should want to learn."

"Under our resolution, we propose a curriculum that serves to build the self-esteem and self-confidence within a young individual, to support a belief that they have the ability to make better lives for themselves. This belief leads to desire. When kids have this belief, they develop an appetite for knowledge as the means to build a better life. Without that belief, that appetite is suppressed."

"I have witnessed many hundreds of young children transform within a few weeks of our introducing them to the concepts we teach. With our training, we take kids on the precipice of self-destruction, pull them back, and transform them into productive, happy, successful young men and women."

"Ladies and gentlemen, I'd like to introduce you to one of the many of our success stories from Oxnard. Jamal Peterson was a young man on the edge of leaving school for a local Oxnard gang. Today, three years after graduating from our program, he will soon be graduating from Top Gun school and begin his career as a fighter jet pilot in the United States Air force."

"Becoming a fighter jet pilot was a dream he developed using the life learning tools we provided him. Very shortly that dream will become a reality." Jon looked up into the gallery to his right. "Jamal, please stand and say hello." Jamal, dressed in Air Force whites, stood, and waived to the House floor. "Also in the gallery is the managing director of the Win-the-Day Foundation, Ms. Connie McIlroy, the public education veteran who assisted me six years ago in developing our curriculum and currently serves as our Foundation's Managing Director. She is the person most responsible for changing the lives of hundreds of underserved young people in the city of Oxnard. Connie, please stand."

"My third guest here with us today you all know. In the gallery is my predecessor in Congress, the honorable Earl Gregory." Gregory stood, and the sight of him brought all the Congressmen on the House floor to their feet in a respectful round of applause. Earl was well liked on Capitol Hill, and most had not seen him since his stroke six months prior.

"Mr. Gregory today serves on the Win-the-Day Board of Directors and since his retirement from Congress has taken an active role in the organization. He, Connie, and Jamal will be in my office following our session and will be available to answer any of your questions about the work Win-the-Day does. Work which serves as the inspiration for our resolution before you today."

"Distinguished members of Congress, allow me to present to you House Joint Resolution 1641, the Success Training and Youth Life Lessons Education Resolution of 2013, in short, the STYLE Resolution. It is the intent of Senator Harkin to present this resolution to the Senate for adoption as well. A copy of the resolution will be distributed to all members."

"Our bipartisan joint resolution is being proposed to amend the recently adopted Student Success Act of 2013. Our resolution proposes the addition of a curated curriculum to be taught during the fifth grade to all students attending K12 public education in the United States. The curriculum being proposed is designed specifically to teach concepts to fifth graders to improve their opportunities for success in middle and high school, and beyond. Under our resolution all fifth graders in public education would be required to complete the curriculum we propose."

"The curriculum being proposed would serve to teach the following concepts and how they can be utilized by our children as tools to use to become successful and productive adults—universal truths, self-esteem, self-worth, honesty and integrity, personal responsibility, goal-setting and attainment, self-confidence, charity and giving."

"The curriculum would be developed by a commission to be formed by the U.S. Department of Education, and I would recommend that commission work closely with Mrs. McIlroy for that purpose. The children of this nation are its greatest resource. It is incumbent on us, as this country's legislative body, to develop this resource to its maximum potential by cultivating and nurturing it. H.R. 1641 proposes to change the style of our public education such that we teach not only subject matters, but also life matters."

"Fellow colleagues, please stop by my office today to meet Jamal Peterson and Connie McIlroy. And to speak with Earl Gregory. Come to an understanding of what we are proposing and, when given the opportunity by the speaker, approve H.J. Res 1641 so we can begin to educate our kids with the tools they need to make themselves productive, confident, and morally centered young adults. Thank you."

To the surprise of many in the chamber, there began a round of applause by House members and staff as Jon concluded. It started small and as Jon made his way away from the podium, the applause grew. He was stopped constantly on his way back to his seat by members of

Congress wanting to shake his hand. By the time he made it back to his seat virtually the entire House was standing and applauding.

Speaker Boehner leaned over to catch Majority Leader Ryan's ear. "It's like the goddamn President making the fucking State of the Union address."

Thirty-seven

"Good morning from Washington, DC. It's Sunday, September 29. I'm Wallis Kriss, and welcome to Big News Sunday. Our first guest today has been with us twice previously. During his first appearance on this program last year, following his appearance at the Republican National Convention, he stated he had no interest in politics. On his second visit, he announced he was running for a seat in Congress in a special election. And now we wish to welcome Congressman Jonathon Braxton back to the show. Welcome, Congressman."

"Wallis, can I ask you a question before you start the interview?"

'Here we go again,' thought Wallis. "Of course, Congressman."

"Would you mind calling me Jon or JB, if that suits you better?"

"Uh, alright, uh, Jon, uh, JB. Why would you ask that?"

"The last time on your show, I told you I didn't consider myself a politician. I think you just implied I misled your audience as a politician may have done, and you know that it is not the case. So, from now on, when you and I talk, I'd like it to be as if we were just two guys in a bar, enjoying a beer and shooting the breeze. No pretensions, no sniping. Will that work for you?"

Kriss ignored the question.

"OK, uh, JB, let's discuss your busy week last week. On Wednesday, you introduced a bipartisan joint resolution to the House, a resolution that was cosponsored by Paul Ryan, Kevin McCarthy, and Senator Tom Harkin, the Democratic chairman of the Senate Health and

Education Committee. This is somewhat unprecedented. We're still researching, but it's possibly the first time a first-term Congressperson has sponsored a joint resolution with bipartisan cosponsors. How were you able to accomplish this feat?"

"Two reasons, Wallis. One, the resolution has tremendous merit. And two, the resolution has tremendous merit. I'd say it's a good thing when merit trumps politics. Wouldn't you agree?"

Kriss ignored the question. "And why did you wish to present it in this manner, seeking Senator Harkin's co-sponsorship, as opposed to only presenting it to the House?"

"Wallis, we're two guys in the bar, right? No one else is around?"

"OK."

"I want to see this resolution adopted by both houses as soon as possible. I don't have the patience to slow-walk it or play politics. The fastest path to have this legislation signed into law is having it adopted by both houses simultaneously is to limit the number of rewrites. By having Senator Harkin cosponsoring, we are hoping to see it voted on and adopted within the next two weeks."

"You refer to your resolution as the STYLE Resolution, the Success Training and Youth Life Lessons Education Resolution. Will you describe it briefly for us?"

"There have been three landmark education bills in the modern era passed by Congress. Starting in 1965 the Elementary and Secondary Education Act as part of LBJ's war on poverty. By 2001, that legislation was woefully outdated, and Bush 43 amended it with No Child Left Behind. Then just last month, Congress passed the Student Success Act to fill in some gaps from NCLB."

"Unfortunately, neither of these three acts address the core reasons why kids fail in school or drop out. Our resolution was drafted to move Congress to address those core reasons. If it's adopted, we'll amend the Student Success Act with the ideas I've put forward. All of which Ryan, McCarthy, and Harkin have signed onto."

"What are the core reasons in your estimation?"

"It's not an estimation on my part. We have the proof. Wallis you have kids, right? What ages?"

"I do. Nine and twelve."

"I'll venture to say that both your kids do well in school. True?"

"Yes."

"Why is that? I'll answer. The primary reason is they have a good role model. You. They know you place value on education, which led you to a good profession and a nice living. Imagine your kids were not yours. Assume they live in a broken home at the poverty level with no role models. Under those circumstances, would your kids do as well in school as they are doing now?"

"I'm not sure."

"Many kids overcome difficult circumstances and develop an appetite for learning. But the overwhelming majority of kids coming from those circumstances do not. This is the reason for STYLE. These kids need lessons on life they do not learn at home. Our bill is focused on providing these lessons. We know our ideas work in the right private sector setting. Our success in Oxnard is proof. Our challenge going forward will be adapting our concepts to a public education setting."

"Thank you, JB. We'll return after a word from our sponsors."

———≈———

One evening later that week Heather Carrington was in her residence watching CNN. A commentator is describing the action earlier in the day in the House.

"And on Capitol Hill a bit of history was made today. First-term Congressman Jon Braxton's education reform resolution, known on the Hill as STYLE, was adopted jointly by both houses of Congress with massive bipartisan support. We asked Congressman John Kline, the sponsor of the Student Success Act legislation which this resolution seeks to amend his thoughts."

The station switched to a live interview with Congressman John Kline, the sponsor of the Student Success Act.

"I like JB's ideas. His proposals make too much common sense to ignore. The fact he has put his principles into successful practice in the private sector made it easy to support his resolution. I, like many of my colleagues, believe the life lessons we will soon be teaching the fifth graders in this country will significantly improve the chances for success in life for these kids."

Heather switched off the TV with her remote, closed her eyes, and sat silently with her thoughts and insecurities.

Thirty-eight

The STYLE Resolution was adopted by both houses of Congress in early October 2013. The vote in the House was 420-8. In the Senate, 93-7. Legislation to amend the Student Success Act to include Jon's curriculum was written—titled 'The STYLE ACT of 2013'— and approved by year-end. Jonathon Braxton's legacy was now officially under construction. Many of his colleagues were amazed and commenting on how he made such a significant mark on Capitol Hill within seven months of arriving. The goodwill generated by STYLE among the voting public towards Republicans was highly favorable, and Jonathon 'JB' Braxton was quickly approaching household name-recognition status.

Wallis Kriss—recognizing Jon was not a Republican Party shill—became one of his biggest fans and offered Jon an open invitation to appear on Big News Sunday. He could come on virtually whenever he wanted with their conversations always featuring two friends in a bar shooting the breeze—only with millions watching.

Jon's appearances on Big News Sunday, happening at the rate of once per month, were becoming must-watch TV. In Thousand Oaks, when Jon was scheduled for a Sunday morning appearance, it was brunch time at the Braxton household. Angela would host a houseful including Tanoro, Taka, Abby, Earl, Connie, Rob, and their entourages. It was also must-watch TV on the East Coast on Sunday mornings at eight for the Hale brothers, Lance Reibus, Paul Ryan, Kevin McCarthy and Heather Carrington. Even Jeffrey Claymore moved his regular Sunday eight o'clock sermons to nine on the Sunday's Jon was appearing.

One thing, however, not measuring up to Jon's satisfaction in Washington were the results of his efforts to increase pluripotent cells research funding. That war pitted Jon against Big Pharma and other special interests in the medical community vying for the same funds. His battles were difficult, time-consuming, and—to a large degree—unsuccessful.

As the calendar rolled into 2014, Jon faced the decision of running for reelection. He was missing his family greatly and was not comfortable in the middle of the DC swamp. While harboring feelings he could better spend his time elsewhere advocating for pluripotent cells research, he followed advice from Heather and Paul Ryan to be patient. He entered the 2014 race for the House seat he currently occupied.

That November, Jon was reelected to Congress in a landslide victory, 855 days following Luke's T1D diagnosis. No serious Democrats ran against him. They saw that decision as futile and career-ending. A sacrificial far-left candidate was offered up to push specific leftist agenda items. She carried eight percent of the vote. It did not go unnoticed by the likes of the Hale brothers, Heather Carrington and Lance Reibus that Jon had significant appeal to voters of both parties. They were all watching Wallis Kriss' election night coverage on November 4, as were John Boehner, Paul Ryan and Mitch McConnell from Boehner's office.

The TV in Boehner's office was tuned to the Big News channel. Wallis Kriss was moderating a panel discussing the evening's election news. "The results are clearly pointing to a big night for the Republicans. We can now confirm that they have won a majority in the Senate and Mitch McConnell will become the new Senate Majority leader."

Boehner looked at McConnell. "Welcome to the party baby. You're the man now." He hoisted a glass of cabernet sauvignon.

"Thank you, John. It's nice to be in the majority and I'm guessing I have Braxton to thank."

Paul Ryan answered. "I think that would be in order. All our polling indicates the goodwill generated by STYLE for Republicans across the country being the catalyst."

They stop to watch Kriss.

"The Republicans will also maintain their majority in the House. And in one race of particular interest, California Congressman Jon Braxton was reelected to his seat with an unprecedented 92% of the vote in his District."

A pundit from Kriss' panel comments. "I'd say Jon Braxton has a bright political future ahead."

Kriss replied. "Perhaps. But does he want it?"

———————≈———————

When Jon returned to Washington after the holiday break—919 days following Luke's T1D diagnosis—Paul Ryan requested a meeting. It was scheduled for nine in the morning.

"Good morning, JB," was the cheery response from Ryan's Washington office receptionist. "Mr. Ryan asked me to send you in when you arrived. He's expecting you."

"Thank you, Gracie."

Jon walked into Ryan's office. John Boehner was there as well. "Good morning JB. Thanks for taking the meeting. Happy New Year and congratulations on your landslide reelection victory. Ninety-two percent? Wow. Folks in your district must really love you. I'm not sure I've ever seen a Congressional candidate capture ninety-two percent. Have you, John?" Boehner shook his head no.

"Thank you, Paul. I've got a great staff in my district. Rob Wiley knows the vote there like no one else, and Earl Gregory's support is big."

"Don't be so modest. Listen, JB, the Speaker and I are interested in hearing some of your legislative thoughts and ideas. We want to set the 2015 agenda for our caucus in the next few weeks and want you to be part of the process."

Boehner clumsily interjected. "JB, the STYLE Act provided our party with tremendous goodwill with the voting public. We believe it was a large reason we were able to hold majority control in the House and win a majority in the Senate. As Paul mentioned, we are interested in your thoughts. Are you planning to introduce any legislation to the House this year?"

"I am."

———≈———

The former First Lady was dressed in a light-peach jogging suit with white Nike running shoes. In 651 days, she would have the opportunity to make good on her promise. She walked down the first-floor hallway in her Washington DC home and knocked on the study door of her husband, the former President.

Knock, knock, and she was in. Wil Carrington was to her right, seated on a burgundy leather sofa adorned with brass buttons, facing an unlit ornate walnut-paneled fireplace. He had his reading glasses on, reading that Sunday morning's edition of The Washington Post.

"Wil?"

"Good morning, honey. Please come in," he said sarcastically, annoyed she was now knocking and entering without his consent.

"Kriss is on with Braxton in a few minutes. Why don't you watch with me?"

"I'm not watching Wallis Kriss, not after what he did to you in '08. And I'm not watching Braxton. I don't like him. He's a Republican, remember?"

"I'm not so sure JB's a Republican. I think he looks at the party as a rental car. He's just using it to get where he wants to go."

"Oh, it's JB now?"

———≈———

"Good morning from Washington DC. It's Sunday, January 27. I'm Wallis Kriss, and welcome to Big News Sunday."

"Last week, the big news in Washington was made on Tuesday when Barack Obama delivered his State of the Union address to a joint session of Congress. This week, the big news promises to be generated by Congressman Jonathon Braxton of California. Braxton, no stranger to our show, is likely to create some fireworks on Capitol Hill as he did last year when he brought his STYLE Resolution to the House floor, initiating historic change to public education in the United States. Today, we're pleased to have Congressman Braxton back with us for the first time since he was reelected to his House seat last November. Happy New Year, sir, and congratulations on your mammoth victory. Ninety-two percent of the vote. Impressive."

"Thank you, Wallis. It's nice to be back, and Happy New Year to you as well."

"OK JB, tell us your plans for the House next week. I heard you have some big ones"

"Wallis, I'm buying this week, so make it the same as last time? Guinness?"

Kriss smiled and half-heartedly chuckled. "Sure, JB, a Guinness for me and—based on what I understand you're about to tell me—make it a tall one."

Jon said nothing and just stared at Kriss, who was becoming slightly agitated. He liked crisp back-and-forth dialogue, not pregnant pauses. Finally, from Kriss: "Well?"

"Well, what?"

Ordinarily Kriss would be indignant toward this kind of interchange, but it was JB.

Kriss smiled and slowly restated his question. "Aren't you going to tell us about your legislation?"

"Of course, I thought you'd never ask." Laughter could be heard from the production crew on set. "Wallis, what's the single biggest problem facing this country?"

"I'd say the way you annoy the heck out of me when you come on my show." More and louder laughter from the production crew.

"OK, the second biggest problem facing this country?"

"Please tell us—I mean me, since it's just the two of us."

"Dirty money in politics. There are common sense solutions to all our other problems, but they never see the light of day. Why? Because the people sent to Washington to develop these solutions can't do it. They are either the wrong kind of people, playing the game solely for money and power. Or, they have the talent and desire to do the people's work but can't escape the shackles of the swamp. They rationalize taking dirty money to stay in office to get the job done. But the money eventually compromises them. The biggest problem in our country today— the one preventing us from solving all our other problems? Dirty money in the form of campaign financing and lobbying."

"So, what are you proposing? Quietly, just between you and I."

"Getting the dirty money out of politics."

"Oh, that should be easy. Let's order another beer, shall we?" More production crew laughter.

"Wallis, next week I am introducing to the House our ELECT Resolution of 2015, 'Election Law Everyone Can Trust.' We'll propose forming a new Department of Elections within the legislative branch. This department will have jurisdiction for funding all campaigns for federal legislative offices. All candidates who survive their primary would be allocated a fixed amount of money, based on the office and their location. No outside money would be permitted, and all candidates would be responsible for detailed accounting of their funding."

"For primaries, campaign funding would not come from federal money. Primaries would be funded as they are today with a few modifications. All primary campaign funds would be maintained outside of a candidate's reach. Their campaign funds would be controlled by a separate individual the candidate designates upon filing to run as their Campaign Finance Manager. The Campaign Finance Manager would be responsible for disbursement of any funds contributed to the primary campaign. The candidate would be prohibited from being a signatory on this account. This account would also be subject to potential full auditing by the Elections body. Should any monies remain in a primary campaign following the primary election, those funds would be due and payable to the federal treasury and the account closed, regardless of whether the candidate wins or loses."

"In the general, only funds coming from the Department of Elections could be used. This keeps the playing field level, from a campaign finance perspective, for candidates running for the same office. No longer would a candidate—simply because he has better fund-raising abilities—have an advantage over his opponents. And all unused monies from all general campaigns would be returned to the federal treasury within thirty days following the election. We want to rid the landscape of campaign war chests. Wallis, just between you and me—sound good?"

"This resolution sounds very complex and I'm certain would come under intense scrutiny from your colleagues on the Hill. Do you truly believe you can move this kind of legislation through both houses and bring it to a vote? Notwithstanding the sheer miracle it would take to get this legislation that far, there's not much chance, in my opinion that Obama, or any successor, would sign it into law. Unless of course you happened to be his successor."

"Thank you for the thought but we know that's not going to happen. I know it's not a perfect solution and would face hurricane level headwinds in Congress. But we want to solve the country's problems and we must start somewhere. Any solution will be uncomfortable to put an end to the way our politics are played. But dirty money in politics is the fundamental problem to solve. I've seen first-hand being in Washington for almost two years now how poorly we govern because of outside undue influence. So, let's start the work to fix this country. Let's work to bring the best and the brightest problem solvers to Washington as elected officials. We're still two guys in the bar, right Wallis? No one else listening?"

"Nope. It's just you and me."

"If the swamp is too deep, at least we'll know we gave it a shot. You know my story. Before Luke's diagnosis and Earl's stroke, I didn't have the slightest interest in politics. If ELECT fails, I'll gladly go home to my beautiful family and resume my advocacy efforts outside of the swamp. I don't need politics. I've been in Washington long enough to know this life doesn't suit me. I love solving problems, but with all the dirty money in the way, it's almost impossible to solve anything in Washington. I'll go where I can be effective."

"Well JB, you were able to make history in 2013 with STYLE. This one, I think, is going to be much tougher. Thank you again Congressman for joining us on Big News Sunday. We'll be back with our panel to discuss the Congressman's resolution right after these messages."

Heather Carrington switched off her TV with the remote control. She had intently watched every minute and heard every word. After the screen went dark, she again closed her eyes and sat motionless for twenty minutes. She thought about her father. She thought about her years in the White House and in the Senate and at State. She reflected on her entire life's body of work. She questioned what she wanted for her future. She yearned for her father's wisdom. Finally, she opened her eyes and stood. She put on her Washington Nationals baseball cap and oversized dark glasses and headed outside into the crisp Washington winter day for a five-mile walk—her Secret Service detail in tow.

Thirty-nine

In the year 2015, politics in Washington D.C. was a smoking hot mess. Factors contributing to the continuing and growing discord within the U.S. government included foreign and domestic terrorism fueled by the growing influence of ISIS, legislative gridlock in Congress, racial injustice and the resulting riots and protests, increasing homelessness and drug abuse, the resignation of John Boehner as speaker of the House and replacement with Paul Ryan, continued animosity between Barack Obama and now a fully Republican Congress, the growing federal deficit, ongoing backlash against the Affordable Care Act, and increasing stress on the U.S. immigration system. The toxicity between the executive and legislative branches of the U.S. government was at unprecedented levels.

Adding to the combustion were indictments of two sitting House members—Chaka Fattah and Bob Menendez—on racketeering and corruption charges. Two others resigned after federal investigations. Former House Speaker, Dennis Hastert, was indicted on illegal banking charges.

The looming 2016 presidential election was generating friction and conflict across the spectrum, and the ground was being laid for the most expensive presidential campaign ever. The 2012 election cost the two parties $2 billion. For 2016, projections were $5 billion.

As if this were not enough to grind the wheels of government to a halt, discussions on Jon Braxton's election law reform legislation were ripping the scabs off in Congress. Despite the acrimony and turmoil,

Jon remained focused on his three personal primary agenda items. Along with election law reform, he was spending his newly acquired—and not insignificant—political capital to significantly increase funding for diabetes research and to build support for rewriting the U.S. federal income tax code.

With all the issues Congress was grappling with, Jon was encountering significant headwinds moving his primary agenda forward at a pace he could be satisfied with. While election law reform and improving the federal tax code were important issues to him, nothing was more important than finding the cure for Type 1 diabetes. Jon was becoming increasingly impatient in the swamp, and again thoughts of conducting advocacy outside the halls of Congress were occupying his consciousness.

———≈———

Paul Ryan had asked Jon to meet with him. Ryan was concerned about Jon's mindset in early March after the ELECT resolution went down to defeat in the House by a 230-203 margin. There was not enough appetite in Congress for campaign funding and finance reform. Though surprisingly, 140 House members voted across party lines.

The issue spawned serious debate and forced a lot of House and Senate members to choose a side. Interestingly the split was not along party lines. The divide seemed to be along character lines. There were many members of the House and Senate, from each party, who had spent years building their financial pipelines and campaign war chests, for whom the resolution was unappealing. But there were also surprises. Many long-term members of Congress were supportive, relieved with the thought of being released from the bondage of special interests. Jon had been correct in his assessments. Many congresspeople were in office for the wrong reasons. And some were in for the right reasons but were compromised and ineffective because of their dependence on dirty money for reelection. The concept of election law reform was debated heavily in the media. Some networks and publications were highly supportive, and others highly critical. It was apparent dirty money was in play there as well. A network or a publication was all-in one way or the other—with each of their journalists or broadcasters always in alignment with the others in their shop. A fact that did not escape Jon and was the subject numerous off-air conversations with Wallis Kriss.

Ryan's receptionist greeted Jon. "You know the way Congressman."

"Hi JB, good to see you. Thanks for coming by."

"What's up Paul?"

"Just wanted to take your temperature after the vote on ELECT. I know you're not happy and I just wanted to give you my perspective."

Jon was not in the right frame of mind to hear swamp-speak from the Speaker. "Honestly, Paul, I'm not in the mood for any 'this is the way it is' BS. This place is what we all know it to be."

Paul was sympathetic. "It is exactly that. And it will be what it is until someone comes along to change it. I'm not sure who that is or will be. Maybe it's you. Maybe it's not. But I wanted you to know that I am with you, even though a lot of shitheads in your own caucus are not."

"Thanks for your sympathy Paul, but you can save it. I don't need it. What I need is to be somewhere I can do my thing. It's clear that Washington is not that place."

"What are you saying Jon?"

"I'm saying I don't fit in Washington."

In Thousand Oaks things were in much better condition than in Washington. Luke was now fifteen and had found his footing in his ongoing battle with Type 1 diabetes. He was still pricking his fingers, injecting insulin, and watching his carb intake. But he had assumed complete responsibility for managing his blood sugar and was doing a masterful job. His sugar spikes were under control, and outside of schoolwork, his attention was focused on girls, surfing, and exercising.

Spectre Systems, under Abby's guiding hand, was continuing to outperform its competitors and bedazzle its customers. Sales numbers continued to grow at above-average industry rate. Personnel turnover was almost non-existent. Customer satisfaction levels were at all-time highs, as was the Spock Market.

Earl Gregory had recovered from his stroke and took on the role, with great enjoyment, being Connie's right hand running Win-the-Day. He had also assumed the role of lead fundraiser, and due to his fund-raising prowess, the foundation was set to open a second campus in the nearby San Fernando Valley. The foundation's work was now benefitting 1,200 kids per school year.

Ventura County was enjoying the nine new companies and the 3,300 new good-paying jobs that had relocated to the county resulting from the 2012 County Economic Conference and the efforts of Larry Morris. Unemployment in the county was at an all-time low.

———≈———

When Jon returned home during the August 2015 recess, he and Angela had many conversations centered on his retiring from Congress. They discussed his returning full time to the work of the Lucas Braxton Foundation. The more they talked about it, the better it sounded.

He was leaning towards saying goodbye to Washington DC.

While home, Jon decided to stop by Spectre and catchup with Abby. They were in her office he was seated across from her.

"Well Mr. Congressman what is going on with you?"

"Washington's beating me up, Abby. I can't seem to get the funding increases we need. Too many competing agendas, all with big lobby money attached. Everything in Washington is so polluted with money and influence and corrupt politicians. I knew it would be bad but had no idea how much so. I It feels like I'm wasting my time there. I feel I could be more effective outside of the cesspool."

The day prior to this meeting Angela had spoken with Abby about Jon's discontent. She wanted Abby to be ready to respond if Jon mentioned his frustrations to her. She was more than ready. "Thank you for that Mr. Braxton. Are you quite finished?"

"What?"

"Are you quite finished with your little pity party? I hope so because I would like to say a few things to you. First, this moaning and groaning is not like you and may I add very unbecoming. So please give me the little crying towel you walked in here with so I can shred it. Second, let's talk about Luke shall we? You do know he is growing into an amazing young man don't you? He will not let diabetes get the best of him and his work locally helping newly diagnosed kids and raising money and awareness is unbelievable. And just where do you think he gets his inspiration Mr. Braxton? Third, our company is growing market share like crazy, and WTD has never been better. And it is you—Mr. JB your highness—who is making all this happen. Even from 3000 miles away. The sacrifices and the efforts you have made and continue to make are inspiring more people than you can ever imagine. Don't you know what your brewski stops with Kriss are doing to this country? Millions of people see who you are and what you want. And they want you right where you are to fight for them. Don't let the fog of Washington cloud your vision. You were right when you first decided to run that your best chance to develop the cure was to be close to printing presses. And that's now where you are. OK so maybe it's not happening fast enough. Well then, let's figure out how to make it happen faster. But leaving Washington isn't the right move. So, if you want to continue to bitch and moan, feel free but just don't do it in my office. I'm not interested in hearing it. With all due respect your majesty."

———⋙———

Jon returned home after his therapy session with Abby to take call from the Speaker of the House.

"JB, Paul Ryan."

"Hello Paul."

"When you come back to DC, let's meet. I want you to take over chairmanship of Ways and Means."

"That's quite an honor Paul. But I need to get back to you. I'd like to think on it a little bit."

"OK, is tomorrow enough time?"

"OK, I'll call you tomorrow.

———⋙———

Later that evening the Braxton family was at the dinner table.

"Luke, mom tells me you've got a girlfriend."

"Nice mom. Yeah dad, she's cool."

"What's her name?"

"Madison, but I call her Maddie."

"When do I get to meet Maddie?"

"Whenever you want. She wants to meet you too. Her dad is impressed that his daughter is dating your son. He wants to meet you as well."

Angela interjects. "Did I hear you on the phone with Paul Ryan earlier today?"

"You did."

"And?"

"He wants me to take over the chair of Ways and Means."

Luke dropped his fork on his plate. "Dad! Are you serious? That's the most powerful committee in the House. They control funding and budget processes, right?"

"Yep."

Angela—"That's right where you need to be. You're getting closer."

———≈———

Luke's life as a Type 1 diabetic had consumed 1161 days of his fifteen-year existence when Jon returned to Washington following the August 2015 summer recess. He had Abby's ass-kicking in his head and new conviction in his heart. Paul Ryan was putting together the final packaging to hand Jon the chairmanship of Ways and Means, arguably the House's most powerful committee. It was an unheard-of precedent considering he was serving in only his second term. Given the not-so-positive impact ELECT had made on many of Jon's colleagues, Paul knew he would face stiff opposition within his caucus. This move would cost Paul considerable political capital and had to be well-planned, coordinated, and strategic. He calculated it was worth it.

———≈———

Only 427 days remained until Heather Carrington would have the opportunity to fulfill the promise she made to her father fifty-nine years ago at the age of seven. She was in her DC residence watching CNN when a commentator came on with breaking news.

"And on Capitol Hill an anonymous source just informed us House speaker Paul Ryan has installed Congressman Jonathon Braxton of California as the new Chairman of the powerful House Ways and Means committee."

Heather switched off her TV, reached for her cell phone and called Jon.

"Hello, Heather. Good to hear from you."

"Jon, my god, Ways and Means? In your second term?"

"I guess that's congratulations, so thank you."

"You, my young friend, are a magician. I've never seen a political career like the one you've launched. You are making history on a regular basis. You know that, right?"

"I'll leave that for the media to decide. I have a meeting just about to start. Can I call you back in thirty minutes?"

"No need, I just had a quick ask, and I don't need an answer right now."

"OK, what is it?"

"Switch parties and be my running mate next year."

.

Forty

She had Mark Parker set two State Department meetings in Philadelphia for her the following week. She then cancelled them both as the Gulfstream G450 entered Pennsylvania airspace. She was on her way to Sharswood. She needed Jeffrey.

This visit she had no staff entourage, and there were no Secret Service on the plane. She had instructed her detail to meet her at Chester County Carlson Airport upon her arrival at ten. She was to be alone in her thoughts, as confusing as they were.

By 10:35, the State Department black Chevy Yukon SUV arrived at First Pentecostal. Two Secret Service personnel went inside the quiet, empty house of salvation. They surveyed for five minutes and came back to the vehicle. Heather exited with one on each side and walked in. She asked her detail to stay in the church foyer. She was early for her meeting with the pastor and decided to make her way alone into the sanctuary. The sanctuary had twenty rows of seats, divided by a six-foot wide center aisle, with each side slightly angled to face the pulpit.

Jeffrey's office, where they often would meet, was to her right behind a set of closed walnut single-panel double-doors. She looked at her watch and noticed she was twenty minutes early. She took a seat in the tenth row to the left of the pulpit.

She sat still for a moment, eyes fixed straight ahead, anxious for the outcome of this conversation with the only one she could confidently share her insecurities and doubts with.

Suddenly her eyes felt heavy. She was awake but as her anxiety mounted, she found her eyes closing. She then did something she had not done alone since the age of eleven. Sequestered in her thoughts, she started to pray. In this house of worship, she prayed for guidance and good judgment. She prayed for understanding and for forgiveness. She prayed alone for fifteen minutes, and soon felt a presence she had never felt before. It was a presence that had nothing to do with Jeffrey Claymore, who had entered the sanctuary five minutes earlier. Unbeknownst to her he sat to her right without making a sound and joined her in silent prayer.

Heather's eyes suddenly opened. She turned to see the pastor at her side, silent and motionless. His eyes still closed, and his hands folded over his knees. She reached her right hand over his left and set it down gently. She looked at him. He opened his eyes and returned the gaze. Her look was a blend of despair and confusion. His of reassurance. "I'm glad you're here, Heather."

Neither felt the urge to move, and the conversation started slowly with the two of them seated in the sanctuary. Both now gazing at the pulpit some thirty feet away.

"Jeffrey, thank you for meeting me. As you can see, I'm a bit of a mess. I have a crucial decision weighing on my mind, and I am at a loss for what to do."

"I'm always grateful for the opportunity to help you. Tell me the nature of your dilemma." It was a question for which he already knew the answer.

"I made a promise to my father when I was seven. I promised him I would break the glass ceiling and become the first female president. And, for the last ten years, I've made the same commitment to thousands of others. Because of my words, so many people have put their credibility on the line, their money, their integrity, their reputations, all on the line for me. And now, as in 2008, that promise is within my grasp to keep. Everything is in place and ready to go. Everything that is except me. Jeffrey, I have so many doubts about my ability and my desire. I can't decide what to do. One day I feel committed, the next I want to run away and hide."

"If I were to leave the race, I would be letting so many people down. So many would pay a heavy price. I'm not sure I could live with myself. But I can't get comfortable with the idea of staying in and likely winning. I would be more comfortable staying in the race if I knew I was going to lose. Listen to me, does this make any sense at all? Do I sound like a world leader? Jeffrey, help me. I don't know what to do."

"Heather, you came to the right place to ask your question. But you are asking the wrong question. Now let me ask you one. Let us say you did not have these doubts and you ran, and you won. Now it is four years later, and you have had a full term in office. Look back and tell me what accomplishments you achieved. And tell me, assuming you achieved those accomplishments, how you would feel about the decision you made to run?"

Heather tried to answer but could not. The question was too insightful. She tried to look inward for the answer but could not find one. She turned her gaze from Jeffrey back to the pulpit. She closed her eyes. Jeffrey waited for her to respond, but she was silent as she stared at an image of the Christ raised on the wall behind the pulpit.

"Heather, ours is the only species on Earth with the capacity for free will. God, in His infinite wisdom, gave us two systems for exercising our free will. He intends for these two systems to counterbalance one another. One system is embedded in our brain, the mind if you will. The mind uses reason and logic to make its calculations. The second system is embedded in our heart, metaphorically speaking, and uses a formula dominated by our conscience, our spirituality, and our morality."

"The brain and its ability to reason is best suited to make decisions based on sensory input such as sights and smells. Or on information. Or previous experiences. In other words, hard data. When logic is needed to make the right decision, God wants us to use our brain."

"The heart is best suited for decisions that call for morality, ethics, and principles. When there is no sensory input or data to call on, God wants us to use our hearts for our decisions. When people despair is when they fail to or are unable to use the right system."

"For many decisions, input from both systems is called for. If an individual uses both systems to arrive at their decision, that decision proves to the best possible one within their capacity."

"People with the ability to consistently choose the right system are those who are the most well-adjusted, the happiest, the most authentic. When you make the best decision for yourself, you know it in both your heart and your mind. This bipartisan—if you will—decision generates harmony and soothes the soul."

"If you decide to stay in the race, make sure you do it for the right reasons. Assess all the factors involved in your indecision. Then assess how to use your systems. The first question in your assessment should be, do I really want the job? And if so, why? If the answer to the first question is no, then your decision is clear. Don't stay in, even considering the fallout with colleagues and supporters. You owe it to the country, and yourself, to not run if your heart tells you not to."

"If your heart assures you that you want the job, give your mind the chance to uncover the reasons why. Give both your heart and your mind the opportunity to give you the right answer. Give both your heart and your mind their due, and the ultimate choice will become clear. And it will be a choice you can live with."

Forty-one

By December 2015, the presidential campaigns of all candidates from both parties had come into focus. All had announced earlier that summer and had been jockeying broadcast, journalist, and social media with their messaging.

Even with Barack Obama terming out, and precedent concluding the White House would switch parties, the race was perceived to be Heather Carrington's to lose. She was the favorite for the Democrat nomination and the betting favorite to win the general. She had the full endorsement of the popular Democrat President and had her people in strategic positions throughout the important swing states and the Democrat National Committee. She had only one serious challenger, the progressive far-left Senator from Vermont, Bernie Sanders.

The Republican race was more complex. There were several strong and viable challengers for the nomination, including Ted Cruz, Marco Rubio, Jeb Bush, Chris Christie, Mike Huckabee, Rand Paul, Carly Fiorina, and a host of others. According to Carlton and Cornelius Hale, all of whom had virtually no chance of winning against Carrington.

From the Republican field all who had declared their candidacy were in the market for consequential endorsements. One of the most coveted was that of the second term Congressman from California, Jonathon Braxton. All had been seeking meetings with him upon Congress' return to Washington from the Thanksgiving weekend—all except for Ohio Governor Anthony Jacobs. All except Jacobs had been seeking Jon's endorsement and all asked Jon a similar question—

"What are your thoughts about potentially joining the ticket if I were to win the nomination?"

To all Jon expressed the same sentiment: "I'm going to wait until after Super Tuesday before considering any endorsements. I have no interest in being on the ticket. I can be more effective with my agenda as Chairman of Ways and Means."

———≈———

Carlton and Cornelius decided to rendezvous in New York City to discuss next year's presidential election. They met for dinner in mid-December. They were sitting with their cocktails awaiting their dinners.

"Well Corny, it's that time again. Lance Reibus called yesterday. He wants to know where we stand on the field."

"What did you tell him?"

"That we don't much like our chances against Carrington. And we haven't started working with anyone yet."

"Carl, how do you feel about Tony Jacobs?"

"I like the fact he's a governor and he's from Ohio. We'll need that state. And I love he's fiscally conservative. But he doesn't have much national name recognition. Why?"

"He wants to take his campaign to the next level and wants our help. I told him we'd pay him a visit and hear him out."

———≈———

The two most influential Republican power brokers in the country visited the Ohio governor's mansion the following week. Neil Hale felt moderate Ohio governor, Anthony Jacobs, was the only Republican candidate with even a remote chance of contending against Carrington. But winning he felt, was not going to happen.

But he was pleased Jacobs had reached out for consultation and was anxious to hear his views.

"Gentlemen, I'm grateful you took the time to come to Ohio and meet with me. I imagine all our guys have been reaching out to you."

Neil replied. "They have and we've turned them all down. Fact is we like you Tony. Of all our guys, you best represent the values of the Hale Brothers. So were here to hear what you have to say."

"Thanks Neil. How are you sizing up the election next year? And how would you assess my chances against Carrington?"

"It will be tough. She's got lots of money, the media and ground ops in the battleground states. We should hold our own in the Congressional races, but at the national level a traditional Republican campaign will not put us over the top. Carl and I have been debating this since McCain's loss in '08. If you play their game you lose, as Romney did four years ago. And as Cruz or Jeb, or Carly, or Rubio or Rand or anyone else on our side will do next year if they don't do anything different. The Democrats are too well situated. Our only hope is to run a campaign unlike any other we've tried."

"I've come to the same conclusions, and I've got some ideas for a campaign I want to run by you."

Jacobs spent the next sixty minutes detailing a unique campaign strategy that had the Hales nodding with approval. When he concluded his presentation Neil responded.

"I really like your ideas and your vision, Tony. Give Carl and I little time to reflect and we'll get back to you."

"Thank you, Neil. And just one more question. I'd like to ask Jon Braxton for his endorsement. Any thoughts on that?"

"I'm not sure how much Jon knows about you. Knowing him as I do, he would think highly of your positions. They're not too far from his. But I would recommend you not ask him until you survive the primaries and win the nomination should that happen. He's already been approached by all the others and has turned them down. He's not prepared to offer any endorsements until after Super Tuesday. If you're still in the race at that time, you'd have a shot with him."

At that moment three children entered the room to pass through to the kitchen. Tony's son (15), daughter (14) and niece (9).

"Hey guys, say hi to my friends Carl and Neil."

The kids all said hello and left the room a few seconds of entering. Neil was curious.

"I thought you only had the two teenagers. Who's the young one? And what was that device on her hip?"

"That's my niece, Lauren Woods. It's an insulin pump. She has Type 1 diabetes."

Forty-two

"Good morning from Washington, D.C. It's Sunday, February 28. I'm Wallis Kriss, and welcome to Big News Sunday. This week, we are pleased to have back to the show California Congressman and Chairman of the House Ways and Means committee, Jonathon Braxton. I've got us two seats at the bar, and we have a couple of brewskis being poured as we speak. So, let's get started with the always entertaining and informative JB. Congressman, welcome back to Big News Sunday."

"Thank you, Wally. It's nice to be back. Before we dive into our beers, let me applaud you on the mammoth new contract you just signed to continue to host this show for another four years. So, congratulations, and you're welcome."

"I'm welcome? For what exactly?"

"Well, your ratings have quadrupled over the last two years since I've been hanging out and drinking beers with you."

"Granted. But your star has been rising swiftly since you started appearing on this show as well. So maybe we have a case of you scratch my back, I'll scratch yours going on."

"Agreed, let's toast to back-scratching." The production crew laughs in the background.

"You know I haven't been called Wally since I was six years old."

"Maybe when you were six your mom stopped because she started watching Leave It to Beaver."

"Yes, I'm sure that's the reason. And you're likely predating most of our audience with a reference to that TV show from the mid '60s."

"Gee Wally, I didn't realize that. Will they forgive me?" More production crew laughter.

"Either that or they'll check YouTube to see what you're talking about. Now I know you're not here to discuss comedy. I've got a few things for you, but I'll give you the floor first, since you usually take it from me anyway. What's on your mind?"

"You say I'm not here to discuss comedy, but may I remind you I work in the U.S Congress." More production crew laughter. "The comedy of some of the decisions we make on the hill cannot be understated. But in Ways and Means we're working to get a bit more serious about solving the nation's problems."

"And I understand you are here to tell us about some of the workings of the Committee which you've been chairing for over a year now. Many members of the committee have been appearing on cable and network news commenting how well the committee is operating under your chairmanship. Can you give our audience the reasons why your colleagues, even from across the aisle, are so complimentary of your work?"

"Wait, audience? Thought this was just you and me. And when are our beers coming?"

"Yes, right, just between you and I. Bartender! Our beers please. OK, so what's going in Ways and Means? I won't tell a soul."

"What is your first sense when you wade into something, and you sense it's just not right? Or when someone puts a plate of food in front of you and you get the idea it's not going to taste good?"

"It smells bad?"

"Right, Wally, exactly. Something doesn't smell right. When something doesn't smell right, it usually isn't. The sense of smell is our most trustworthy sense. I often used the smell test in my business to help my decision making. It always worked well, and now the members of Ways and Means are using their noses a little more."

"Is this what the members of your committee are talking about when they say how well bipartisanship is now functioning and the legislation coming out of Ways and Means is better?"

"I believe so."

"Just between us, can you tell me how all this smelling works?" Production crew laughter.

"Have you ever been in a formal debate?"

"Not since high school."

"I decided to take the formal debate process and apply it within our committee as the method we use to evaluate the aroma of the legislation we work on. My expectation was following a formal process of argument, followed by rebuttal, and followed by rebuttal to the rebuttal, we would promote intelligent dialogue and, as a byproduct, build bipartisanship. And if there were any foul odors, we could apply some air freshener before sending the legislation to the floor."

"What have been the results?"

"What you've been hearing from my colleagues. Many of them are former attorneys and they enjoy reliving the formal debates of their law school days."

"These debates are what's leading them to proclaim the return of compromise and bipartisanship?"

"Yes, and better legislation because the arguments for both the pro and con positions are delivered with structure and civility. As a result, we see proposed legislation from better viewing angles and the pieces of paper we sign into law just smell better."

"I've also heard from some members of the committee that your debates also include a unique format for opening arguments. Can you describe that for us?"

"The committee members responsible for opening arguments for both positions have responsibility for three things. First, show us the data supporting their position. Second, put that data into proper context. And third explain why the American people should believe their position."

"Why do you take this approach?"

"If the legislation makes it out of committee and is eventually passed into law, we want members of Congress to be able to show their constituents the validated data and supporting arguments behind our vote. We believe the American people have the right to know the reasons behind our decisions."

"That is certainly a novel approach. Are any of the other committee chairs in Congress considering following your lead?"

"Paul Ryan likes what we're doing. The other committee chairs not so much. They've been in the swamp a long time, and the stench has likely compromised their sense of smell. But I'm hopeful we can clear the air in more committees soon."

Forty-three

The calendar turned the last page from a tumultuous 2015. As the new year dawned it was formally election year in Washington, and the race for the U.S. presidency was revving up. The candidates were circling the track and the pit crews were in position. The Iowa caucuses were only weeks away, and Washington had overnight felt the effects. In Congress, members committed to running for reelection had taken their eyes off the ball labeled *for the people*. And fixed them squarely on the ball labeled *one more term, whatever it takes*. It was Jon's first taste in office during a presidential election year. He marveled at the absurdity.

Despite Washington's preoccupation with the upcoming presidential election, the business of the House Ways and Means Committee was being conducted in a fashion as never before. Jon's methods to drive bipartisanship, even though he still believed compromise often came at the cost of efficacy and efficiency, were now adopted by a few other committee chairs. Jon had successfully integrated many of the concepts he had used over the years at Spectre and WTD. His skill at adapting the concepts used in managing his company, where it was one-party rule, into the workings of a Congressional committee to where two-party acrimony ruled the landscape was adept. He shepherded the members of Ways and Means together in a fashion Congress had not seen for years.

Jon made it protocol to have the Congressional record transcripts of Ways and Means debates posted online and excerpted through social media. These transcripts were often part of the barroom discussions taking place between Jon and Wallis Kriss during their monthly Sunday morning meet ups on Big News Sunday, discussions being witnessed by an ever-growing audience. Their talks had transformed from politics and policy to Jon's creative ideas for fixing government. A regular viewing household was Heather Carrington's. Two TVs were now typically tuned in—one in former President Wil Carrington's study.

The primary season of 2016 rolled through February without any surprises. On the Republican side, Iowa, New Hampshire, Nevada, and South Carolina had all been captured by a different candidate, leaving the eventual party nomination in doubt. On the Democrat side, Heather Carrington carried all four contests by a comfortable margin. Everyone paying attention—except one—knew it was inevitable she would be the Democrat nominee.

As each day passed during the early months of 2016, Heather's internal conflict intensified. She was querying both her mind and heart for the answer. She constantly recalled the words of Pastor Claymore and tried prying open her heart. But her mind was stronger and was winning the fight for the chairmanship of the exploratory committee that had formed within her soul.

Super Tuesday was two weeks out. The pressure on her to resolve her inner conflict was becoming unbearable. When she awoke on Sunday, February 29, nine days before Super Tuesday on March 8, she went into her home office to pray for guidance.

After twenty minutes of silent reflection, she reached for the remote control. It was time for Big News Sunday.

By June 2016, the presidential primary season was in the books. Following the California primary on June 7, Heather Carrington had accumulated enough primary delegates to secure the nomination, though her margin of victory over Sanders was smaller than anticipated.

On the Republican side, Governor Anthony Jacobs of Ohio gained momentum on Super Tuesday and rode that momentum to secure enough delegates to earn the nomination. The Hales had been instrumental in mentoring Jacobs across the finish line, and the party was coalescing around him. The Republican Party leadership was now turning its sights to the vice-presidential choice and the national convention to be held in Ohio—Jacobs' home state—from July 18 to 21.

In Washington DC, Jon remained laser-focused on his agenda. Still at the top of list was significantly increasing federal funding for diabetes research, restructuring federal election law, and rewriting the federal income tax code. While public education reform under the STYLE Act was proceeding at an accelerating pace, his other agenda items were not.

Jon's ELECT Resolution had gone down to defeat in 2015, and his attempt to bring it back to the floor proved unsuccessful. Dirty money was out in force to stop his efforts. Similarly, his efforts to significantly increase diabetes research was continuing to stall. While he was able to secure between ten percent and fifteen percent annual increases for each of the three years he had been engaged, the increases were not significant enough to generate the level of progress with pluripotent cell research needed to determine if that science held the keys to a cure for Type 1.

Another thought on Jon's mind was reelection. While two years ago, he was ready to throw in the towel, his ascent to Ways and Means Chairmanship had given him hope he was now positioned to move his agenda forward more quickly. That had not yet proven to be the case, but assurances from Earl Gregory, Mitch McConnell, Paul Ryan,

Kevin McCarthy, and Heather Carrington to be patient a little longer convinced him to announce his 2016 reelection bid. Rob Wiley assured him very little money and very little of his time was needed for campaigning. Jon's name-recognition and growing legacy in his district assured him of victory. The betting line favorite was he would run unopposed.

A few days after the California primary, a phone call came into Jon's congressional office. "Mr. Braxton, Cornelius Hale calling for you."

"Thank you, Rosemary. Put him through. Neil, long time no talk. You and Carl OK?"

"We are. Just extremely busy these days as you can imagine. Hope you, Angela, Luke, and Darla are well."

"We are and congratulations on Jacobs. I know you both worked hard on his behalf and feel he gives the party its best shot."

"Thank you, JB. We're not confident in his chances, but Carrington's weaker than expected primary showing gives us a little cause for hope. We were surprised how much momentum she lost by Super Tuesday. Seemed her heart wasn't in it. But listen, the reason I called. Carl and I are wondering if you are going to be home in T.O. this weekend. If you are, we'd like to stop by the house to see you and Angela on Sunday morning. Any chance we can all meet Sunday morning around ten?"

"Of course. We'll be home. You're welcome to stop by. Anything I should be ready for?

Neil ignored the question. "Great. Look forward to seeing you and Angela on Sunday."

———— ≈ ————

It was a picture-perfect early summer day in Thousand Oaks as the Town Car pulled into the circular driveway fronting the Braxton residence. Jon and Angela, upon hearing the car in the driveway, approached the front door and stepped outside to greet Carlton and

Cornelius. The brothers gave their driver instructions they would be two hours and she was to wait. Warm embraces were shared by all, and the foursome proceeded inside to the family room. The brunch the Hales had sent over earlier was spread out on the kitchen counter.

Jon was expecting a pitch to support Jacobs. The first words from Neil were: "Thank you for having us over, Mr. Vice President."

The reason for the Hales visit was now in focus.

"JB, as you know, we've been consulting with Tony Jacobs. Since he now has a clear path to the nomination, it is the time for us to chart his path for a victory in November. Truthfully, his chances are not great. You know our feelings about how the Democrats have learned to play this game much more effectively than we have. Carrington has a strong ground game in all the swing states and the mainstream media behind her. Her fundraising machine is tuned up, oiled, and ready to go. The odds are against us."

Big brother Carl clumsily interrupted. "JB; I, Neil, Jacobs, and Reibus all see only one path to victory for Tony. That path happens to go right through the Braxton home. Now we realize this may be a bit overwhelming, but we know how important your agenda is to you personally. We've told Tony not to talk to you unless he was prepared to back your agenda 100 percent. And he is. He's willing to go all the way for increasing diabetes research to the degree you need. He's strongly behind reintroducing ELECT to Congress. And he loves your ideas on income tax reform. He will give you his word he'll support your top agenda items all the way if you join him on the ticket."

Jon and Angela were stunned by the content and directness of the message.

"OK, Carl. I get it. What if we say no? Does that mean he says no to our positions?"

"If you say no, he loses, and it won't matter. You've probably come to learn by now that politics is a blood sport. The road to the promised land isn't always lined with roses, but that doesn't mean the road is not worth traveling. If the destination is that important, then the road deserves its due respect."

Neil jumped in. "Let's say you join the ticket and lose. Think of all the opportunities you will have had to bring awareness to your agenda during the campaign. Since the ticket's chances would be somewhat slim, you should view this more of an opportunity to advance your agenda than to be Vice-President."

At that moment, Luke came bounding down the stairs. He saw the spread on the kitchen counter. "Can I grab some food, mom?"

The four sat in silence while Luke filled a carb-free plate, then waited until he headed back upstairs and out of earshot.

"Neil, Carl, would you excuse Angela and I for a few minutes while we go out back?"

"Of course, take all the time you need."

The Braxton's, still in shock from the offer, walked out back. Their property backed an open hillside. They leaned on the iron fence and gazed out at the dried brush and yellow grass that was their summer landscape. "If we say yes and win, we move to Washington. Would you want that, Angie? I've already disrupted everyone's lives enough the last few years. Would it be worth it?"

"Jon! Aren't you missing a few things here? Don't you think it would be nice for you and I to live together full time again if we won? Don't you think your kids would be incredibly proud of you? Don't you think you would be in a better position to secure more research funding? Honestly, I don't understand your hesitation."

"But you, Angie, your life. Your parents are here. In Washington you'd be under a microscope as never before. You would have very little privacy. And the kids; new schools, new surroundings, no friends. I'm not sure I want that for you guys."

"Come on, Jon. Don't lose sight of your mission. If we say yes and we win, look at the good you'll be able to do. All those families we met when Luke was first diagnosed. Think of the difference you can make in their lives. And if we don't win, we still win because you would have so many opportunities to tell your message during the campaign."

Jon was conceding. "The good WE will be able to do. And if we do this, we don't go in with the mindset of losing. If you have any misgivings about picking up our lives and moving them to Washington, don't hold them back. I only want to do this if you are in all the way with the expectation we win. Not ninety-nine percent. Only 100. But also consider if Neil's right and we say no and Jacobs loses to Heather, we still have a friend in the White House and I'm still Chairman of Ways and Means. And if I say no and he happens to win, we're still in a good position to move the agenda forward and we don't have to pick up our lives."

"Honey, you're only Chairman of Ways and Means next year if the Republicans hold onto the House majority, right? Isn't it possible Heather's coattails could be long enough to flip the House? And couldn't that put all your agenda at risk? When I used to stress out as a kid, my dad would say to me, *'Anzuru yori umu ga yasushi.'* The literal translation is, *'It's easier to give birth than to think about it.'* He was telling me not to worry. The fear is greater than the danger."

Jon turned to look at Angela, realizing she was right on everything. She turned to him and put her arms around his shoulders and pulled him close. They kissed passionately. Angela moved her lips to his left ear and whispered. "Let's win and go to Washington. I know that's what Luke would want. His heart is your heart."

"Mrs. Braxton, your husband became the luckiest guy in the world when he met you in psych twenty-five years ago. And he still is."

They walked hand in hand back into the family room. "Anyone else hungry?"

———≋———

Luke had been living as a Type 1 diabetic for 1443 days when Neil, Carl, Jon, and Angela entered a small conference room at the

Harborside Hotel in Washington DC. Awaiting them were Anthony and Renee Jacobs. Tony needed a candidate for vice-president to join him on the ticket. Jon needed a meeting to determine if they could work together. Angela and Renee needed to be there to keep their men in check.

Tony had chosen the 'off beaten path' location for the first formal interaction between a future president and vice-president of the United States. "No need for the press or any other lawmakers to see us talking at this point," was Neil's explanation to Jon after advising him of the time and place.

"Tony, Renee, permit me to introduce you to Jon and Angela Braxton."

Tony was gracious and excited to meet Jon. "Speaking for both Renee and I, it's so great to finally meet you. We've been following you since your speech at the convention four years ago. And always watch you and Wally Kriss together. We never miss the show you're on. Otherwise, truthfully, I can't really stand him."

Jon laughed. "Thank you, Tony. It's good to meet you as well. From what Neil has told me, sounds like we have much in common. I'm looking forward to hearing some of your ideas."

"Same for me Jon. I've been reading about your positions on election law reform and taxation. Very innovative. And your education initiatives are doing wonders for us in Ohio. Test scores are way up from the kids that go through the curriculum. But we have lots of other problems to tackle so let's sit down and start covering them. Let's see if you and I would make a good team."

The first formal meeting between Tony Jacobs and Jonathon Braxton went beyond anyone's expectations. Tony had been coached well by Neil Hale. In prep for this meeting, he had researched the STYLE Act, the ELECT Resolution, and pluripotent cell research. He and Jon had in-depth, substantive discussions on all three agenda items, and Jacobs expressed sincere admiration for Jon's positions and efforts. He emphatically declared his full support for all. They also discussed Jacobs' agenda items. He asked Jon to start thinking about potential solutions for the problems on his short list plaguing the country—reforming immigration policies, rectifying trade imbalances, resolving Middle Eastern conflicts, deconstructing social injustice and combating terrorism, among others.

It was a policy wonk's dream meeting. The two fast-becoming friends reeled off large amounts of data and discussed potential solutions. They seemed a perfect team, with Jacobs' executive experience in government, running the state of Ohio for the last eight years. And Jon's executive experience in business and unique problem-solving approaches. Both shared their disdain for politics as it was currently being conducted. Both shared their sense of concern with the country's loss of traditional, American-style values. Both expressed commitment to practical solutions and both shared a willingness to stretch the fabric of Washington at the risk of their political careers, to shake things up.

The Hales marveled at the growing chemistry between the two dynamic personalities. The two ladies in the room were mostly silent but exchanging lots of smiles. When Tony would make a point she approved of, Angela would look at Renee and smile with a nod. Renee returned the show of satisfaction when Jon hit a bullseye for her, which occurred frequently during the two hours of discussion.

As their time for the meeting room was winding down, Neil offered his comment.

"Well gentlemen, that was quite the discussion. I've listened to both of you individually and now to hear the two of you speak to one another—if you two decide to join forces—I believe our voters are going to love their ticket."

Tony nodded. "I couldn't agree more. Jon, Angela, it's been a long day for you coming from the West Coast. You must be famished. Please join Renee and I for dinner. I've already set us up. We're in a dining room just down the hall."

The six of them vacated the conference room and headed towards the room where their dinners would soon be served. Angela and Renee were walking behind Tony and Jon. Renee queried Angela.

"How is Luke doing? Is his condition under control?"

Angela was surprised by the question. "Yes thankfully, he's doing very well. Do you know much about Type 1 diabetes?"

"I do. My sister's daughter, Lauren, she's nine. Was diagnosed when she was four. I was so moved by your husband's speech at the convention four years ago. She had just been diagnosed and then there's Jon on national TV fighting for her. I've been on Tony's ass to introduce us all. When he won the nomination, I told him to get Jon on the ticket or we were divorcing." She was perfectly serious.

Angela grabbed Renee's hand and walked around Jon and Tony. She stepped right in their path to leave no doubt their two spouses were hand in hand. Jon could decline Tony's offer at his own peril.

During their dinner, Jon accepted. After dinner and some serious hugging, the Braxton's left for their DC residence and the Jacobs retired to their room at the Harborside. Carlton and Cornelius headed to the bar for a nightcap.

Their Hendrix Gin Gibsons—straight up—arrived a moment after they ordered. Carl raised his glass and looked to Corny to do the same. "Well, little brother, you are a miracle worker. We have the best possible ticket to take the White House back. I'm not sure how we pulled it off, but here's to getting back on top."

"Thanks, Carl. Believe it or not, my previous pessimism notwithstanding, I think we can win this thing."

———— ≈ ————

A few days later, and only 145 more until Heather Carrington would have the opportunity to keep her long-standing promise, she was home in her DC residence watching CNN when a breaking news story was aired.

"And on the political front we have breaking news. Presumptive Republican presidential nominee Governor Anthony Jacobs of Ohio has just announced he has offered the Vice-Presidential position on their ticket to Congressman Jonathon Braxton of California."

Heather froze for a moment. She then attempted to stand and immediately fainted to the floor, knocking over a vase on the table next to her chair. The loud crashing noise caught the ear of Wil down the hall in his study. He raced into Heather's office to find her on the floor, unconscious. He knelt by her side and cradled her head. She slowly regained consciousness but was unaware of where she was or what had happened. Wil reached for her cellphone on her desk and dialed 911.

While waiting for the paramedics he brought a pillow to the floor and rested her head on it. He then soaked a washcloth and cooled her head. She was slowly regaining awareness. He helped her up and into their bedroom.

The paramedics arrived to find her resting comfortably in her bed. Wil, mindful of the negative press this would generate, moved to damage control.

"She's OK. Just an upset stomach. I was panicking when I called 911. I shouldn't have. I overreacted."

The paramedics left, satisfied with the explanation from the former President. They would file a report labeling the call a 'misdial'.

———≈———

The call from Neil Hale to Jon's cell phone was on day 1449 since Luke's T1D diagnosis. He called unaware if Jon was in California or DC.

"Good morning, Neil."

"Not so, Jon. Where are you?"

"Home in T.O. What is it?"

"I'm not sure how to say this so I'll just say it. Anthony Jacobs was killed in an auto accident in Columbus about an hour ago."

Jon closed his eyes. "Oh no. Oh no. Renee and their kids?"

"They weren't with him. They were home. Tony was on his way to the airport to come back to Washington. I'll call Rob and have him draft a statement for you. You're going to be in the media crosshairs now. I'm sure you'll hear something from Reibus soon, I'm not sure when. And I'm not sure what will happen with the RNC. I'm sorry. I know you and he had become friends. Things are going to get difficult my young friend. I wish you all the best to make the right decisions now for whatever comes your way. I'll call you as soon as I know more."

Jon went to Angela, and they both cried. Angela thought of Renee, and then she thought of the pastor. "Jon, give Jeffrey a call. Talk to him."

———— ≈ ————

The following day was chaotic in Washington. As news of Jacobs' death was digested by everyone in the political sphere, the media went on a rampage for information. Jon decided not to cancel his flight back to Washington. He knew he would soon be in a firestorm and wanted to shield his family by being away from them and back within the Beltway.

The spotlight began to focus on Lance Reibus. Most of the difficult decisions to be made were now his. He called Neil Hale for perspective.

"The convention is only four weeks out. You've got to make your move, fast. If you're asking for my recommendation, to my thinking, there's only one person who has even a remote chance to take on Carrington."

"I know you like Braxton, and I like him too. But Jesus, Neil, he doesn't have much experience. He knows virtually nothing about foreign policy. He has no real appeal to Blacks or Latinos or LBGTQ.

His appeal to the Evangelicals is precarious. Can he really compete with Carrington for the women's vote when she has the chance to break the glass ceiling? We haven't had the chance to vet him the way we vetted all the other candidates in the primary. He's a huge risk."

Neil was undeterred. "He's our only chance. Get into the head of Republican and Independent voters. What do they want? They want better government. Who can give it to them? The last eight years have been a shit-show, right? The divide between the parties is so wide that Republican voters can't even think straight anymore. There's a lot of fatigue out there. A lot of them have given up on the party and will not bother to vote if you go with another establishment type. Where did McCain and Romney get us? The only guy we have that can bring them back is JB. Consider what he's accomplished and how he's done it. Look at his legislation. What he's done with Ways and Means. The way his colleagues talk about him. The passion he has for his agenda. The fact he doesn't chase money. The fact he doesn't lie. His attributes far outweigh the negatives you listed. He can be a transformative figure in the history of this country. He's another JFK in my book—but better."

"OK, let's say we offer the nomination to Braxton, will he take it? And what do we do about a VP for him? Do you think he'd go for Rubio? I'd like to know all this before I go to bat for him with the committee.

"I don't know. Let's ask him."

Neil arranged for he, Jon, and Reibus to meet at the RNC offices in DC after business hours. Neil asked Jon to be discreet in travelling over. The media was in a feeding frenzy, and he wanted to keep the meeting out of the news.

Jon was anticipating the conversation and had concluded to

accept, with the full approval of Angela. They both agreed this was all about Luke, Renee's niece, and all the others. His mind was on the conditions he would require.

At their meeting, Reibus was unusually passive. He was now talking to a potential president and the possible future head of their party. Given the unorthodoxy that was Braxton, Reibus was having trouble getting into his normal rhythm and the conversation quickly became disjointed.

Neil Hale took the lead.

"JB, I believe you have a legitimate chance to be the next president of the United States, if you want it. That's what Lance needs to know. Do you want it? He's ready to put his good name and reputation on the line, and back you with the RNC and his backing will most likely lead to your being offered the nomination. We don't know this for sure, but we believe the party is ready to coalesce around you. While we believe the odds are against you winning, it's possible you can defeat Carrington and help maintain the Republican majorities in both the House and the Senate. Should this all come to transpire, your agenda will be front and center, with no opposition in Congress. Think of the reason you started your political career. Your objectives are within your reach. And even if you were to run and lose, your agenda will have had enormous exposure. And you would be in position to advance it even if not from the White House."

None of the words spoken by Neil Hale took Jon by surprise. He had considered all.

"Gentlemen, I'll accept the nomination on one condition. I choose my VP."

Reibus was visibly flustered. "JB, we have to be strategic in our VP choice. There are some holes in your resume, and some of your flanks are weak. The right VP choice is crucial to our success."

"Crucial to get elected? Or crucial to govern properly?"

Forty-four

Later that evening Wil Carrington was at his desk. Heather was sitting across from him. She had recovered quickly from the unexpected and unprecedented panic attack she suffered the previous week. She was back in politician mode and, though still confused by her thoughts, following the happenings of the last few days with intensity. Her psyche was still in disarray. She was contemplating the most difficult decision of her career and was still undecided as to what, how and when. The Democrat nominating convention was only two weeks away. As if she weren't distracted enough by her own insecurities, she was now also unsure of who her opponent would be.

"You look much better today honey. The best you've looked since the panic attack. How are you feeling?"

"I'm good. You wanted to see me about something?"

"Yes, I've been making some calls and it looks like Ted Cruz is going to be your opponent. And I doubt Braxton will be on the ticket. Cruz doesn't like him. With the convention coming up so quickly, I just wanted to see how you and your team were doing getting ready. And you know you've got to decide on your VP in the next day or two. To my thinking, Tim Kaine is your best choice."

"Thank you, Wil. I'm meeting with Donna and Debbie tomorrow and the VP pick is front and center."

It had been 1454 days since Luke's T1D diagnosis when the RNC met and voted to offer the 2016 Republican nomination for President to Jonathon Braxton. All the other candidates who captured primary delegates pledged them to Jon. This included Ted Cruz who saw the inevitability after a pep talk with Neil Hale and Lance Reibus. It was now unanimous. The news left the RNC at ten that evening. Enough time to hit the morning edition of The Washington Post.

It was now only 135 days until Heather could deliver on her promise when one such copy of The Post slid across her front porch and stopped abruptly at the foot of her front door in the early hours of the following morning. With the sun thirty minutes into its day, the presumptive Democrat nominee was now dressed in a plush pink bathrobe over blue-gray silk pajamas and fluffy white slippers. With a cup of coffee in hand and confusing thoughts in mind, she stepped onto the porch to retrieve the newspaper. Normally she would not open it until back inside and seated at her kitchen table. Today she would open it on the porch to scan the headline.

Washington Post News

IT'S BRAXTON'S TURN
RNC Goes All In With JB
VP Pick Undecided

She looked at the headline then immediately closed the paper and looked skyward. Her first reaction was disbelief but that was immediately replaced by a huge sense of relief. She mouthed the words '*thank you*' and then went inside—without second thoughts or uncertainty— to wake her husband. An hour later Sidney Rosenberg's cell phone rang with 'CallerID unknown' in the Blackberry display.

He answered cautiously: "Hello?"

"Who you going to call?"

"Anyone but Ghostbusters."

"Hello, Sidney."

"Hello, Mr. President."

"Sidney, something about Heather you need to know."

"Should I sit down and drop the sharp objects I'm holding?"

"Probably a good idea."

———≈———

Jon was back in Thousand Oaks. His thoughts were scattered. The net result of the events of the last ten days had not yet been fully processed. And now he had to present himself as a candidate for President? Face the press? Write an acceptance speech? Choose a VP? Get educated on policy matters? And Heather, his friend, was his opponent? How did this happen? The word surreal seemed woefully underpowered to sum up how both he and Angela viewed the totality of events that had occurred in such a compressed period of time. The vibration of his cell phone interrupted his bewilderment.

"Hello Jeffrey. Good to hear from you. I'm sorry I haven't been in touch."

"Understood considering everything you're dealing with. You must be under great stress given recent events. I have a reflection for you. Is this an OK time?"

"Yes, please."

"Jon, please know that I pray for you and your family every day. You and I have often discussed how God works in ways we cannot understand. Tony Jacobs' death was for a reason, a reason for which we are not enlightened enough to comprehend. But I believe there will be some light to comfort all of us who mourn him shortly. I pray Jon, you will look at Tony's death in this context. You are part of a plan God has designed for you and your family. Recognizing he has a plan, even without understanding it will give you comfort and the resolve to push forward."

"Thank you. I will try. Did you know Tony Jacobs?"

"I did not, but I heard many good things about him over the years from Heather. If you were not aware, their paths crossed many times when she was in the White House and the Senate. She spoke highly of him, and they had a friendship."

"I was not aware. I should call her and offer condolences. I didn't get the chance to know him well, but from the brief time I spent with him, he seemed like a good man."

"Indeed. Jon, allow me to change the subject if I may. I would like to meet with both you and Angela, if I could, as soon as possible."

"In Philadelphia or here in T.O.?"

"In Washington."

"OK, Angie is travelling with me back to DC next Wednesday. Do you want to set something up for next Thursday?"

"That would be perfect. It would be in the evening if OK with you. I'll be in touch when I get to DC. God bless you, Jon."

———≈———

Jeffrey asked Jon and Angela to meet him at seven at the Downtown Hampton Inn. They were seated in the lobby, waiting. She was curious.

"What do you think Jeffrey wants to talk to us about?"

"I'm not sure. I imagine more spiritual guidance, but I have an uneasy feeling."

At that moment Jeffrey exited a lobby elevator and walked towards them. He had a look of peace and comfort as he silently embraced them both. "Come. Let us go. We have another destination."

In silence, they walked out of the hotel and into a waiting limo. The moment they were all situated Jon's curiosity intensified.

"Where are we headed?"

"Heather's home."

"Ok, why the mystery? What's going on Jeffrey?"

"Heather has some news for the two of you. She has not yet shared this with anyone but her husband and myself. She wanted to relay her news in person. I do not mean to be so mysterious, but she asked me only to escort you. We will be at her home in five minutes, and you will have all your questions answered. In the meantime, tell me how are Luke and Darla."

The limo pulled into the driveway of the Carrington residence that ran adjacent to the side kitchen door, a much more private entrance than the front. No one thought having the two 2016 presidential candidates seen together a good idea. Heather opened the side door on their arrival. She stood in the doorway awaiting them. As the three ascended the four steps to enter the kitchen, Heather opened the door wide. Wil was standing next to her.

"Jon, Angela, this is my husband, Wil."

"Angela, you're more beautiful than I imagined. Welcome. Jon, it's great to finally meet you."

"Thank you, Mr. President. An honor to meet you, sir." Wil smiled, thinking, 'OK, pretty good so far.'

Heather suggested they all move to the living room, where, to the surprise of Angela and Jon, sat Carlton and Cornelius Hale. Jon's mind was now in overdrive, trying to ascertain what was happening. Heather had their cocktail server make sure everyone had their drink of choice before leaving the residence. A beautiful spread of appetizers and hors d'oeuvres was laid out on the three-by-five cherry wood coffee table. The seven took their seats, Jon and Angela on a sofa. Heather, Wil and Jeffrey in comfortable high-back chairs facing them. Carl and Cornelius in a love seat adjacent to the sofa. When they were all settled, Jeffrey spoke first.

"Heather before you start, let us observe a moment of silent prayer for Tony Jacobs."

They all bowed their heads for a moment before Jeffrey concluded with a soft amen. Heather was anxious to get her thoughts out. They had been bottled up for too long.

"Jon, Angela, thank you for coming. I apologize for the mystery and having Jeffrey kidnap you. You will understand everything in a few minutes. First, let me congratulate you, Jon. I haven't spoken to you since before your VP selection. And now, through such unfortunate circumstances, you are a presidential candidate and my opponent. Imagine what the media would do if they saw us meeting like this?" She laughed uneasily. No one else did as the sense of melancholy for Tony lingered.

"I still remember that night in 2013 at your victory party after the election for Earl's seat. I remember no alcohol and no sweets in honor of the Type 1 kids. You were such a breath of fresh air for me, especially compared to the other politicians and bureaucrats I am always surrounded by. I know this is going to sound trite, but from that day, I have been a different person. I didn't truly understand how different until recently. After working in government all these years, I came to realize I've been working with a faulty belief system. I believed the desired ends of my actions always justified the means. My belief system always proved me right, regardless of outcome or circumstance. I believed whatever I needed to do, I could just do and justify it after. But with that belief system, I made some very horrible choices which led to terrible consequences. I lost close friends while at State. They died because of my inability to see things clearly. My vision was always clouded by my ambition. These thoughts have been haunting me the past few years, but they were not enough to stop me from pursuing the promise I made to my father when I was seven that I would be the first woman president of the United States. I failed in 2008 but remained committed to that promise. So, I declared for 2016, even though I had my doubts. But thank goodness for Jeffrey. He knew exactly how to guide me. I shared I was not sure I wanted to be President. I felt emotionally inadequate and unprepared to do the job." Heather paused as a lump formed in her throat. She took a sip of club soda.

"Even though Jeffrey showed me the path to make the right decision, I couldn't bring myself to leave the campaign. I would be letting so many people down. I didn't know how I could face them. I couldn't see how I would face myself. I was missing something that would help me see things clearly. But now, everything is in focus. Tomorrow first thing in the morning, I'm having my campaign call a press conference for the afternoon. The media is expecting me to announce my running mate, but that's not going to happen. Jon, Angela, tomorrow I will be announcing I am leaving the campaign, taking my name out of consideration for the nomination, and resigning from the Democrat Party. And I'll announce, Jon, I am endorsing you for President. And I will ask my supporters to do so as well." She bowed her head. The room was silent. Jon and Angela looked at one another. Wil stood and walked behind Heather, putting his hands on her shoulders, and then glared at Jon. Jon made eye contact with Wil and then stood. He turned and walked to the large living room picture window facing out to the street. He puts his hands in his pockets and stared outside at a dusky sky ready to turn into nightfall. As if the recent string of events were not enough to twist his brain inside out, Heather had just added the impossible to the improbable. All eyes in the room were fixed on him.

Jeffrey ended the awkward silence. "Jon. I'm grateful Heather consulted with me on her uncertainties and her ultimate decision.

When she asked for my help, I found many insights from you. Being effective as an elected government official is beyond the ability of the great majority of human souls. There are too many distractions, temptations, and human frailties for elected officials to overcome, so they yield to traditions and norms. As a result, most fail to serve effectively. People like you do not offer their services for good reason. The level of sacrifice to their morality and their humanity they must make to survive—they consider too great. You were of this mind before Luke's body and Earl's age led you to Washington. I am sure you have contemplated the circumstances behind your journey. As a man who has yet to partner with God, you likely see them as coincidence. As a man who has a forty-five-year relationship with God, I know differently."

Silence again descended on the room before Neil Hale found words. "Before we learned of Heather's decision, Carl and I gave you a one in five chance of winning. Now there is nothing in your way to becoming the 45th President of the United States. Considering the torrid sequence of events of the last few weeks, combined with the overall trajectory of your brief political career, I'm not sure we can even imagine what you're thinking at this moment. From an outside perspective of what is likely firing in your head, step back and consider what a magical moment this is in the evolution of this country. It remains to be seen what the political landscape and both the Republican and Democrat parties will look like after the dust settles. I'm sure we won't recognize either of them. And it remains to be seen what the future of this country will look like during and after a Braxton presidency. I, for one, happen to think that future looks very bright. And I feel I'm speaking for everyone in this room."

Wil frowned—unnoticed by all in the room—begging to differ.

"But this is still the USA of 2016, and our politics will not transform easily. While the road now looks clear, rest assured there will be potholes, and fallen trees, and downed power lines. And all kinds of obstructions. But Mr. President and Mrs. First Lady to be, Carl and I want you to know that we have total confidence in you. And to know that all our resources and connections and influence are squarely behind you. We have your backs."

Heather was ready for more explanation.

"Jon, I was struggling with insecurity for many months while Jeffrey was counseling me. When I first read you were replacing Tony, I flashed back to your last appearance with Kriss. He asked why you do what you do, and you said, 'I love my son and my country'. When I heard those words from your lips they rocked me, but I was uncertain why. When I read the Post headline last week you were to be the nominee, I understood. I realized I too love the USA, but I have not been a very good lover. My decisions always catered to my ambition and my ego. This last decision would not. This last decision would be for my country. My heart would make this last decision, and I came to believe that you, Jon Braxton, in all your inexperience and all your quirkiness, that you are the best person for the job. I realize now this country needs you. You are much better equipped to be the next president than I. And to Jeffrey's point, who am I to stand in the way of God's will?"

Jon was still staring outside and then turned to look at her.

"What does this mean for you, for your career, for your life in Washington?"

"I'm not sure. Maybe you can find me a job."

———— ≋ ————

Later that evening from the Carrington residence, after Heather's guests had left, the former President made a call. Sidney Rosenberg's cell phone rang with 'CallerID unknown' in the display. He answered cautiously.

"Hello?"

"Who's buried in Grant's tomb?"

"Marilyn Monroe."

"Hello Sidney."

"How'd it go?"

"About what you'd expect. Now get us some dirt on him."

Forty-five

The Republican National Convention was ready to start in Cleveland, providing Washington DC a much-needed breather. The sudden death of Tony Jacobs, the ascension of Jonathon Braxton to the top of the Republican ticket, the resignation of Heather Carrington from the campaign and the Democrat Party, and her decision to support her former opponent had created an unprecedented media frenzy. It was too much for DC to handle. The federal government was paralyzed.

Lance Reibus was in his makeshift office at the Cleveland convention center. His TV was tuned to the Big News Channel. Wallis Kriss was on air commenting. "Washington DC continues to reel in the wake of Heather Carrington's decision to drop out of consideration for the nomination. There is no shortage of theories on what prompted her to leave the race and endorse her would be opponent. President Obama has been diplomatic in his responses to questions on the matter, but sources in the White House say he is livid with the situation. It's clear this move by Carrington has put the Obama legacy at risk. And in another bombshell report just received, we now know the DNC has offered the Democrat nomination to Vermont Senator Bernie Sanders."

———— ≈ ————

Every newspaper in the country sent their reporters to DC to scoop a story. Every media outlet from websites to social media to bloggers to twenty-four-seven cable and broadcast TV was trying to make sense of—or at a minimum convey—what happened. The news cycle was all Heather Carrington, all day, and all night.

The blow back against Heather was fierce. Anonymous threats were made against her life. Conspiracy theories abounded. Absurd stories circulated. Heather was called everything from a Russian operative to Jon's secret lover. Salacious lies, rumors, and *according to sources'* reporting filled the airwaves.

The focus on Heather gave the DNC and the Democrats some time and space to regroup around Sanders. The move energized the left wing of the party, and their enthusiasm helped Democrats regain some momentum. But no one outside the far-left wing of the Democrat Party felt Sanders had any chance against Braxton. The combination of Jon's growing legacy and Heather's passionate endorsement created volumes of enthusiasm. So much enthusiasm Wallis Kriss was begging Jon to make an appearance, which he gracefully declined. More out of respect for Tony Jacobs than anything else.

———— ≈ ————

Lance Reibus was frantic at the cusp of the convention that Jon had still not selected a running mate. He was constantly pushing Jon to make the choice and fill him in. In three days, it would be the VP's night to be introduced, placed into nomination, and approved by the delegates. Jon was weary of Reibus' constant harassment. He asked Neil Hale to meet he and Angela for a drink. He wanted an intervention.

They were at the most discreet table they could find, in the most intimate cocktail lounge in their hotel. So far, they had been successful at avoiding the throngs of convention delegates and the press. "Neil, I've made a decision on the VP pick."

He spent the next thirty minutes explaining who and why and answering Neil's questions. Jon fully understood his limitations in experience and wasn't concerned about making the pick to assure victory. That was almost now a given. His thoughts were on governing and how to best bring the country together and work to solve its problems. His choice needed to be one to help restore civility and intelligent debate, to help bridge the divide that had fissured over the last sixteen years of the Bush and Obama administrations.

"OK, that's sure to send Reibus into cardiac arrest. Are you sure? You've thought this through?"

"I have. I don't plan to serve more than one term. Given my lack of experience this makes the most sense. And one more thing. I want to change the convention protocol a little bit and introduce the pick on Wednesday night myself. I know it's traditional to lay low and only speak on Thursday, but this is what I want. Let Reibus know I won't take no for an answer."

Neil held up his drink for a toast. "To what promises to be a most interesting four years."

———— ≈ ————

The first two nights of the Republican National Convention ran smoothly and delivered all that was intended, including a sincere and heartfelt tribute to Tony Jacobs. Lance Reibus had this convention gig down pat—all except for the quirks of the man now leading the party.

It was Wednesday night. The drama building all day surrounding the pick among the delegates, was now at a fevered pitch. Who was going to be JB's running mate? The delegates discussed among themselves every possible option and then some. "He's going to pick his wife." "It's got to be Marco Rubio—he needs the Latino vote." "He's going for a woman—probably Meg Whitman." "No question—it's Jeb Bush to win Florida." "He's got to win the Evangelicals—look for Mike Huckabee." "Ted Cruz was runner-up to Jacobs in delegates—he deserves it."

Wallis Kriss was on air from the convention center at the Big News desk discussing the matter. "Tonight we learn Jon Braxton's pick for Vice-President. No one in the media is aware of who it will be but there is plenty of speculation. We don't even know who will be putting the vice-president candidate's name into nomination here in the next few minutes. There's plenty of mystery here tonight in Cleveland. Bridgett Masterson, your thoughts on who the pick will be."

"Wallis, speculation continues to center around Marco Rubio and Lindsay Graham. Sources tell me Braxton is focusing on foreign policy expertise, and at this point is not considering a woman. He feels Carrington's endorsement is sufficient to do well with that demographic, and the speculation it will be Angela Braxton is ridiculous."

The convention program agenda had the vice-presidential nominee listed for speaking at 9:30 p.m. Normally there were two or three nomination speeches for the VP pick. Tonight, there would be only one. It was listed on the program in the nine-p.m. slot as '*Vice President Nomination*'. There were no other references.

Just before nine, Paul Ryan was concluding his address. It had plenty of praise for his protégé. Not even Ryan knew who would be following him to the podium. He exited to polite applause which soon abated into silent intrigue.

The stage remained empty, and the convention hall remained quiet for two minutes following Ryan's departure. Without any fanfare or music, from the left side of the stage, Jon appeared. He started approaching the podium with two young people by his side. On one side was Luke, on the other side was Tony Jacobs' niece,

Lauren Woods. They both were holding one of Jon's hands and were flanked by Renee Jacobs.

The floor of the convention, upon seeing Jon, Luke, Lauren, and Renee, broke into a roar of applause and cheering that nearly blew the lid off the auditorium. Lance Reibus was looking on from the right side of the stage, out of view from the convention floor. He shook his head and looked down. He realized again, as he had done in 2012, that he had underestimated Jon Braxton. He made a mental note to never do so again.

The applause and cheering went on for what seemed an eternity. The four of them had stopped just to the left of the podium and were now in full view of the delegates. Jon, Luke and Lauren waved to the roaring crowd. Renee stood majestically, her hands clasped in front of her. Finally, the crowd decided they wanted to hear from Braxton and silenced themselves. He had a wireless mic.

"This is my son, Luke. He is sixteen years old." Then dialing up the volume. "He has Type 1 diabetes, and he is kicking its ass!" Jon exalted, slowly putting emphasis on the last three words. The roar from the crowd obliterated the noise meter. After a few minutes, the crowd wanted more and again silenced.

"And this beautiful young lady is Tony Jacobs' niece, Ms. Lauren Woods. Lauren is nine years old, has been living with Type 1 diabetes since the age of four, and she's doing her share of ass kicking as well." Another deafening response.

Jon turned to face Lauren, put the mic on the floor, knelt on one knee, and hugged her. The words he whispered in her ear were picked up by the mic and inadvertently delivered to the delegates. "Don't worry sweetheart and stay strong. Your uncle is resting peacefully in Heaven. He's there to help us find the cure for diabetes."

He then picked up the mic, stood, and turned to Luke to give him a high-five first and then a powerful hug. "My son has a few words. Luke?" He handed the mic to his son.

"Hello everyone. To all of you here at the convention, and to everyone watching from home helping us fight for a cure. Type 1 kids, families, medical professionals. If you give my family the honor to move into the White House, I have four words." Luke gripped the mic hard as a look of confidence took over his face and he raised his voice a few octaves. "Type 1, you're done!"

Luke's words of defiance whipped the delegates into a frenzy. A contingent started chanting and within two repetitions all the delegates joined in. "Type 1, you're done. Type 1, you're done. Type 1, you're done."

Luke, handed the mic to his dad, hugged him, took Lauren's hand, and walked off stage with her. Jon and Renee were left to the chanting delegates. He motioned Renee to the podium, where she stood at the stationary mic. He was off to her right and behind her. The crowd silenced.

"Good evening, everyone. I will be brief. Thank you all for the love and the best wishes you've directed toward my family over the last few difficult weeks. Tony would be so touched to see how many people loved and cared about him. I know he is resting peacefully with the knowledge that he lived a great life and proudly served the people of Ohio for so many years. I know he's taking solace in knowing that in his absence the torch is being passed to Jon. Jon is simply the best. There is no other way to describe this man. Please, everyone, when you go home to your districts, tell everyone that Jonathon Braxton deserves your vote for president and tell them why." She turned to Jon, they embraced. She let go, turned, and left the stage, waving to the sea of cheering admirers.

Jon waited until the noise dissipated and the curiosity of the VP pick returned. "Ladies and gentlemen, four years ago, I was offered the opportunity to come before you and talk about my quest for finding a cure for the insidious autoimmune disease known as Type 1 diabetes. At the time, I had zero political aspirations. As you know I was, and frankly still am, disgusted by politics. And yet here we are, just you and I and a whole country we need to take care of." Another round of boisterous applause and cheering.

"I told you four years ago my inspiration was my son and it should be no surprise he still is. He's a pretty good-looking young man, right?" If a second applause meter had been brought online, that one would have melted down as well. "Make no mistake, that young man is my hero!" Jon loudly proclaimed among the cheers which lasted another moment before he motioned for quiet.

"When Tony Jacobs offered me the VP spot on the ticket, my wife and I had to make a decision that could potentially lead to our family moving to Washington. In Southern California, Luke had settled into the life of a typical sixteen-year-old, except for the finger-pricking, carb-counting, and insulin shots. His four-year fight with Type 1 had not been easy, and I was having trouble getting comfortable with a possible move for us. His life and his condition had stabilized. He was enjoying his friends, a school he loved, a new girlfriend, the beach, and his surfboard. How could I possibly take all that away from him, given what he's had to live with the last four years? But that son of mine, when he learned from his mom about what we were contemplating, he told me there was no way we were not going if I had the chance to be VP. He knew we needed a lot of money for research. He knew the difficulties I was having in Congress getting the requisite research funding. He understood the significance of his dad having access to the White House. He understood the suffering of Type 1 diabetics, as well as anybody. He knew Tony Jacobs was fully committed to helping us go after that funding. And so we accepted Tony's offer to join him on the ticket, knowing the possibility we could be moving to Washington. Luke would not let me turn it down." The floor was silent.

"So, just as it was four years ago, when I told you I stood before you because of Luke, I am here tonight again because of my son. Did I tell you yet he is my hero?"

The crowd could not have cheered any louder. After another eternity passed, Jon motioned for quiet. "But things are different now. Tony is not here. And it is not the job of VP in front of us. It is a much bigger job. It is a job candidly I'm uncertain I am prepared for, but a lot of people in our party seem to feel differently. And it was offered. And because Luke would not let me say no, I am accepting. Although that comes tomorrow night."

"The job of president is too big and too important to remain focused on only a single issue. Of course, I understand that. It is a job that requires tremendous peripheral vision. It requires expert multitasking. It requires keen instinct. It requires empathy and compassion. It requires the ability to consume great volumes of information and render sound judgments. It demands experience, much of which I do not have. So, if I'm going to win this job and do it, I must do it well, for you. To do it well, I need the right partner. I need the right vice president to work with. In my case, because of my relative lack of experience in the ways of Washington and the rest of the world, we need a vice president who has experience that I do not. We need a vice president who has shown the courage to make tough decisions, a vice president with strength and conviction. And we need a vice-president that can help us bridge the large political party divide in the federal government."

"OK, that's enough of my thoughts for tonight. We'll talk more tomorrow. For now, permit me to introduce you to my choice for my partner on the ticket, the next vice president of the United States, the former First Lady, Heather Carrington."

———— ≋ ————

At the mention of Heather's name by Jon, two very loud sounds could be heard on the east coast—one in Washington DC and the other in Manhattan. They were the collective jaws of Heather's husband and her senior strategic advisor hitting the floor at the exact same instant.

A moment later Sidney's cell phone rang. He answered cautiously. "Hello?"

"What color is the little red wagon?"

"Blue, Mr. President. And I had no idea."

"None? You didn't see this coming?"

"You live with her. You didn't see it coming?"

"She didn't say anything. With all the negative coverage lately, she's been holed up here at home in her office since the press conference. Yesterday she told me she's going to Philadelphia to see Jeffrey to help her handle everything."

"What are you going to do."

"Sidney, I think nothing. Come to think of it, being only a heartbeat away isn't that bad a place to be. Now get me that dirt on Braxton."

———— ≈ ————

Two weeks after the Republican National Convention dispersed, with a scheduled break in campaigning, Jon had a chance to return to Thousand Oaks. It had been six weeks since he checked in with Abby. He surprised Roberta when he walked into the executive office lobby area unannounced at nine on a Tuesday morning. He saw the door to his old office closed.

Roberta jumped up to greet him, squealing and hugging.

"Is she busy?"

"Not that busy. I'll let her know you're here." She buzzed Abby's intercom, barely containing her excitement. "Mrs. Martin, it's the next president of the United States here to see you."

Roberta's intercom buzzed back.

"Does he have an appointment?"

THE END

To Stay Current with JB ★ For JB's BLOG
To Join Our Mailing List ★ For Sequel and Motion Picture Development Updates
www.braxtonsturn.com

CPSIA information can be obtained
at www.ICGtesting.com
Printed in the USA
LVHW081201110723
750869LV00008BA/68/J

9 781737 303862